CHAPTER 3

Josie

When I was a young and impressionable college student, back when I thought there was a glamorous job waiting for me on the other side of the university rainbow, I dreamed of a cool townhouse—one of those big ones in New York City. It would be my sanctuary. There would be a kitchen three times as big as the one in Anke's old apartment. I would have a six—no *eight*—burner range and three ovens. The kitchen would have an island to seat the humongous family I totally would have. I would make awesome, tasty meals and wear a cute apron and kiss my attractive husband when he came home from work. I would have a craft room, with pretty bits of ribbons, paper, and shiny markers. Best of all, I would have a candy wall displaying glass jars of all different kinds of colorful, sweet treats. When I wasn't crafting or cooking, I would take inspirational photos of my house and curate them on Instagram.

The tiny house that was waiting for me the next morning in the parking lot behind Ida's General Store never featured in my dreams. It never even featured in my nightmares. In its heyday, the tiny house might have been described as modern rustic. Now it was just dilapidated. It was also, well, it was *tiny*. I could stretch my arms out and touch both walls. The linoleum countertop was peeling. The walls were cracking. The cabinetry looked askew, probably from all the bouncing around on the road. There was a sink the size of a soup bowl, a cruddy toaster oven, and on a shelf above the sink was a display of mason jars holding a dusty array of various pastas.

I made a mental note to put candy into them. If this was as close as I would ever get to my own home, I was making the most of it.

"You're just giving this to her?" Willow asked the hipster. His name was Homer, and he wasn't wearing any shoes. His feet were black.

Homer shrugged. "The lady who had it got married and moved into her new husband's tiny house." He shook his head. "It isn't even that tiny. It's a luxury trailer. This"—he slapped the side of the little cabin on wheels, and the house shook ominously—"this is what tiny-house living is supposed to be—small and low impact."

"Does it have a bathroom?" Willow asked.

Homer picked a piece of gravel out of his foot. I was going to have to scrub the house at some point if he had been walking all over it. "It has a composting toilet and a wet room," he replied, pointing to a tiny door that looked like it was made for elves. I peeked inside and tried not to barf.

"This is a well-traveled tiny house," Homer said, banging on the wall again. The house shook, and a piece of the wood veneer on the ceiling fell down, exposing the insulation.

"It's fine," I assured him, needing him to stop destroying my new home.

"The truck comes with it," Homer added, gesturing us out of the house.

Hitched to the trailer bed was an old Ford pickup. If it had been lovingly maintained, I might have called it a classic pickup. In its current condition, there were brown rust patches, and the door handle was missing.

"I hope you can drive a stick shift," Homer said.

I nodded.

"It guzzles gas but pulls like a champ," Homer said, slapping the truck. One of the chrome pieces fell off, swinging by the remaining screw. The screeching of metal on metal made me wince.

"Enjoy your new home!" Homer said. "Go tiny!" He pumped his fist in the air. I raised my fist halfheartedly and looked up at the sky. It looked like it was going to rain. Maybe it would clean Homer off. Willow and I watched him lope down the road.

"Where is he going?" I mused.

My friend shrugged. "I have to go. My team is meeting at a coffee shop on Main Street before we head over to PharmaTech." Willow hugged me. "Enjoy! We'll catch up later."

I walked back inside the tiny house, sagging. I was still hungover from last night. I remembered falling asleep in the Uber then throwing up outside Willow's hotel.

My head pounded. I needed to go to work soon. I checked the time on my phone. I didn't have to be there until nine a.m. I had plenty of time. I lay down on the scratchy mattress.

CHAPTER 4

Mace

As always, I woke up the next morning at five thirty. Routine was important. I led my younger brothers on a run around the large estate. They trailed behind me in two lines of twelve. My eldest brother Remington, Remy for short, ran with us, wearing a big weight vest.

"Top of the morning!" he said through his huge bushy beard. The big ex-marine had let his hair grow out after he left the service. He looked wild, but the kids loved him. I loved him, too, though he was more like a kid himself than any real help with our younger siblings. Still, he was probably one of my favorite brothers.

Jack Frost was in the dining room when we returned from the run. On the table was another box of baked goods

"My girlfriend, Chloe, made breakfast muffins," he explained. "It's not sugary. They can have that, right?"

Nate and Billy clasped their hands together, silently pleading.

"I guess so," I relented. "Though I can't believe you all don't want vegan nut bread."

Jack laughed as my little brothers clamored for a muffin.

"Line up!" Hunter ordered, looking over his newspaper. "Act civilized, and say thank you to Jack."

After the kids were sitting nicely at the table, Jack offered me a muffin. "It's a steak and potato soup muffin. Chloe is developing a new line of breakfast muffins."

I shouldn't. It wasn't health food. "Come on," Jack cajoled. "Take it from a reformed Grinch whose soul was saved by the wonders of baking. This will change your life."

"It does smell good," I said, relenting.

"It's all protein. There's so much cheese and steak in it it's basically keto."

I peeled back the paper and took a bite. It was like eating a big plate of steak, eggs, and hash browns at a small-town diner. "That's really good," I mumbled around the food.

Remy picked one up and took a huge bite. My hand twitched. Crumbs were in his beard. "She should open a franchise in Harrogate," he said.

"She's still swamped with the one in my tower," Jack said, smiling.

I walked into the office at exactly seven thirty a.m. Yesterday had been a bust, but today was going to go exactly as planned. I dropped Henry off at the in-office daycare.

Adrian, who had been acting as my assistant, said, "Jack and Liam, as well as several executives, are here for the Platinum Provisions meeting at eight thirty."

"Perfect," I said. "Liam's actually early."

"Bro!" someone shouted down the hallway.

It was Archer, my identical twin. I could see the tattoos on his collarbone and on his forearms as he wrapped me in a hug, half climbing on me.

"You're messing up my suit," I complained, pushing him off. "Why are you here?"

"Harrogate is the hot spot," he replied. "Besides, I came to see you. Hunter said you were wigging out."

I resisted the urge to find a comb and tamp down his hair.

"You should come to the meeting," my older brother Greg said, pausing before he went into the conference room. "It might benefit you to learn something."

"I can't believe he's even up," I remarked.

"I never went to sleep!" Archer said proudly. "Though if Mace is giving a presentation, I'll doze right off."

"I don't know," my CFO and brother Garrett said, walking up, laptop under his arm. "He's been experimenting with PowerPoint effects. It's going to be very entertaining."

"Presentations aren't supposed to be entertaining. They're supposed to be informative," I retorted.

"Cramming a paragraph of twelve-point font on one slide is not helpful," Liam said. He threw an arm around my shoulder. "You need a girlfriend. Look at Jack! He used to be as uptight as you. Now he has a baker."

The Platinum Provisions executives and some of their marketing team were already in the room. Adrian had put out the nut bread I had brought as a snack.

"Throw that in the trash," Liam hissed to him. "That stuff is disgusting."

"I think it tastes great!" Adrian said, picking up a piece and chewing it.

"Adrian's a sycophant and a liar!" Liam announced. "You should have come to work with me. Mace is a bad influence."

"Yes, he is," Greg said and turned to give me an icy glare. "Adrian is not here to make copies and lay out snacks. He's here to learn how to run a business, not be your coffee boy."

"Aww," Liam cooed, wrapping his arms around Adrian and picking him up. "Adrian's trying to be a serious business man."

"Stop it, Liam!" Greg said irritably as Liam put Adrian down. "Adrian, has Mace been teaching you anything?"

"I got the whole office smoothies, and they were still frozen!" Adrian said proudly.

Greg shook his head slowly. "Why am I not surprised?"

"He's learning logistics," I protested.

"This ends today," Greg said.

I cut off the tirade that I knew was coming. "I need to start the meeting. Don't want to get behind schedule." I walked to the front of the room, pleased to see my PowerPoint was loaded onto the screen. "Good morning, everyone, and a warm welcome to the representatives from Platinum Provisions. I'm glad that our two companies are able to partner and branch into medical device development. We're currently in the process of locating a site for the new light manufacturing plant. We will also be building more research and development facilities."

I heard a *thunk* and looked over to see Henry, face suctioned onto the glass door of the conference room. He wasn't wearing any pants or shoes.

I shook my head at him, but he pushed the door open and came in, looking around. Some of the attendees giggled.

Go to Liam. Go to Archer, I chanted silently, willing him to hear my commands. Henry made a beeline for me and clambered up my pants leg.

"We offer daycare here, and obviously one escaped," I said, picking him up and glaring at my brothers. Not a single one moved. Adrian finally came over to drag Henry off me.

Henry did not want to go. "I don't like it! They're mean! It's prison!" he wailed. There was more unintelligible shrieking as Donna, one of the daycare workers, ran in.

"I'm so sorry," Donna apologized. It took her, me, and Adrian several minutes to peel Henry off of me. I had to pry each of his fingers out of my hair, all while he screeched in my ear.

My ears were ringing when they finally left.

"My apologies." I checked my watch. "The schedule has a break now anyway. This PowerPoint will be emailed to everyone." Annoyed that the timetable had been disrupted, I walked over to the table and grabbed a bottle of water.

Through a mouthful of cookies that he procured from who knew where, Liam said, "Thank God for the interruption. You really outdid yourself. That has to be the worst presentation you ever gave. I particularly liked it when each letter of 'research and development' came in like a hail of bullets."

Garrett snickered. Then he and Greg exchanged a look.

"I'm going downstairs to check on Henry," I said, scowling at my brothers. "I'm sure he needs his clothes at least."

Greg followed me as I walked through the office. "What are you plotting?" I demanded, picking up Henry's pants. "It better be about finding me help with the kids. I'm the only person who cares about them."

"You're hardly the only pillar holding this family together," Greg retorted.

"Yes, I am! Hunter was supposed to help, and he's never here. He's off running his latest scheme. None of you guys who live in Manhattan ever show up to help. And now you and Garrett are plotting something."

"I don't plot," Greg said, picking up Henry's shoe.

"Garrett plots."

"Garrett has expressed concern about your mental health."

"My mental health?" I snarled at him. Greg raised an eyebrow.

"My company is doing great. We're branching into a new sector. We've never been more profitable. Tell Garrett my mental health is fine. You know how he is when he starts fixating on something. I don't want to be his target." I found the rest of Henry's clothes behind a plant.

Greg followed me down to the daycare to return the clothes. "I know you need help," Greg said, "so I have a surprise for you."

"I don't like surprises," I said as we cut through the lobby to go back upstairs to the conference room. But Greg stopped in the middle of the atrium.

"I know that. That's why I wasn't going to tell you. I hired you an assistant. She was supposed to be here by now, though." He looked around the lobby.

"That's a good sign," I said with a sigh.

CHAPTER 5

Josie

I woke up to my phone blaring.

"Marnie?" I answered, yawning.

"Where are you?" my friend yelled into the phone. "It's almost ten a.m.!"

"Oh crap!"

I raced around the tiny house, grabbing my things. As I shuttered the windows, I felt my shirt pull, and I heard a rip as my blouse caught on a nail someone thought would hold a cute knickknack.

"Why is this happening to me?" I shouted. I was late to my new job. Not just a little late—I was a lot late. And now I had to change; I couldn't show up in a ripped shirt. I pulled it off and then saw my bra had a huge hole in it too.

"Screw you, tiny house!" I yelled as I dumped my entire suitcase out on the floor. Pawing through it, I grabbed the lacy bra I never wore, which usually sat at the bottom of my pile of clothes. Then I hurriedly buttoned up a new blouse.

I ran outside just as the first few drops of rain hit me in my face.

"You were supposed to get it together!" I said, cursing my terrible life skills. It started pouring rain, and I pulled and twisted at the trailer hitch. I couldn't decouple the tiny house from the truck.

"Fine! You're coming to work with me," I told the tiny house and jumped into the truck cab.

I prayed as the engine turned over and over then cheered when it started. I could barely see through the rain as I trundled out of the parking lot and onto the main road that led up to the Svensson PharmaTech factory. My heart was pounding. I couldn't get fired on my first day. Surely they would give a girl some leniency.

"What the—" I muttered as a car came down the street directly at me. "Why are you in my lane?" I yelled at the headlights. As I approached them, a train horn blared, and the huge diesel train engine loomed in front of me.

"Crap! Crap!" I swerved, and in the rearview mirror, the tiny house fishtailed behind me, barely clipping the train that was barreling down the middle of the street.

The logo on the train cars said Svensson PharmaTech.

"What kind of company lets their train run down the middle of the street?" I shrieked, my breath fogging up the window. I rubbed at it with my sleeve, but it didn't help.

"Can't stop! Just keep moving!" I sang to myself off-key.

Today was supposed to be the first day of the rest of my life, and here I was late, dripping wet, and almost killed by a train. At least the adrenaline surge seemed to have chased off any lingering hangover.

I was shaking when I finally made it to the PharmaTech offices. They were a series of beautiful glass buildings set up on a hill overlooking Harrogate. I didn't have time to admire the picturesque scene; I was late. I parked the tiny house way in the back of the parking lot—the only place I could get enough space—grabbed my bag, and sprinted through the freezing rain to the front doors.

Wrenching the glass door open, I ran in and promptly tripped over the floor mat and landed on the floor.

"Oof!" Thankfully, my bag took the brunt of the fall. I jumped up, hoping no one saw me face-plant. Two tall blond guys in suits looked at me in shock as I dusted myself off and looked around, pretending like I didn't just face-plant in front of them. The lobby was gorgeous. There were actual live trees among the white terrazzo floor and warm wood accents highlighting the glass elevators and open stairs that crisscrossed the large atrium.

The men approached me. They looked almost identical.

"Hey," I said, trying to ignore the throbbing in my knee. "I know you! I poured chocolate sauce on you in the vegan restaurant, remember? I guess you're just so hot women just drop to their knees in front of you."

The Chad Michael Murray look-alike seemed horrified.

"Can't stop and flirt!" I said, trying not to shake from the adrenaline. "I'm very late for my first day on the job. You know how that is." I hobbled over to the reception desk.

"I'm here to meet Mace Svensson," I told the woman in a rush. I could feel the water from my hair dripping down my face into my already-soaked shirt. "Just, can you not call him yet? I need to go to the restroom and get myself together. You wouldn't believe the day I had!" I laughed loudly. The receptionist looked at me wide-eyed.

Maybe this place wasn't all that friendly.

The receptionist slowly pointed to the men behind me. "That's Mr. Svensson there." I turned around. The hot guy from the vegan café was still in the same spot, along with his doppelgänger, watching me.

"I see," I said, turning back to the receptionist. "Well. Thank you for your time."

Squaring my shoulders, I marched back over to the men.

"I'm Josie," I said, holding out my hand. "I believe you're my boss."

I saw Mace's eyes flick down to my chest then immediately back up. He ignored my outstretched hand.

I looked down at my chest. Through my soaking-wet white blouse, I could see my also white lace bra, and through that I could see, well, not everything but a lot.

"As you can tell," I said, gesturing to the rock-hard nipples that were outlined through the wet fabric, "I am very excited to work here."

CHAPTER 6

Mace

"This is not going to work," I hissed to Greg while we waited for Josie to dry off.

"Nonsense," Greg retorted. "Marnie recommended her. You know Marnie is a great assistant. Besides, we don't have the best track record of keeping people employed for our family, what with our obnoxious little brothers. If she doesn't run off screaming the first time you ask her to babysit, she's a keeper!"

"She's a stranger," I said flatly. "There's no way I'm leaving any of the kids with her."

"Fine," Greg said. "But be nice."

I looked over at the carpet where she had tripped. I had already called the facilities manager to deal with it. "What if she had broken her neck? She could sue us."

"You always overreact," Greg said with a snort. "You need to relax. That's why I hired an assistant for you. She'll help make your life easier."

Josie came out of the restroom. She was wearing a PharmaTech T-shirt. "Don't worry," she said. "My bra is still on under here."

Greg handed Josie a packet. "All the company information along with your email login and server access is here. Also, here's a phone."

"Sweet!" she said, taking the phone. She immediately dropped it.

Greg sucked in a breath. "I guess I'll leave you two to it," Greg said after a moment. Josie scrambled to pick up the phone. The screen was shattered.

I scowled at the girl. She already ruined one day of my life. Was she going to ruin the next week, the next month? Exactly how long did Greg expect her to stay here?

"So," Josie said, following me up the stairs to my office, "what do you need assistance on?"

"Nothing. I'll have to give you to Tara. She'll find something for you to do."

"So, what is it you guys do here, and why does it involve running a train down the middle of the street?" she demanded.

I turned around, my eyes narrowed. "The pharmaceutical products we make need raw materials brought in, and the finished product is shipped out by train. I picked this location because it already had the active rail right of way. It's one of the things that make us logistically competitive."

"The train almost killed me. There weren't any gates or anything!" she said loudly.

"Everyone else in this town manages just fine," I retorted, not bothering to hide my irritation.

She gave me a dirty look.

"This building is for research and development," I told her as we continued the tour.

"So was that other tall, good-looking blond guy your brother?" she asked, interrupting me.

"Half brother," I corrected.

"Dad got around, huh?"

"That's not any of your business." When I got to the fifth-floor landing, I turned to watch her stagger up the stairs. "I don't know what you heard about this job description, but you are my assistant, which means that you are here to make my life easier not more difficult."

"Uh-huh," she said. "Give me a minute. I need an energy boost." She took a small bag of pink-and-white candy out of her purse, opened it, and put three pieces in her mouth. I shuddered.

"This office is healthy food only," I admonished, plucking the bag out of her hand.

"I was eating that!" she protested as I crumpled the candy bag in my hand.

"There are healthy snacks and water in the breakrooms. There's one on every floor," I said as I ushered her to the large white kitchenette.

Josie picked up a packet from the basket on the counter. "Seaweed?" she said, wrinkling her nose.

"It's good for you. It contains antioxidants."

She opened the package, sprinkling seaweed crumbs all over the floor. "Oops! I guess I'll clean that up." She looked around.

"Just leave it," I ordered and texted facilities. Then I texted IT to bring a new phone.

We stopped outside the large conference room where we were having the presentations for Platinum Provisions. I texted Adrian to come out.

"Oh my God!" Josie exclaimed, looking into the room through the glass walls. "There are more of you! How many kids did your father make?"

About a hundred, but I didn't want to go into that with her.

Archer followed Adrian out, and Josie looked between Archer and me.

She did the double take everyone did when they saw us together.

"I'm the more attractive twin," Archer said.

"Clearly!" Josie told him. I scowled.

"Adrian, this is Josie. She's going to be doing things like serving coffee and making copies. Send her an email with a list of your duties. I'm putting you on the big marketing team. You'll be working with Tara, making sure she and the consultants have all the information they need."

He nodded enthusiastically. "I won't let you down!"

"You better not. This is an important campaign. I'll be working closely with you, so don't get too cocky. I'll be back down in a second after I introduce Josie and Tara."

IT met us in my office and swapped out Josie's phone.

"Don't drop this one," the technician said, handing it to Josie. We looked up when Tara walked in.

"Mace," she gushed. She was the marketing director, but she always volunteered to do things for me that were outside of her job description. I had gone for one drink with her, and now she was there any time I turned around. At least now I could pawn Josie off on her.

"This is my new assistant, Josie," I said. Tara's smile seemed a little strained. "Tara is our marketing director."

"Nice to meet you," Josie said, extending her hand.

"Maybe you can find her something to do?" I said to Tara.

"Anything to help," she purred, lightly touching my arm.

I hurried back to the conference rooms. I had the rest of the Platinum Provisions meetings to get through. And I had completely missed Garrett's presentation, thanks to Josie. On the way I looked out over the parking lot. There were pristine rows of expensive cars. But in the back of the lot, I saw a rust-bucket pickup truck attached to a tiny house that looked like it was listing. The contraption was taking up about eight parking spaces.

I had a sinking feeling it belonged to Josie.

CHAPTER 7

Josie

"You didn't have anything else to wear?" Tara asked, thinly veiled distain on her face.

"I'm showing team spirit! You know—being a wonderful member of the PharmaTech family," I replied.

Tara blinked at me. She was wearing high-designer clothes with these yellow suede ankle boots that I coveted.

"It was raining, and my shirt was wet and white and see-through," I explained. "I think it made Mace a little too excited."

"Don't talk about him like that," Tara snapped at me. "Mr. Svensson is a great man, and you can learn a lot from him. This company is innovative and groundbreaking. It's a wonderful place to work."

I made a noncommittal noise and nodded. Tara made Svensson PharmaTech sound like a cult. I guess she and I weren't going to be friends after all.

"You need to take this job seriously," Tara continued, flipping her straight, glossy hair over her shoulder.

"I thought all I was doing was making coffee and sending emails!" I joked.

"Which is an integral part of our operations," she said. "There's a lunch order coming in for the Platinum Provisions meeting. You can set that out. It should be here soon."

I saluted.

"That office adjacent to Mace's is the assistant's office," Tara said, pointing. "Mace is a very private person, so stay out of the way."

I sat down at the desk and spun around in the chair to look out of the floor-to-ceiling glass windows. The view was pretty nice. Maybe this wouldn't be so bad after all.

"So, what should I do until lunchtime?" I asked Tara. She looked down at me, her nose twitching slightly.

"Check your email inbox. I'm not your supervisor. I'm the director of marketing. I only helped you because Mace asked me to, and I like to make things easier for him." She turned on her heel and left the room. I watched her pause by the coatrack and stroke Mace's coat. Weird.

I logged on to the computer. Sure enough, the inbox was filled with unread messages. "I don't even know how to do half, okay basically all, of what is here," I mumbled and rested my head on my hand as I scrolled through the email inbox.

There were hundreds of requests wanting me to file expense reports, send some documents through a courier service, and help with booking hotels for a conference. Was there a company credit card for that sort of thing?

I leafed through the folder Mace's brother Greg had given me, hoping to find answers. But it only contained a floor plan of the office along with a horribly designed brochure about the company with terrible copy that I itched to fix. I wondered if it was Tara's work. If so, they needed a new director of marketing.

Another email came in demanding that I replenish the supply of VitaMeal drinks. I slammed the laptop shut and tried to resist the urge to walk out of the building back to my tiny house.

"I need this job. I need this job," I chanted to myself as I opened up the laptop and began responding to emails. I'd only been here a few hours. Why were all these people complaining to me?

On a hunch, I scrolled down, down through the emails. Then I saw it—an email from Tara to the entire office with my name and an unattractive picture of me looking like a half-drowned rat. The email told everyone that I would be happy to assist with any task, no matter how small. Great.

My phone rang, and I almost dropped it, banging my arm on the corner of the desk in the process.

"I hate this office," I hissed, rubbing the spot. It was a little softer and fleshier than I would have liked.

"The sandwich order is here!" said Tara through the phone. I hustled down to the lobby, picked up the bags of wraps, went back upstairs to put together a tray of drinks, and then hauled it all to the conference room.

I waited until the presenter finished and slipped inside. The tray of tea and coffee rattled in my hands as I pushed through the door. Mace walked up to the podium and opened a presentation. I could feel his eyes on me as I set out the lunch items.

There was a table in the back of the room, and I tried to keep from shaking as I laid out the food. If I was being honest, I was too nervous, frazzled, and messy to be an assistant. I was a creative writer and a graphic designer. Put me in charge of a big marketing project, and I was in my element.

I was disorganized on a good day. Now I was being paid to organize Mace's schedule. The billionaire was standing up at the front of the room, droning on about medical devices. Tuning him out, I mentally fantasized about taking the tiny house out into the middle of nowhere and defaulting on all of my debt. But I didn't think the truck could make it that far, and I didn't know if the tiny house could survive a Midwest winter.

One of the glasses toppled over, and Mace paused. My face flamed as I righted the cups and finished arranging the food. I just wanted to go home and eat some mac 'n' cheese and cookie dough. Maybe I would go to the little general store on Main Street.

As I wheeled the cart to the door, I looked up at Mace's PowerPoint, and before I could stop it, a laugh popped out.

Everyone turned to look at me.

"Sorry," I said.

"Do you have something to add?" Mace asked irritably.

I choked down the laugh. "I mean, it's just... this is a joke, right?"

He glared at me.

"Like, this is the worst PowerPoint I've ever seen. No one makes PowerPoints like that." Mace's brothers were smirking. Adrian looked terrified. But I couldn't stop the critique. "There's so much text. Nothing on the slide is aligned, and is that a knockoff of the Comic Sans font? And what is that picture? Is that supposed to be ground beef?"

"It's a robot inserting a stent," Mace said through his teeth.

"I mean, I've seen a clearer picture of Bigfoot, but okay." His brothers roared in laughter.

"If we could return to the presentation…" Mace said, his voice an authoritative drone.

I fled the room, mentally berating myself.

Tara ran out after me. "That was rude and unprofessional!" she scolded

I shrank back. *Way to go, Josie—getting fired after only a few hours on the job. This must be some sort of world record.*

"Do you even want to work here?" Tara asked, hands on her hips.

No, but I need the money, and I owe Marnie for getting me this job, so…

"Sorry," I apologized. "I didn't mean to insult Mace. I have a marketing background, and I have developed hundreds of presentations and marketing packages. If he's trying to sell PharmaTech's services, this is not the way to do it."

Tara's nostrils flared. "I am the director of marketing, and I say this is perfectly acceptable."

"Acceptable is the bare minimum," I scoffed. "You should demand excellence, which is what I provide my marketing clients."

"You aren't here to do marketing. You are here to fetch coffee, book hotels, and answer the phone," Tara hissed. "You are not paid to have an opinion on the way Mr. Svensson runs his business. Do you understand?"

"Yes, ma'am."

CHAPTER 8
Mace

I couldn't believe Josie had the nerve to insult me in front of my employees and the Platinum Provisions representatives. I fumed through the rest of the day's meetings.

"I am so sorry. I don't know what's wrong with Josie. You should fire her immediately," Tara said, coming up to me after I escorted the Platinum Provisions representatives to the lobby.

That was tempting. With Josie gone, life could return to normal.

"Your PowerPoints are amazing. She doesn't know what she's talking about," Tara continued.

I nodded. "She's just a coffee girl. What does she know?"

"You seem really overworked," Tara said, touching me lightly on the arm. "Maybe we should go for a drink? There's a new distillery nearby. I know you enjoyed that one we went to a few months ago." Tara did her fake laugh that always grated on my nerves and was one of the reasons why I had avoided repeating our drink date.

"I can't. I'm busy," I told her and escaped back to my office.

But it was not an oasis of peace. When I walked in, Josie and everything around her was covered in the powdery toner ink used in the laser printer. She whirled around and looked at me, eyes wide.

"I-I-I'm sorry," she stammered.

"Go home," I told her in disgust. Josie slowly collected her belonging as I called the facilities department *again*.

While the maintenance workers cleaned up the ink, I stood at my window and watched Josie walk to her tiny house. She could not stay here. I would have to fire her. She was the worst assistant in the world.

I shook my head. I couldn't keep wasting time on Josie. I was behind schedule. I sat back down at my desk to go through my notes for the big address to the company that I made every quarter. It was in a few days, and I wanted to have everything prepared.

I barely made it through the first page when a little voice shrieked, "Mace!"

"Hi, Henry. How was your first day?"

"Terrible," my little brother declared.

Donna, one of the daycare workers, came in behind Henry and handed me a slip of paper.

"This is his report card," she said.

I scanned it. "Henry, you got Ds and Fs on everything! This says you don't play nicely with others, that you bit someone, *and* stole a toy that someone else was playing with." I looked down at him. "You can't do that."

My brother ignored me and stomped around the room, pretending to be a T. rex.

"Listen, Mr. Svensson," Donna began.

"Mace is fine."

She pursed her lips. "I know you own the company and pay for the daycare but—" She clamped her mouth shut.

"You can tell me the truth," I said, setting down the report card.

"Henry needs more individualized attention than I think we can give him," she said carefully.

I sighed. "He had a bad childhood."

"I know about your situation."

"He's younger than any of the other kids who are shipped to us," I explained.

Donna's expression was carefully neutral.

"Can you bear with him for a little longer?" I pleaded. "Give him another chance. Please?" It was not in my schedule to find Henry his own private nanny, and he was too young for school. If the daycare that *I owned* wanted to kick him out after only one day, I was positive no other daycare in town would take him.

"We'll try, but be aware, Henry is on probation. If there is another incident, we will have to kick him out. It's a liability issue," Donna warned me. "The lawyers will back me up."

"I understand. I'll talk to him about it. Thank you."

"I think—" She sighed before she left my office. "I think he needs to spend more time with you and your brothers. This is a big change for him. He needs some assurance that his world isn't going to fall apart again."

Henry waved goodbye to Donna as she left then ran to plaster himself against my leg. I needed to work on my presentation, but Henry wasn't having it. He complained he was hungry but wouldn't eat any of the seaweed crackers or drink the VitaMeal smoothie.

"I want pizza!" Henry whined.

"Have you ever even eaten pizza?" I asked him. They hadn't served it on the compound when I lived there.

"Yes! On the train!" he said, nodding. "It was tasty!"

Archer waltzed in, Greg following behind, the ever-present look of annoyance at the world in general on his face.

"Henry!" Archer yelled.

"We're heading back to New York City," Greg said as Archer picked up Henry and tossed him up and down. Henry shrieked in glee.

"Can't you stay and babysit him?" I begged.

"We have meetings in the morning," Greg told me.

"Is Hunter going to be there?" I could feel the scowl form on my face. Greg's look confirmed my suspicions. "You all were supposed to help with the kids," I said. This was a usual topic of conversation whenever I was with my brothers.

"Get Garrett to do it." Greg's tone was dismissive. I looked across the hall to Garrett's office. Through the glass walls, I could see him studiously ignoring us.

"You've handled it thus far," Greg said with a sigh. "It isn't as if anything's changed."

"Yes, it has. All the college-aged kids are back at school after spring break. It's just me."

"You're so dramatic."

"Adrian can help," Archer said.

"Adrian is not a babysitter," Greg countered. "He's supposed to be learning about how to run a company. That's why I procured an assistant for you."

"Yes, and she's just a fantastic assistant—very organized and efficient," I said.

"I detect a hint of sarcasm," Archer said, snickering.

"I think I need to fire her," I told Greg.

"No," Greg said. "You're not going to make Adrian do that menial work."

"She's incompetent, disorganized, and she eats candy," I countered.

"The horror," Greg said. "Marnie highly recommended Josie. I know you hate surprises, but give her a chance."

"I'm the CEO. I make the decisions here. This is *my* company."

"That I invested in."

Dealing with Greg was so frustrating. "I'm going to fire her anyway."

"Do not," Greg warned. "Garrett and I talked about it. Garrett was adamant that you needed an assistant."

I clamped my mouth closed. If Garrett had decided that I needed an assistant, I didn't really want to blatantly cross him by firing her. He had a habit of screwing you over if you didn't do what he wanted. I had a suspicion that he was one of the reasons the younger boys were being shipped off to us instead of dumped in the desert, which was what usually happened in polygamist cults.

"The only reason you hate her is because she said something mean about your PowerPoint!" Archer hooted. "You need someone to keep your ego in check. This will be good for you. It will give you something to fixate on," Archer joked.

"Go home, Mace," Greg said, disentangling Henry from Archer.

"I just need to finish up my presentation," I said.

"Have Josie do it," Archer called out as he and Greg left.

Henry played on my phone while I typed out some more notes. But I couldn't concentrate over the clang of the specialized cleaning machine the custodian was using to remove the printer toner stain from the floor. The racket made me even more furious with Josie.

A thought came to me, cutting through the noise and frustration: just because I couldn't fire Josie didn't mean I couldn't make her quit. After today, she seemed like she was on her way to quitting. I smiled, the headache lessening. Then maybe we could regain some order.

CHAPTER 9

Josie

"This was the worst first day ever," I said to Marnie over the phone. It was on speaker in my lap while I tried to maneuver the truck and tiny house combo through the town to the general store. At least it wasn't raining. "I think Mace is going to fire me." I was on the verge of tears.

"It's fine. Don't worry about it," Marnie said soothingly. "Everyone's first day is rough."

"No, you don't understand." I paused and sneezed. The acrid smell of the toner stung my nose. I hadn't been able to remove all of it. I had tried to blot it with paper towels in the restroom but just succeeded in smearing it around on my shirt.

"I spilled things, broke a phone, and sprayed toner everywhere." I sneezed again.

"Those printers are tricky," Marnie said with a laugh. "On a more serious note, have you heard anything from Anke?"

"Not in a while. The last time I talked to her, she said it was a big misunderstanding, the bank had frozen her account because she was international, and that she would absolutely pay me back. That was several months ago. I keep emailing for updates but haven't heard squat. Have you?"

"No, and she still owes me three thousand dollars," Marnie said.

I sagged over the steering wheel. "I wish that's all she owed me."

"I think you should go to the FBI," Marnie urged. "What she did has to be some sort of federal crime."

"That's not what the credit card company said," I replied, feeling the clench of shame at being scammed by Anke. "They wouldn't accept the police report I filed. They said I stayed at the hotel and I have to pay. Now I'm going to lose my job." Behind me, sirens blared, and in the side mirror, I saw a police cruiser signal to me.

"Crap, I have to go."

It can always get worse. That's what I always forget.

"Miss," the officer greeted me. She was a dark-haired woman with high cheekbones, and her hair was pulled back into a severe bun. "Do you know why I'm pulling you over?"

I couldn't have been speeding. The house wouldn't go that fast. Maybe the lights weren't working?

"No," I answered.

"You can't use a phone while driving," the police woman clarified.

"I wasn't texting!" I protested.

"You aren't allowed to talk on a speaker or a headset while driving. It's dangerous and against the law. I'm writing you a ticket."

I started sobbing. "I can't pay a ticket. I didn't know! I'm not from here!"

"That's not an excuse. Don't use a phone and drive. It costs lives."

The police officer wrote me the ticket while I sniffled. I didn't even look at the sum when she handed it to me. Whatever it was, I couldn't pay it.

I pulled the house back into the parking lot of Ida's General Store. Wiping away the tears, I checked the candy jar in my purse. Empty. I needed a refill.

Ida's General Store was high-end. As soon as I walked in, I felt out of place, with my toner-stained clothes and generally bedraggled appearance.

A well-dressed woman looked at me in fear.

Her daughter pointed at me and said, "You look weird."

"This is going to be you in a decade," I told the kid.

The woman pulled her daughter away. I grabbed a basket and looked for the candy aisle. I found it near the front of the store. It was well stocked, and I felt my mood start to lift as I contemplated my options.

"Ooh, saltwater taffy. Now we're talking!"

An older woman with a shock of white hair and bright-purple lipstick walked up to me.

"Those are a good choice. They're locally made," she said.

"They look delicious." I read her name tag. "Are you Ida, from Ida's General Store?"

"That's me, sweetheart," she said proudly.

"This is a great candy selection," I said.

"You have a great candy selection yourself!" she said, making me laugh. "I'm sure all the guys are after your gobstoppers."

"Hardly," I said. "I think I'm too much of a mess. I scare them off. I'm sure all the men in Harrogate want the health-food, vegan-goddess types. I'm more the carbs, cheese, and cake troll that lives under the bridge."

"Please," Ida snorted. "I've been around. Trust me—wave those things at a guy, and he'll come crawling under that bridge with you. Men like a little something to grab onto." She winked.

I grabbed milk, three kinds of cereal, a few packets of microwave mac 'n' cheese, and a box of bottom-shelf wine. There was also a display with organic chocolate chip cookie dough, but it was expensive. I sighed longingly and put it back. I bet it was delicious.

Ida waved me over to the cash register.

"Pro tip," she said, pointing to my shirt. "Put hair spray on those ink spots, and let it sit forty-eight hours. Wash it off in cold water, and it'll be good as new."

"I'll do that," I said gratefully as she rang up my groceries.

"Also"—she waved a packet of organic chocolate cookie dough in my face and put it in my bag—"this is on the house."

"I can't," I protested, but not all that hard if I was being honest.

"I know a kindred spirit," Ida said, blowing me a kiss.

I was feeling a lot lighter when I walked into my tiny house. Ida seemed cool. Hopefully she was cool with me parking my house in the lot behind her store for a little bit.

After taking down two of the pasta-filled mason jars, washing them, and filling them with the candy I had just bought, I took off my shirt and sprayed it with hair spray.

"Let's see, Ida. You came through with the cookie dough. Hopefully this works. I can't believe I ruined two shirts in one day." The bra I just had to assume was ruined. It wasn't like anyone was going to see it. Mace wasn't planning on ripping my clothes off. I felt a bit tingly between the legs at the thought.

"Ugh, what am I doing?" I shouted to the tiny house. "I can't stand him. He's the worst, and he clearly hates me."

My stomach growled. I looked at the cookie dough then put it down.

"No, you need to be a responsible adult. Eat the instant mac 'n' cheese first." The tiny house was supposed to be furnished, and I poked around for a bowl. I wrenched an upper cabinet open, and the door flew off the hinges and hit me in the face.

"Ouch!" I clutched at my head. "Why is this happening to me?" The tiny house creaked ominously. Rubbing my head, I pulled a bowl out of the cabinet, filled it with water, and looked around for the microwave.

It was then that I discovered the tiny house did not have a microwave.

"Why does my life suck?" I yelled. "I'm eating cookie dough for dinner, and you can't stop me!"

I grabbed the handle of a drawer then stopped myself from wrenching it open. "Not this time, house." I carefully opened the drawer and took out a spoon.

"See? I'm nice to you. You can be nice to me." The front face of the drawer fell off, landing on my foot.

I think my tiny house is trying to kill me.

I ripped open the packet of cookie dough, poured myself some wine, and went to town. Sadly, this was not the worst thing I could be eating. I have been known to eat butter with sugar. Pro tip—put a little vanilla extract in the mixture, and it's like eating buttercream frosting. Yes, I have a problem.

It started raining again sometime after my third glass of wine. I woke up to a wet mushy piece of insulation falling on me.

Oh no.

I looked up; dirty water dripped in my eyes. A piece of the ceiling had fallen off, and the rain leaked through. Cursing my bad decisions that had led me to this point, I found some duct tape and a plastic bag and patched the leak as best as I could.

> **Josie:** *I hate this house. It's raining inside*
> **Willow:** *I'll come help you tomorrow. This PharmaTech project is the worst. The management is problematic*
> **Josie:** *Let me guess. Tara*
> **Willow:** *Uh yeah*
> **Willow:** *Is there something going on between her and Mace? She's always like saying how wonderful he is.*
> **Josie:** *Gross. I hope not. Though probably. He has terrible taste. You should see his PowerPoints*
> **Willow:** *Have seen one. Thought I was going to have a stroke. It's like that with everything on this project, though. You needed to be on this team. You'd whip them into shape*

Josie: *I wish I was doing marketing. Anything is better than being Mace's assistant*

Sticking my phone in my mouth, I hauled myself up the ladder to the loft. I curled up on the musty mattress and passed out.

I woke up with a start the next morning and looked at the time on my phone. Crap! I was going to be late again. I ran around, throwing the jars of candy, the mac 'n' cheese packet, and a bowl into my purse. Then I walked outside into the sunshine and looked solemnly at the trailer hitch.

Nope, still couldn't figure it out.

"You're coming to work with me, tiny house!" I shouted and jumped into the truck.

"Being mindful of any wayward trains," I ordered myself over the grinding of the engine. I prayed that the truck would hold out as I trundled down Main Street and up the hill to the Svensson PharmaTech offices.

Belching exhaust, my truck pulled up beside a cute little sports car. I looked over. Tara was giving me a sour look through the window.

"Good morning!" I said cheerily. She didn't wave back, just zipped her little car into a parking space.

The tiny house wasn't going to fit that neatly. I drove it over to an empty part of the lot and parked the trailer as best as I could. Something creaked in the house, but I decided to ignore it.

I checked the time on my phone—three minutes before nine. I sprinted to the building. Tara was waiting for me in the lobby. The ground was still wet from the rain last night. I saw the mat I had tripped over yesterday and braced for impact. My foot hit the mat, and instead of slipping and falling, I was stable.

"I had someone fix that," I heard Mace say. Tara beamed at him. I was satisfied to see that he only gave her a professional smile back. Wait, what did I care? If he wanted to hang around no-taste Tara, that was his problem.

"I see you're a man with foresight," I told him. "Nicely done." He looked annoyed. "Today is a new day," I promised him. "I am a new me. I'm not going to let you down, boss." I clapped him on the bicep. I had to reach up slightly because he was very tall. He also had a very muscly arm under that designer suit. Not that I cared, of course.

Mace looked down at my hand on his arm. "See that you do. This is a streamlined operation. I can't have a repeat of yesterday. You've been highly recommended by my brother's assistant. Her reputation as well as yours is on the line."

I saluted him. "Won't happen again."

"I highly doubt that," he replied and directed me to the stairs. "There are quite a few things that need your attention," he told me as we climbed the five flights of stairs up to his office. I was huffing and puffing once we made it to the landing.

Mace looked at me. I bent over, my chest heaving. "I only ate wine and cookie dough for dinner last night," I told him. "I'm a bit low on energy. Give me a second."

His mouth turned down in disgust.

"You take those stairs really fast. You should slow down and admire the view." I snickered to myself. "Although I guess the view from behind you is actually much better. "

I heard him suck in a breath, and I looked up at him, giggling internally at the expression on his face.

"Sorry," I said, "that was totally inappropriate. I swear I'm turning over a new leaf. Girl Scout's honor."

He gave an incredulous snort.

"Hey!" I exclaimed when I walked into the office. "All the ink's gone."

"And I see you also removed it from your skin," Mace remarked. I looked down.

"It's still on me, it's just that this shirt is a little higher collared," I explained as I unbuttoned the top two buttons and pulled the shirt down to show him the faint ink stains. My boss reddened ever so slightly as he looked at my chest. Then his gaze went quickly to the ceiling.

"I didn't mean it like that," I said. "I was just trying to make conversation since you brought up the ink."

"*You* brought up the ink," he corrected.

"But you brought up ink on my skin." I looked at him. "Do you have any tattoos?"

"Excuse me?"

"Like your twin brother, Archer. And you have another brother, Hunter, right? And one named Garrett?" I chuckled. "That's so weird. Did your mom name you all after war instruments? Was she a video game geek?"

Mace glared at me, gray eyes steely.

"My mother was only thirteen when she was coerced by my father to join a cult. She got pregnant at fourteen with her first child and had eight more in as many years until she left. So, yeah, that's what she named us. What do you expect? She was basically a child; she had no education. But good on you for mocking a victim. I bet you feel real superior."

"Oh," I said, feeling stupid. "I put my foot in my mouth. It's an unfortunately regular occurrence with me. I'm so sorry."

"Grow up," Mace snapped at me. "You are a useless person. I don't want you here, and I'm going to make sure you quit before the week is out."

I looked down at my shoes.

"Your work assignments are in your inbox," Mace said. "I suggest you start your day."

CHAPTER 10

Mace

I couldn't believe Josie. How dare she make fun of my mother?

"I need to get rid of her," I fumed.

I went across the hall to my brother Garrett's office while I watched Josie through the layers of glass. She set out jars of candy and pulled a bowl out of her purse.

"What are you doing in here?" Garrett, my CFO, asked.

"I hate that assistant," I told him.

"Hate is a strong word and should be reserved for people who dump puppies on the side of the road, people who don't use an Oxford comma, and our father," Garrett said from behind his computer screen.

"She insulted our mother."

"Do you see me?" Garrett asked, not looking up from his spreadsheet. "I'm rolling my eyes. Mentally. You can practically hear them scraping the back of my head."

"You never liked Mom."

"Of course I didn't like Mom," Garrett sneered. "By the time I was born, she was five kids deep and threw anything within reach at you if you came near her or interrupted her TV-viewing time."

"She was a victim."

"No one forced her to live in that compound."

"She was a child," I argued.

Garrett shrugged. "So were we."

"I forgot what an asshole you are," I snapped at him, though I knew I was going to regret it.

My younger brother looked at me, eyes cold. His military-short haircut made him look dangerous. It was not an inaccurate conclusion to draw. I'd seen Garrett bring companies to their knees and devour their carcasses.

"I have zero sympathy for people who make bad choices," Garrett said in a clipped tone. "Now you are starting to get on my nerves. You need to calm down."

"You could help," I said churlishly.

Garrett waved his hand. "How do you think everything gets funded, hmm? You think Greg and Hunter are *that* smart?"

"No?" I said cautiously. Talking with Garrett was like dancing with a snake that had a knife duct-taped to its tail. I was always going to be on the losing end.

"The only way we're able to keep our family afloat is finances. This company would be bleeding to death in a ditch if it wasn't for me." Garrett tapped his pen on the desk, punctuating each word. "Do you know I have headhunters regularly calling me, wanting me to save the Fortune 500 Company du jour that's been run into the ground? Do you even appreciate the sacrifices I have made?"

"I do, but I'm just tired of being the only person taking care of the kids. If you could help out—"

"I'm already helping Archer with his stupid little conference center idea. He's thinking about buying that defunct zoo and bringing in penguins. Penguins! I am obviously trying to steer him in a more profitable direction, but I can't have you having a nervous breakdown," he warned me.

"I'm not having a—"

"You've wasted enough of my time. Go put together another one of those seizure-inducing PowerPoints for the quarterly address to the company. You're going first. Presenting after you always makes my slides look better," he ordered.

I slunk out of my brother's office. I usually tried to avoid him. Garrett was odd, even when we were kids. He had all the star charts memorized, and he could count prime numbers to the hundredth digit. He and Remington spent too much time together, I decided. The two craziest brothers shouldn't be that close. It was dangerous. Who knew what they were plotting?

Not wanting to be that close to Josie, I went to an empty conference room. Normally I liked all the glass walls since it was usually so cold and dark this far north in New York. But now I wanted some privacy. Hoping no one would bother me, I quickly searched on my phone for information on how to convince someone to quit.

One article had a whole list. The first recommendation was to play favorites. I could do that. I could tell she and Tara didn't get along.

The next suggestion was to assign an overwhelming number of tasks. I sent out an office-wide email replying to the one Tara had sent out a few days ago reiterating that anyone needing help with anything should contact Josie.

The article also suggested making the undesirable employee stay late. I could definitely do that, especially if I insisted on unreasonably short deadlines for all my assignments.

The biggest recommendation was to demand success in areas the person wasn't trained or hired for. What project could I put her on? I didn't want Josie to work on something that was actually important. The company quarterly presentation was coming up. That would be a perfect opportunity to send her over the edge.

"See, Garrett?" I muttered as I put away my phone. "You're not the only one who can plot."

Tara was walking down the corridor to one of the conference rooms as I headed back to my office.

"Is Josie still upstairs?" I asked her.

Tara made a face. "She's making microwave pasta."

"She what?"

"Don't ask. You know, Mace," Tara said. "You work too hard. Maybe you should get out more. The cider brewery just opened a restaurant. Maybe we should go?"

I nodded noncommittally. Tara constantly wanted me to do stuff with her. I had gone to get a drink with her once, just for business, and now she was constantly around me or doing things for me.

"I *am* stressed," I told her, trying to divert her attention. "But Josie is the main source of my stress."

"She does seem to have trouble fitting in," Tara said. She looked up at me from under her lashes. "Maybe you could fire her?"

"I can't," I said, "at least not anytime soon. But if she quits, it won't be a problem."

Tara winked at me. "I think things might just work out in your favor."

I felt a little guilty for trying to make Josie quit. But then I remembered how she had mocked my family situation. That particular sore point was more tender than I liked to admit. No, it would be best if she quit. Especially since she somehow always seemed to ruin my carefully managed day.

As I rounded the corner, there, like a ghost that just wouldn't quit, was Josie, sitting in the middle of the hallway. Irritation bubbled to the surface.

CHAPTER 11

Josie

I slumped down at my desk. I had had no idea about Mace's mother—I bet that was a real sore point for him. There was no way he would keep me around after I made a mean joke about her. I really needed to learn to keep my mouth shut.

Promising the employment gods that I would absolutely do better if only I wasn't fired, I opened my email inbox.

Someone needed a hotel reservation. Someone else wanted some samples sent to the Palo Alto branch. Closing the email program, I rested my head on the desk, feeling overwhelmed. I needed some breakfast before I could deal with all the demands.

I took out the mac 'n' cheese packet and the bowl I had thrown into my purse. After heading to the breakroom, I mixed up the water, noodles, and cheese packet, then I checked the snack selection while it cooked.

Tara came over to me as I was picking through the plain rice cakes and little packets of something called chickpea butter.

"I have a marketing meeting," she told me. "You need to prep conference room 25-T."

"Sure," I said, taking the pasta out of the microwave.

Tara looked disgusted as I stirred the neon-orange food. "You aren't a good fit for this company. If I were you, I would consider finding somewhere else to work and bowing out gracefully."

"I am going to prove that I am an invaluable member of this organization," I bluffed. Truth be told, I figured Mace would have me out of there by tomorrow evening. "I'll have that room ready to go," I told her.

I grabbed my bag and filled a container with trace paper, card stock, and boxes of pens and markers from the supply closet near Mace's office. Balancing my bowl of breakfast pasta on the plastic container of brainstorming material, I walked to the conference room. Except I couldn't find it.

"The map says it's supposed to be here," I muttered. I set down the container and sat down on it, taking bites of pasta and contemplating the floor plan that had been included in my welcome packet.

"What are you doing?"

"Hey, boss!" I said to Mace. He walked around my impromptu seat to stand directly in front of me. I had to crane my neck up to see him. I tried not to make a comment about how my head was strategically at crotch height to him. Probably best to keep that to myself.

"Just trying to find a conference room."

"You're eating pasta."

"Wanna bite?" I asked, offering the bowl to him. "I think it's organic. I bought it at that hippie general store down the way."

"I told you only healthy food is allowed in this facility."

"Pasta is healthy!" I told him.

He held out his hand.

"Seriously?"

"It's company policy," he said, half smiling at me.

I put the bowl in his hand, and he tossed it into a nearby trash can.

"That was my only bowl!" I yelled at him, running to the silver bin.

"*Don't*," he ordered, grabbing me and wrenching my hand back just as I was about to stick it into the large metal trash can.

I stared up at him, feeling apprehensive. I didn't think Mace was the physically violent type, just the glaring, broody type who loomed around corners and broadcasted his disapproval.

"It's a compacting trash can," he said softly, releasing me. "It could have crushed your hand."

"Oh. Well, thank you for saving my hand." I swallowed. "You should probably not have those things just lying around. Sounds like a liability issue."

"There's a huge sign on the front of the trash can"—he pointed—"and one on the wall behind it. It's never been a problem until now."

"Great. As always, it's been a productive conversation, but I have to prep a conference room."

He stood there silently as I picked up my box, said a little prayer, and picked a direction.

"This seems right," I said, feeling sweaty as I walked away from Mace. My body echoed with the sensation of his large hand on my arm and the heat from his body.

I looked at the door numbers in the short hallway. Where was the conference room? I turned a corner and saw Mace standing there expectantly. Fuck. I was right back where I started.

"Are you lost?" Mace asked with a quirk of his eyebrow.

"Nope," I said. "Just enjoying some exercise."

"What conference room?" he asked, the hint of a smile playing around his mouth.

"I don't need your help," I countered. "I'm just admiring the view."

"But you're standing in front of me," he said.

Did he just—

"There you are!" I heard Tara screech. "Mr. Svensson is very busy. Stop wasting his time."

Tara did a bad imitation of the longing sigh of a Disney princess in Mace's direction then gestured impatiently for me to follow her. We turned left, not right, and then we were at the conference room. I set the box on the table.

"What is all of this?" Tara asked as she opened up the lid to the box I had filled with paper, colored markers, and stickers.

"You said you were brainstorming, right?" I said. "So you need something to get the creative juices flowing. I brought a few things."

"You need to bring refreshments," Tara sneered. "That's what you do. You fetch coffee. You are not part of the marketing team."

"If I wasn't supposed to bring this, then where's all your brainstorming stuff?" I argued.

Tara pointed to one solitary easel.

"That's it?" I asked, incredulous.

"This is all we need," Tara said.

I was about to make a nasty comment about the state of Mace's PowerPoints and the marketing collateral generally, but I was trying to make it through the week without being fired. I couldn't ruin Marnie's reputation—she had stuck her neck out for me. The least I could do was not insult people every five minutes, even if they deserved it.

"I'm off for coffee, then," I told Tara.

I filled pitchers of water and coffee from a nearby breakroom and was setting them out on the table when Willow walked in. She gave me a brief hug.

"Stay strong," I whispered to her.

"No promises."

Tara stood in front of the room and cleared her throat, watching me. "You can go now."

"Let me know if you need anything else!" I chirped.

See? I'm turning over a new leaf.

CHAPTER 12

Mace

I made Josie stay late that night. She was organizing the notes from the Platinum Provisions meeting to send out. I watched her through the glass partition wall. She seemed stressed as she typed up the notes. Good. She would be gone for sure by the end of the week.

I sent her several emails with busywork like reorganizing the supply closet and inventorying the breakroom snack supply.

"Did you receive my messages?" I asked her from the doorway between our offices. She looked up at me. A few tendrils of her curly hair had escaped from her bun. I longed to tuck them back into place… but only because I wanted it to be orderly, not because I wanted to touch her hair.

"You want that done tomorrow?" she asked. I noticed a slightly hysterical edge to her tone.

"Of course," I replied. "While you're at it, survey everyone in the office to see if they want different break-room snacks."

"I'm sure they do," she muttered.

"What was that?"

"Nothing!" she said in a fake-pleasant tone.

"You are free to leave after you send me the notes to review," I informed her.

Josie sighed. "I'll have it done in a few hours."

"See that you do." My plan seemed to be going well.

Josie didn't send the notes out until close to midnight. Garrett was in the study with me at the house when Josie's email showed up in my inbox.

I opened it, expecting to see a mess. Instead it was nicely formatted with pictures and callouts for the conclusions.

"I see your assistant is working out nicely," Garrett said.

"I wouldn't say that. This is the only thing she's done right, so don't act so smug."

Josie was back to her disorganized self the next morning. As I was pulling into the parking lot, she almost ran over me with her tiny house.

"I can't stop! It doesn't brake easily," I heard her yell through the window. I needed to have a talk with her about not leaving that monstrosity in my parking lot.

"I'm early today!" she sang as she ran up behind me in the lobby. "I had candy for breakfast, and I am pumped!" I ignored her as she followed me up the stairs.

Josie stepped in front of me when we walked into my office. "I want to apologize for yesterday. I was acting shitty and unprofessional. I'm going to show you I'm a great assistant. This is the start of a brand-new me!"

"Your shirt skipped a button," I told her. She looked down at her blouse. I wondered if she was wearing that bra from two days ago when she showed up soaking wet. Then I cut that thought off. Josie was my annoying assistant. I was not thinking about her in *that* way.

But I spent the whole morning obsessing over her. My schedule said I was supposed to be reviewing Garrett's latest financial report and preparing for the quarterly presentation. Instead I watched Josie through the glass wall that separated her office from mine. She had dumped out what looked like the entire contents of her purse, and they were piled messily on her desk.

Phone pressed to her ear, she typed furiously on the keyboard. In between phone calls, she would swear or eat something from the pile of stuff on her desk. As soon as I finally managed to stop wasting my time watching Josie and actually do some work, I heard the unmistakable sound of a phone hitting the floor.

"Did you break another phone?" I yelled, running into her office.

"It slipped out of my hand," she shouted. "Why don't you all have cases for these phones?"

"No one else has had a problem."

Whoever was on the other end was still talking from the receiver. Josie shushed me and knelt over the phone on the floor.

"Hello? Hello? Are you still there? Yes, I need to book a block of hotel rooms for September. Yes, for that conference... perfect, thanks!" Josie looked up at me and smiled. "At least I got that done. I made a list," she said proudly, showing me her notes scrawled messily on a scrap of paper. I couldn't even read Josie's handwriting. It looked like gibberish. She crossed out one of the rows of scratched writing.

"I don't know how you stay organized. Give me the phone," I growled.

She picked it up, and it basically disintegrated. The battery popped out, and the screen puffed into glittery dust. Josie handed me the phone. "I think I need a new one."

As I tried to put it back together enough to give to IT, Josie slumped dejectedly in her chair. Her computer glasses were perched on her nose, and tendrils of her curly hair had escaped from the messy bun and hovered in her face. She blew the hair away and shuffled the pile of stuff on her desk.

Pulling out two mason jars, Josie took out a piece of candy from each and shoved them both in her mouth.

She swallowed the candy and grinned when she saw me watching. "Admiring my candy jars?" she asked, holding the jars up to her chest. I could see her breasts strain against the fabric of her shirt with the motion.

"I'm not—"

She blew me a kiss. "I know you want to taste my candy."

"I don't eat candy."

"You'll like *my* candy," she said, leaning forward, her breasts straining at her shirt. "Go on, just stick your hand in."

I swallowed. *Put my hand in her candy jar?* I could feel heat start to creep up my neck. "I hope you aren't implying what I think you are," I said through gritted teeth.

Josie gasped and hugged the candy jars to her chest. "Get your mind out of the gutter, Mr. Svensson," Josie said in shock. "I'm merely offering you a piece of candy. I have gummy worms and saltwater taffy. They're all organic and locally made."

"My apologies," I stammered and hightailed it back to my office. What was I thinking? That was highly inappropriate. What if she filed charges? She could sue. My company could be ruined! I looked through the glass, and I saw Josie smirk as she ate another piece of candy.

So she *was* teasing me.

CHAPTER 13

Josie

I laughed to myself, thinking about Mace's reaction. He had the face of a man who needed to get laid.

Josie: *I think Mace wants to put his hand in my candy jar*
Willow: *Like your actual jar of candy or your you know*
Josie: *He wants the candy jar between my legs so to speak*
Willow: *I mean it's not so to speak about anything. You just said he wants to finger you*
Josie: *Well yeah... he's a terrible boss, but he IS good looking*
Willow: *I thought you were trying to keep this job*
Josie: *I am, but I think he wants me to quit*

Willow: *I know Tara wants you to quit. She seriously spent 10 minutes this morning complaining about you*

Josie: *That woman needs a life*

Willow: *I think she thinks Mace is going to be her life. She gushes about him and every other sentence is something he said, did, or thinks and what a great man he is*

Josie: *Gag. He's not that great. He's sexy and has a face I'd like to sit on, but he's too inflexible and he is terrible at marketing*

Willow: *LOL! He came and did a presentation for us to introduce us to this new product. Worst. Presentation. Ever. I would think it was satire if he wasn't so serious*

Josie: *Got to go... speak of the devil*

Tara had come into Mace's office while I was texting Willow. She was perched on Mace's desk and was so obviously flirting with him. She leaned over to touch his collar. I scowled as her glossy hair flicked in his face.

I poked one of my errant curls back into my bun. Back when I thought Anke was the answer to all my problems, she and I would go to a dry bar to have our hair blown out every week. Now I couldn't afford that luxury, so I had to make do with my natural frizzy hair. All the rain, drinking, and early mornings weren't doing it any favors.

Tara was still talking to Mace, so I resisted the urge to put my head down and sleep. My sugar high was wearing off fast, and I could feel a crash coming on. My computer pinged with a notification. I read it and smiled.

Poking my head through the doorway, I ignored Tara and addressed Mace. "Your schedule says you eat lunch right now."

"Do you want me to have something delivered?" Tara asked brightly.

"No, thank you," Mace said firmly. "I brought something."

I smirked at Tara. "I'm sure you have really important marketing director things to do. Don't you worry about Mace's lunch; I'll make sure he's *well* taken care of."

Tara shot me a dirty look as she left the office.

"I'll have everything ready for you soon," I assured Mace.

I found a tray in one of the cabinets in the breakroom. Mace's lunch was in a glass container in the fridge. I sniffed it. The square dish contained a dense, half-frozen mass of raw fish, quinoa, uncooked vegetables, and strips of dark-green seaweed. It smelled disgusting. I popped it all in the microwave for six minutes. That should do it.

I arranged silverware and a glass of water nicely on the tray.

"Josie!" Lennie, one of the IT guys, said, sticking his head into the breakroom. "I have a new phone for you. I just need to swap out the old one." He followed me to my office, and I handed him a plastic baggy with the broken phone.

"Don't you have a case?" I asked him. "I'm terrible with electronics."

"We can have one ordered," he replied. "Do you have a color preference?"

Before I could answer, an earsplitting *woop woop* shrieked out, and the fire-alarm lights flashed in the hallway in time with the siren.

"I don't think there's supposed to be a fire drill today." Mace poked his head in, concerned. "It may be a real emergency."

Lenny and I followed Mace out into the hall. As soon as I took a breath, my nostrils were assaulted by the acrid smell of burning fish.

"Your lunch!" I looked at Mace in horror then ran in the direction of the breakroom.

"Josie, stop!" Mace shouted.

Thick black smoke was billowing from the kitchenette when I ran in.

"Just leave it for the fire department!" Mace yelled as I wrenched opened the microwave door. Coughing, I ignored him and dumped the dish into the sink. It spattered as I turned on the tap.

"What is wrong with you? Why would you microwave it?" he asked, incredulous, as he waved the smoke out of his face.

"It was cold, and it looked raw," I explained.

"It's *poke*—it's raw fish and rice," he said angrily. "You just mix it together."

"I've had *poke*. I'm not a complete idiot," I said defensively. "Poke is expensive tuna, rice, and yummy grilled vegetables. I've never seen *poke* that looks like something that died on the side of the road."

I looked out through the glass walls enclosing the breakroom. The fire department arrived. The men in their helmets and bright-yellow gear marched through the open floor plan, their boots clomping on the floor.

"You need to evacuate in the event of a fire," one of the firemen admonished when he went into the breakroom.

Mace gestured to me in irritation. "She wouldn't evacuate."

"It's fine," I assured the fireman. "Just a little cooking accident." Mace shook his head while one of the firemen took a crowbar and wrenched the microwave out of the wall.

"It doesn't look like it's on fire," he explained, "but better safe than sorry."

"Cliff's right. There may be an electrical issue. Don't want to burn down this nice facility, right, Mr. Svensson?" another one of the firemen added.

"Were you microwaving fish?" Cliff asked me.

"I think it was the seaweed," I said, poking at the mushy blackened food in the sink. "I bet it acted as tinder."

"She's my new assistant," Mace said. I didn't have to look at him to know he was glowering in my direction.

"No judgement here!" Cliff said with a chuckle.

"I'll have some lunch ordered in," I offered meekly.

"Don't bother." Mace sounded disgusted. "I need to deal with this. Just cancel lunch on my schedule."

I wish I hadn't. Mace was hungry and angry the rest of the afternoon. He paced around his office, barking on his phone. Periodically he would glare at me through the shared glass wall of our offices. I wished he would leave; I longed to sleep. Waking up early was not normal for me. I couldn't believe Mace started work at seven thirty in the morning.

"Did you finish anything on your list?" he asked, coming into my office, the irritation visible on his face.

"I'm still working on the inventory," I explained to him.

"You need to work faster. Everyone at my company strives for a high level of excellence. Except you."

That man was so enraging. I gritted my teeth and reminded myself that I needed this job. "I will have this done by tomorrow," I promised.

His eyes narrowed. "I need you to work on something else first." He came around to my desk and leaned over me, grabbing the computer mouse, and navigated to a folder on the server.

Being that close to him, I could feel the heat radiating off him, and his masculine scent enveloped me. I started wondering what it would be like if he did stick his hand in my candy jar.

"Are you even listening?" he asked.

"Yes," I lied, forcing my attention back to what was displayed on the screen.

Mace made a disgusted noise. "I have the quarterly presentation to the entire firm. It's broadcast live to all of our offices. You need to polish my script. I already wrote it, and I have the slides done. Just read through all the reports in this folder, and make sure the information is correct. The presentation is tomorrow morning. Be here early because I want to review your work."

I looked through the material after he left. It was dry and boring, and his presentation deck was basically his script copy-pasted onto each slide, with tiny blurry pictures.

"Gross. We're just going to delete all of this," I said. Clicking through the server, I found some older presentation recordings. Mace came off as stilted and uninspired. I felt sleepy by the first minute. His voice was professional, but he talked in a convoluted manner. It was worse, though, when he tried to tell a joke.

"You're like a sad little robot," I said, tapping the image of him on my screen. "Don't worry. We're going to punch up your script. What you have here is not going to work." I bet Tara had had something to do with the presentation. You would think the PharmaTech marketing director would know better, but you would be wrong.

I loved developing marketing material. The creativity, the graphic design, the wordsmithing to make sure the text was informative, entertaining, and a little funny—it was what I excelled at.

I worked on Mace's presentation for the rest of the afternoon and into the evening.

"You're still here?" Mace asked, sticking his head through the door that connected our two offices. He seemed surprised. "It's not *that* difficult."

"I just want to make sure everything is perfect," I chirped. "Remember I'm going to prove to you that I am an invaluable assistant!"

I unwrapped a piece of taffy and put it in my mouth. "One for the road?" I asked, holding out another piece to him.

"No, thank you," he said as he shrugged on his coat.

"My candy jar is always open!" I called after him. Was I mistaken, or did I see the barest hint of a smile? Not that it mattered—I would be here all night.

Fortunately my tiny house was on the premises. I made a thermos of instant coffee, took it back to the office, and set to work. PharmaTech had some nice-looking images, but they were buried on the servers. I pulled together the best photos into a presentation, edited together a little background video from some footage I had found, and chose a nice sans serif font to add headers and punctuate key points in the presentation. It was masculine but not aggressively so.

I rewrote Mace's text to seem friendlier and more conversational without sacrificing the content that he was trying to deliver.

It was five in the morning by the time I was satisfied. I ran through the presentation myself out loud to make sure the pacing felt right.

"Perfect!" I crowed.

When Mace arrived at the office at his usual time, I had changed, put on fresh makeup, and was perched on his desk, waiting for him with coffee and a breakfast rice cake I had snagged from one of the breakrooms that wasn't wrapped in caution tape.

CHAPTER 14

Mace

My morning started poorly. Henry did not want to go to daycare, and it took a while to disentangle him from me. When I finally brought him in, Donna didn't look all that pleased to see him either.

"Are we going to have a good day today, Henry?" she asked as Henry fought me while I tried to help him out of his coat.

"No!" he shrieked. "No!"

"You're late," Garrett remarked when I walked by his office. "Did you prep at all for the presentation? It's in thirty minutes."

"Has the room been arranged?" I asked him.

He shrugged. "I thought your assistant was fixing it up."

"So nothing's been done."

Josie was sitting on my desk when I walked into my office. She was in a pencil skirt with her legs crossed, and she beamed at me when she saw me and uncrossed her legs. I wondered what it would be like to slide my hand up that bare leg and stick my hand in her candy jar.

She opened her mouth. Her lips were as red as a candy apple.

"I want you," she said. My whole body jerked. Josie looked at me in bemusement. "I just wanted you to know I didn't sleep last night," she said. "I was here all night."

I watched her warily as I hung up my overcoat. "Why were you here?"

"I did what you asked," she said. "Actually I did more than you asked. Rice cake?"

"No, thanks."

"But it's healthy!" She took a bite. "Yum, it tastes like cardboard and the tears of children."

"I don't understand how it took you all night to do one simple task," I said irritably.

"It wasn't one simple task," she countered. "I had to fix not just your script but your whole presentation. Now everything looks amazing. This is going to be the best presentation of your life."

Henry making me late had thrown off my schedule, and I was having trouble recalibrating. "The broadcast room needs to be set up," I said, moving around Josie to look for my notes on my desk.

"Everything's set up already," she said. "Here's your script. Read it over, and familiarize yourself with it."

I took the papers and scanned through them as we walked to the broadcast room.

"You aren't going to be reading from it, obviously," Josie said, "so I'll have a teleprompter app on my tablet going in case you forget what you're supposed to say."

"This isn't right at all!" I complained when I followed Josie into the room we were going to be livestreaming from. "Where's my chair?"

"You can't sit down at a table hunched over," she countered. "You need to stand up tall. Be confident. We have to go live soon. Did you read over the script?"

"This isn't what I wrote at all," I grumbled as Garrett stuck his head in the room and looked around appreciatively.

"It's better," Josie told me. "Trust me."

"Garrett, we can't do the presentation like this."

Garrett gave me an annoyed look. "It's not anything that serious. Most of the employees just ignore it. You should see the glazed looks," he said to Josie.

"You won't have any glazed looks with what I've prepared," Josie promised. Garrett came over and flicked through the slides.

"She changed everything," I said.

"It looks great," Garrett replied. "All the information's here."

"Broadcasting in ten," Lenny said from behind the camera.

Josie stepped up to me and swept a hand through my hair. "You look a little frazzled," she said. "Smile! You're a good-looking guy. Be the confident CEO. Also, let's get rid of this."

She unbuttoned my jacket. The muscles in my stomach twitched as her hands grazed my abs.

"We're a conservative pharmaceutical company," I protested. Josie tossed the jacket on a chair then undid my cufflinks, pocketed them, and rolled up my sleeves. Then she undid my tie. She draped it around her neck and undid the top button on my collar. The part of my mind that wasn't reeling from the abrupt change to the presentation format was wondering what she would look like wearing that tie and nothing else.

"Are you undressing me?" I asked her.

"Not like that!" she said and winked. "Though maybe tonight." She stuck her tongue out at me. "I just want to make you seem more approachable." She fussed with my hair some more. My skin felt tingly when her nails grazed my scalp.

She stepped back, inspected her work critically, then smiled broadly. "You look good!"

"Broadcasting in three!" Lenny announced. I could see a few hundred employees gathered in the lobby below, watching the presentation on a large screen.

Josie mimed, *Smile*, as Lenny cued the camera to start.

As I gave the presentation, I had to admit it flowed much better than anything I could have created. Josie mouthed along with the speech as I talked and made exaggerated gestures when she wanted me to emote more. The little jokes and funny comments she had written into the script helped break up the dry, corporate information. Out of the corner of my eye, I could see that the people below in the lobby were all engaged and attentive to what I was saying. I even heard them laughing at the jokes, which had never happened before.

When I finished, Josie gave me a thumbs-up. I felt a grin spread on my face.

Tara was waiting outside the door when we left. "That was inspirational," she gushed, clasping her hands together. "You were amazing!"

"It was Josie's doing," I admitted.

Tara's expression went dark. "She made your presentation?"

Josie smiled blandly at her. "You know, just helping out my boss, doing assistant things."

"You did much more than that," I told her seriously. "Greg didn't tell me you were so good at graphics and communication."

"She's just full of surprises, isn't she?" Tara said, the skin around her eyes tense.

"It was nice of you to come by, but I guess you have that super-duper secret marketing meeting you need to go to," Josie said to Tara.

"Don't let us keep you," I told the marketing director. "It's very important that the product launch go well."

"I had breakfast delivered," Josie said as we walked into my office. There was a bag of sandwiches sitting on my desk.

"Are you planning on feeding the whole office?" I asked as she rummaged through the paper sack.

"I might have ordered extra for lunch," she said, selecting two croissants. She held one out to me. "Did you eat?" she asked.

"I had oatmeal."

"Then you can have a second breakfast."

"It's not in my schedule."

"You're scheduled to do planning for the next week," she informed me. "So we can work and eat." She sat on my desk and unwrapped the croissant sandwich. "It has sausage, egg, and cheese." Josie waved it in front of my face. "Take a bite," she whispered. "It's tasty."

She looked tasty perched on my desk. I could see the faint outline of her panties through the skirt. To quell thoughts of her underthings, I took a bite of the offered sandwich.

"Good, right?" she asked. "Once you have a taste, you'll want to eat the whole thing."

Yes, I thought.

Josie made notes as we went through my schedule. I didn't see how she could read that chicken scratch she wrote in. It looked like alien writing.

"Hunter and Greg are here," Adrian announced, opening the door. "Wait, you have breakfast sandwiches? That's not healthy!"

I stuffed the last bit into my mouth and threw the wrapper in the trash can. "I'm not eating it," I said around a mouthful of food. Adrian glared at me. "Josie was eating it," I told him. "I didn't have any."

"You're lying!"

"There's plenty more," Josie said, offering him the bag.

"It's going to be fine," I heard Hunter bark at Garrett.

"No, it's not! You need to apologize to her," my CFO shouted. "This is outrageous. I have to pull over every time someone calls me. And it's *your fault*."

"I said, *drop it*," Hunter growled at Garrett.

We all stared at Hunter and Garrett as they pushed past Adrian into the room. Greg came in behind them, scowl firmly in place.

"Do you need anything for your meeting?" Josie asked.

"You can bring Hunter some balls," Garrett snapped. Josie dutifully took out her notepad.

"Don't write that down," Hunter huffed. "I swear, Greg, I thought Mace was exaggerating with how useless this girl is."

Josie looked shocked. Adrian froze midbite of his sandwich.

"Apologize," I told Hunter. My voice sounded flat and cold. My older brother glowered at me but didn't say a word.

"You aren't allowed to insult my employees," I continued. "Josie has been very valuable."

Garrett sniffed. "I see, Hunter, you still haven't learned your lesson about not screwing over women."

"My apologies," Hunter said to Josie after a moment.

"Sure," she replied. Her voice sounded a little faint. I hoped she was okay. "Breakfast sandwich?"

"See, Hunter," Garrett said, his voice laced with venom. "An apology isn't that difficult. Just go to Meg, tell her truthfully that you're a big fat idiot, and ask if she would please have the cell phone law repealed."

"Wait, that law is because of you?" Josie blurted out. "The police pulled me over and wrote me a ticket. I can't pay that fine!"

"Expense it," Garrett said. "And I'll have the company bill Hunter."

"Seriously?" Josie asked.

"Yes. Give me some paper; I'll write down the code you need. I made a special one just for this situation." He glared at Hunter as Josie handed him her notebook. Garrett stopped for a moment, cocked his head, and looked at the notepad.

"Her writing is pretty bad, isn't it?" I joked. "I don't know how she reads it."

Garrett turned his head to look at me, his expression dripping with distain. "I know you're not all that smart, Mace, but Lord help us, you really don't know *anything*, do you." I looked to Greg. His expression was blank.

Garrett waved the notepad in my face. "This is shorthand. She's writing in *shorthand*. It's a lost art that was ubiquitous in the early twentieth century but has since become a dying skill. Tell me, where did you learn this?" my brother asked Josie.

Josie shrugged. "From YouTube. Seemed like a useful skill to know, and it wasn't that hard to learn."

I peered over Garrett's shoulder at the notepad. "Huh. Well, how about that?"

"I told you she came highly recommended," Greg remarked.

CHAPTER 15

Josie

Tara came into the office as I was cleaning up. The Svensson brothers had gone off to a meeting, and I was looking forward to napping at my desk.

"Do you need something for your super-duper secret marketing meeting?" I asked Tara.

"I wanted to see if Mace was around," she replied.

"He keeps a very tight schedule," I told her. "You should probably make an appointment if it's urgent." I took out my phone and scrolled through the calendar. "He has some availability next week."

"Stop acting like you're not trying to steal him," Tara spat.

I laughed. "As if."

"I see how you're flirting with him," Tara demanded. "Pretending to be a klutz so he thinks you're some wounded little bird that needs his protection."

"Uh, no, I don't do stuff like that," I countered, suddenly angry. I couldn't believe she was accusing me of going after Mace. I wasn't my mother. My standards were low, but they weren't *that* low.

"Stay away from him," Tara said.

"Sure, whatever. I don't even like him. He's a self-absorbed nutcase, and you two deserve each other," I shot back.

Tara glared at me. "I think you're supposed to be rearranging a storage closet. Oh, and I need coffee and tea in my meeting. Chop-chop!" Her nose twitched.

"I'll be down with coffee in a little bit," I said, giving her my most insincere smile.

The breakroom still smelled like smoke, and there was caution tape wrapped around it like a yellow spider's web. So I went to the breakroom on the next floor down and grabbed cups, a pot of coffee, and a kettle of hot water and put it all on a tray.

Willow was huddled in a chair in a corner when I went into the conference room.

"I can't take this anymore," she whispered to me as I set out the refreshments. "I hope there's cyanide in that pot of coffee. This is the most disorganized marketing contract ever."

"No cyanide," I said, "but—" I slipped her a breakfast croissant.

Willow took a big bite and said around the food, "Tara made us watch that quarterly presentation."

"It was good, wasn't it?" I said. "I spiced it up."

"It was too spicy for Tara. She bitched and complained through the whole thing," Willow told me in a low voice.

"Lordy. Are they paying on time at least?" I asked.

Willow nodded.

"That's the important thing," I told her.

When I walked back to Mace's office, I stopped in front of the storage closet that served the C-suite office.

"Yikes," I said after I opened it. I fully admitted I was a disorganized person, but even I thought this closet was a wreck. I hadn't fully appreciated how bad it was yesterday. "We are about to Marie Kondo this shit up," I said.

I took everything out of the closet and piled it in Mace's office, covering the floor, his desk, and the sofa.

I was lugging a projector screen out of the closet when the strap broke, sending it crashing into the glass wall of Mace's office. Little squares of glass rained down all over me and the floor.

"Are you trying to destroy this office?" Garrett asked. "You're going to single-handedly raise our insurance premiums."

"Sorry," I said to Mace's brother.

"What are you even doing?" he asked.

"Reorganizing the closet."

"That's not part of your job description," he retorted.

"Mace told me to. He wanted me to reorganize the closet and make an inventory of all the snacks and create a survey for the office of people's favorite food items," I rattled off.

Garrett looked taken aback. He shook his head. "No."

"No?"

"No. That is beneath you."

"He's my boss..."

Garrett snorted. "Mace likes to think he runs this company, but finances are the backbone of any empire. Your talents are wasted on tidying. You're good at all that communications business, correct?"

I nodded.

"I'm emailing you some links," Garrett said. "I need a presentation done. I'd like for you to work your magic."

"What about all this stuff?" I asked hesitantly.

"My presentation is more important," Garrett replied.

"But the window."

"I'll have facilities come clean it up," Garrett assured me.

I looked around uncertainly. Mace's office looked like Godzilla had rampaged through. "Mace isn't going to like this," I said.

"Mace is the one who wanted you to organize the storage closet." Garrett smirked. "Play stupid games, win stupid prizes."

CHAPTER 16

Mace

"You and your assistant are getting along really well," Liam said as we walked downstairs to one of the smaller conference rooms.

"She's growing on me."

"Pants getting a little tight?" Liam waggled his eyebrows. "She's cute. Maybe you need a little workplace romance."

What was with my brothers today? I bodychecked Liam and slammed him into the wall.

"Let's make one thing clear," I told him as he wheezed dramatically. "You don't get to be disrespectful to my employees, especially not my female employees. You were raised better than that. Understood?"

"*Yes,*" Liam gasped.

I released my younger brother and patted him on the head. "The kids look up to you. Set a good example. Also we've seen what happens when you don't respect women. The nuclear fallout is long and painful."

To highlight my point, Deputy Mayor Meghan Loring was waiting in the conference room. She did not look happy to see all the Svensson brothers.

Hunter was standing in the doorway, the tension visible in his jaw and the line of his back.

"I guess we aren't getting that factory anytime soon," Liam sighed.

"No, you certainly are not," Meghan said in a sharp voice.

"We're honored that you're here, Deputy Mayor," I addressed Meghan. "Can we have tea or coffee brought down?"

"I don't want you to go to the trouble of burning down your facility for me."

Liam snickered.

"Thank you for making the trip. We just wanted to reach out to the city of Harrogate," Greg told her, "and make sure that we're all on the same page."

Meg snorted. "Cut the flattery, boys. You want to build several huge factories and research facilities. It will change the skyline and tear up acres of meadow and forest." She leaned forward. "I'm not going to send old Mrs. Levenston from the planning department up here so you can flatter and sweet-talk her into signing off on whatever harebrained scheme you've come up with." She sat back. "Harrogate is my town, not yours."

Hunter's jaw was so tense I thought he was going to crack a tooth. "You're doing this to mess with me," he growled. "This is just business, Meg, but you're making it personal."

"No, I'm doing my job," she countered. "This isn't feudal England. The Svenssons are not going to treat Harrogate like their personal fiefdom. There are rules and regulations that you *all* need to follow."

"This is beyond following regulations and procedure!" Hunter said, slamming his fist down on the table.

Adrian jumped, but Meg didn't even flinch.

"You block our developments at every turn. You implemented the cell phone law. You're doing this because you hate me. You said that you were going to make my life here a living hell." The pair glared at each other.

"I'm not trying to ruin your life, Hunter," Meg said, "though it is a nice side effect of making sure Harrogate is a welcoming place for all citizens, not just a breeding ground for you Svenssons and your billions. But let's talk business. You want a factory? What are the concessions you all are willing to make?"

Liam looked at me then said, "Since we are planning on tearing up some green space, we were hoping a transfer of development rights—"

Something *thunked* against the glass wall of the conference room.

Meg looked over. "What was that?"

I stood up and looked down.

Henry was plastered against the glass partition. "They're going to feed me to the bears!" he said, his breath fogging up the glass. Donna walked up to the door and knocked. Adrian opened it, and Donna picked up Henry by the arm. He had gone completely limp.

"I'm an octopus. *Glurb, glurb.* That's the sound an octopus makes." Henry waved his legs.

"Mr. Svensson," Donna said, raising her voice over Henry's noise. "Unfortunately, Henry has been expelled from daycare."

"I'm shocked," Meg said, her expression implying she was anything but. Gathering her things, Meg said, "It seems like you all have your hands full. We'll continue this meeting at a later date. I suggest an attitude adjustment."

"Thank you for stopping by, Deputy Mayor," I said over the racket Henry was making.

"We're all on the same side. Let's all work together to make Harrogate the most desirable city in the country." She flashed a toothy smile.

"You know," Liam said after Meg left, "she says that, but her smile says she has us by the balls."

"This is your fault," Greg spat at Hunter. "If you hadn't fucked up, we would have had a much easier time."

"Get off my case," Hunter snarled at Greg, standing up so quickly his chair crashed to the floor.

Donna looked between them. "I see where Henry gets it."

I bent down in front of my youngest brother. "Henry. Henry, look at me."

He stopped yelling and patted my shoulder. "I want a cookie."

"You just got expelled from daycare. You don't get a cookie."

Henry threw himself down on the floor and wailed.

"What was he expelled for?" Liam asked as I picked up Henry. He was all limbs, and I winced as one of his hands hit me in the face.

"Aside from the fact that he cannot follow directions, that he has to be the center of attention, and that he yells if you don't bring him whatever it is he thinks he has to have at exactly that moment?" Donna remarked.

"Sounds like Archer," Greg said.

"Is that another one of your younger brothers?" Donna asked.

"He's in his early thirties," Greg said, "but yes, technically."

Donna sniffed. "Obviously we could handle those issues on their own and teach Henry more socially acceptable behavior. But we had to expel him because he keeps trying to run away. Not only that, he tries to convince the other children to run with him. I don't suppose that has anything to do with your upbringing?" Donna asked delicately.

"Probably," Greg replied.

"This is an insurance issue," Donna said to me. "Henry is a liability to the other children. He needs one-on-one attention. We cannot accommodate him. You can push your weight around, and I'm sure the director will take him back, but when he maims another child and the newspapers and lawyers get involved, well, I won't say I told you so, but I'll be thinking it."

Liam opened his mouth, and I knew he was about to say something inappropriate.

"Do not say anything," I growled at him. I'd had a lot of family time, and I was ready for them all to leave so I could return to my business, which I had been admittedly neglecting of late.

"Thank you for your concern, Donna. We'll make other arrangements for Henry."

"So, what *are* we going to do with Henry?" Liam asked after Donna left.

"I'll try and find a daycare." I sighed. "I guess we'll just leave him with Remy for now."

"That may not be the best idea," Hunter said.

"Why?" I asked. "He obviously can't stay here."

Hunter and Greg exchanged a look.

"What is it? You're keeping something from me. I know it." I looked between my older brothers.

"We didn't want to tell you," Greg began, "because we knew you'd overreact."

"Stop keeping things from me," I hissed.

Hunter looked pained. "Payslee is trying to take Henry back."

I hugged Henry to my chest. "She can't do that!"

"She's his mother," Hunter said, "so legally she could."

"She abandoned him and all of her other children!" I protested. "You need to do something!"

Hunter held up a hand. "I'm working on it," my older brother assured me.

"Work harder." I felt a swell of panic that I usually kept stuffed down. My family was more important than anything. Henry couldn't go back to the compound. I would not allow it. "Henry has to stay with one of us at all times," I insisted.

"That's probably overkill," Greg said.

I shook my head. "He could be snatched. She could take him to South America. We'd never see him again."

"Well, I can't be expected to take care of Henry," Greg said. "He's practically feral."

CHAPTER 17

Josie

Two workmen came and swept away the glass and placed some caution tape in the empty frame. I tried not to think about how annoyed Mace was going to be. But his brother, who was the CFO, had told me to work on his presentation. And if I was being honest, making a pretty slide deck was way more fun than organizing a closet.

I was eating cereal out of a bag. It was an off-brand mix called marshmallow wheat loops. Pro tip, you can buy just the marshmallow bits on Amazon and mix them to make marshmallow-heavy cereal. It was a little stale, but beggars can't be choosers. It wasn't like Mace kept the breakrooms stocked with anything tasty.

Garrett walked in.

"I'm not done yet," I told him. "Still working. You can't rush perfection."

Garrett gave me a small smile. "Oh, I'm not here to bug you about that. I know you'll have it done. No, I'm here to watch the fireworks, as they say."

"Cereal?" I offered. We heard Mace coming down the hall. He was talking to someone loudly over the screech of some sort of wild animal. Garrett selected a single shooting-star marshmallow and snapped it between his teeth as Mace grabbed the door handle to his office.

"What the—" he said. Garrett and I watched as Mace paused for a moment and looked between the door, the broken glass pane, and the piles of stuff all over his office.

"It's like Disneyland!" the small child in his arms exclaimed. He wiggled down and took a running leap at a pile of envelopes I had put on the sofa.

"Henry, no!"

"Too late," Garrett remarked as envelopes and labels went flying.

Henry shrieked and made snow angels in the carnage.

"I don't understand," Mace said, still standing in the doorway to his office.

Garrett blinked at his brother. "You asked her to reorganize the storage closet."

"I did?" Mace sounded like he was in a daze.

"Marie Kondo says you have to take everything out, ask each item if it brings you joy, then reorganize it. I had only gotten to the first step of taking everything out," I explained, "but then Garrett wanted me to help him on his presentation, and well"—I gestured with the hand that held the bag of cereal—"I'll finish organizing after I'm done."

I grabbed a handful of cereal and stuffed it in my mouth.

"Are you eating a bag of marshmallows?" Mace asked, disgusted.

"No," I said, swallowing. "There's wheat bits in here too."

"It looks like it's all marshmallows."

"Girl's gotta eat. It's energy. Plus marshmallows are great. You can put them in coffee. You can decorate with them. I bought a forty-pound bag online. It was only ten dollars. So you're going to be seeing a lot more of them."

Henry ran toward us, a roll of trace paper swirling out behind him. He ran into a stack of colored posters, sending them cascading to the floor.

"My work here is done," Garrett said, stepping around Henry.

Mace sighed and grabbed Henry. The little kid squirmed in his arms.

"I need you to babysit," Mace said to me.

"That is not in my job description," I countered, looking at Henry suspiciously.

"Neither is working for Garrett." Mace scowled. "Just, can you watch him, please? There are some snacks in my cabinet if he gets hungry." He handed Henry to me. The kid was heavy. He shrieked as Mace walked out of the office. I set Henry on the floor.

I liked kids in theory. Henry didn't seem like he liked me in theory or otherwise. The towheaded boy looked at me and scowled. I had to laugh because he looked just like a mini version of Mace in that moment.

"Don't laugh at me!" he yelled and crossed his arms.

"Sorry," I said. "Shhh people are working." Henry let out a high-pitched screech, and I winced at the noise. I always wanted a big family, but I sort of assumed that it would be far down the road and that I potentially may die under an avalanche of English toffee and empty wine boxes before it ever happened.

"Henry, do you want a snack?" I asked him. He stopped screaming and looked at me expectantly.

"I want pizza and ice cream," he announced.

"Me too, but I don't know if Mace has any of that." I rummage around in the CEO's cabinets and found a Ziploc bag filled with slices of some sort of crumbly bread. Opening it, I sniffed it.

"This smells—" I sniffed it again. "Oddly familiar. Is this from the vegan place?" Dry to begin with, I was sure the bread was almost inedibly stale by now.

"Pizza! Pizza!" Henry chanted.

"I don't have that," I said, "but I do have this amazing, delicious vegan nut bread." Henry didn't seem like he believed my hype. Breaking off a piece of the bread, I handed it to him.

He inspected it, took a tiny nibble, then spit it out on the floor.

"Yuck, it's gross."

"What is this racket? There are people trying to work," Tara said as she came into the office, a pinched look on her face.

Does that woman seriously not work? Why is she always hanging around Mace?

"Do you need something?" I asked Tara.

"I need to talk to Mace. You need to clean up this mess. I should have known a simple organizing job would be beneath you. You and your incompetence are harming Mace and hurting the company. If you had a shred of integrity, you would leave."

She looked around at the mess and noticed Henry, who was grinding the bread into the sofa.

"Don't do that," Tara chided, kneeling down beside him. "Why don't you come with me, and we can find Mace?"

"No!" Henry yelled and pushed her away with the hand that held the bread. I winced as Tara cursed. The nut bread was smeared in her perfect hair.

"Say sorry, Henry," I told him. "That was rude." Inside I was secretly laughing.

"Sorry," he said with a pout.

Tara turned on her heel and left.

"Serves her right," I said.

Henry resumed his yelling and dancing and general destruction. I pulled out my bag of cereal and popped a marshmallow in his mouth. Henry's eyes lit up.

"Yum!" he said. "This is amazing!"

"I know, right? Come to my office. Let's leave all this stuff alone." Henry followed me like a little puppy begging for treats.

I worked on Garrett's presentation slides in between playing seal with Henry. He would jump around and clap, and I would throw a marshmallow at him. Henry would try and catch it in his mouth. We played all afternoon. A generous portion of the bag was gone between me taking handfuls to make it through the presentation and throwing pieces at Henry to keep him occupied.

"Okay here's two," I said, throwing them at him.

"I missed one," he said as he crunched through one of the marshmallows.

"Go find it. We don't want ants," I told him.

Henry scurried around the room, looking for the treat. "I can't find it."

"Keep looking," I said, not looking up from the screen. There was one thing I wanted to finish on the slides.

"Wait, here it is. I found it."

"Don't eat it," I said absently.

"But it's mine."

"I'll trade you for a fresh one," I said, not looking up.

"Okay, but I want a star because this one's a star, and they taste better—oh." Henry went silent. I looked up.

Mace was standing in the doorway. He looked furious.

"Sorry about your office. I'm still trying to do Garrett's slides," I explained.

"Did you feed him sugar?" Mace asked, advancing on me.

"Just a little..." I said, feeling apprehensive about the look on Mace's face.

Henry started spinning around and around. "I'm a rocket ship."

Mace grabbed him and picked him up, inspecting his little brother. "His face is covered in sugar." I looked at Henry. He did look like he'd been in a fight with a clown. He was also looking a little green, which I didn't think had anything to do with the shamrock marshmallows.

"I think you should—" I started to say.

"No." Mace interrupted, walking over to me. "You can't just ignore every instruction I give you and feed him garbage."

I scooted back. Henry was licking his lips. He looked a little drooly. I'd done enough college drinking to know what was coming next.

"It might be a good idea if—"

"Could you listen to me? You need to make a change."

Henry leaned his head against Mace's chest and puked rainbow colors all down his suit. Mace strangled a curse.

"I'll grab some paper towels," I said.

CHAPTER 18

Mace

"I can't believe you fed him all that sugar," I snarled at Josie as she stood up from her desk.

"I'll bring him some water." She hurried out and came back with water and paper towels to clean up the mess. Henry for once wasn't in motion. He seemed a little stunned. I held my hand to his forehead. He felt warm.

Josie swiped at me with the paper towels and tried to convince Henry to sip some water.

"Don't bother," I said, setting my brother down and taking off my jacket. "I'm taking him to the emergency room."

"Is he really that sick?" Josie cried, taking my jacket. "Mace, I am so sorry."

"I can't say I expected anything better from you," I snapped at her.

On the way to the pediatric emergency room, I had to fight off visions of Henry succumbing to fever or some other ailment like in those old Victorian-era novels where one day a kid was fine, and the next, they had one foot in the grave.

Hunter met me at the emergency room; Archer was there with him. Hunter took one look at Henry and snorted. "He looks fine. The way Josie was carrying on when she called me, I thought Henry was on death's door."

"She was hysterical," Archer added.

"I made a rainbow," Henry said proudly. He ran to Archer to try and give him a hug.

Archer grimaced. "I can see the rainbow all over your shirt. And on Mace."

"I can't believe they won't see him," I complained. "Why is the wait so long? I've donated a lot of money to this hospital."

Hunter shook his head and said irritably, "I can't believe I'm wasting my time on this. He's fine. Just take him home. I need to make you his guardian if you're going to overreact to every little thing."

"He might not be," I countered. "What if his pancreas is about to shut down?"

Hunter ignored me and walked outside to take a call.

Archer sat down in a chair next to me. "You always overreact," said Archer. "My poor, high-strung twin."

"Why are you even here?" I asked.

"Looking at sites for my new hotel," he replied.

"At least if there was a conference center, we wouldn't have to have meetings at my office," I grumbled.

"You love seeing us. Besides, I'm good for you." Archer patted my hair. "I don't know how you and Garrett manage day-to-day. Both of you are control freaks."

"I'm not a control freak. And I function better than you."

Archer snorted. "I wasn't the one who thought he had diphtheria after he read *Little House on the Prairie*."

The doctor saw us several hours later. Josie had called me several times, but I ignored her. Henry was fine, and I felt bad for overreacting.

Henry chatted away with the doctor while she checked his pulse and his reflexes.

"Stick out your tongue," the doctor said. Henry obliged. "Wow! You did have a lot of sugar. You have quite the rainbow on your tongue." She turned to me and said, "He's going to live."

"Praise the lord!" Archer exclaimed.

The doctor struggled to hide a smile. Women couldn't resist my brother.

The doctor giggled then said, "I would say, have him drink lots of water and eat a salad. He'll be fine. In the future, maybe don't feed him so much sugar."

"It was my assistant," I explained.

"Don't be too hard on her," the doctor said.

I nodded noncommittally. Any warm feelings that had started to grow for Josie were gone. I didn't tolerate anyone putting my family in danger.

CHAPTER 19

Josie

I felt terrible about Henry. It was yet another bad decision, just like trusting Anke, except this time it could have cost Mace his brother.

I ran out into the hall and almost bumped into Garrett.

"Henry is hurt! Mace is taking him to the hospital!" I said in a rush.

Garrett rolled his eyes. "Of course he is."

"Mace said Henry could die!" I pressed.

"Uh-huh." Garrett did not seem as upset as I though the situation called for.

"Aren't you going to meet him at the hospital?" I asked.

"No," Garrett replied. I detected a hint of irritation. "I can't pander to Mace's hysterics."

"Someone should go," I insisted.

Garrett pursed his mouth then pulled out his phone, scrolled through the contacts, and pressed the call button.

"Tell Hunter," he said, handing the phone to me. "And send me the presentation when you're done," he called out as he went back into his office.

"What is it, Garrett? I'm about to start driving," I heard Mace's older brother say through the phone.

I started sobbing. "Mace took Henry to the hospital! I'm so sorry."

"Who is this?" Hunter asked.

"Josie."

"What? Where is Garrett?"

"Tell him I'm not interested in talking," Garrett called out. "But if Mace is at the hospital, Hunter should be there since he's the legal guardian."

I started to repeat the message.

"I heard," Hunter said with a sigh. "I'll go deal with it."

Dabbing the tears in my eyes, I worked on Garrett's presentation. I tried calling Mace, but he didn't answer his phone. I only reached his voicemail.

I sent Garrett his presentation and then set about cleaning Mace's office. I didn't have the energy to organize it, so I just shoved everything back in the supply closet and shut the door. It was just one more thing that I screwed up and that I was going to stick my head in the sand about.

Willow was waiting for me in the lobby when I came downstairs.

"Rough day?" she asked sympathetically. "Did you hear any news about Henry?"

I shook my head.

"Let's get a drink. I'm sure he'll be fine. Little kids bounce back," my friend assured me, putting her arm around my waist.

"I guess."

"You need to find a better place for your tiny house," Willow told me as we walked to the old beat-up pickup truck.

"I can't even unhitch it," I told her as we climbed into the truck cab and I started the engine. Or tried to anyway. It churned over and over.

"Come on!" I pleaded. "Not today." It finally started, and I let out the breath I was holding.

"Does it always make that weird clicking noise?" Willow asked as I slowly navigated us out of the parking lot.

"I think so?" I said. "But I just turn on the radio."

"That's probably not a good idea."

"Story of my life."

"I think your trailer might be busted too," Willow said, looking in the side mirror. The house listed side to side even though I was driving slowly. I was tense as I drove, trying not to hit anything.

The sweat was dripping down my scalp as I parked the house. I had to pay for two on-street parking spaces, and the top of the tiny house scraped against the tree branches when I pulled in.

"Do you think the house is going to be okay on the street?" I asked as Willow and I walked into the busy bar and followed the hostess to a table.

"Do you really think anyone is going to steal that death trap?" Willow remarked as we looked over the menu that featured high-end pub food. "After the day you've had," Willow said, "I think you need a cocktail."

When the waitress put down our drinks, I took a long sip.

"That straw is just for stirring," Willow said, pulling the glass away from me. "You're not supposed to drink it like water."

"I need it," I said, pulling it back from her.

The waitress brought an order of pretzel bites to the table, and I was distracted by the gooey beer cheese and the tangy mustard dip long enough for Willow to take the straw out of the cocktail.

"These are amazing," I sighed. "I wish I had an actual kitchen where I could cook food like this."

"You haven't been cooking in the tiny house?"

I snorted. "I can barely survive in the tiny house. I think it's trying to kill me."

Willow laughed. "It can't be that bad."

"It doesn't even have a microwave."

Willow grimaced. "Svensson PharmaTech is about to not have microwaves. Tara wants to have them all taken out because of that fire you started."

"You're supposed to make me feel better, not throw my shortcomings back in my face," I complained.

When the hamburgers arrived, she pushed mine toward me. "Here. Eat your feelings."

"That's the plan!" I replied, looking up to see the waitress set down a mason jar filled with a gooey golden liquid.

"Thanks?" I said confused. "I didn't order this."

"You look like someone who's had a bad day," the waitress explained. "Trust me, this will make it all better."

"Do I drink it?"

"I mean you can," she said. "It's cheese sauce." She picked it up and poured the whole jar all over my burger and fries.

"This is something I never knew I needed in my life," I told Willow through a mouthful of cheesy burger. "I'm having a religious experience."

"You have cheese sauce all over your face."

I licked it off with my tongue.

"You know," Willow said, swiping one of my cheese-covered fries, "I was going to make a joke about you having jizz all over your face, but this cheese is too miraculous to be sullied with a dirty joke."

"Yeah, this is the closest thing I'm having to a sexual awakening," I told her, taking another giant bite of the cheese-covered burger.

"I guess Mace is off the table."

"He was never on the table."

"Actually I think that he probably wants you on the table." Willow snickered.

"Doubtful."

"I saw the way he looked at you." Willow waggled her eyebrows suggestively.

"I doubt he's in lust with me. I think he's going to fire me tomorrow," I said, contemplating my burger. It was grilled medium rare, with the smooth taste of high-quality beef. The tomatoes were juicy, and the cheese sauce brought it all together.

"If you are fired, there's a tiny house village a few hours from here," Willow said as she swiped another fry. "Josie?"

I didn't answer her. I was staring at my phone.

"Is it Mace?" Willow asked.

I shook my head, trying to breathe. I felt like my food was going to end up all over the table like Henry and his marshmallow cereal. "It's not Mace. It's Anke. She wants to meet," I said.

Willow looked at me. "Why now?"

"She wants something," I said. "She's going to try and convince me to do something for her. And I'm so stupid, I'll probably do it."

"Or maybe she just wants to give you the money," Willow offered.

I wasn't so sure. Nothing with Anke was ever that easy.

CHAPTER 20

Mace

Henry was up before five thirty the next morning. I had an uneasy dream that something was chasing after me. I woke up to see Henry inches from my face, staring at me, motionless.

"I'm hungry," he whispered.

"Dude."

"I'm hungry! I'm hungry!" he repeated while I dressed and walked downstairs.

"I guess you aren't any worse for wear," I said, ruffling his hair.

"I want marshmallows," Henry said, bouncing around my legs.

"Never again," I told him.

Archer was in the kitchen, burning an omelet.

"You could have had Archer fix you something," I told Henry as I opened a window to air out the kitchen. Henry ignored me and climbed up on a stool at the large kitchen island.

"Why are you up so early?" I asked Archer. "Wait, let me guess. You never went to sleep."

"We creative geniuses work best in the dark," Archer said as he scraped some of the eggs onto a plate and handed Henry a fork.

I looked at the food. "You really want to eat that?" I asked Henry as he gingerly took a bite.

"Don't hate on my food," Archer said. "At least I cooked. Normally I have people to do this for me."

"I think there's some nut bread left," I told Henry, trying to take the plate away from him.

"There's not," Archer said, sitting down next to Henry. "I gave it to Remy and told him to bury it in the yard."

"You wasted food!" I said, shocked.

Archer snorted. "Nope. Remy said he was going to vacuum pack it, that the bread would survive a nuclear apocalypse and we would all be glad to have it later. He stashed it in the bunker."

I snagged a bite of my brother's omelet. It tasted as bad as it looked.

"Maybe I should try and find a chef," I mused.

"I thought you tried that before, and the kids couldn't handle it."

"Right. Maybe we won't repeat that," I said.

"You could find a live-in girlfriend," Archer said and made a suggestive gesture.

"Not in front of Henry," I admonished.

"Josie should be your girlfriend," Henry said, a piece of egg falling off his fork. He grabbed it with his hand and slurped it up. I handed him a napkin. "I hope she doesn't leave."

"Mace isn't allowed to fire her," Archer said, smirking. "Greg said so."

Henry beamed. "Good. I like her. She's cool." He looked thoughtful. "And pretty."

"She is pretty," my twin said, smiling broadly.

"Don't even think about it," I growled at him.

"Someone's possessive!"

I thought about that. I wasn't, was I? Strange. I didn't even like Josie.

Henry rode with me to work. I sagged as soon as I walked into the building. Right. He was expelled from daycare.

"What am I going to do with you?" I asked him.

"Send me to Australia," he said.

"I'm not sending you to Australia. You don't even know where that is."

Josie was waiting for me in my office. The glass was still broken, but at least everything was picked up.

"How is Henry?" she asked, worry on her face.

"He's fine."

"I just want to apologize—" she began.

I grimaced. "It's fine. I have a tendency to overreact. I just... my brothers are all I have."

She looked up at me. "I understand if you want to fire me."

"I can't really afford to fire you," I admitted. "I need someone to watch Henry."

"What about inventorying the snacks?" she asked.

"What—no. Let's forget about that."

Tara knocked on the doorframe and stepped inside. Josie's eyes narrowed when she saw the marketing director.

"You have the visit to the hydroelectric plant," Tara reminded me, "with the city officials and the economic development director of the State of New York."

"Yes, I'm heading over in a few minutes," I replied.

"I thought maybe I should come along," Tara offered. "I am the director of marketing, and I think it would make a great advertising piece."

"That's a good idea. But I need Josie to watch Henry while I'm there doing the tour. Why don't you tell her what you need, and she can interview officials for quotes and coordinate with the photographer who's coming on-site to take pictures?"

Tara jerked back like I'd slapped her. "Josie?" she said, her voice rising an octave. "She wrecked your office, almost burned down the building, and made Henry sick."

I turned my palms up. "I don't understand what the problem is," I told Tara. "Josie can handle it."

"Can she?" Tara seemed skeptical.

"Can you?" I asked Josie.

"Absolutely!" she said. "I won't let you down."

Josie was silent in the car ride to the hydro plant.

"Do you still want me to quit?" she asked after we had been driving for twenty minutes.

"Of course not," I said, glancing quickly at her then back to the road. "I shouldn't have acted so horribly to you. It was unprofessional."

"I shouldn't have given Henry the sweets. I didn't mean to make him sick." She turned around in her seat to look at my younger brother. Henry had fallen asleep in his car seat. "What did the doctor say?"

"That he should eat a salad," I said wryly.

Josie laughed. She had a great laugh—it was sort of a snort, and it sounded genuine.

She pulled a small notebook out of her purse and flipped it open. "So for the marketing stuff. I've looked through your marketing collateral. I think you need a brochure or commercial or something to highlight green energy. It shouldn't be for just the hydroelectric plant but for all the buildings in the complex."

"We have something Tara put together," I said.

Josie barked out a laugh. "That is *not* good, like at all. It's a small flyer with some random pictures and words."

"It's not that bad," I protested. I could feel her glare at the side of my head.

"Except it is that bad. You need to tell the story of your business—that you care about people's health and their environment."

"But people do know that," I countered.

"I bet a lot of them don't, and the ones who do need a firm reminder," Josie said firmly, her pen scratching on the paper. "You have to set the narrative about your company being innovative, cutting-edge, and just plain awesome."

"Our work speaks for itself."

"No," she said. Her dangly earrings chimed softly as she shook her head. "That's not what marketing is. You can't just leave these things to chance. You have to not only set the narrative but dominate it. Svensson PharmaTech needs to foster some goodwill. It will help shareholders, the general public, and government regulators to have more confidence in your company. You absolutely cannot be reactionary and play defense. You must set the narrative. If PharmaTech ever wants to make a risky play or take chances on a new technology, setting up the narrative that your company is cutting-edge and has a record of excellence will mean that a new idea isn't a stupid risk. Actually it's a bold move that will create a new market and make tons of money."

I nodded along as she talked. What she said was simple but brilliant.

"I'd never really thought of marketing that way," I admitted. "I always concentrated on the formulas, products, and logistics."

She huffed. "Most people think marketing doesn't matter, or they assume marketing is facts and figures. But you can't make bold visionary decisions on last quarter's numbers. You have to set the trend. Marketing can grease the tracks, so to speak, and let your vision launch. It's not just pictures and a website. It's everything—the way you talk, the way you dress. It's graphics, photography, and social media. All those elements need to work together to sell the vision and the brand of the company."

"Tara has all that together for us," I said curtly.

"No she doesn't," she snapped, then her tone softened. "Surely you have some visions for the company beyond just making new drugs? While that's important, there are other aspects of the medical industry that would be smart to branch into."

"We are already looking into new market sectors," I admitted. "This is strictly confidential, but we're unveiling a new gene therapy product at a big medical conference next month."

"See?" Josie exclaimed. "That's the type of product you need a real marketing plan behind."

"Tara's working on one."

She snorted.

"The next time I talk to Tara, I'll bring up your ideas," I assured her.

I heard her mumble something.

"What was that?"

"Nothing. Are we almost there?"

Throughout the tour of the plant, Josie directed the photographer, chatted with the state and local officials, and all the while, wrangled Henry and made pages of notes. Henry thankfully didn't stray. He stayed glued to Josie the entire tour.

"How did you keep him quiet?" I asked her after the handshaking and photo ops were completed.

"I let him pick the restaurant we're going to," she said, looking guilty.

"I have lunch at the office," I said. Henry's face screwed up like he was going to start yelling. "But since we're out, let's grab lunch," I added quickly.

"Yes," Josie said, pumping her fist. "Free food!"

"Free food!" Henry yelled and laughed.

The restaurant he had chosen was a hip farm-to-table-type place.

"I don't know if Henry's going to like this," I whispered to Josie.

"You should give him a chance. He has opinions."

"What a lovely family!" an older woman exclaimed as she walked by our table. She must have been out with her women's group. I recognized Ida and several other senior citizens from town.

"Your son looks just like both of you," the elderly woman gushed.

"Oh, ah," Josie stammered. "We're not—this is my boss."

The woman's eyebrows rose up into her hair.

"Don't be such a prude, Dottie," Ida exclaimed. She turned to Josie. "Sleeping with the boss, eh! That's how I met my former husband. It's a tried-and-true way to find a good man."

Josie was red in the face. "She gave me free cookie dough," she explained when the women had left, cackling.

I smirked. "Ida is a local character, isn't she?"

Henry looked at the menu while Josie read it out to him.

"They have panfried fish with a fresh salad and a lemon butter garlic sauce. That looks amazing!" Josie said.

"There's a pasta dish; you might like that, Henry," I said. I did not want him to order something exotic, hate it, then make a scene.

"You can order what you want," Josie assured Henry.

"I want the lamb," Henry decided.

"You should order the fish," she told me. "I'm having the duck with plumb sauce."

"Could we also order the pasta?" I asked the waiter. If Henry didn't like the lamb, maybe he would eat the noodles.

When the food came, though, Henry dug in. He took a bite of the chards, and I winced, waiting for him to start complaining.

"This is good!" he announced. I wanted to tell him not to talk with his mouth full, but he was eating vegetables, so I didn't want to jinx anything. Henry reached for a whole lamb chop.

"Let me cut that for you," Josie said, making neat kid-size pieces with her knife and fork.

"Can I try some?" Josie asked him.

Henry nodded, his mouth full.

"Yum! It has a nice Mediterranean seasoning. It's very tasty," she said.

Henry nodded, his cheeks bulging.

"How's your fish?" Josie asked me.

"Good."

She looked at me expectantly.

"What?"

"Uh—"

"*What?*" I set down my fork.

"I want to try some of your food," she said sheepishly. "When I go to restaurants, I basically treat them all like tapas places because you can sample a lot of different dishes!"

She seemed so delighted that I couldn't help but smile.

She reached out with her fork. I took it and cut off a piece of fish. But when I extended the fork across the table, she didn't take it. Instead she bit the piece of fish off the fork. It felt strangely intimate to feed her a piece of my food.

"Mmh!" she said, pleasure on her face. I felt the breath leave my body. "That is *so good*."

CHAPTER 21

Josie

I had no shame. I stole bites off Mace's plate all through lunch. The fish was amazing; it was slightly crunchy, and the sauce was tangy and almost sweet.

"You can have it if you want," he finally said.

"No, but I'm giving you some of my duck." I speared one of the thin slices of sweet and tangy duck with my fork and held it out to Mace. I wondered if he would bite it off, but he took the fork from me. His hand was warm where our fingers touched.

"Don't you love how it just melts in your mouth?" I gushed. "I love food. I love cooking it and eating it!"

I hadn't had the money to eat at nice places since the Anke debacle, and I'd forgotten how awesome it was, especially if someone else was paying.

Henry ate most of his lamb and some of the pasta. Mace watched him, amazed.

"I can't believe he finished all of that," he said.

"It was good. We should come back here," Henry said.

"I mean, if he's going to eat vegetables, we might have to," Mace muttered.

"Are we interested in dessert?" the waitress asked as she set down boxes for the leftovers.

"No," Mace said.

"Yes," I told him. "You can't skip dessert."

"The coconut cream pie is very good," the waitress said. "It's from the Grey Dove Bistro."

"Chloe's shipping stuff all the way out here?" Mace asked, obviously impressed.

"You know Chloe?" I asked him seriously. Watching *The Great Christmas Bake-Off* over Christmas had been the only thing keeping me from completely falling apart after Anke left me with all that credit card debt.

"She's my brother's cofounder's girlfriend," he explained. "When Jack comes to Harrogate, he always brings food that she's made."

"Okay, see, you should have led with that," I told him. "Chloe is so cool! I follow her on Instagram. You should see her kitchen. It's amazing."

"I've been to their penthouse."

"What? You're killing me!"

The waitress set down two pieces of the pie.

"See?" I showed Mace. "You would probably actually like it. Chloe said she developed a new recipe that doesn't have all the cream. It's denser and less sweet. She puts salt on the coconut before toasting so you can really taste the flavor."

I cut a piece off with my fork.

"Try it," I demanded. This time, he didn't take the fork, letting me feed him.

"So the next time Chloe comes to Harrogate, you have to let me know," I said as we walked out of the restaurant. "I want to casually be there for some fake reason. I feel like we would be friends after I finish fangirling all over her shirt."

Mace laughed. It was a nice deep chuckle that ended in almost a purr.

"Are you ready for a nap?" I asked Henry as Mace opened the car door.

"He's going to be up all night," Mace said with a sigh. "You need to stay awake," he told Henry as I buckled him into the car seat.

"You just want a siesta after you eat that much." I yawned and stretched. "Ah, I forgot—"

"Your purse and your leftovers." Mace held out the bags to me. I took them sheepishly.

"Is this a regular occurrence? Your leaving stuff lying around?" Mace asked, a hint of a smile on his lips.

I stuck my tongue out at him. "My life is kind of a shit-show right now," I said as he opened the car door for me.

"Oh yeah? Why's that?"

"My boss is a nutcase."

"Really? Because I thought he just bought you lunch and let you eat all of his food."

I smiled and leaned against the window. "That fish was really good."

When we arrived back to the office, I transcribed my notes and wrote an email to the photographer. For the first time since Anke had disappeared, I felt actually relaxed and happy. Henry wasn't even running around. He sat quietly on the rug in my office and colored.

Don't get me wrong, Mace was still a weirdo who didn't like dessert and who was way too uptight, but I had to admit he was actually sort of fun to be around. It had been nice to spend the day with him. The tension in the office even felt like it had dissipated.

However, the knot in my shoulder set back in as soon as I returned to my tiny house. It took me three tries to start the old Ford truck, and I swear the house looked like it had shifted so much it could cameo in a Dr. Seuss movie.

As I drove back to Ida's General Store's parking lot, I wondered what I was going to do about Anke. I still hadn't responded to her text. I had almost given up on her paying me back the money like she had promised. To hear from her now, almost six months after the fact, I suspected it wasn't for anything that would benefit me.

Still, if she did have my money, it would be a huge help for me. PharmaTech wasn't issuing my first paycheck for another ten days, and I was down to my last few hundred dollars on my credit card.

I parked the tiny house at the far end of the small parking lot. Taking my leftovers, I had to shove my shoulder against the tiny house door to open it. It was muggy and smelly inside. I opened a window, called Marnie, and slumped on the couch.

"How's the job?" she asked when she answered.

"Slightly better."

"Good because apparently Mace wanted to fire you," my friend said.

I sighed and rifled through the takeout bag. Pulling out the container of pasta, I cursed again that I didn't have a microwave. Fine. I would eat it cold. "It was a rocky start."

"You burned down the office."

"Just a kitchen."

"Never change, Josie!" my friend said, laughing.

"Hey, so," I said around the pasta. "A weird thing happened—I heard from Anke."

"That seems suspicious," Marnie said. "I'm going to the FBI about her."

"The FBI!" I half-choked on the pasta. Coughing, I asked, "How is that going to help?"

Someone banged on the door.

"Sorry, let me call you back."

"This is the police," announced an authoritative female voice.

Hands shaking, I wrenched open the door and stepped outside.

"Ma'am." It was the same officer who had given me a ticket earlier in the week. "You can't park a tiny house on this property."

Ida came running out of the general store. "Susie, stop harassing my customers!"

"Ida," Susie said in exasperation. "It's a code violation. Tiny houses can only be parked on residential properties, not commercial, and certainly not in view of the street."

"Police brutality!" Ida announced loudly. "I'm going to be protesting in front of your office, young lady. Why, in my day—"

"In your day, Ida, the majority of these properties were vacant, and unemployment levels were some of the highest in the nation. We're trying to do better in Harrogate. We can't have RVs and campers just parked everywhere."

"This place has become so bougie," Ida complained. "It's those Svenssons. Though they are good-looking." The old woman looked thoughtful.

I slumped down on the steps of the tiny house, fighting back tears. "What am I going to do?" I groaned.

A sleek black car pulled into the parking lot and slowly crept toward us. We all peered at it. A window rolled down.

"Josie!" Henry called, waving at me.

The driver's door opened, and Mace stepped out. He was so tall he just unfolded from the car. He buttoned his suit jacket as he walked toward us.

"Is everything all right, Officer?"

"She cannot park the house here," Susie explained.

"I say she can! It's my property," Ida exclaimed.

"You and Meg just have it out for my family, don't you?" Mace asked, his face dark.

Susie didn't seem perturbed at all by his threatening expression as she looked between Mace and me. "Is she a Svensson sister? A Svensson cousin?"

"She's the future Mrs. Svensson," Ida said.

"Ida—"

Mace didn't look as upset at the idea as I thought he would. His face remained neutral. "She's my employee," he said finally.

Susie looked down her nose at Mace as much as she could since he was so much taller.

"She cannot park here. She needs to move in the next five minutes, or I'm having this tiny house impounded."

I started crying. I was not a cute crier; I was an ugly crier, and I preferred to do it in private, not in front of my attractive boss. "I don't have anywhere to go," I said, gasping through my sobs. "I'm going to be homeless and then kidnapped and eaten."

Mace sighed the sigh of a long-suffering man. He stared up at the sky, a pained look on his face. "I guess." He looked down at me. "I guess you can come stay at my place."

CHAPTER 22

Mace

"I can't believe I'm doing this," I muttered. Taking Josie to lunch was one thing. Having her live at my house. Well.

"We're having a sleepover!" Henry sang.

"She's not sleeping in the house," I warned Henry. "She can park her tiny house monstrosity on the property. *Temporarily.*"

I wondered what Hunter was going to say.

We made a strange caravan, Josie following me in her clanking historic truck towing the wobbly tiny house. Henry squirmed in his seat, trying to see out the back window. Using a remote, I opened the gate to the property, and Josie chugged in behind me. We parked in the roundabout.

"This is amazing," Josie said, standing in front of the large manor house.

"It was originally the Harrogates' estate. They made millions in steel and manufacturing in this town and had this huge estate built."

"How did you buy it? Are you related to them?" she asked.

"No," I replied as I unbuckled Henry. "The Harrogates lost their fortune, and the property was in disrepair when Hunter bought it. He landed a good deal on it. There're hundreds of acres out back. We can put your house there for the time being."

She looked down at her feet then up at me. "Why are you helping me?"

Why *was* I helping her?

"You work for me. Plus, I can't have you parking in the Svensson PharmaTech parking lot anymore. That's not good marketing."

Henry raced up the wide front steps and banged rapidly on the door.

"I shouldn't have let him sleep in the car," I told Josie.

I heard the yelling of my dozen youngest brothers as soon as we walked inside the house. The teenagers were probably doing homework or still at after-school activities. The youngest ones were, as usual, running wild.

Henry ran off to join the fray.

"Wow!" Josie said. "Are all of these your brothers?"

"It's a small portion of them," I said, hoping she wouldn't ask any more questions.

"A small portion?" she asked, looking at me in shock.

"Who's that?" Nate asked, well yelled, really. He was climbing on the outside of the railing along the stairs.

"Get down from there!" I barked at him.

"This is Josie," Henry said. "She's my best friend."

"Where is Hunter?" I asked Nate. He shrugged. "Don't shrug. It's rude," I scolded him.

"Hunter's out," he said and glared at me.

Of course he was. That was why the kids were out of control. I wondered if Josie thought it was weird to have so many brothers. Sometimes even I thought it was strange.

"Josie, come see my room!" Henry shouted.

"All of you, outside!" I ordered them. "Outside now!" I pulled Nate off the banister and shooed the kids outside.

"Sorry," I said to Josie, looking for signs of revulsion on her face. But her eyes sparkled in delight.

"This is so cool! You have a gigantic family! I always wanted a big family," she gushed as I led her through the house out to the sprawling backyard.

"Incoming!" I heard Remy call. I looked over to see two of the teenagers, Isaac and Bruno, walk by, guiding our oldest brother Remy, who was driving a tractor towing a full-sized school bus.

"Won it at a storage-unit auction," Remy said, flashing me a thumbs-up. "Just needs some elbow grease and new tires."

"You know how I feel about school buses," I told him.

"I'm gonna sell it," Remy assured me.

"You better."

Remy maneuvered the bus into the large carriage house and dusted off his hands.

"Hi," Josie said, holding out her hand.

Remy wrapped her in a hug. "Welcome," he greeted her.

"Remy, put her down," I said. But Josie just laughed.

"I like your beard," she said, petting it. "It's glorious." Remy beamed. "Maybe you're the most attractive Svensson!"

Remy went red through his beard, and I scowled at him.

"I'm growing a beard too," Isaac said.

"No, you aren't," I said. "You're going to look like a gutter-punk kid."

"I told her she could park her tiny house out back by the cottages," I informed Remy.

"You have cottages on the estate?" Josie asked.

"Yeah and a big garden and a castle!" Bruno said excitedly.

"It's a fake ruin that the Harrogates built. It was all the style back in the eighteen hundreds," I told Josie.

"It's like the royal family in Britain!" my assistant gushed. "They have the Windsor Estate and Sandringham."

"It would be a lot nicer with some goats," Remy said, rocking back on his heels.

I looked up at the ceiling. "We're not getting any goats."

Leaving Remy to help Josie unhitch the tiny house, I went back inside to answer emails and make a few phone calls. I knew my younger brothers always wanted me to play with them, but with the launch of the new gene therapy product, there was still a lot of work to do.

I watched through the window of the home office as Remy used a tractor to tow Josie's tiny house to a flat spot near the cottages. They had originally been built for guests or extended family. It was on the to-do list to renovate them. If they had been habitable, I would have just set that tiny house on fire and had Josie stay in a cottage.

My phone rang, and I picked it up.

"I just wanted to touch base with you," Tara said as soon as I answered. She sounded sort of breathless. "You know, we could meet at a bar. There's a great little place—"

"I'm at home," I said, cutting her off.

"Of course. I didn't mean to bother you."

"How is the marketing launch going?" I asked her.

"Great!" she chirped. "I think we're making real progress."

"You know," I said, thinking of Josie, "you might ask my new assistant for some of her thoughts. She seems to have a knack for marketing. We had a good discussion about it over lunch today."

That seemed like the wrong thing to say. I heard Tara take in a breath.

"Hello?" I couldn't tell if she'd hung up.

"I don't think your assistant needs to be on the marketing team, Mace," she said with a laugh. It sounded fake.

"Whatever you think is best," I told her.

I went back to stand at the window. Remy had put the house in position. It looked like Josie was pointing something out on the house while Isaac and Bruno wedged rocks under the wheels.

"Are we going to be ready for the conference?" I asked Tara. "You know, the presentation—actually no," I corrected, remembering what Josie had said. "The whole marketing package needs to tell the narrative about how we are a cutting-edge company and innovative. It can't just be about the product. It needs to be about the larger brand."

"We're already on that track," Tara assured me.

Henry ran into my office a few moments after I ended the call.

"Can we go visit Josie?" he asked.

"Sure," I said, picking him up.

Josie had changed into jeans and a T-shirt and was on the roof of the house with a giant container of Gorilla Glue and some duct tape.

"I'm not sure you're supposed to just glue a house back together," I called up to her. She yelped and almost fell off the roof. I ran to catch her, but she righted herself.

"You startled me," she said.

"At least make Remy do that. You can't break your neck on our property," I pleaded as she shimmied over to the ladder.

I would be lying if I said I didn't notice how nice her ass looked in the jeans as she stretched to climb down the ladder. I reached up to steady her, my hand on her waist.

Her foot slipped on the top rung, so I just picked her up and swung her to the ground.

"You're accident-prone."

"Yes, but you're always looking out for me," she said, smiling up at me. Then she tapped me on the nose with the bottle of glue.

Henry pushed past us.

"You need to ask before you go into her house," I chided him.

"Can I go inside?" Henry asked.

"What else are you forgetting?" I prompted.

"Please?"

"You're always welcome in my tiny house, Henry," Josie said, bending down to his level.

Henry sprinted inside yelling, "This is so cool!"

"Are your accommodations satisfactory?" I asked her.

"Er, Remy said there's no sewer hookup, so..." She fidgeted.

Henry stuck his head out of one of the tiny windows. "This house doesn't have a potty."

Josie looked a little red. "The ills of a tiny house."

"You can use ours," Henry said. "We have an indoor potty. And a shower. It's better than where I used to live. We only had a big hole. I almost fell in."

"You almost fell in a hole?" Josie asked. Henry nodded.

I felt sick. Josie looked shocked and horrified. The rush of shame at my upbringing flooded through me, and I grabbed Henry and dragged him back to the estate house before he could fill Josie in on what exactly all the Svensson brothers were running from.

CHAPTER 23

Josie

I didn't know what was going on with Mace. One minute we were having a moment. The next, he just shut down and stalked off.

> **Josie:** *So I'm living with Mace now*
> **Willow:** *Say what?!*
> **Josie:** *Not in his house. He let me park my tiny house in his backyard*
> **Willow:** *Oh well, thank God you're just camping on his lawn. Because living in his house, well, that would be weird*
> **Josie:** *It's not like camping. It's a big backyard. It's more of an estate*
> **Willow:** *Geeze how loaded is this guy?*
> **Josie:** *Pretty loaded*

Willow: *Maybe you should, you know, hitch up the boobies and actually wash your hair. You might land yourself a billionaire*

Josie: *No, thanks. I'm not going to be like my mother. Besides Mace is weird*

Willow: *He can't be that weird. I saw the free lunch you posted on Instagram*

Josie: *I can't go for a guy just because he buys me nice food*

Willow: *That seems like as good of a criterion as any*

Josie: *I'm not sure. Sometimes I think he's attracted to me but then he shuts down*

Willow: *Maybe Tara put him off of women. I don't know what happened. She was on a call with him, then when it was over, she just went off yelling about how assistants need to know their place and shouldn't be gold-diggers going after their bosses*

That stung more than I cared to admit. I never liked the way my mother treated her boyfriends. She always seemed to go after decent guys because she could use them for money more easily. In her rare phone calls to Aunt Myrtle's, she would never ask me about school or friends or anything like that. She would just brag about how she had convinced this or that guy to buy her a car or take her on an expensive vacation. She would gleefully tell me about how she lied and made the poor guy think she was in love with him. Then, when she'd drained them of money, or if they got sick or just needed her to be there for them, she would dump them and leave, usually stealing something of value on the way out.

I didn't want Mace to think I was after him for his money. He seemed like a nice guy—he took care of his family, and he offered me a spot to park my tiny house. He also didn't fire me, which was worth quite a lot.

I needed to find some way of contributing to the Svensson household. Maybe a nice thank-you gift? But Mace could just buy anything he wanted. I'd need to think on it.

Though I didn't want Mace to think I was using him, I was stupidly excited to use his shower. The tiny house had a wet room, but it provided only the barest trickle of water. It smelled like moss, and I never really felt clean after using it.

It was dark outside already as I picked my way across the lawn, a canvas bag with toiletries and my pajamas slung over my shoulder.

"A shower! A shower! I'm going to have a shower!" I sang to myself. I was so looking forward to a real shower.

When I walked into the house, I realized just how huge it was. There were supposedly thirty-odd people living there, and I didn't see a soul. It was a little spooky.

"Don't eat me, ghosts," I whispered as I crept down a dark hallway and up what seemed to be an old servants' staircase.

"If I were a shower, where would I be?" I muttered as I wandered down a wider hallway. There were old portraits of people I assumed were the Harrogates. This hallway smelled cleaner than the back stair, as if it had recently been painted. My feet padded on the plush carpet runner covering the hardwood floors. Where were all the lights?

I started trying doors at random. Surely there was a bathroom somewhere?

The first door I tried seemed to be a bedroom. It too was dark. The next room looked like an office. The next was...

"Ah, a bathroom! Or part of one." It was one of those fancy kinds where the toilet, the shower, and the sinks were separated. It even had a little room with a bench.

The door to the shower opened, and I came face-to-face with Mace. Actually it was more like face to chest—a very bare, very muscular chest. My boss was cut. Like, very cut.

"Excuse me!" he said. He seemed like he was going to reach for the small towel that slung low on his hips and use it to cover his chest then realized that that probably would be worse.

"Hey, you can stand half naked in front of me anytime!" I joked. Mace blinked at me. A few droplets of water clung to his skin. I wanted to lick them. "I just was looking for a shower."

"Guest showers are on the other wing. I thought Remy told you."

"He just pointed in the general direction of the house," I replied. I was still standing directly in front of him. The polite thing to do would have been to move back, but I didn't. He smelled really good. I wondered what product he used. I needed it. I wanted to smear it in my pillow and drift off to sleep with it.

Mace cleared his throat. "I would give you a map, but I'm not sure that would help, seeing as how you got lost in my office with one."

"I can just shower here," I told him. He looked down at me. Really I wanted to steal his body gel or aftershave or whatever that scent was. I started grinning like an idiot when I walked past a guy who smelled really good. Mace smelled so amazing that I just wanted to bury my face in his chest.

"You'll have more privacy in the guest wing," he said firmly. "Let me change, and I'll show you where it is."

When he reemerged from his bedroom, he was in a T-shirt and gray sweatpants that were slung low on his hips.

"I'm digging the hot casual look," I told him. He rolled his lips between his teeth. I could tell he was trying not to laugh.

The bathroom he led me to was nice; it was even nicer than the other one. This bathroom had an actual fainting couch in the little seating room before I went into the bathroom.

"The architect we hired to renovate the house wanted to make it as historical as possible. She said having a proper dressing room before going into the bathroom would have been desired."

"I bet they didn't use it for dressing," I told him. "They probably enjoyed a little morning action then went to wash off. It's super convenient because there's no walk of shame to the bathroom."

Mace did laugh at that. It rolled low and deep around the luxurious room.

"You are really something," he said.

"You haven't seen anything yet!" I quipped. "Now, I'm sure you secretly want to watch me shower, but I warn you, I'm going to be in there a while, so you might want to grab a book. I have about a week's worth of tiny house living to wash off."

"Wait you haven't been bathing?" he asked, laughter still around the edges of his voice.

"Sponge baths, man," I told him, setting down my bag on the vanity counter. He didn't follow me through the doorway though I left it open. Was I hoping he would follow me in?

"Is that why you still smelled like smoke?" he called after me.

I turned to look at him. "That microwave was defective." His mouth quirked. "It totally wasn't my fault!" I said, and he laughed as he left the bathroom.

The shower was just as good as I thought it would be, even if there was no Mace in it.

I'd like a little Mace in me.

Wait, no, I wouldn't. Oh, who was I kidding? Of course I did! He was tall and good-looking. I wasn't trying to marry the guy or tie him down. I just wanted him in my candy jar, just once. Just a taste. I liked to sample things. Mace was like a perfectly handcrafted chocolate truffle, the kind festooned with little gold flakes. It was a totally indulgent, once-in-a-lifetime opportunity—an experience to have once and remember fondly on your death bed.

Hair washed and wrapped up in a T-shirt, a trick I'd learned on a forum for people with unmanageably curly hair, I skipped out of the bathroom, turned right, and opened the door to another set of servants' stairs Mace had said would take me out to the backyard.

Except there wasn't a staircase there; it was another bedroom.

Let's try door number two. It was a small library.

"It's cozy, and I would say that I would come back here and read, but let's be honest—I'm never going to find it again."

After I ran around and tried every door, I finally found the stairwell.

Finally.

Except it didn't take me to the backyard. I found myself in a kitchen—the most glorious kitchen I'd ever seen.

"*It's so beautiful*," I half sobbed and sank down on the floor. There was a huge island, and I mean *gigantic*. The glossy bright-yellow stove had eight burners. The opposite wall contained a bank of four ovens nestled among cabinetry with white uppers and dark bottom cabinets. It was the kitchen of my dreams. There was even a cozy glass-enclosed nook that would be perfect to grow little pots of herbs. The floor was a white terrazzo, and the whole space gleamed.

The three blond men sitting at the island looked over at me.

"Josie?" Mace said.

"Don't mind me," I told him. "I'm just over here having a religious experience. This is a really nice kitchen. Also," I admitted, "I'm lost."

Mace grunted.

"Did I mention how freaking sexy your kitchen is? Like seriously," I said, unable to stop the word vomit.

"Your tiny house is through that door," he said, pointing.

"Right, well, have a good evening. Thanks for letting me squat on your property," I said with a wave. Mace and his brothers watched me head out the door. I thought I saw light and a bit of green up ahead. That must lead outside. But no, it was some sort of conservatory that contained a few lone plants.

"They need to up their plant game," I said, walking around. I turned around to go back the way I came in. There was more than one door in the conservatory, and I picked one at random.

Mace and his brothers stared at me when I opened it.

"This house is ridiculous!"

CHAPTER 24

Mace

Josie got lost again the next morning.

"This house is not intuitive at all," she said as I guided her to the bathroom.

I wondered if she would not-so-subtly invite me to join her. I was ninety percent sure that that was what she was doing last night. A part of me wanted to throw caution to the wind and take her up on her offer, but then, she liked to tease. What if she didn't mean it? Would she have been upset if I actually watched her take a shower? I wondered what she looked like standing under the water, her back arched into the spray.

"Did you hear me?" I felt her grab my bicep. Her hand was warm through my long-sleeved workout shirt. "I asked if you wanted me to find a daycare option for Henry, or a nanny?"

I shook my head. "Can you look after him? There are some… complications with his situation."

I had to be in the office early, so I left Josie to find her own way. There was a meeting scheduled with Tara and the biomedical engineers and Owen Frost, Jack's brother. He was a wiz at computing and had made billions from cryptocurrency though that was just something he had done for fun.

His day job was being the CEO of a data-analytics and cryptology company. Owen's company was a key partner in my gene therapy product. The whole procedure hinged on quickly, economically, and accurately decoding the genome of a cancer cell and the host patient's own cells then parsing it against other data. Both of our companies' values would skyrocket if this procedure was successfully mainstreamed—or would crash and burn if it wasn't.

"Thanks for making the trip," I said, greeting Owen.

"We cannot afford to have anything go wrong with this gene therapy rollout," he said, shaking my hand. He had the same platinum-white hair and ice-blue eyes as his younger brother, Jack.

Henry was weaving between my legs.

"You coming to the meeting, little man?" Owen asked Henry.

"I like dinosaurs," my little brother said.

I made a helpless gesture. "He's clearly CEO material."

"I'll say! Kicked out of daycare, disrupting meetings—if I didn't know any better, I'd say your company cloned Archer," Owen said with a laugh.

Tara was already in the meeting room with the marketing consultant team. Parker, my brother and chief biomedical researcher, was there too. No one looked that happy except for Tara.

"I want—"

"Hush, Henry," I hissed at him. "Josie will be here for you soon."

Tara pursed her lips but then smiled widely when she saw I was watching.

"We needed to have this meeting," Parker began, "because we cannot have the marketing team making promises about the product and treatment that are unrealistic. I've told Adrian about this."

Adrian shrank down in his seat.

"You have *Adrian* running this project?" Owen turned to me, glaring.

"He's just my eyes and ears," I assured Owen. "I'm completely in charge."

"He's not," Parker muttered. I kicked my brother under the table.

"Do you all understand the product?" Owen asked, leaning forward over the table. He was a big man and cut an imposing figure.

"Of course we do," Tara assured him. Parker snorted derisively. "I told them I could handle it without wasting your time," Tara said to me.

I stopped her. "It's not a waste of my time. This product could make our company billions of dollars or completely ruin our reputation if it goes south. It is critical that this therapy launch correctly."

Tara nodded.

"People need to understand that we don't have a cure, per say," Parker insisted. "It's a personalized treatment plan based off the genome of your specific type of cancer. It has a very narrow focus."

"But it has the potential to help a lot of people," I interjected.

"Also keep in mind that you're going to be presenting to medical- and science-minded people," Owen added. "You need to have some information about the algorithms."

Tara looked annoyed. "I've been doing marketing for a while now. I think I can handle this."

The door slid open, and Josie crept in. I nodded to her, and she reached for Henry. He wrapped himself around the table leg. Josie shimmied under the table to try and pull him out.

Parker looked to me. I could feel Josie crawling around under my legs.

"Sorry," I said. "I'm listening. Henry is just being a pill."

He nodded. "There's a whole education process about what this type of therapy is and what it isn't. I don't think this marketing presentation has enough nuance."

Josie had managed to unwrap Henry from the leg of the conference table. I knew this because he had started to crawl up my legs.

"Just give me one second," I said as Tara began flipping through the slide deck.

Henry was clambering on me, and I felt one of Josie's hands grab for him. She missed, and her palm landed on my inner thigh. I looked down into Josie's red face that was dangerously close to my crotch.

I froze. Josie grabbed for Henry, but he scampered up to wrap his arms around my neck. I scooted my chair back.

"Ow!" Josie yelled. Everyone watched us.

"My earring is stuck," she said in a muffled voice.

"Stuck *where*?" Tara's voice was icy.

Henry climbed off me and waited patiently by the door as if he hadn't just caused all this commotion.

"She's stuck on his button," Parker said, looking over at me then down. "It's exactly the button you're thinking of."

Tara hurried over. "Honestly, Josie," she hissed and reached for my crotch.

"It's fine!" I declared, pushing Tara away. "We'll just go to the bathroom."

I bit my lip as Josie fumbled around my crotch, trying to undo her earring. Parker's lips were pressed together, and Owen was struggling not to laugh.

"Willow, help!" Josie called. I tried to ignore how hot her breath was as her friend came over.

"Willow, Mace, Mace, Willow," Josie introduced us. I needed her to stop moving her mouth against my junk.

"We've met," Willow said. "You passed out drunk in his car, and I couldn't get you out."

"I did that?"

Willow deftly unclipped Josie's earring, and she was free.

"Whew!" she said, sitting up and immediately banging her head on the underside of the conference table. "Ow!"

"Why don't you go put some ice on that?" Tara said. She and Josie exchanged some sort of look.

Josie blinked up at me. "Do you need some ice?"

Parker barked out a laugh.

"No, thank you," I said firmly. Tara looked scandalized.

The rest of the meeting didn't go much better. Aside from the brief amusement Parker had from my predicament with

Josie, for the rest of the meeting, he was mad about everything. Owen didn't seem all that pleased either.

"Please keep me informed on everything. I've allocated a lot of money and resources to this project," he said when the meeting was finally over that afternoon.

"It doesn't make any sense," Parker complained. "You see that, right, Owen? Also the graphics and everything are just plain ugly. You need to fire that marketing team."

"Tara recommended them," I said. "And they've done other really nice campaigns. Now that the team has more information about the gene therapy procedure, the next draft will be better. We'll regroup in a few days."

When I returned to my office, I looked through the notes and the presentation. Was it really that bad? I didn't have the best eye for marketing.

Josie came in from her office and looked over my shoulder. I could feel the puffs of breath on my neck. I remembered how hot her breath had felt against my crotch.

Do not go down that road...

"It sounded like there were some structural problems with this marketing campaign," she said diplomatically.

"They have some time. Hopefully this meeting helped Tara's team get on track," I said, rubbing the bridge of my nose.

"I could look at it if you want," she offered.

"Don't worry about it," I said. "I know you have a lot to deal with since I dumped Henry on you plus your other work."

"Of course," she said, straightening up. She seemed colder and more professional somehow. Gone was the funny girl who got lost in my house.

Did I say something? Was she upset by the incident this morning? We could not afford a sexual harassment lawsuit.

I cleared my throat. "I just want to apologize for this morning—"

"Don't worry about it," she said. "I'm disaster-prone." She smiled, but it wasn't quite as warm as usual. Maybe I was imagining things?

Henry also wasn't as well-behaved as he was yesterday.

"I don't think he likes being cooped up inside," Josie said when I complained to her about it. "Yesterday we did a lot of walking at the hydroelectric plant, and there were things for him to see. In addition, we had a nice long lunch. He had your attention for several hours when you weren't on your phone or staring at a computer screen."

I glared at her. "Look, I know this isn't ideal, but I don't need you to throw my shortcomings in my face."

"You asked," she retorted. "You can't complain about the weather when you're the one making it rain vegan nut bread. I know you think I'm the dumb girl who just hands out coffee, but even I can read a basic psychology book and see what's going on here."

"I never called you dumb," I snapped at her.

"Never mind," she said, picking up her computer and her coat. "I have some work to finish. I'm going to an empty conference room."

"What is wrong with her, Henry?" I murmured to my brother after Josie left. He didn't acknowledge me. He was running around from the back window to me to the piece of plywood covering the broken window on which he would scrawl with the large black sharpie he was carrying.

"Why isn't this fixed?" I asked aloud after Henry made a particularly squeaky black line across the plywood.

"I don't know. Why don't you ask someone whose job it is?" Garrett said, pulling the door open. Henry ran to him. Garrett plucked the sharpie out of his hand before Henry could scribble all over his pants. "I'm leaving," he announced. "Archer wants me to look at some property. We're going to grab food before. Coming?"

"I have that land-use meeting. Hunter wants me to go, but I have to take Henry home first. I'll walk down with you," I told him, closing my laptop. It took a moment to wrangle Henry, and Garrett looked on impatiently.

"We really need a new plan for his day," I remarked. I wondered if Hunter or Garrett had done anything about Payslee, Henry's mother, yet. I didn't want her to snatch Henry. But having Henry stuck in my office all day wasn't a great solution either.

When I walked out to my car, Henry trotting beside me, I heard loud clanks and a woman cursing. When we approached the next parking bay, Josie was bent over her rusted-out truck, the hood propped open.

"What on earth?"

She stood up when she heard me and blew a tendril of her hair out of her face.

"It won't start!" she exclaimed.

"Mace can fix it," Henry said.

"No, I can't."

"I thought you were an engineer," Josie said, hands on her hips.

"I'm a chemical engineer. Liam's the car guy. He and Jack used to build engines from scratch in college. Speaking of which—Jack is calling me over video chat," I said, pulling out my phone.

"Can we talk about the land-use meeting tonight?" Jack Frost asked when I answered. "I heard it didn't go that well with Meghan last time. We should have a strategy. If we're going to put this factory out in Harrogate, this process can't drag out for years."

"I agree. I'm going to bring Hunter in on this call," Liam said. I ran a hand through my hair in agitation. They sounded like they were settling in for a long conversation.

"I have to take Henry home. I can't get another ticket for driving while on the phone. Hold on," I told them. I looked at Garrett.

"My evening schedule is full," he said.

"Someone needs to take Henry home."

"Are you seriously arguing about who's going to drive home?" I heard Hunter's voice come out of the phone speaker. "I can't believe you put me on this call, Liam."

"This is your fault, Hunter," Garrett said loudly. My jaw clenched. The easiest way to work Hunter up into an angry froth was to blame him for the new cell phone law.

"Stop it," I hissed to Garrett. "You're not going to have to deal with him!"

"I heard that," Hunter said. "Have Adrian drive."

"He's working on the marketing push," I replied.

"Have Josie drive, then," Garrett said. "There. Problem solved."

I looked at Josie. She looked a little nervous.

"In my car?" I asked dubiously.

"Yes, Mace, in *your car*. Her car is broken," Garrett sneered. "You know, sometimes I wonder how you made it this far in life."

I waved him away and went back to strategizing with Jack and Liam while I buckled Henry in.

Josie sat down in the car, and I resisted the urge to stop her as she pulled the seat forward, adjusted the mirrors, and fiddled with the radio settings. I would never be able to put everything back how I liked it. It would take months. I was sure of it.

"Are you even paying attention, Mace?" Liam asked through the phone.

Josie clenched both hands on the steering wheel and slowly pulled out of the parking lot.

"Sure," I told my brother. "I'm thinking that if we offer to pay for park improvement and—"

Screeeeech!

"Ignore that!" Josie shouted.

I looked over. "Why were you even driving that close to the light pole? This is a huge parking lot! You have all the room in the world!"

CHAPTER 25

Josie

Mace looked shaken when I parked the car in front of the large estate house. I took Henry out of his car seat, and we all inspected the damage.

"You can probably just buff that out," I said with more confidence than I felt. The scratch looked deep.

Several of Mace's brothers ran out of the house.

"Hey, Arlo. Hey, Otis. Hey, Calvin! How was school?" Mace greeted his brothers.

"Boring. Come play tag," they begged, pulling at Mace.

"I have a meeting," he said apologetically.

"You always have a meeting," Otis complained. His brothers looked sad. Mace looked guilty.

"I'll come play with you," I told them. "Just let me change."

Mace smiled at me then got in his car to drive off. Or tried to. His little brothers and I watched as he took several minutes to readjust the seat and the mirrors.

"You're not driving anymore," he rolled down the window and told me before taking off. "You're so short I could barely fit in the seat."

"You're just freakishly tall," I countered.

I thought about the marketing meeting while I changed into athleisure wear. Anke and I would go on regular shopping sprees for clothes, but to scrounge up some cash, I sold most of what I had bought. Not that I was sad—I had gained enough weight from stress eating that none of them fit right. But I kept the yoga pants; they were so comfortable, and they still fit.

> **Willow:** *Did you recover from your exploration of Mace's crotch area?*
> **Josie:** *You don't have to make it sound so dirty*
> **Willow:** *Except it was. It looked like you were giving him head*
> **Josie:** *Ugh*
> **Willow:** *If Tara didn't like you before, now she really has it out for you. Her nose was twitching nonstop. She kept going on and on about how you were going to drive Svensson PharmaTech into the ground*
> **Josie:** *If anyone's ruining that company it's her. No offense, I know you worked on it, but that marketing scheme is exceptionally bad*
> **Willow:** **sigh* yes I know and no, no offense. I just hope the last check from PharmaTech*

> clears before they realize what an abject disaster it is
>
> **Josie:** *I feel like we shouldn't just let her ruin the campaign. The gene therapy procedure is a big deal for Mace*
>
> **Willow:** *Feel free to come up with something better. I'll text you a link to where all the work so far is*

I checked the link to make sure it worked then made a mental note to review the material that evening. Little fists banged on the tiny house door, and I closed my laptop. I had an appointment.

"Who's banging on my tiny house?" I roared in my best troll voice. "I'm going to eat you up!" Mace's little brothers all shrieked in delight as I raced after them.

The back lawn was perfect for running around. It was a little overgrown, but I could see how, back in the days when the ornate, beaux-arts style was all the rage, a designer had carefully planned the grounds. The lawn was mostly flat but rolled slightly to give the appearance of a natural meadow. Large trees framed the edges, carefully planted to frame picturesque views of the house and the outbuildings. Entrances to bridle and walking paths were visible at the edges of the vast lawn. As it grew dark, lights came on, marking the pathways and illuminating the grand house.

By that time, Mace's teen brothers had joined in the game as well, and we all gathered on the terrace as Henry pretended to slay the troll witch—me—and my two crazy dragons—Isaac and Bruno.

"I'm hungry," Henry announced, flopping down on top of me.

"Me too. What would you like to eat?"

"Pizza!"

"We can order some," Isaac said.

"Mace lets you order pizza?" I asked him.

"No, but he's not here, so…" He shrugged

"Why don't I make you pizza?" I told them.

"You can do that?" Otis asked as the whole squad followed me into the house. I stood in the hallway for a moment, looking around.

"Kitchen is that way," Calvin said helpfully.

The kitchen was just as big and beautiful as it was when I first saw it.

"And it's even well stocked," I remarked, opening up the cupboard and the large refrigerators. "And you have a stand mixer?" I exclaimed as Isaac carried the large shiny-red mixer out and placed it on the island.

"We have three!" he said proudly, bringing out a yellow and a blue one.

During my YOLO days with Anke, I took various cooking classes, starting with Italian cuisine because, hello? Carbs and cheese. Needless to say, I was pretty good at making pizza.

While the dough proofed, we chopped toppings. It was fun being around the kids, but I had to stay on them. I was a little nervous with the knives, but the older kids helped the younger ones. All the while, the Svensson boys told me about their older brothers.

"Archer is the best," Nate said.

"No, Liam's the best!"

"I'm sure they're all great," I said.

Calvin nodded. "Remy's cool. Greg is mean."

"He's not that bad!"

"Mike always brings toys even though Hunter doesn't want him to."

"Yeah, he brought us a bunch of drones! But now most of them are stuck in the trees," Nate admitted.

They all agreed Hunter was scary.

"What does he do?" I asked.

"Nothing. He doesn't yell or anything. He gives you the evil eye," Billy said and pretended to glare at Calvin. He laughed.

"What about Mace?"

"He's probably actually the best. He's always here. Or he used to be," Bruno said.

"He's really busy lately. I'm sure it's temporary," I assured them.

"I guess," Calvin said and shoved his brother. Otis picked up the pepper he was cutting to throw it at Calvin.

"Nope," I said. "We aren't throwing food."

"You're mean!" Otis yelled at me.

What the—I hate kids.

"No, she's not," Bruno scolded him. "She's a thousand times nicer than Mom. Mom would never cook or play tag."

Otis hugged me, getting flecks of pepper and basil on my clothes. "I didn't mean it. You're the best. And you're pretty too."

"So are you," I told him.

Yeah, I love kids.

CHAPTER 26

Mace

I felt bad about working so much. I promised myself that as soon as the launch of the gene therapy product was done and the Platinum Provisions factory was approved, I would spend more time with my little brothers.

But I was feeling admittedly less than confident about the marketing campaign since the meeting that morning. And as for the factory… as soon as I walked into the ornate meeting room in the city hall building, I could see that Meghan was not going to make it simple.

The meeting was open to the public, and it was a full house. Any time the Svenssons made any sort of change to the town, people wanted to know.

Mayor Barry Loring, Meg's great-uncle, was there. So were her two little sisters. They did not look happy to be there.

"This is a preliminary planning meeting for the proposed Svensson PharmaTech and Platinum Provisions research facility and factory," the mayor said. "Before we call this meeting to order, I'd like to thank Jack Frost for bringing refreshments." He held up one of the cookies.

Jack stood up, impressive in his dark-blue suit. "My girlfriend, Chloe, provided them from her bakery."

"We're all fans of the Grey Dove Bistro!" Mayor Barry said.

"Depending on how this evening goes, she might bring a franchise to Harrogate, or you could run us all out of town," Jack joked. The crowd laughed, and Liam gave Jack a fist bump.

"We have this in the bag," he whispered.

"Let's not confuse cookies with the fact that the Svenssons' new facility is going to tear up trees and destroy green space," Meghan said.

In a normal city, the deputy mayor wouldn't speak out against a particular project. But this was a small town, not New York City. Even though there had been growth, Harrogate retained the small-town anything-goes mentality.

Liam stood up and walked to the front of the room, where we had several site plans and renderings displayed.

"Obviously our company is very environmentally conscious," he said. "We are cutting down a minimal amount of trees, and anything that is cut down, we're putting in the new park we're going to build for all residents to enjoy."

There was a smattering of applause.

"While a pocket park is... nice, the fact is," Meghan stated, "that your property is not zoned for any more development. This town is surrounded by protected rural land. The voters and taxpayers bought land out here with the expectation that it would retain that character."

"Hear! Hear!" someone shouted.

"I birdwatch out there," an elderly man told us.

"There are native apple trees in the woods," a young woman complained. "I pick those for my jam business."

"We're bringing much-needed jobs to the area," Liam said, not losing any of his charming demeanor.

"Are you going to hire any of us old folks?" Ida countered. "Save Harrogate!" she started chanting, and the rest of the crowd joined it. The meeting went downhill from there.

When it was over and people were filing out, talking about plans to protest in front of our property, Hunter stalked over to Meghan. I hurried after him. The last thing we needed was for him to go off on his ex-girlfriend.

"You're doing this on purpose," Hunter snarled, shaking me off as I tried to pull him back. "It's like the cell phone law. You're hurting the residents of this town just to spite me. You know this research facility brings good jobs to the area. I can't believe how selfish you are."

"How selfish *I* am?" she spat. "I know those factories use mostly robots. You're not providing low-skilled jobs. You can't just walk in here with cookies and a sexy smile and expect people to fall over themselves to do your bidding."

"You certainly did," Hunter said. I winced. Meghan hauled back and slugged Hunter in the jaw.

"That's that, I guess," Liam said as we watched Meghan leave. "Pack up and find somewhere else for the factory."

We walked out to where we parked on the street. Hunter was rubbing his jaw, and Liam and Jack were arguing about alternative factory locations.

A thin woman with sunken cheeks stepped out of the shadows. Her blond hair, bleached from the harsh desert sun and years of hard living, was bright in the streetlamp light.

"Where is Henry?" Payslee said. She looked old—older than I knew she actually was. She was one of my father's younger sister wives, but I knew that after they had a few kids and the charm of being the newest youngest wife wore off, he neglected the poor women.

"You stole my boy," she said, pointing at me, jabbing a sharp nail in my direction.

"You never took care of him," I said to her. I couldn't believe she was here. "You've sent every single one of your sons away, and they always arrive in the worst condition—scraped up, covered in bugs, bruised."

"You don't know how hard it is to be a mother," Payslee said with a fake sob.

Hunter stepped in front of me and held out three one-hundred-dollar bills. Payslee's eyes were greedy as she watched his hand.

"You want this?" Hunter asked, his tone low. "Then you need to leave. That's part of the stipulation for my giving you cash. You can't just come here begging for more money."

"Yes, yes, I'll leave." She snatched the money out of Hunter's hand and hurried off.

"What is she doing here?" I snarled at Hunter when he turned around. "*You said you had it under control.*"

"Calm down," he retorted.

"She's in town," I said, moving into Hunter's personal space. He glared at me but didn't move. "She could be trying to kidnap Henry."

"And I thought my life was a soap opera," Jack muttered.

Liam held back a laugh. "You think she's going to kidnap Henry?"

"Yes," I insisted. "Do none of you see how serious this is?"

"You are severely overreacting," Hunter said, brushing past me.

"He needs to get laid," Liam said sagely. "It will take the edge off. Think of your heart and your cholesterol. You're almost in your midthirties, Mace. You're ancient."

"Dad doesn't want the boys back," Hunter said as he headed to his car. "And their mothers are too brainwashed to take them back. You saw what condition Payslee is in. She just sees us as a bank account."

"And you just taught her that she can come here for a handout," I snapped.

"I'm paying her off with peanuts," Hunter scoffed. "I make more money moving money around than I use to pay her off. I have it under control."

"You need to tell me every time she contacts you," I said, wrenching open my car door. "And I'm going to have Remy put the concertina wire back up."

There was laughter from the kitchen when I returned to the house. Hunter arrived home at the same time I did, and when we walked into the kitchen, there was Josie, with all of our younger brothers. Even Garrett and Archer were sitting around the island, putting toppings on oblong pieces of dough. The scene was domestic and relaxed.

"What?" she asked when she noticed us standing in the doorway. "It's a crime not to use this kitchen for what God intended!"

CHAPTER 27

Josie

"We're making pizza," I announced. Hunter made a disgusted noise and turned on his heel. I wasn't sure what I'd done. "Am I not supposed to be here?" I asked, confused.

"Ignore him," Mace said. He regarded me; his eyes seemed warm.

"Sit down, Mace. I'm going to make you a surprise pizza."

"How was the meeting?" Adrian asked him.

Mace shook his head slightly. I wondered what was up. "Did you do all this?" Mace asked, surveying the scores of little bowls filled with chopped ingredients.

"Me and all my sous chefs," I said. "Now what should we put on Mace's pizza?" I asked them.

"Candy," Henry said, handing me a bowl.

"You're putting gummy worms on pizza?" Mace asked with a frown.

"I'm making a dessert pizza," I told him. "I have extra dough left. Don't worry. I won't put candy on yours."

I coated some dough with olive oil, spread the garlicky cream sauce on it, then sprinkled olives, sausage, and peppers. Satisfied with how it looked, I slid it carefully onto the hot pizza stone in the oven. Then I helped several of the kids make their dessert pizzas.

Henry, perched on a stool, took a big handful of chocolate chips and dumped them on his pizza.

"You need to put ninety percent of that back," I told him as I walked to the oven. Mace's pizza smelled done. I opened the oven, but before I could take out the pizza, Mace was there. He took the hot pad out of my hand, and using a spatula, scooped the pizza out onto a plate.

"I can't make you do all the work," he said with a small smile.

"It's hot," I warned him.

He blew on the pizza. "Just like something else in this kitchen."

Had Mace been flirting with me?

The thought rolled over and over in my head. We'd exchanged witty banter before, but in the kitchen last night, he'd said explicitly he thought I was hot. Well, not explicitly; he implied it. The thought nagged at me like the bent safety pin that jabbed my side whenever I turned in the driver's seat to check for traffic.

What kind of boyfriend would Mace be? But maybe he didn't actually want to be my boyfriend. Maybe it was simple lust. I had invited him to watch me take a shower for goodness' sake.

A scream from Henry jolted me out of my fantasy.

Mace did not want me to drive this morning, but he had to take a call. Before even leaving the property, I had dented the front bumper on the stone mailbox in front of the estate as I turned out of the gate. I also cracked the windshield on a tree branch, which was not my fault. The city really needed to keep the roads clear. Now Henry had taken to screaming whenever I made a turn in anticipation that I would hit something. The screaming of course would make me jerk the wheel.

"Henry, stop," Mace told his brother, not looking up from his phone. I made a mental note to take Henry out during the day so he wasn't cooped up inside.

There was a box of cookies on Mace's desk when we walked into the office.

"Jack must have had the leftovers from last night's meeting sent here," Mace explained as he situated Henry on the floor in my office with some coloring supplies.

I admired the elegant yet minimalist label of the Grey Dove Bistro as I opened the box. There were five exquisitely decorated cookies. They looked like little miniature versions of the Harrogate city hall building.

I took a bite of one. The sugar cookie was soft but still had some bite. There was a hint of almond, and the royal icing added a sweet note to contrast with the almost savory sugar cookie.

"This is the best cookie I've ever eaten," I said around the mouthful.

"It's almost eight in the morning," Mace said. "You're eating a cookie?"

"And water," I added, holding up my glass water bottle. "That basically cancels it out."

I held out the cookie to him. "Take a bite. It's a happy little treat to start your morning."

"You look like a treat in that blouse," he said to me.

Yep, he was definitely flirting.

"And you look like a snack in those pants," I told him, taking a seductive bite of the cookie, as much as one could.

"I look like a snack in my pants?" He seemed amused but confused.

"Are you kidding me? Expertly tailored dress pants do something *else* to a man's behind," I said. "I don't know what it is, but wow."

Mace was grinning at me. His hair and his jaw were doing that thing that made me want to drag him off to my tiny house and have my way with him.

"So you're saying you notice me," he said, rubbing his jaw.

"Are you kidding me? I'm surprised Tara hasn't hauled me down to human resources for checking your butt out. I don't know how your tailor did it, but it's like you pants fold *under*. Like the pants should fall, but they go around it."

"Huh. Almost like your tits in that shirt. Especially when you were wet. In the rain," he clarified.

Right, because I'm not wet right now.

His eyes narrowed slightly. "I didn't know that women checked men out like that."

"Of course we do! It almost makes me wonder if I should start a company for butt bras for men. Like it would lift everything up and give you a little butt cleavage. I'd call it Victor's Secret."

Mace cocked his head. "I think we need to focus-group that name. It's very unsettling."

"Fine," I said. "Herbert's Sex Dungeon it is, then. Happy?"

"Not yet," he said. He walked up to me, the intoxicating smell of him surrounding me. I took another bite of the cookie to calm my nerves.

"Do you want a bite of something else?" he whispered.

"I'm the one who offered a taste of my candy first," I told him around the cookie. I had taken too big of a bite. I picked up my water bottle to take a swig. Mace's hand crept up my side. Of course I couldn't have a sexy flirtatious moment with a gorgeous man who was a relatively normal person and not a homicidal maniac. Mace's hand hit the faulty safety pin, and it jabbed me in the side. I screamed, sloshing the water all over Mace's front.

"I am—that is totally my bad," I said.

What the hell, Josie? Get it together!

"I sure know how to ruin a moment, huh?" I said as I dabbed at his shirt. "I think this probably needs a dry cleaner," I told him as I helped him remove his suit jacket.

"You know," he said, "if you wanted me to take all my clothes off, you didn't have to ruin my suit to do it."

"Ha ha," I told him as I carefully unbuttoned his shirt before the water soaked through any more. "I hope you have a change of clothes."

"Of course. I plan for all sorts of situations."

He bent down over me, touching our foreheads together. I was very close to him, my hands on the farthest button. The outline of his abs was visible through the soft undershirt. The warmth made me shiver.

"You know," he breathed, "I may want a bite of candy after all."

"Lord have mercy!" I heard Tara say.

"It's not what it looks like!" I shouted, jumping back. "I sprayed him with water."

It wasn't just Tara's nose doing that twitching thing. Her cheeks and forehead looked like they were twitching too.

"I need you to look over this marketing direction, Mace," Tara said finally.

I clapped Mace on the back. "I have him all warmed up for you!"

CHAPTER 28

Mace

My brother Parker was at the marketing meeting, and he was even less happy with the new direction.

"This isn't even how any of this works!" he shouted at me.

"I understand—"

"Do you want to get sued? Because promising all these things and confusing potential customers is how the federal government rains hellfire down upon you."

I was becoming seriously worried. "The conference is in less than a month," I told the team. "You have four days to come up with something good."

"Tara, do you have this under control?" I asked her as Parker stormed out. "I can bring in outside help."

"No," she insisted. "We will have something by next week."

"Everything okay?" Josie asked me when I walked back into the office.

"Just this marketing thing. Don't worry about it. Tara is going to fix it."

"Uh-huh." She didn't sound all that convinced. I had to admit I wasn't feeling all that confident myself.

"I'm taking Henry out," Josie said. "He's antsy. I made a little scavenger hunt for him. You should come! Fresh air and exercise are good for you."

"Says the person who eats fistfuls of candy," I retorted.

"Especially for the person who eats fistfuls of candy. It's all part of a balanced life," she said, tossing me my jacket.

Over the next few days, Josie and I took Henry to run outside a couple times a day. I had to admit taking a break did help me feel more relaxed.

"Maybe you shouldn't be so much of a workaholic," Josie said, peering at me over her sunglasses.

"You're being a workaholic though," I told her. Ever since the blatant flirting on the day she'd dumped water on me, Josie hadn't been acting like she would be receptive to any more flirtatious behavior. She was busy working on something. She locked herself in the tiny house all weekend.

"The kids want you to come play," I told her through the little round window that evening.

"I have to finish this sustainability brochure," she told me.

"No, you don't. It's not important."

"Just—" She sounded a little frustrated. "You go play with them. I'll make lasagna for dinner."

I played several rounds of hunt the ogre witch troll, which apparently was a game.

"Josie invented it," Henry explained.

"What are the rules?"

"You run around like this." He mimed making Hulk motions and pretending to smash things. "And these are your evil hench-dragons." He pointed to Garrett and Remy.

"You're playing?" I asked Garrett.

"I know how to play," Garrett scoffed. "It's a useful skill. Wolves play with the pups so that when they actually go hunt, they know what to do."

It felt good, like we were a real family. Were we still a little dysfunctional? Yes, but having several of my little brothers hanging off of me as I spun around felt nice. I never really got to be an older brother, because I was too busy being their parent.

"You guys want dinner?" Josie called out from the terrace.

Huge trays of lasagna steamed on the long buffet in the grand dining room.

"I like cooking for a crowd," Josie said as we all sat down at the table.

"You should move in," Remy told her, lasagna staining his beard. I handed my brother a napkin.

"I'm sure you all can cook," Josie said.

"Remy makes a mean breakfast burrito," I said. "Other than that, I think we're a bit lackluster."

I didn't make the kids help clean up after dinner.

"They should shower," I told Garrett when he looked perturbed.

"Uh-huh," he said and ushered the kids away.

"You know," Josie said as she grabbed plates, "if I didn't know any better, I'd say you were trying to get me all alone."

"That would be devious and underhanded and highly accurate," I told her, trying to keep my tone light. I wasn't exactly sure what her feelings were. I didn't want to put her in a bad spot since she lived here. "I can clean up everything if you have other stuff to do," I offered.

"I do have other stuff to do," she said, "but there's nothing sexier than a man doing housework, and I don't want to miss the display."

"So it's like that," I said, grinning at her.

"Yep. I just need you in an apron."

"Not in a frilly one, I hope."

"No, a nice thick leather one. And nothing else."

"I can't tell if you thought about this before or if this is just something random that popped into your head like the butt bra," I said.

"That was a well-thought-out plan!" she protested as she loaded the dishwasher.

"I'm not even sure how that would work," I said.

"I feel like it would look like a jock strap."

"Those don't lift anything."

"But they look damn fine," she said. "It's like a little bondage strap or something. No, I'm picturing something more like a shelf bra."

"A what?"

She wiped her hands then put a palm under each boob.

"You know what a pushup bra is, right?" she asked, demonstrating.

"I guess so?"

"I was wearing one the first, well, I guess second time I met you. I was soaking wet, remember?"

"I do seem to have that effect on women."

"Don't get too cocky," she said, giving me a slight shove. I caught her forearms. I just wanted to push her back against the counter and fuck her brains out.

"You know," she told me as I held her arms so our bodies barely skimmed each other, "considering that you hated me the moment I dumped chocolate sauce on you and now I've moved into your house, we might be moving a little fast."

Her eyes were dilated, and her breathing was slightly erratic.

"I'm not trying to back you into a corner," I said. "I just want to stick my hand in your candy jar."

"Once you taste my candy, you're going to want to stick your whole *face* in my candy jar." Josie smirked and stepped back, releasing her arms.

"Keep talking to me about this shelf bra," I said lightly. I was a little worried I had pushed too far.

She smiled. "It is what it sounds like. It's just the shelf of a pushup bra." Her hands were back under her boobs, pushing them up to demonstrate.

"Wait a minute," I interjected. "But then what's the point?"

She shrugged. "Support? If you have boobs like mine, you can't go braless."

I mean she could, but then I really wouldn't get any work done.

"Like, if you were wearing a really low-cut dress. You would wear a shelf bra to keep everything up, but obviously you would wear a pasty to not show anything too risqué."

"I think I'm going to need to see a demonstration," I said. "You know, to compare and contrast."

"For science?" she asked, one eyebrow raised.

"For science."

CHAPTER 29

Josie

The blatant and heavy flirting with Mace had left me feeling like a Twizzler left in the sun. My jellybean was jumping, and I wanted Mace to suck it and make it better. I wanted to march back up to the house and tell him to put his face in my candy jar. But I didn't have the best track record with making decisions based off of the YOLO philosophy. Maybe it was better to put the brakes on and really think about what I was doing.

But thinking made me think about Mace doing naughty things to me. I squirmed. My candy jar was feeling very gooey and melty.

> **Josie:** *I want Mace's face in my candy jar*
> **Willow:** *And I want Tara to take a long walk off of a pier made of my broken dreams and murdered ambitions*
> **Josie:** *Marketing not going well?*

Willow: *No*

Josie: *I'm working on something. I've been sketching out ideas all day. Going to hard line everything tonight and tomorrow*

Willow: *I hope it's amazing, because this is like the blind leading the narcissistic bitch over here*

Josie: *You guys still at the office?*

Willow: *Yes. Not just the office but trapped in one horrible, smelly conference room. I'm going to have tinnitus after all this is over from Tara's screeching*

I ate the last of the candy from my stash to distract me from the fact that Mace clearly also wanted a taste of my candy. It didn't work, so I turned my attention to the marketing project.

Between talking to Mace and the hundreds of documents in the folder Willow had sent me, I had a pretty good idea of the marketing direction for the gene therapy product. Actually it wasn't a product. I decided that was what Tara was missing. This was a procedure—an idea, a vision for the future of purely customized healthcare.

I spent Monday polishing everything, only taking a break to take Henry out for his midday energy burn-off. I spent that night working, finalizing everything and tweaking the words and graphics. Willow was up all night too. I periodically got text updates from her about how Tara was making them change all the colors on the slides from, in her words, puke green to puke yellow.

\The next morning, we all met in a large conference room. I was there only to hand out coffee, but then I was supposed to leave. I had my presentation on a flash drive. I was planning on showing Mace privately after the meeting so as to give him something to compare and contrast.

The room was packed with what looked like mainly Svensson brothers and one guy who looked a lot like Chloe's boyfriend, Jack Frost. I sighed, thinking about Chloe and her perfect life. I religiously followed her on Instagram and Pinterest. Everything she made was beautiful. Lately she'd been posting pictures of the renovation of her and Jack's penthouse. I had to wipe the drool off my face when I saw the plans for the craft room.

"Thank you for coming this morning," Tara said while I slowly handed out coffee and tea. "This is the marketing material thus far for the gene therapy product."

"It's a procedure," I muttered under my breath.

"What was that?" she asked sharply.

"Just asking if he wants any water," I said with a fake smile.

"So, everyone knows my background. I was originally at a marketing firm that specializes in pharmaceuticals." A basic big-pharma bitch. Figures. Pharmaceutical sales were known for their mediocre commercials and marketing. They were all geared to sell unnecessary medicines to the anxious elderly. I had worked on those types of campaigns; it always felt like a scam. If that was Tara's mentality toward the gene therapy procedure, then it was no wonder it fell flat.

"Could you move this along?" one of the Svensson brothers asked. He was wearing a white lab coat and looked unhappy and annoyed to be there.

"You don't have anywhere to be, Parker," Mace said to his brother.

Tara launched into the presentation. It was worse than Willow had said. My friend was sitting in the room, staring unhappily into her water glass.

Parker interrupted Tara as she was explaining the contents of a slide with a logo that looked like two beavers going at it like rabbits.

"I don't know what you all were doing the past few days," Parker said. "Mace, this is unacceptable. You're paying people for this crap?"

"You don't need to be rude, Parker," Mace said.

"But he's right, isn't he?" Garrett asked. "I mean look at this. And we're only weeks out from the conference."

"I agree," Greg said. "I hope you have all of this insured."

"Doubtful," Hunter said.

"If we could just finish the presentation and hold questions until the end," Tara pleaded. She sounded a little hysterical.

"Or you could just kill it, bury it, and spare us all," I muttered. I was having real issues holding my tongue.

Tara turned her sharp gaze toward me.

"Like the eye of Sauron," Willow whispered.

"Do you have something to add?" Tara asked nastily.

All the heads in the room swiveled toward me.

"If you have something to say," Mace said, "speak up. Maybe fresh eyes would be good." He looked a little desperate.

I cleared my throat. "Actually, yes I do have something to say. You see," I said as I walked up to the lectern and plugged in my flash drive. "There is a fundamental flaw in the team's thinking. The gene therapy treatment isn't a product. It's a procedure. It's a method, an idea, and a vision for purely customized healthcare. It is fundamentally about the future."

My slides flashed up. They were minimalist but still sexy—a splash of blue, a thin-line circle for the logo. I flipped through the deck.

"This procedure is about hope. But it is also grounded in the realities of today."

I flashed up a slide of a blue-eyed cat.

"Computing power has never been cheaper. It's so inexpensive to do this kind of analysis. Right now all that data space is taken up with cat memes. Not that there's anything wrong with that, but maybe a little less memeing and a little more lifesaving." I saw Mace smile.

I clicked through the graphics I had made that clearly explained how the gene therapy worked. I was particularly proud of the diagrams, a brilliant blue against a deep charcoal.

Next was a picture of Henry looking up in wonder at the hydroelectric equipment.

"This gene therapy procedure also ties into our sustainability mission. PharmaTech cares about people's health and a safe environment, and we're innovating in both. It's a future-looking ideal of purely customized healthcare. Except that the future is now."

Willow flashed me a thumbs-up.

Tara was incensed. "She's just an assistant! She gets coffee and answers the phone. You can't seriously be listening to her."

"These are just a few things I've been working on," I told the room. "Take it and run with it, or keep beating your heads against the wall. I have done several campaigns for FinTech companies and medical device companies. I can do a lot in a short amount of time, especially with a good team, but we are fast approaching the point where nothing can be done well. You must have time to vet the language and the graphics."

I hoped I sounded authoritative and not shrill. The Svensson brothers looked thoughtful. Owen stood up and walked to the front of the room. He seemed angry.

Why are all of these men so tall?

He approached me, and I resisted the urge to step back. Owen extended his hand.

"Thank you," he said. "I think you just saved us billions of dollars."

"And some jail time," Parker piped up.

"I'm glad you like it," I said as he shook my hand, "but why do you look so mad?"

"Because Mace should have hired you to do marketing instead of wasting your talents serving coffee."

CHAPTER 30

Mace

As soon as I saw Josie's presentation, relief flooded through me—and desire. Seeing her standing up there, dominating the room and being so authoritative, showed me a different side to the klutzy girl who was hell-bent on destroying my car.

I liked her, and while I found the klutzy girl endearing, this woman I needed. I wondered why she wasn't working at one of those hyper-creative, super-cool New York City marketing firms. What was she doing out here?

"When did you have time to put this together?" I asked her after we had spent hours in the meeting going over more of her vision for the marketing campaign and the rollout at the conference.

"I have a confession to make," she said, turning to look up at me. "I still haven't organized the CEO's supply closet or inventoried the snacks or—"

I wanted to kiss her to silence her, but I settled for holding a finger up to her mouth.

"None of that is in your job description. You're marketing full-time now."

She wrinkled her nose. "You haven't seen the state of the supply closet."

I wanted to push her against the wall, kiss her, stroke her, make her mine. Instead I watched her return to her desk. I ran my fingers through my hair in frustration and tried not to plaster my face against the glass wall separating our offices and stare at her like a creep.

I patted my hair back into place. Josie was eroding my self-control. But I had to act professional. I didn't want to be like my father. He would get so infatuated with his newest wife, then when she moved out to the desert with him and had a few kids, he'd ignore her for the next one.

But Josie was in my brain. It was like all the frustration and annoyance I'd felt toward her had flipped one hundred eighty degrees and turned into desire. I didn't know what to do. She was all I could think about.

The ironic thing? I had an excessive number of brothers and none I dared ask for advice about this.

I was assured that Josie had a handle on the gene therapy. But I still had another problem. The next day we had another meeting with Meghan about the factory. For that, I didn't think Josie would have a solution.

"Why are you here?" I asked Archer the next morning when I saw him sitting in my office, eating a bowl of gnocchi.

It smelled like the dinner Josie had made yesterday. I needed to talk to Jack about how he kept trim eating all of Chloe's food. If Josie was going to stick around, I needed to change my workout regimen. Would she stick around? Did I really want her to? I knew I needed her to.

"Where did you get that?" I asked my twin, pushing his feet off my desk.

"I made Adrian bring me some. He was raving about it on the group chat."

"Josie does make great food," I said, sighing happily.

"Holy smokes," Archer said around the mouthful of food. He jumped up, set the bowl down, and snatched my jaw, peering into my eyes. "You like her."

"I don't," I protested, trying to push Archer off me.

"Yes, you do! This is too much," he crowed. "You can't keep anything from me." He lowered his voice. "*We're the same person.*"

"We are not."

"Tell the truth!" Archer thundered, pointing at me with the spoon.

"Fine. Yes, I think I like her."

"Mace has a girlfriend! My baby is all grown up." Archer wrapped his arms around my neck and pulled me into a half headlock, half hug. "Your first crush. You're a late bloomer, but—"

"I'm not a late bloomer! I'm never telling you anything ever again," I complained. "Why are you even here?"

"Mike wants me to sit in on the land-use meeting. He wants us to have a better heads-up on what happens when we go for the new conference center."

"Did you find a location yet?" I asked him. "There are a lot of old industrial sites around here, especially near the river, that would probably make really cool conference centers."

"We have a few on our short list. When is Meg coming by?"

"Not until this afternoon. We're meeting to strategize first though. The last meeting went poorly."

"I would have paid good money to see Meg punch Hunter in the face. Greg was appalled when he found out," Archer cackled, leaning back in my chair.

I shook my head.

"He's used to those planning meetings in New York City. A brawl would never break out in one of those," Archer said, chuckling.

"That's how we roll here in small-town America," I replied, gathering up my notes.

Of all of us at our strategy meeting, Archer, because of all the hotels he'd had to secure approvals and permits for, was probably the most knowledgeable. Though my twin could be annoying, he could dominate a public meeting like no one else.

"You guys need to promise something," he said when we went over our strategy. "The community wants to see that they're not getting pushed out. That's why all my hotels have a publicly accessible restaurant on the ground floor or something like a high-end bodega. One hotel has an Italian grocery store that sells imported goods. It was smart because it also tied in with the history of the neighborhood, which historically had a strong Italian immigrant population," Archer explained.

"We're offering to build a park," Liam said, tapping his pen on the table.

"Ah, yes, the good old transfer of development rights," Archer said, rolling his eyes. "That's fine if you need to fulfill some legal requirement, but you need to have something directly related to your new building."

"The residents are mad about the amount of land we're going to be tearing up and the meadow and forest," I told him. "I'm not sure another restaurant is going to help that."

"It can help drum up more support from younger people," he said. "You can use your cute marketing genius."

I kicked him under the table. I could see my twin struggling to keep his mouth shut. I shook my head at him.

But Archer blurted out, "Mace has a girlfriend."

"I don't! I told you that in confidence!" I yelled at him.

"Wait what?" Liam asked. "Greg said you hated her."

"Hate is a strong word," I replied.

"He's embroiled in passion for her." Archer snickered. "And in typical Mace fashion, he's imagining worst-case scenarios and way overthinking things."

"You're terrible," I grumbled.

"Just make sure you go down on her first," Archer said. "A helping hand helps her first and all that."

"That is inappropriate!"

Archer ignored me. "You should ask Hunter for some tips." Hunter's face said that if for some reason I was dumb enough to ask him, it would be the last thing I ever did.

"If we could get back to the meeting…"

"So you can get back to Josie?" Archer waggled his eyebrows.

I did want to go back to Josie, but after the meeting was over, Hunter grabbed me.

"Don't get involved with Josie," he said, face serious. "It can only end badly. Trust me."

CHAPTER 31

Josie

My infatuation with Mace was at a simmer. I wanted it to boil, but I also didn't want to screw it up. My friendship with Anke had progressed fast too. When I liked something, I went all out. I was worried that my desire for Mace was overriding the minimal amount of good judgement I had left.

At least I had the excuse of working on the marketing campaign to stay away from him. I avoided him last night and made the kids help me with cleanup after dinner so I wouldn't be tempted. Then I locked myself in my tiny house to work at the cramped drop-down desk.

I had pawned Henry off on Garrett while I met with Willow and the rest of the marketing team that morning on the promise that I would take him to the park with the dinosaur slide for lunch. When I returned and peeked into Garrett's office, he and Henry were deep in conversation.

I smiled and left them be so I could take a breather for a minute. I loved marketing, but Tara was making it very stressful. She would challenge every one of my ideas and complain nonstop.

Mace wasn't in his office thankfully, so I sat down at my computer and checked my personal email. My heart dropped when I saw the message from Anke.

> *Dearest Josie!*
> *Many apologies. Life is like that sometimes. You're my dearest friend. Please don't think poorly of me. I've sent some of the money I owe you. Don't worry. I have a plan for the rest. I'll need your help though, but I know we'll make it work. You are a beautiful spirit! I'll be in town soon. We should get together.*
> *xoxo*
> *Anke*

Wait, did she actually send me money? What did she mean she had a plan? My hands shook as I scrolled down and opened the email from PayPal.

Anke sent you $5000.00.

I clicked on the link. Maybe it was imaginary money? But no, the website said it was available to transfer. I sent it to my bank account then slumped at the desk, my mind reeling.

Maybe Anke hadn't been lying, and it was all a big misunderstanding. Maybe things were going to work out!

A flush of relief swept through me. Everything was going to be okay. Anke had paid a chunk of the money she owed me. It wasn't out of the question that she had a legitimate plan for paying me back for the rest. All of my problems would be solved.

I grabbed my bag and skipped out the door, feeling as light as cotton candy until something grabbed my purse strap and jerked me back. I yelped as I fell backward and squished my eyes shut, bracing for impact.

"I thought our high-powered marketing person wasn't going to keep falling down everywhere."

I opened my eyes to look up into Mace's gray ones.

"It wasn't my fault," I said. "Your door tried to kill me."

"It's probably revenge for the window you broke," he said, tipping me back up and disentangling my purse from the metal door handle that was at perfect purse-grabbing height. "Why are you looking at the door handle?" Mace asked and reached over to tilt my chin up. "Did I do something?"

"What? No. You've been great."

"I didn't start off that way," he said. "And I regret that. You've been a positive force in my life. You know, Josie, I really like you."

I had been holding back because of the anxiety that I would screw up Mace's life as epically as I let Anke mess up mine. But now Anke was paying me back, and Mace said he liked me. I deserved a little treat—a bonus for getting my money back and finally using my degree. I wasn't going to eat the whole box of chocolates, just one little truffle.

Mace was very close to me. I wanted him to kiss me, and I wanted to kiss him.

I reached up on my toes and pressed my lips against the corner of his mouth. His lips were soft, and I smelled a hint of that yummy aftershave or body wash or whatever it was that he used. I seriously needed to steal it.

He grinned when I dropped back on my heels. Then his hands came up slowly on my hips. One stayed there as the other moved up my waist to my lower back. Mace pulled me close to his chest, dipped his head down, and gave me a real kiss. It was like chocolate cake, deep and rich. It felt as good to kiss him as I thought it would. Actually, no, it felt better. I hadn't imagined how delicious it would feel to have the ridges of his abs against me.

When Mace pulled back, he was smiling. His hair was slightly messy from my fingers running through it.

"Did I ever tell you I had a real thing for blond guys when I was a teenager?" I said, sounding slightly breathless.

"I'm glad to see you didn't outgrow it," he said. His hands were still at my waist, and he casually caressed my hips. "You're lucky there are glass walls," he said, his voice low, almost a purr. "Otherwise I'd kneel down and—"

"Eat my jellybeans?" I prompted. "Twirl my toffee? Stick your cake pop in my whipped cream?"

But we were probably moving too fast. I didn't want to YOLO into trouble just when I was starting to find my way out of it. Sleeping with my boss was probably in that category though he was an awesome kisser.

"As much as I'd like to introduce you to the finer side of the dessert menu," I said, fixing his tie, "I already have a hot date lined up with one of your brothers."

"Which one?" he growled. The hands on my hips squeezed possessively hard.

"Why, the cutest one, of course—Henry!"

Mace relaxed, laughing. "Cock-blocked by my own brother."

There was a knock on the door. Henry was standing there with Garrett.

"He said you were supposed to meet him at twelve thirty," Garrett said.

"Did you have fun with Garrett?" I asked Henry. "I saw you doing serious business in there."

Henry nodded solemnly. "He taught me about the Great Emu War."

"It was a stain on Australia's history," Garrett added.

"Coming?" I asked Mace.

He shook his head. His eyes flicked from my chest to my mouth and up to my eyes. "I have to prep for a meeting this afternoon."

"It's just you and me, Henry," I said.

The first stop was Ida's General Store. I needed to pick up lunch.

"How's my favorite tiny house lass?" Ida asked, coming up to hug me in front of the premade sandwich display. I hugged her back.

"Is that a Svensson boy?" she asked, looking down at Henry.

"Of course."

"Those Svenssons are tearing up the land," she complained. "They're building a new facility that Bert said is going to ruin the songbird habitat. He's been distracted by it lately and won't even acknowledge my most obvious request to make fondue. Birdwatchers are very detail oriented, if you know what I mean. Those Svenssons and their nonsense are ruining my sex life."

I looked around wildly. Fortunately Henry was picking out his snack and didn't seem like he was listening to Ida.

"We're having a protest," Ida declared. Mace wasn't going to like that, and it would be bad publicity for PharmaTech.

"Before you go to the trouble of making signs," I said. "Let me talk to Mace about it and see if we can't find another solution."

"Talk. *Right.*" Ida smiled at me knowingly. "Ah, the power of pussy. It can bring men to their knees—willingly!" The elderly woman winked at me as we walked back to the register.

"Sign up for the farming co-op?" she asked as she rang me up. "Ernest runs it. Nothing like fresh produce!"

"Why not?" I said, taking the tablet Ida handed me. "If you live in a small town, you might as well enjoy the bounty."

Mace was doing a lot for me. This would be a nice thing to do in return, I thought as I paid the modest fee.

"You wouldn't believe how good that man's eggplant tastes!" Ida crowed.

After a picnic of turkey, avocado, Swiss cheese, and arugula sandwiches on really good ciabatta at one of the tables in the park, I ate my salt-and-vinegar chips while Henry played with a few of the other kids. I promised Henry he could come back tomorrow as I buckled him in the car seat.

A light on the dashboard blinked when I turned on the car.

"I think we're out of gas, so I'm going to fill up before we head back," I told Henry.

And I'm going to use the money that Anke finally sent me!

I practically floated out of the car when I pulled up at the gas pump. Today was going great. Mace kissed me, and

I didn't scratch up his car. It did take me a while to find the gas tank. It took some muscle to pry the cap off, but I did it. It was also one of those weird kinds that didn't have a screw-on lid.

"Taking care of business!" I sang as I swiped my credit card. I only put a few gallons in. I still had debts after all. But it felt good that I wasn't a total mooch. I didn't want to be like my mother, using men only for their money, but now I was contributing. I was helping save Mace's gene therapy launch. I made dinner. I put gas in the car.

Sunglasses on, I pulled out of the gas station. I grinned stupidly as I replayed the kiss. I knew Mace wanted more. Henry screamed as I turned on the main road.

"Henry, you can't keep yelling every time I turn," I scolded him.

"Fire!" Henry said.

"A fire truck?"

"No! *Fire!*"

I took off my sunglasses. Thick black smoke was billowing out of the trunk of the car.

"Oh my God! Fire! Fire!" I yelled. Someone honked as I swerved the car off to the side of the road.

Quick as a monkey, Henry unbuckled himself from his car seat and climbed to the front of the car over the center console.

"Why is it on fire?" I yelled, coughing as I dragged Henry out of the car. "Crap, my purse!" I lunged back and grabbed it while Henry yelled. I jumped back in the nick of time as flames shot up out of the back of the car.

"Call the fire department!" Henry said, jumping up and down.

"It seems like someone already did." Sirens blared in the distance, and people were stopping to take videos of Mace's burning car.

"We're going to be on TV!" Henry said happily.

"That's just great. I can't have one good day without a car spontaneously combusting."

A compact silver car pulled up, and a kind-looking brunette jumped out. "Are you all right?" she asked in concern.

"Just a little singed," I said. The woman pulled us away from the car as it popped and sparks shot out.

"Look, a fire truck! It's a fire truck!" Henry exclaimed in excitement as the large red truck pulled up alongside the burning car.

"I was going to ask if he was okay, but he doesn't seem any worse for wear," the brunette said dryly.

"This is the best day ever," Henry said, his eyes sparkling. We watched as the firemen hustled out of the truck and started dousing the flames with water.

One of the men sauntered over to us.

"Meg," he greeted the brunette. He peered at me and pulled the kerchief off his face. "Hey, aren't you the girl who burned down Svensson PharmaTech?" The fireman started chuckling.

"I didn't burn it down," I huffed. "The microwave spontaneously combusted."

"We have to stop meeting like this," Cliff said and winked at me.

"She's already taken," Henry announced then coughed.

"You should come away from the flames," Meg said. "Those battery-powered cars can just explode."

"We should block off the street," Cliff agreed.

"Wait," I said. Meg and the fireman looked at me. "It's a battery-powered car?"

Cliff nodded. "I'm surprised that it just randomly caught on fire. Normally they're a bit safer than that."

"Funny how those things happen." I felt faint, and I didn't think it was from the smoke.

"What's that leaking out from under it?" Meg asked, pointing to the back of the car. "Is it melting?"

I coughed dramatically. "I think I need to get out of this smoke."

"Meg, can you take them out of here?" Cliff asked.

"Sure thing," she said, pulling her keys out of her purse. "Where are you guys headed?"

"I don't want to go! I want to watch the explosion!" Henry said and jumped up, making a sound effect. I winced.

"Sorry he's…" I made another helpless gesture.

"A Svensson," Meg said, her mouth flat. "The pervasiveness and lack of variety of their insufferableness is beyond belief, isn't it?"

"They are a unique bunch."

Meg drove us to the PharmaTech offices then parked in the visitors' parking.

Was she walking us inside? I wondered.

But when we got into the lobby, Meghan marched up to the reception desk, Henry and me trailing behind her.

"Good afternoon. I'm Deputy Mayor Meghan Loring, and I'm here for a meeting with Mr. Svensson," she said.

"Which one?" the receptionist asked, picking up the phone.

"All of them."

CHAPTER 32

Mace

I thought the kiss with Josie would slake my desire. But it only made it worse. She had felt so good melting against me like chocolate. I shook my head. Josie and her love of candy had gotten to me.

"Anyone in there?" Archer asked, rapping his knuckles against my head.

"Stop it," I said, pushing his hand away.

Garrett held the door to the conference room open for Meghan, and we all stood up. She looked angry. This was going to be another awful meeting.

"She even smells like hellfire and brimstone," Archer whispered to me under his breath.

"I heard that," Meg said.

"How is the lovely deputy mayor?" Archer exclaimed. "I'm expecting you to announce your run for president any day now." He pulled out her chair for her. "Please sit down. I'm so sorry you have to deal with all of my brothers. They're uncultured! Uncivilized! Also I locked Hunter in the supply closet." He smiled broadly. There was a slight smile on Meg's face. Maybe the meeting wouldn't be so bad after all.

"I know I'm your favorite Svensson," Archer said, pouring a glass of water for Meg. "So let's chat."

Meg seemed to relax slightly until Hunter rolled into the room, practically yanking the door off the hinges.

"What the hell is wrong with you, locking me in a closet?" he fumed at Archer.

"You actually locked him in a closet?" Meg asked, laughing into her water glass.

"I mean, yeah, that's what I said. Unlike some people, I don't lie."

"Archer, what were you thinking? Hunter could have starved to death in there," I admonished my twin. "Or suffocated for lack of oxygen."

My twin snorted, and I could see Meg tamping down a smirk.

"Look at this big lug," Archer said, whapping Hunter on the back. Hunter snarled, and Archer jerked his hand back. "He'd have survived weeks."

"He didn't have any water," I countered.

Archer hummed a few bars of the "Circle of Life."

By the end of the meeting, I knew we had completely wasted our time. Meghan didn't like any of our potential design options.

I had also found it difficult to concentrate. I couldn't stop thinking about Josie and the kiss. I wanted to push her against my desk, slide my hand under her skirt, and feel the soft skin underneath.

When I finally escaped from my brothers, I found Josie in her office, chewing on her lower lip. Her glasses perched on her nose, and one of the buttons on her blouse looked like it had come undone. I could see the hint of her lace bra in the gap.

I went to her and wrapped one arm around her waist. The other hand snuck through the gap, cupping her breast. Josie gasped as I tipped her head back, taking her mouth like I wanted to take her body.

"Wow," she said after I drew back. "You fogged up my glasses, and I'm half undressed." Sadly she buttoned her shirt.

"That was already undone," I said. I wanted to kiss her again, but Josie seemed tense. I immediately was on edge.

"Look," I told her, "I know this is weird. You work for me and everything, but I really want to be with you. I could set you up with a separate consultancy company if it bothers you to be employed with Svensson PharmaTech."

She smiled softly. "No, this is fine. You're too nice to me."

Was I though? All I could think about was sleeping with her, waking up wrapped around her. It was like my brain had latched onto the idea.

"I promise this isn't some workplace affair with a childish billionaire playboy who just uses and abuses women," I insisted, needing her to see I was serious about pursuing a relationship with her.

"Feel free to use me any way you want. I enjoy a good workout," she purred. "And you'll need it, too, after eating all my candy." She snorted at her own joke.

"Let me take you out," I offered. Archer was taking Henry home and spending time with the other kids, so I was free to spend the evening with Josie.

"Out where?"

"On a date," I said, grabbing her coat. "I know a place that has great drinks, and they put candy in them."

"Sounds like my kind of establishment," she quipped.

I pulled out my keys as we walked to the parking lot then stopped short. "Where's my car?"

"Funny thing," she said, her face beet red. I looked at her.

Josie sagged. "The car didn't make it." I looked at her incredulously, and she handed me her phone. On the cracked screen played a video of my car engulfed in flames.

"How did this happen?"

"It was just one of those things." She smiled, but it was more just showing her teeth.

"You could have died!" I said.

"We're fine," she assured me.

"Henry—"

"Is fine," she insisted, grabbing my arm and stroking it. "He was very excited when the fire department showed up. I believe his exact quote was, 'Best day ever.'"

I shook my head. "I'm going to complain to the manufacturer. Cars shouldn't catch on fire like that. What if you had died?"

Josie reached up on her toes and kissed me, and I swept her up in my arms, deepening the kiss.

"I'm never going to get tired of this," I told her, setting her back down. "And I want to continue kissing you, but first we should call an Uber. It's going to take a while since most drivers usually go to New York City to work the bar scene."

"We could take my truck," Josie offered.

"I thought it was broken."

"Maybe it's fixed? Let's try. I'm not waiting around. I was promised a candy cocktail with actual candy. Although," she said, taking my arm. "I wonder what a cocktail with an actual cock would taste like."

"I hope it's not just a disembodied one," I joked.

"Yeah, that would be fine on, say, Halloween, but for a simple after-work drink, maybe not. Unless it was attached to a good-looking guy," she said as she wrenched open the door to the truck. I opened the passenger side, and paint flaked off the door.

"Think lucky thoughts," Josie said as she cranked up the truck. It clunked, shuddered, then started. "It's our lucky day," Josie said as she put it into gear.

The truck seemed like it had lost all of its shocks sometime back in the seventies. My head almost bumped the ceiling a few times when we jerked over the railroad tracks. The truck was in such poor condition I was afraid my head would go straight through the roof.

"I need a drink after all of that," I muttered after Josie parallel parked the truck, running halfway up the sidewalk and almost hitting a tree. To her credit, she did straighten out after a few tries.

"And I didn't hit anything," she said, slipping her arm in mine as we walked into the bar.

"You weren't joking about the candy drinks," Josie said happily as we sat at the reclaimed-wood table and looked at the menu. "I want to try them all."

When the server came over to take our order, I said, "She wants a Dark and Stormy."

"With candy?"

"Of course!" Josie said. "Extra candy!"

"Do you want that as well?" the server asked me.

"I'll have a whiskey."

"Any apps?" she asked, making a note on her pad.

"All of them," I said. "One of each."

Josie clapped her hands together when the server left. "You know me so well. *All the appetizers!*" She rubbed her hands together gleefully.

"Of course I know you. You've been living at my house, and I spend more time with you than my own family, it feels like. And," I said, lowering my voice, "I'd like to get to know you even better."

I heard someone clear their throat behind me.

"Can I help you?" I asked, turning around.

"Detective Brown with the Harrogate PD," the man said. Susie was there next to him, a hand on her utility belt. They looked serious. I stood up from the table.

"Mr. Svensson," the detective said. "We were just up at your office. The receptionist said you'd left already."

"What's this about?" I asked.

The officers looked at each other. "Sir, do you know of anyone who would want to kill you or your family?"

CHAPTER 33

Josie

I kicked myself for not coming clean earlier. Why did I always do that? I had to ruin this thing with Mace with my stupidity.

"The fire department looked into it after they had the fire under control," the officer explained to Mace.

"I heard the battery caught on fire," Mace said. He looked furious.

I sank down in my chair.

"No, fortunately not, or that car would still be burning," Susie said. "The fire department was able to control the fire before it pierced the protective casing surrounding the battery."

"I don't understand," Mace said. His eyes shifted between Susie and Detective Brown.

"Someone doused your car in gasoline," Susie said.

I felt faint. I was going to be arrested. Where was that drink? "I uh—"

"Don't worry, Josie," Mace said. "I'll find whoever did this. They'll pay for trying to hurt you." His face had this blank look that scared me.

"Actually I um… I'm the one who put the gas on the car," I said.

"What, why?" Susie asked.

"I didn't know it was electric!" I started sobbing. "I thought I was helping, but I'm an idiot."

I could tell Susie and the detective were trying not to laugh.

"It's not funny!" I gasped.

"Actually it kind of is," Susie said. "Those electric cars don't even have gas caps. How did you pry a piece of the car off?"

"I'm made from sturdy stock," I said, wiping at my eyes with a napkin. "And I eat a lot. Mass moves mass."

"Still. Maybe you should take up boxing or MMA fighting if your grip is that strong," the female police officer chuckled. I didn't dare look at Mace.

"I guess we'll close the case," Detective Brown said. "Love it when my job is easy."

"Don't I need to sign a statement or something?" I asked meekly.

"Let's not get carried away," Susie said. "No one likes extra paperwork."

"Grab a drink on me," Mace said, shaking their hands and signaling to the bartender.

"Aren't there rules about police officers accepting gifts?" I asked when he sat back down across from me. I expected to see that terrifying blank look turned in my direction, but his eyes were warm with humor.

"This is a small town," Mace said with a shrug. "People don't get too worked up over that stuff."

He took a sip of his whiskey then laughed. "Only you would set my car on fire."

"Don't remind me." I drained my glass and used the little plastic straw to scoop out the crumbs of the SweetTart candies.

"Need another?" Mace asked.

"I need, like, three more of these," I said as the server set down our appetizers. "Yum! Cheese," I said, swiping a pretzel bite through the cheesy sauce. "And French fries. This is the best date ever! This is basically my dream come true—go to a restaurant and order every appetizer."

Anke wasn't a big eater; she was a big drinker. But I was with Mace now. I wasn't going to let Anke spoil my evening.

She'll come through with the rest of the money, I promised myself. *I just have to believe.*

The server brought me another drink that had a whole stick of Airhead candy in it to use as a stirrer.

"This is so clever," I cooed. "And everything here is so cheap. New York is so much more expensive."

"Another bonus of a small town," Mace said, reaching over and taking a goat cheese fritter.

"It's not that small," I said. "There're a lot of buildings, and Main Street seems busy."

"A large number of families live here," Mace explained, "because of my company. Though that is slowly driving up prices." He looked annoyed for a minute, then his features smoothed out.

"Is that why all the old people are protesting your new facility?" I asked him, biting off a piece of the Airhead candy.

The annoyance was back on Mace's face.

"Ida says you're cock-blocking her," I told Mace. "She wants old Bert to bring his detail-oriented bird-watching self to her bed and make her sing. But he's too distracted to play the peacock, so to speak."

Mace worked his jaw. "I really didn't want to know, frankly, any of that," he said finally. I laughed and ate a bite of duck slider.

I held out my hand to feed him the other half. His lips brushed my fingertips when I placed the bite in his mouth.

"I don't know what I'm going to do if all the senior citizens start picketing in front of my building," Mace said after he swallowed.

"I asked Ida to hold off, and she agreed," I said.

"How did you manage that? She doesn't seem like the type to be dissuaded," he said, eating a French fry.

"I told her I would use the power of pussy to convince you to reconsider."

Mace started coughing.

"Have a drink of this," I told him, handing him my cocktail. He took a swig.

"That is *very* sweet."

I leaned over and kissed him. "Yes, but it tastes so good."

I could taste the lingering sweetness later that night as Mace parked the truck in front of the estate house.

"It's good that you drove," I whispered to him in the dark. "I think I'm too drunk."

"You hit those candy cocktails pretty hard," he said. His hand inched up my thigh.

"I had to celebrate," I said, reaching for him.

"Celebrate what?" he asked as he leaned over me. "Burning up my car?"

I giggled. At least I had enough non-drunk brain cells to refrain from blabbing about my terrible decision-making with regards to Anke.

He leaned into me, kissing me. His mouth was warm, and I could taste the lingering spice of the whiskey. I moaned softly as his tongue pushed my lips open. I tangled my hands in his hair as he tipped my head back, his tongue stroking my mouth.

"Dinner and drinks were fun," I said breathlessly when he released my mouth. One of his large hands was on my waist, the other under my skirt, caressing my thigh. I wanted it higher. I pulled him back down by the tie.

"Now I want my dessert," I whispered against his mouth.

"I thought you had enough candy today," he said. One hand moved up to cup my breast and rub at my nipple through the fabric.

I moaned. I could feel his cock through his pants, hard against my thigh.

"I never have too much candy," I told him. "But you didn't have any dessert."

"I'm having it right now," he said as he unbuttoned my shirt.

I whimpered and arched up against him. "My jellybeans are down there."

His hand pushed up under my skirt. I could feel his fingers through the wet fabric of my panties.

"I can't tell if I'm weirded out or turned on by the candy innuendoes," Mace said, kissing my neck and jaw and nipping at my lips.

"You like the candy innuendoes." I gasped as he rubbed me through my panties. "Besides you would get really flustered if I flat out told you I wanted to feel your tongue on my clit and that I wanted you to turn me into a moaning mess, then stick your hard cock in me and—"

He kissed me hard, shutting me up. "Holy smokes," he said, eyes dark.

"See?" I grinned at him and ran my hand down his back. "You're all flustered."

"No," he said, kissing my neck. "I'm incredibly turned on."

His fingers worked under my panties. I tipped my head back, moaning as he stroked me. Then I screamed as someone appeared in the car window and knocked on the glass.

Mace cursed and jerked up. I heard a *crunch*, and he swore.

Clutching his head, Mace wrenched open the door and called out, "Archer, you piece of—"

"No swearing!" Archer yelled. Feet crunched on the gravel as Mace took off running after his twin brother. Concentrating on the damage to the car roof, I adjusted my clothes and tried to calm the throbbing heat between my legs.

Little cracks of light peeked through the ceiling of the truck. I stuck my finger in the hole, and part of the top of the truck caved in.

"What the—" I jumped out of the car and took off running after Archer, screaming, "You put a hole in my car roof. You better fix that!"

CHAPTER 34

Mace

I woke up the next morning with a headache. It was either from the drinking or the new sunroof I added in Josie's truck. I also had the worst case of blue balls in upstate New York. I was going to kill my brother. He specifically delayed his trip back to New York City so he could harass me.

Josie was in the kitchen when I went downstairs. She was nursing her own headache with what appeared to be a mixing bowl filled with cereal. There were three boxes of various cereals in front of her on the island, all pure sugar. I knew I didn't buy them. I wondered if cereal and candy just appeared wherever Josie went.

Several of my brothers were racing around and around the kitchen island, shrieking.

"I can lock them in the bunker," I offered, sitting down next to her on a stool. "And we can finish what we started."

She reached out and slowly felt my head. I took her hand and kissed it.

"You are more fit than me," she stated. "Don't you have a concussion?"

"I feel fine," I said. "Well, fine enough to, you know."

"Mm." She took another bite of cereal. "You want some?" She offered me the spoon.

"Only if there's whiskey and painkillers in it." That earned me a smile.

"I could use a nap," Josie said.

"I know a great spot," I whispered in her ear, kissing her neck to punctuate the words.

"You said you'd help me with my art project," Otis said, tugging at Josie. I needed to do something with my brothers.

"Do you really need her help?" I asked Otis harsher than I meant. Josie looked at me accusingly. I bit down a curse. No happy naps today.

"Do you have everything laid out?" she asked. She picked up the mixing bowl and walked after Otis while I watched in agony.

Eating my usual tofu scramble didn't help my mood. It also looked like she was settling down for a long day of homework helping. Josie had set up shop in the dining room, where she was helping with various school projects. Periodically one of the boys would sprint out of the room to the kitchen, grab cereal or marshmallows, and scramble back to the dining room.

"She needs fortification," Theo clarified as he ran through the kitchen. Henry was not fortifying, and Josie kicked him out of the dining room after an hour.

He spent the next several hours whining. He whined through lunch. He whined while I made him clean up the food he had thrown during lunch. He whined while I helped Isaac with his chemistry homework.

"No, it's easy," I told Isaac over Henry's wails.

"I'm not a freaking chemical engineer," he snapped.

"Watch your language," I scolded him. Henry wrapped himself around my leg.

"You're mean!" Henry wailed. "I'm going to see Josie."

"Don't bother her," I said as I wrote out a formula for Isaac. "She's helping the people who didn't get expelled from school."

"She's done. She went back to her hobbit house," Bruno said, opening the fridge.

I laid out on the warm flagstones after Isaac was done with his homework. Henry had run off to harass Josie. I would probably need to wrangle him back at some point.

I stood up. Everyone else had seen Josie today, but I hadn't had any of her time. Crossing the yard, I knocked on her door.

"Your house is so comically small," I said when she answered. I had to duck to walk through the doorway.

It felt even smaller inside. I hunched over and banged the side of my head on the hanging lamp.

"It's not for tall people," Josie said, sitting down on the tiniest couch I had ever seen.

"I feel like a giant in here." I peeked over the loft railing. Henry was scrambling around up there, running from window to window.

"He likes it in here," Josie said. "It's just his size."

I sat down next to her on the couch.

"That's the one good thing about the tiny house," I said, snuggling her close to me. "You have to sit practically on top of me."

"You shouldn't do this in front of Henry," she whispered.

"He's not paying attention," I whispered back, kissing her.

The tension left my neck, and the headache subsided as I wallowed in the nearness of her. She was wearing a soft athletic shirt, and I pulled it up to rub my hand across her back and under her bra, cupping her tit.

I moved her to straddle me. I caressed her thighs and ass through the tight yoga pants. I was about to suggest that we go inside to somewhere more private and with a lock on the door when there was a *crack* and the *pop, pop, pop* of several glass mason jars hitting the floor.

"Henry!" I yelled at my brother, jumping up and narrowly missing the sloped ceiling. "You destroyed her house!"

He immediately started crying.

"It's not his fault," Josie said as I picked Henry up out of the glass and inspected him for any damage. "My tiny house is trying to kill me. It's not just this shelf. Stuff randomly fails in here."

"I wanted to see the candy," Henry cried.

"You need to ask before you touch other people's stuff," I told him, patting his head.

"Don't cry, Henry," Josie said, tweaking his cheek as he buried his head in my shoulder. "This is a good thing! This means we get to go shopping!"

CHAPTER 35

Josie

Unfortunately I had to go shopping in the Svenssons' kitchen. It was late, and the stores closed early in small towns.

Mace fixed my shelf, and I was carefully filling my new mason jars with candy. Henry had wandered off to play with his brothers.

"This should be pretty sturdy," Mace said as he tested the shelf.

"I don't know how much longer this tiny house is going to be with us," I said. "I feel like, sometime in the near future, it might be crossing the eternal threshold from tiny house village to freedom."

Mace chuckled and unplugged the drill. "I just wish they had made the ceiling a little higher," he said, ducking under the hanging light.

"Does all this candy have you inspired?" I said, moving past him with my newly filled jars. I felt him come up behind me as I reached up to place them on the shelf.

His lips were on my neck, and his hand moved between my legs. "I'm feeling very inspired." His other hand caressed my breasts. "I want to eat your candy," he said. His voice was an octave lower, making my jellybean melt.

"I thought you didn't like candy," I said breathlessly as his hands slowly pulled down my yoga pants.

"I think I'm going to like this," he said.

"If you want to see if you like something or not, you have to taste it." He blew softly on my bare skin, and I almost came right then and there. "And find out."

He kept one hand on my lower back while the other pulled my pants down to the floor. I stepped out of them as he pushed me forward.

The hand on my lower back traced down my ass to the wet, tight opening that was honestly ready for a good fucking from his cock. His fingers trailed through the slick, wet heat to my clit. I moaned when he rubbed it and whimpered when his hand went back up to dip in my opening.

"Can I taste your candy, Josie?" he asked. His tone promised all pleasure.

"That's what it's there for." I gasped as his fingers teased me, doing this thing like he was spinning taffy. "Don't play with your food. Just eat it."

"Or eat it out." Mace chuckled.

He grasped my hips, and then his mouth was on me. His tongue was warm, and he moved purposefully, licking me, tracing the lines of pleasure, moving to nip and kiss at my clit then back up. One of his thumbs moved to my opening, pushing in to rub me while his tongue teased my clit.

I bucked against him, but his hands held me steady.

"Mace," I pleaded, "I want you to fuck me."

He ignored me, his tongue making steady rolling strokes, teasing me, bringing me to the edge then back.

"I'm gonna come. You should fuck me. *Fuck,*" I gasped, my fingernails scratching at the laminate countertop, causing it to peel up.

I knew I was close. My legs trembled and tightened. Mace was completely holding me up because, if I were on my own, I would have collapsed on the floor in a melted puddle of syrup.

His tongue made two more twirls around my clit, and I was done. I bit down a scream as I came. I slumped over the countertop as he continued to stroke me.

"I'm toast."

"I thought you were candy," he replied, his fingers drawing out the aftershocks of pleasure.

"Toasted almond crunchy gooey caramel delight candy," I mumbled.

"That's not even a real thing." His hand was still stroking me. I felt the stirrings of pleasure.

Normally I needed a breather between rounds, but something about having that attractive man wanting me, totally content to bring me over wave after wave of pleasure, had me aching and wet for him all over again.

I licked my lips. "You going to use that Twizzler?" I asked.

"I'm almost insulted," Mace replied. I squeaked as his hand moved back down to my clit, and I moaned as he rubbed it.

"They make giant Twizzlers," I gasped. "Like really big, thick ones."

He hummed, his voice low and echoing through me. He came around to the side of me. One hand still moved between my legs while the other slid under my shirt to cup my breast, pinching at my nipple. Then he pulled me upright and kissed me hard.

"Fuck me," I begged him, pulling off my shirt and bra.

"Not after that Twizzler comment," he said, nuzzling my breasts and kissing each nipple.

Mace set me on the couch, still sucking and biting my nipples as his hand stroked me. This time my hips were free, and I bucked against his hand, gasping as he teased my clit. His mouth moved to plant kisses from my tits to my neck to my mouth, where his tongue mimicked the motions of his hand.

I was splayed over the tiny couch, my hips rolling against Mace's hand, my fingers tangled in his hair as he made me come again.

"Give me a minute, and let's see if you can do three for three," I slurred.

But I was the one who couldn't last. I woke up an hour later and pushed off the blanket he had laid over me. Yawning, I looked around the dark tiny house.

My phone blinked. I had new messages.

Marnie: *You will not guess who's asleep on my air mattress*

CHAPTER 36

Mace

I was shocked at how quickly Josie fell asleep. I didn't know if I should be proud or miffed about it. But she had been working hard, and like Owen said, she probably was saving us billions of dollars with salvaging the marketing rollout of the gene therapy procedure.

I walked into the house, trying to tamp down my desire. Being with her was what I had fantasized about for the last week or so. Eating her candy, as she put it, hadn't slaked the desire, just dialed it up to a thousand.

The old Harrogate estate house had a large room that the architect told us was the clubroom. It had a built-in bar and was completely clad in wood. In the middle of the room stood a giant globe that I wouldn't let the kids touch because it was some sort of priceless antique. The furniture consisted of large leather chairs—a mix of what had been left over in the house when we bought it and pieces the architect said were period appropriate.

Usually, we kept the room locked because that was where we stored the liquor. I needed a drink. It wasn't locked when I walked in, but it was dark. If Isaac or one of the other teens had pilfered the liquor, I was going to—not hit them because I refused to be my father, but there were quite a lot of windows that needed cleaning in the house.

But the teenagers weren't there. Instead, when I turned on the light, I saw Hunter slumped in one of the chairs. He looked rough. His hair was a mess. His eyes were red, and his tie was loosened and draped over his rumpled shirt.

A bottle of cognac was on the table next to him, with a generous amount missing.

"Are you all right?" I asked him, taking the half-filled glass away from him before he could drink it.

"Don't get involved with women," he said, staring at the glass. "I think that's the mistake Dad made. He should have just stayed in the military."

"Dad made many more mistakes than leaving the military," I said carefully. I knew this had to be about Meg. I wasn't sure what had happened between them. Archer had sold it that they were madly in love and Meg was going to move in. Then the next thing I knew, she was in the Harrogate government and hell-bent on making the lives of every grown Svensson male as difficult as possible.

"All women are like Payslee, deep down," Hunter continued. "They're out to make your life as miserable as possible."

"No, they aren't," I admonished him. "Josie's nice. She's nothing like Payslee."

Hunter snorted. He looked a little green. I didn't want him to throw up on the carpet. I drained the rest of his glass and set it down.

"You're not thinking right," I told him. Slipping an arm under his armpit, I lifted him out of the chair.

"What you're doing with Josie is a mistake," Hunter slurred as I carted him down the hall. "Trust me. This isn't going to end well. We're cursed. We'll never be happy."

I couldn't stop thinking about Hunter's words as I tried to sleep that night. Was Josie a mistake? How well did I really know her? My father would show up randomly with a young woman, declare he was in love, and inform us she was our new sister mother. Maybe he and I had more in common than I'd wanted to believe. Maybe I was just infected with whatever sickness my father had.

But when I saw Josie the next morning, I knew that even if it was a bad idea, I wanted nothing more than to make mistakes with her.

She had an easy effectiveness with my younger brothers. Wearing a big straw hat and a sundress, Josie was organizing my little brothers for the picnic outing at the train park. They hung on her every word and were calm and well-behaved, more or less.

"Mace, did you see these picnic hampers?" she asked. Her eyes sparkled with delight, and my heart swelled. I couldn't help but lean in to kiss her.

"The Victorians had the best stuff!" she exclaimed.

"It's Edwardian," Garrett said as he strode past us from the carriage house, carrying a box of papers. "Can we try to use correct facts?"

I glowered. My brothers could be the worst sometimes.

Josie didn't seem fazed by his curt attitude. "Are you coming with us to use these glorious *Edwardian* picnic baskets?" she teased Garrett.

"Some of us have to work." He snorted. "You keep dumping Henry on me, and I can't get anything done."

"You're going to have to keep watching him," I said. "The marketing rollout needs to take priority in the next few weeks."

"Or you could find another daycare or a nanny," Garrett retorted. "There are any number of adequate solutions."

"You know that's not an option," I said, my gaze cold. I didn't want to ruin the day with the Payslee situation. Garrett scowled and went into the house.

"The train is coming soon," Otis said, bouncing up and down. "We have to go, or we'll miss it!"

"I probably should have been nicer," I said. "Then he could have driven." I sighed. "You can take Hunter's SUV. I don't think he's going to need it. It holds nine. Maybe if I go stroke Garrett's ego, he'll drive a batch."

Josie looked giddy. "We don't need to caravan. Remy and I have it under control."

I heard the rumble of an engine as we trooped around to the front of the house. Remy pulled into the roundabout with a school bus. It wasn't a nice new model—it was old and painted a familiar army green.

"I thought he was going to sell it," I grumbled.

"Why would you sell it?" Josie asked horrified. "It's your very own school bus!"

"Is this the one you bought at the auction?" I asked Remy while the younger kids loaded the picnic hampers in the bus.

"Five hundred dollars, can you believe it?" Remy hooted. "It needed some new parts for the engine. I thought I was going to have to buy a new one, but I fixed her up!"

It must have been all internal because the bus looked about as bad off as Josie's truck. I could see spots of rust through the paint.

"You're so clever!" Josie said, jumping up and down.

"It's perfect." Remy beamed.

"I'm not riding in that," I said flatly. I was having flashbacks to the compound. My father had a fleet of crappy school buses and vans. That was the only way to transport us kids to school or on the rare family outing. One of the reasons Liam was so good with machines was that as one of the youngest at the time, his hands had been small enough to fit in the engine. It was a miracle his arm hadn't been mangled.

"It hasn't been decorated yet," Remy said. "Josie's helping me decide how to brand it. My vote is for goats."

Funny, because I was thinking of how to quietly dispose of it in the night.

"I was thinking it would be like the von Trapps," she said. "Mace can be the mean father."

"Why am I the mean father? What about Hunter?" I complained. The bus shuddered as my little brothers jumped over the seats.

"It should have a name," Josie said as we took our seats.

"What about Buster?" Otis said.

"I want to name it 'The Boat,'" Theo called out.

"We'll have to have a meeting," Josie said, turning around to shout at the kids over the roar of the engine, "and take a vote."

"I want to name it Henry," Henry said.

"You can't name it after yourself," I told him.

The ride to the rail park was thankfully short.

"Watch the china," Josie said as the boys hauled the large picnic hampers down from the back bus door.

"You brought china?" I asked her.

"Of course. That's what's in the picnic basket."

"They're going to break it," I warned as the boys dragged the oversized wicker hampers off the grass.

"I had a chat with them about it. They'll be fine. If not"—she shrugged—"you can buy replacements online. Why have a bunch of dishes you can't even use?"

We set up at two of the tables. The whole park had been an abandoned switching yard back when more than just the one train to the Svensson PharmaTech factories went in and out of Harrogate. The landscape architects had used the old tracks to host tables on wheels that could move back and forth.

"This is such a nice park," Josie said in admiration. "I love how they have all the old locomotives and historic train cars displayed."

"My company built this park," I told her. "It was part of the deal for the last research center and factory expansion."

"Not to brag of course," she said.

When the kids had finished eating, only two plates were broken.

"Better than I thought," Josie said. The sweet scent of her bloomed in the sun, and we lay on the grass while the kids played. Her bare foot slowly rubbed against my ankle.

"Why don't you just build another park?" she asked sleepily against my chest.

"Hmm?"

"For the new factory and the meadow destruction."

"We floated the idea, but the city didn't seem to go for it," I explained. "Technically all the land outside of Harrogate is a greenbelt and a heritage area. I wanted to build there originally because of the freight line, the proximity to the hydroelectric plant, and the connection to the commuter rail line."

"Hmm," she said. I could tell she was spinning the problem over in her head.

"Don't worry about it," I told her. "Mayor Barry likes us. Says we're real men who build things. It will slide through eventually."

"Still, you don't want the bad publicity from the community," she said, frowning. I kissed her forehead to smooth down her features.

"I know," I said, stroking her hair. "We're trying to handle it delicately. Meghan isn't making it any easier."

"Garrett mentioned something about her and Hunter?" Josie asked, nestling against my chest.

I nodded. "They had a thing. It was the only time I've seen Hunter really happy. Then something happened. Now they have a new thing where they just try and make each other's lives as miserable as possible."

"It's time," Otis announced. The train whistle blew.

The park straddled the one remaining active freight line at the point where it came right down Main Street and turned to connect to the main line, and it was an impressive sight to be so close to the large machine.

The kids cheered as the train went by. But I was watching something else. Payslee. She was an apparition through the gaps in the train, watching us from the opposite side of the tracks. I was going to kill Hunter.

I obsessively head counted the kids as I ushered them to the bus. "We need to go. We need to go now."

CHAPTER 37

Josie

I had wanted the outing to be perfect to distract me from the fact that Anke was back and couch surfing with Marnie. My friend was sure Anke had another scam brewing. I did talk Marnie out of contacting the FBI. I had just finally convinced one man to stop seeing me as a ditz. I didn't need a bunch of FBI agents looking at me like a dumb little girl.

But that particular man was tense on the bus ride back to the estate. Out of the corner of my eye, I looked at Mace's stony face.

Was he mad about the issue with the facility expansion? I understood why the residents didn't want any more large research facilities, Ida's lust for Bert notwithstanding. I liked taking Henry out into the meadow, and the trees were nice. I didn't want to see them go. But at the same time, PharmaTech had to grow and expand. There were people who counted on

Mace's company for jobs. Business owners and restaurants in town would also benefit from new employees.

What absolutely could not happen was a bunch of bad press on how a big, bad pharma company was tearing up a heritage area. An important component of my gene therapy marketing push was tying this innovative method of disease treatment into a larger narrative about how PharmaTech had a holistic approach to health.

After we unpacked and situated the kids, there was a quiet moment, and I thought we were going to do the dirty chocolate kiss. But Mace remained tense. He wouldn't let the kids go outside, and he locked himself in the study with his older brothers.

Mace didn't seem in a better mood the next morning when we went to the office. It was like how I first met him, the tendon on his neck prominent, his back ramrod straight.

I kissed him on the front steps, hoping to bring back the tender man I had started to really like. Mace softened slightly and leaned into me.

A rumbling interrupted us. A flatbed truck drove up the drive with a shiny new car on the back.

"Finally," Mace said as the truck driver unloaded the car.

"Aww, and here I was going to have Remy drive the bus to work."

"Please," Mace said, signing the paperwork. "I am not a bus person."

"Of course! You're an expensive-car person," I joked.

"And you're an expensive-car-destroying person," he teased back.

As soon as the flatbed truck was out of sight, Mace pushed me against the side of the car for a heavy kiss. He slid his hand down my back and ran it over my chest, cupping my tits.

"You want to christen this car?" I gasped against him. His hand was hot through my panties, and my nipples were hard.

Before we could go much further, his phone rang. Mace cursed.

"I forgot I had a conference call," he said and answered. "Yeah just give me a moment." He looked at me critically, then he handed me the keys.

"You want me to drive your new car!" I said gleefully.

"Don't scratch it," he warned.

"Ooh," I said, running my hand over the glossy surface. "I've never driven a fresh car before."

I inhaled the new-car smell as I adjusted the seat.

Okay, Josie, I told myself. *Nice and easy.*

I pulled out slowly into the road. So far so good. Mace was looking down at his tablet, making notes as he talked into the phone.

I'm not going to scratch this car. I'm not going to scratch this car.

A car coming toward me swerved into my lane. I screamed and jerked the car.

"We're only two minutes from the house," Mace hissed, covering the mouthpiece.

I slowed to a crawl, and we crept into the Svensson PharmaTech parking lot ten minutes late.

"I would be mad if you weren't so freaking sexy," Mace said, pushing me back into the seat, his hand coming up my leg.

"I have a meeting," I gasped, as much as I wanted him to continue.

Ever since Mace gave me the reins on the marketing gene therapy rollout, I wasn't spending much time in the private office. Instead our team had commandeered several large conference rooms and had set up there.

"The notes on the sustainability research are in your inbox," Adrian said when he saw me. "Also, want any coffee?"

"But I thought you weren't supposed to be bringing coffee," I said with a grin.

"Mace said that we needed this launch to go off without a hitch. I'm embedded in the marketing team to get you all whatever you need: information, photos, resources… *coffee*."

"Yes, that would be lovely."

I was glad to be working on actual marketing again. What I was not glad about was Tara.

"Did you have a good weekend?" I asked her, trying to smooth the tension.

"I was working," she said, turning up her nose. "Unlike some people. You're going to ruin this marketing push. I can't believe they gave so much responsibility to someone with no experience."

"You had ample opportunity," I countered. "Mace chose me, not you. Now if you'll excuse me, we have a deadline to meet."

"You just slept your way up," she hissed.

I turned to her. "I don't sleep my way to get things."

"Yes, you do," she sneered. "You're living in his house, ingratiating yourself with his family. You don't care about him."

"You don't either," I shot back as she huffed out of the conference room.

"She's like this all the time," Willow said as she came in with a puffed-rice round.

"Why are you eating that?"

"It's all they have." She held the rice cake out to me.

I took a bite. "It's so gross."

"I wish they would get better food," Willow said, plucking the rice cake from me and tossing it in the trash can.

"We're ordering in fancy sandwiches for lunch," I told her. "Garrett said I could have an expense account for this project. I can't work off toasted rice puffs."

We worked all morning, tossing ideas back and forth on the marketing. Though I had worked on a basic outline and graphic direction, there was more that had to be refined. Plus we had to write press releases, design, and brochures, and create content for a website associated specifically with the product.

I was starving by the time lunch was delivered.

"Okay, everyone, take a break," I announced. My team looked at me blankly.

"Tara didn't let us take breaks," one guy said after a moment.

"Tara's not here, and I say you need some time to refresh. Meet back in an hour, and be ready to go hard."

"They do have a nice campus," Willow remarked as we walked outside. The view was great, and it really would be a shame if Mace built another factory here. I took a bite of my *bánh mì* sandwich. The tang of the pork made my mouth water. The bread had just enough bite, and the pickled veggies were spicy but not too much. They had also added a hint of spicy aioli.

"Mmh," I said, taking another bite. "I think this is one of my new favorite foods."

"So," Willow said. "Did Mace stick his hand in your candy jar?"

"Stuck his whole face was more like it."

Willow shrieked and grabbed me, making me slosh my drink. There were other people outside enjoying the sunshine. I shushed her.

"Tara already suspects something," I said in a low voice. "I can't be that dumb, idiotic girl who sleeps with the boss. Everyone will think that's the reason Mace gave me this project."

"He gave you this project because you're good at marketing," Willow countered. "You've accomplished more in the last few days than Tara has in weeks."

"I just hope it goes well. This is a really tight deadline," I said, contemplating my sandwich.

"What's the matter?" Willow asked, petting my head. "You're living large. Isn't this everything you always wanted?"

I sighed again. "I guess." My phone dinged. I ignored it, then it rang. "It's Marnie."

"Put it on speaker," Willow insisted.

"Hey, Marnie!" Willow and I chorused.

"Hey, ladies." She sounded frazzled. Usually our friend was unflappable. She had to be to put up with Greg Svensson day in and day out as his secretary.

"Anke left," she said.

"Okay so…"

"She just disappeared in the middle of the night," Marnie explained.

"Good riddance!" Willow said.

"No, I—she didn't sound right. And she didn't look right either," Marnie said. "You know how she was always so put together? I think she owes a lot of money to people more dangerous than Josie. When people are in that position, they do rash things. She kept asking about Josie and her job. Just be on the lookout. I don't know where she was headed, but it might be your way."

"I doubt it's anything that serious," I said. "How much damage can she really do?"

Willow looked at me, incredulous.

"I know you don't want me to," Marnie said, "but it's time to go to the authorities."

"She sent me five thousand dollars!" I protested. "What if she's going to send the rest?" I had just scored this marketing project. I couldn't have the FBI poking around and tipping Mace off to how stupid I was.

Marnie sighed.

"Just, I think we're overreacting. I don't think she's dangerous," I said in a small voice.

"Famous last words," Marnie said.

CHAPTER 38

Mace

I was waiting in the lobby that evening when Josie walked out. She yawned as I wrapped an arm around her shoulders.

"How's everything going? Do you need anything? Are you going to make the deadline?" I asked as I took her laptop bag and let my hand drift down the curve of her hip.

"Of course!" Josie replied. "The only thing I need is fortification. I can't run on seaweed crackers and rice cakes."

"This isn't New York City, with bodegas open twenty-four, seven, but the big wholesale store outside of town is open late on weeknights," I told her.

"Good. I want candy."

This time I drove.

"No Henry today?" Josie asked.

"Garrett has him."

"I'm sure he really likes that!" Josie said, laughing.

I liked her. And I admired her. I had found this old love letter in the house a decade ago, when Hunter first bought it before it was cleaned out. Old Man Harrogate had written all these sappy love letters to someone. At the time I had scoffed, but now I wanted to write her poetry. But instead of a love note, my infatuation with Josie was making me go shopping with her.

I was starting to regret my decision at the store.

"I love shopping! I love clothes shopping and furniture shopping and craft supply shopping, but I really love food shopping!" Josie said as she skipped through the store. I followed behind, pushing an overflowing shopping cart.

"We can just have this all delivered," I told her as she threw more food into the cart.

"But grocery shopping is so much fun!" she exclaimed. "Look! You can buy a whole jar of peanut butter as big as your head and a giant container of marshmallow fluff."

"Who is going to eat all of this?" I exclaimed.

"You have a million brothers," she sniffed. "This is going to be gone in a week."

I surveyed the pile of food in a daze.

"I always wanted a huge family," she said as she directed me to put a giant can of nacho cheese and a big bag of chips in the cart. "With like a hundred kids. The best thing about it would be that you could buy these giant containers of food! My great-aunt would never let me do that."

"But it's all processed junk food," I protested.

"Everything in moderation. Besides, with the food co-op we belong to, there will be a ton of fresh veggies. I'm making ratatouille soon. Ernest says he's going to have eggplants here in another month."

"What food co-op?"

"Oh," she said, grinning. "One of Ida's friends runs it. I put the Svensson family down as members. I figured it would be a nice goodwill gesture with the community."

I looked at her in confusion.

"Because of your land deal," she prompted.

"I told you not to worry about that," I said, taking her in my arms.

"You've rubbed off on me. I'm worrying," she said.

"Just buy all of it," I said when we stood in front of the candy aisle along with a second cart that was quickly filling up.

"There are so many options!" Josie said. "I want them all."

I looked up at the shelves of candy. "Then you're going to be stuck in your tiny house with nothing but candy," I told her.

"I would be okay with that," she said after thinking a second.

"What if you put your factory somewhere else?" she asked as we pushed the carts to the front register. "Right now, you have to run a shuttle up to the research buildings."

"I can't move the factory anywhere else," I said.

"Why not? The train drives right through town. You could put the factory on one of those vacant lots," she suggested.

"We don't own a big enough lot in downtown. We have to have room to build a factory to produce medical devices along with lab space and data-processing buildings," I explained as I handed the clerk my credit card.

Josie winced at the total. "That's a lot of money."

"It's a lot of food."

"Maybe we should put some back," she said uncertainly.

"I refuse to go back in that store," I said, signing the receipt.

Josie argued with me about the factory location on the drive back to the estate house. I was tense and a little annoyed when we finally pulled up in front of the house. Josie looked at me guiltily.

"I didn't mean to make you aggravated," she said. "Actually, I was hoping you would loosen up or loosen me up, at least," she said, squeezing my bicep.

I rubbed my jaw.

"Not having second thoughts, are you?" She asked it flippantly, carefully.

"Never. Just, are you?" I looked at her out of the corner of my eye.

"Are you afraid of a sexual harassment lawsuit? I'm an adult professional," she said. "I don't let my feelings get in the way of my work. It's not like it's serious. We're not going to get married or anything. We can be adults, and you can stick your face in my candy jar, and I'll suck on your lollipop."

"I want more than to have you lick my lollipop," I said, staring at her hungrily. "I want to come in your candy jar."

CHAPTER 39

Josie

Mace followed me into the kitchen, lugging the bags of food.

I could feel him watching me as I bent down.

"See something sweet you want to eat?" I asked, doing my best Jessica Rabbit pose with a bag of chocolate candy.

"Maybe," he said. He voice was deep, and his eyes were heavily lidded. I didn't know if I wanted him to go down on me or push me against the counter and fuck me, but having him stand there staring was messing up my equilibrium.

I opened the bag of chocolate and took out a few pieces.

"Or are you looking for dessert and a show?" I did my best impression of a sexy dance while holding a bag of chocolate.

Unwrapping a piece of the chocolate, I put it between my teeth and crooked a finger. Mace slowly came over and pressed our mouths together, taking it. It was heady.

"I knew you would taste good with chocolate all over you," I whispered against his mouth.

"You really make me crazy," he said. I could feel him hard through his pants.

Mace pulled at my shirt, undoing it. He pulled out a breast and sucked at the hard nipple, making me gasp. His hands slowly slid under my skirt.

"I love how wet you are," Mace rumbled in my ear as two fingers stroked me through my panties, making me moan.

"We should go to the tiny house," I gasped, pushing at him. "This kitchen is so amazing that if you fucked me here, I think I might just disintegrate from too much awesome at once."

"You think I'm awesome," Mace said, grinning against me then moving back up to kiss me hard.

"You gave an impressive debut performance in the tiny house," I replied, grinding against the hand he held against my panties.

"For the past few days, I've been dreaming about fucking your tight, hot pussy, all soaking wet for my cock. And in none of those dreams did it take place in the tiny house," he growled in my ear. Then he picked me up and carried me to the back stairway.

"I fantasized about fucking you in the office," he murmured, "listening to you moan and whimper every time I slid my thick cock into you while you bent over your desk." I moaned.

"I also wanted to fuck you in the car," he said, nipping my ear as he pushed through the upstairs door. My legs were wrapped tightly around him as he carried me down the hallway. I undid his shirt buttons, wanting to feel the hardness of his chest against my bare tits.

"But my bed is closer," he continued, pushing through another door and setting me on the dark-colored bedspread. That delicious smell was everywhere. I couldn't help myself. I turned over and buried my face in the fabric.

"It smells so good," I moaned. There was a soft *whumpf* as Mace's clothes hit the floor. He pulled off my rumpled skirt and shirt. My nipples were hard against the bedspread, and I grabbed fistfuls of it as Mace spread my legs and began to slowly lick me.

"I thought you wanted to fuck," I groaned as his tongue lapped at my pussy, circling my clit.

"I want to draw this out."

"And I want your cock," I gasped. "You're not the only one with fantasies. One of mine involves drizzling chocolate all over you and very, very slowly licking it off."

He laughed against me. "You'll have to table that because I'm the one licking you slowly tonight."

I cursed as he slid two fingers into me, crooking them slightly.

"Why don't you replace those with your cock?" I moaned.

He moved to hover over me. Still stroking me, Mace whispered in my ear, "You want my cock, huh?"

"Yes," I gasped. There was the tearing sound of a condom wrapper, and I almost came right there from the anticipation. I spread my legs and lifted my hips slightly, letting out a cry when he slid into me. One of his hands reached up to pinch and roll my nipple as he slowly thrust into me.

"Harder," I moaned. "I want to feel you."

He ignored me and continued to slowly thrust into me. The pleasure was excruciating. My heart yammered, and my legs felt tight.

"I want you to make me come," I whimpered, my head back, my ass arched up to him. "Faster, I need it faster."

Mace pulled me up on my knees. My arms felt like marshmallows, and I rested on my forearms as he finally started to pound into me. My hips rolled against him, and he held me up while he fucked me. I whimpered in time to his thrusts then cursed him when he stopped.

"I want to see your face when you come," he whispered and flipped me over.

Then he was back inside me. His cock rubbed against my clit every time he thrust into me. I wrapped my legs around him and tangled my nails in his hair as he fucked me. My nipples rubbing against his hard, muscular chest felt every bit as good as I imagined.

My legs tightened as he brought me close to the edge. His thrusts sped up, sending me over a chocolate waterfall of pleasure. He came right after me, kissing me hard.

Mace moved his head down to nuzzle my breasts. "I guess there are certain types of candy I do enjoy after all."

I made some noncommittal noise. In the fading haze of pleasure, my mind spun in the dark. I had just slept with my boss. It wasn't a cute candy innuendo. We had fucked, in his house. And he didn't know the truth about why I was working for him or in Harrogate.

Would Mace feel like I had duped and lied to him when he found out? Was I just like my mother? Worse? Was I like Anke?

CHAPTER 40

Mace

Josie was cuddled against me when I woke up the next morning. It was as perfect as I had imagined. I kissed her awake.

"This is so much better than the tiny house," she said sleepily.

"Your tiny house is very tiny," I said, kissing the nipple that peeked above the edge of the sheet.

"And you haven't even been in the loft," she said, smiling, her eyes still closed.

"I don't think I would even fit," I replied, my hand caressing the curves of her body under the sheet. "It would be very cozy."

I dropped feathery kisses up from her breast to her neck then to her mouth.

"I thought you would be done by now," she murmured against me.

"I'll never have enough of you," I whispered. "You're more addicting than candy."

"Yes," she said as my hand slipped under the sheet to stroke her. "But what kind of candy?"

My phone vibrated, and I ignored it. I had more important things to do. I was kissing down to that more important thing when I heard people running up and down the hall, calling my name.

Josie sat straight up, almost banging into my nose. "You better go; it might be an emergency!"

"This early?" I said, pushing her back down. "One of the kids probably just forgot they had a project due."

My phone rang again. Josie grabbed it and handed it to me.

"We have a problem." Garrett's voice was urgent. "Payslee is at the gate. She says she wants Henry. And she has a lawyer with her."

When I walked outside, I could hear Payslee yelling. The driveway was a straight shot from the front door down to the gate lined with trees. I could make out Payslee's silhouette against the front gate.

"Should we let her in?" Adrian asked. He was standing on the stairs next to Remy, who was holding a large ax.

"Absolutely not," I said. "I know she's your mom, Adrian, but she's acting like a lunatic. Call the police. Where are all the kids?"

"Hunter said just to pay her off," Garrett said, holding up his phone. "He said there's cash in the safe."

"I'm done with Hunter," I growled. "This is insane."

Josie walked out while Adrian called the police.

"Go back inside," I ordered. "We're dealing with something."

"Who is that?" she asked as Payslee started yelling again about how she was going to sue us and send us to jail for kidnapping.

"Evil stepmother," I said, ushering Josie back through the front door.

My brothers and I watched on the security feed as Hunter's car drove up, followed by the police thirty seconds later.

Garrett and I hurried down the driveway. When we slipped through the gatehouse door, Payslee and her lawyer were arguing with the police.

"They have my son. It's kidnapping." Her voice sounded like she was whistling every so often. In the early-morning daylight, I could see it was because several of her teeth were missing. She had to have been only a few years older than me, but she looked decades older.

"I have permission from his father to have guardianship of Henry Svensson," Hunter countered.

As mad as I was at Hunter, he was a lawyer, and I felt more secure having my older brother talk to the police.

"He was abandoned," Hunter continued in that semi-bored, condescending tone he had. "We have the paperwork. He was sent here with a birth certificate and a social security card."

"It was temporary guardianship," Payslee's lawyer argued. "And his mother is revoking it." I didn't like him. He had a doughy face with the cauliflower nose and broken cheek blood vessels of a major alcoholic.

Garrett's mouth twitched. He held up his tablet. "It *was* abandonment. Payslee hasn't seen Henry in fourteen months. She hasn't just abandoned Henry. She abandoned her other six sons, who are here now. Instead of taking care of them, she chose to go to Las Vegas"—he flipped to an image on his tablet—"where she hooked up with this man." A mugshot came up on the screen. "We have eyewitness accounts."

The police officers looked at the tablet.

Garrett kept talking. "Then Payslee came to New York and shacked up with this man." A picture of Payslee making out with the lawyer came up on the screen.

The police looked at the lawyer.

"This is the twenty-first century," he sputtered. "You can't keep a mother from her child just for being a sexual being."

"That's right," Payslee said, nodding. "He's my son."

"Why now?" I countered. Garrett elbowed me.

"I made a mistake," Payslee said. "But I'm ready to fix it. I want to be a good mom. Not just to Henry but to all my boys."

I snorted. I didn't believe her for a second.

"You need to make them give him back," Payslee said to Susie.

The police officer looked between us and Payslee. Was Susie going to take Henry just to spite us? I tried to silently plead with her. She nodded to me then turned to Payslee.

"I can't just hand a child over to someone who says she's his mother. There's a process. I need identification and a Harrogate, New York, residency confirmation. It can be a driver's license, utility bill, or voter identification card. Otherwise it's not my jurisdiction, and I can't entertain the complaint," Susie said.

Payslee opened her mouth to complain, but Susie held up a hand. "You are trespassing on Mr. Svensson's property, and you need to leave."

We watched as Payslee got into the car with her lawyer. She seemed furious.

"I'm going to get that boy!" she yelled through the passenger window as the car sped off. "You don't have any right. No right!"

"Thanks, Susie. We owe you," I said gratefully.

She snorted. "Please. The city of Harrogate may have turned around, but when you go into greater Harrogate, you still have the trailer parks and methheads. I've dealt with too many domestic violence calls to take an innocent child from a lovely home and give him to someone like that." She took her sunglasses off her collar then looked each of us in the eye. "You all need to sort this out, legally speaking," she warned. "Payslee could escalate."

Josie was sitting on the steps of the grand staircase in the foyer with my little brothers huddled around her when I walked in. I stood in front of them, doing a head count to reassure

"You heard Payslee outside, I'm sure. Now, none of you talk to that woman. Don't look at her. Don't contact her, and if you see her, tell me."

CHAPTER 41

Josie

"I don't understand what happened with Payslee," I said to Mace when we were alone in his office at PharmaTech. He had been on the phone the entire drive over. I had heard several men yelling on the call.

"Doesn't she just want money?" I asked. "Could you pay her to make her go away?"

"Hunter tried that. It didn't work. I think it just emboldened her," he said tersely. "And then that leech of a lawyer stuck to her, and I'm sure he's egging her on too."

I rubbed his back, and he pulled me close and wrapped his arms around me.

"I never got to thank you for last night," I murmured.

"Please," he said, tipping my head back and kissing me. There were echoes of last night and promises of future pleasure in that kiss. "It was my pleasure."

"Actually it was mine," I whispered to him. His hands inched under my skirt. "It's too bad your office is glass."

"That doesn't have to stop us," he said, smiling at me wolfishly.

"For someone who doesn't like eating junk food, you sure are willing to take risks in other ways," I said, raising an eyebrow.

There was a knock on the door, and Adrian came in. "We need you downstairs, boss."

"Sure, I'm coming," Mace said, straightening his jacket.

Adrian looked at him oddly. "No, I meant Josie. She's the boss of marketing."

"Ah," Mace said.

I elbowed him in the stomach. Not that it hurt him—his abs were rock solid.

"I'm right behind you," I told Adrian, grabbing my laptop and following him out of Mace's office.

"How are you holding up? This morning was scary, huh?" I asked.

Adrian looked down at the floor. "My mom was always nutty. She believes in aliens and that the government was controlling us with radio signals. We weren't allowed to have anything metal. She was miserable to be around and a terrible mother. It's good you're here," he said, stopping to look at me. "It's nice to just have a woman who's really kind around. And"—he blushed—"for what it's worth, I think you're good for Mace. He's a lot more relaxed and easier to deal with since you arrived."

"Aw," I said, hugging him. He was almost as tall as his older brothers, but I still pulled his head down under my chin to snuggle him. "I wish I could help more," I said after I released him.

Adrian shrugged. "Hunter and Garrett will deal with it. They always do. Though no one else's mom has shown up at the house before. That's a new one."

All that morning, as I worked on the marketing material, I wondered how I could help Mace. Payslee was out of my league, but Mace had other problems I could solve.

"Hey, Adrian," I said. "You busy?"

"Just finishing up pulling some data for Willow," he said, swiveling around in his chair.

"I don't want to take your time away from the marketing project," I told him, "but I was wondering if you could do some research for me on that factory and new research facility your brothers want to build."

"Mace had me working on it," he said, navigating to the folder on the network. "What do you want to know?"

"I want to know if there's another place they could put it," I said, looking at his screen.

"There are lots of good places," he said, pulling up the map. "But we own all this land." He showed a satellite view of the big greenfield and wooded area to the south of the city where PharmaTech was currently located.

"This used to be the town dump. That's why it's on a hill. The land was cheap, which is why Hunter and Greg bought it. Svensson Investment also owns all these other properties, see in purple?" He pointed with the cursor. "But none of them are big enough or in a good location. They ideally need to be on the train line or a track spur."

"Could they buy others?"

Adrian nodded and pointed to an area in orange. "These properties together would be great. They're on the same large block as several of the ones Svensson Investment already owns. Unfortunately, each one is owned by a different entity.

A couple are owned by the city, further complicating the situation. It's highly unlikely any of the owners would sell. And all of them? Forget about it."

"Can't you just make a good offer?" I asked.

"Greg's investment company bought as much land as they could, but now all the residents know that if some random LLC is trying to buy your property, it's the Svenssons. The owners either hold out for a lot of money or flat-out refuse to sell," Adrian explained.

"It's tricky," I remarked. "Can you give me the addresses and names of the owners of those properties you would have to buy?"

He typed a crazy formula into his software, and it spat out a table of properties with the acres and the owners. I took the printout from the printer.

"I'm going to pick up lunch," I told the team. I wanted to visit Ida.

Ida was behind the counter at the general store.

"How's the tiny house?" she asked. "Actually I suppose I should ask you how's the giant man. Is he proportionally big all over?"

I mean, yes, but... I shouldn't tell Ida that.

"There's a pool going on when you two will get married," Ida chattered. "I'm betting April of next year. So don't disappoint me!"

"I'll try not to," I said then pulled out the property list. "I'm trying to fix your bird-watcher problem."

"Oh, Bert!" she said. "Yes, that's all he talks about. You try to get a man fascinated in these"—she cupped her boobs—"and all he talks about are the birds."

"The Svenssons would be open to putting the factory somewhere else." I showed her on the map. "They need to buy all of these properties to do it. But they think they can't convince anyone to sell," I explained.

"Let me see that list," Ida said, putting on the glasses that hung at her neck.

"Hmm. Oh, this one is Art's. He goes apple-picking in the forest."

"Do you think he would sell?" I asked.

She pursed her lips. "Unknown. He always had designs to put a brewery on that spot. Though between you and me, the man is in his seventies, and while he makes good cider, he never keeps enough of it to sell. The man drinks like a fish."

"What about the other sites?" I asked.

"One of them belongs to my sister," Ida said, running her finger down the list. "She hates the Svenssons."

"So that's it," I said, feeling demoralized.

"I'll think on it," Ida said and tapped her head. "We'll figure something out, lass."

I had done all that I could do. Hopefully Ida would come through for me. The French café had the bags of soups, sandwiches, salads, and pastries I'd ordered sitting on the counter.

"Lemon tarts, chocolate tarts, and caramel tarts," the clerk said. "We bring them in from the Grey Dove Bistro."

"I can't wait!" I said, taking the bag.

The clerk looked at me. "My aunt said you knew the Svenssons. Since they're all friends with Chloe, do you know if she's opening up a franchise here? That's what everyone's saying," she said in a rush.

"They are?" I squealed. "I would die if she put a bakery here."

"I know!" the clerk swooned. "Her life is so perfect!" We collectively sighed, and I walked out dreaming of having Chloe's perfect life.

My own life was far from perfect. I made terrible decisions, and as I turned the corner to walk back to where I parked my car, one of my problems was walking down the street toward me.

"Anke?" I choked out.

"Darling Josie!" My ex-friend ran to me, hugging me like she hadn't scammed me out of tens of thousands of dollars.

"You've put on weight. It looks good on you," Anke said.

"What are you doing here?" I sputtered. "And where's the money you promised me? You said you'd pay me back for that luxury hotel suite in Morocco."

"Darling, I told you I had a plan! Marnie told me all about your job. I see you already have your own scheme in motion. You don't need me!"

"The job's not paying that much," I said flatly.

Anke grabbed my hand. "I don't mean your *job*." She winked. "I mean the *man* at the job. I'm impressed, Josie. Marnie says you've already moved into his house."

I would be mad at Marnie, but Anke was so manipulative. She could lull people into a state of complacency and make them think she was their best friend and they should spill all their secrets to her. I tried to stay calm.

"I need that money, Anke. You promised," I reiterated.

"Darling, I will give it to you. I promise. I have a plan for the money. We're friends! I didn't forget about you." She kissed me once on each cheek. "It was delightful to see you. We should go out for a drink. It would be just like old times."

As I drove back to PharmaTech in a daze, I wondered if I should tell Mace. But I shut that thought down. He had enough on his plate, and he finally had started to see me as someone capable and competent. I knew Mace was concerned about Payslee harming his family. I didn't want him to think I was a problem too.

Besides, I thought, trying to relax my grip on the steering wheel. *Anke never stays that long somewhere. She's probably going to be gone tomorrow. This will all work itself out. Right?*

CHAPTER 42

Mace

I was glad I could count on Josie to finish up that marketing project. At least she was someone I could lean on. Though my brothers were passably useful, it was hard being responsible for everyone. Hunter had been scarce lately, and it felt good to have a partner in Josie.

I spent all morning down at the police station with Hunter and Greg, who had driven in.

The chief of police looked at us over her glasses. "She's his mother. Unlike the other children, he's not legally yours."

"I have guardianship papers," Hunter said. "They were signed by Henry's—and my—father."

The police chief sighed. "Yes, but she's his mother. Once she presents me with the proper paperwork and proof of residency, I'm legally obligated to turn the child over to her. I'm sorry."

Meg was in the lobby when we walked out of the station.

"Hunter," she said, her face displaying concern, "Susie told me what happened. I don't understand. Why does she want him back? You can't let that happen."

She stroked Hunter's arm, and he seemed to sag into her touch.

"Meg," he said, grabbing her hand. "I know you hate me, but please, you have to help me."

"Of course," she said, squeezing his hand. Then she seemed to realize what she was doing and suddenly released it. She cleared her throat, and I saw her professional mask fall back into place.

"Why can't you pay Payslee to let you adopt him?" she said. "That would be the easiest route."

"Tried it already," Hunter said. "Someone else is pulling her strings."

I was feeling sick when I returned to the office.

Archer was sitting cross-legged on top of my desk, eating a soup muffin. A large box of them was next to him.

"I brought sustenance, curtesy of Chloe," he said, holding out the half-eaten muffin.

"Here to harass me?" I asked more tersely than I meant.

Archer dusted off his hands, crumbs scattering over my keyboard. They would never come out.

"I needed to make sure you wouldn't do anything rash, like move everyone into Remy's bunker," Archer said. "Also I think I've chosen a site for my new hotel and conference center."

"Oh yeah?" I asked, taking a muffin. It had little bits of meat in it and a gooey, cheesy center.

"It's cheesesteak flavored," Archer said. "Chloe invented them just for me."

"It's surprisingly good," I admitted, taking another bite.

Archer sighed happily. "She said she froze the Cheez Whiz and put it in the center before baking in order to make it explode cheese like that. I'm trying to convince her to put a franchise here and cater for the conference center."

"What site did you choose?" I asked, snagging another muffin.

"The old Mast Brothers' Chocolate factory," he said, pointing out the window to the hulking complex on the north side of town.

"I hope you change the name," I said. "Mast—it sounds a little dirty."

"Only to filthy minds," Archer said. "You want to dip your mast in chocolate? You better not hear Josie hear you talk like that."

"She loves candy," I said, smirking. "She would really go for it."

"Who are you, and did someone replace you with me?" Archer asked, snapping his fingers in front of my face.

"Hardly," I said as my phone beeped in my pocket.

"Is that her?" Archer demanded. "I can tell it is. Your face looks all melty. I should stick a bar of chocolate on your head and call it fondue."

I ignored him and read her message.

> **Josie:** *Sorry you're feeling stressed. If Payslee tries to take Henry I'll pack him up in my tiny house and head to Mexico. We'll live like hippies on the beach. Also did you know they invented chocolate? Sweet fact*

of the day! Here's another treat for you. I was saving it as a reward but I think you've earned it.

There was an attachment, and I watched as it loaded.

"Holy smokes," I said and quickly shoved the phone back into my pocket.

"She sent you a naughty picture, didn't she?" Archer asked in mock outrage. "No, don't show me. I need to retain the image of you as pure, virginal snow. I'll leave you alone with your lustful thoughts." He snatched up the box of muffins and waltzed out, humming that song from the Willy Wonka movie about pure imagination.

I took the phone out of my pocket and stared at the picture. There was Josie. I knew it was her even though she had cropped off her face. I recognized her tits, the curve of her stomach, and the pink flesh between her legs that she spread with her fingers. Her other hand held a large purple lollipop down very close to that glistening pink flesh.

You know where I want your blow pop, the caption stated in loopy cursive text. Funny and sexy, it was pure Josie.

CHAPTER 43

Josie

"Did you receive my message?" I asked Mace when I walked into the office after lunch. The naughty picture had been a spur-of-the-moment decision with me, as most things were. I hoped it didn't explode in my face, though I supposed I wouldn't mind if Mace exploded in my face.

"I did," he said. His grin was downright predatory as he followed me into my adjoining office. I sat down at my desk and opened my laptop.

"I was going to work up here for a few hours," I told him. "That conference room is getting claustrophobic, and I just need to concentrate and knock this out."

"Uh-huh."

"So you should probably go back to whatever you were doing," I prompted. He came up next to me as I opened up the vector illustrator program on my computer.

"You can't send me a picture like that and not expect that it would completely derail my afternoon," Mace said, bending down. His cheek was next to mine but not touching, and I could feel the slight warmth radiating off of him.

"I didn't know you found me that distracting," I teased.

"Oh I think you know that I find you very distracting," he breathed in my ear. I shivered.

"Did you know," he asked, leaning over me, one hand on the desk, the other sliding slowly down my back, "that we specifically had the architect put in glass walls to deter people from fucking in the offices?"

"I did not know that, though it seems like a good call to make." Having him that close to me was starting to make me a little distracted. His hand was sliding lower and lower.

"You probably don't want your employees fucking in the office, do you?" I asked. His hand was at the waistband of my skirt, and he slowly worked his hand under the wide band. I inadvertently spread my legs a little wider. He smirked against my neck. "I can't believe anyone would be so unprofessional and, frankly, have so little control that they just had to screw in plain sight when anyone could walk in." I tried to not sound so needy, but his fingers were under my panties now. One. Two. Three. They started to slowly stroke me, and I gripped the desk.

"Yes," Mace said, "but some offices, like yours actually, now that I think about it, have things like a plant or bookshelves that conveniently block the view from unsuspecting bystanders."

"It is very convenient," I gasped as he stroked me, teasing my clit.

"But since you're up here, let's talk about how your organizing is going," Mace said, his tone annoyingly casual for what he was doing to me.

"What?" I asked, clamping down a moan. My hips rocked into his hand. I tried not to look like I was in the middle of a workplace affair with my boss. Though there was a large plant and a couple of chairs blocking the bottom half of the glass wall, someone walking by could still see inside.

"Did you create the snack survey?" Mace asked, his tone professional as his hand did naughty things to me. I felt his fingers play in my opening, and I closed my eyes, tipping my head back.

"Eyes open," Mace whispered into my ear, nibbling it slightly. "Look at your computer screen. We're just having a normal professional conversation."

"Normal conversation," I repeated. My voice sounded breathy, and in the blank screen of my laptop, I could see my own reflection and Mace's smug one.

"Yes. For example, would you like me to add your favorite snack to the breakrooms?"

"You're my favorite snack," I said. I could feel my heart racing.

"I'm not a snack food," he said. "I'm a main course."

"You're dessert," I said. Mace chuckled, and his fingers moved faster, making this little twisty motion like he was spinning taffy. He was spinning me into a tizzy. I gripped the desk with both hands, my legs splayed as much as I could without ripping my skirt.

His fingers were stroking faster, and my head tipped forward slightly as I bit down on a moan.

"This," he said as his fingers worked me, rubbing my clit then pausing to slide down in the wetness and push into my opening. "This is just a snack. It's just something to whet your appetite."

"Consider it wet," I told him. The words came out in a high-pitched whimper. I licked my lips, and he leaned in to quickly kiss me hard on the mouth as I ground against his hand.

"You need to get me new underwear after this," I gasped.

Mace laughed and said, "Only if I get to keep these."

He increased the rhythm, stroking my clit with two fingers. My hips made little rotating motions.

"I can't wait for you to do this on my cock," he said in my ear. "Fucking you in that tight, hot little pussy. I'll bend you over and fuck you slowly until you feel every hard inch." His fingers moved faster, and I panted as he dirty-talked into my ear.

"I'd like to fuck you in front of a mirror," he whispered, voice low in my ear, "grab your hips, and do it real slow and watch you touch yourself. You'll come, but I'll still be fucking you."

I moaned, my head tipping down.

"Eyes forward," he said to my reflection in the laptop screen. The thought of us doing it in front of a mirror, locking eyes like that while he pounded into me sent me over the edge. Mace clamped a hand over my mouth to muffle the scream as I came, the pleasure rolling over me in waves.

I leaned back in the chair, my chest heaving. Mace smiled at me and licked his hand. "Sweet as candy," he said.

"Next time you do that," I said after a moment and after I had caught my breath, "I want you to suck my tits."

"Do you want me to bend you over and fuck you right here?" Mace growled.

"Oh yeah," I told him, opening my eyes slightly to peer back at him. "I definitely want you to fuck me right here."

For a moment I thought he was going to be the one throwing caution to the wind and YOLO fucking me right there in the office. And I would have loved every minute of it.

Fortunately Mace at least had some self-control because Tara chose that moment to knock on his office door.

"Mace!" she chirped. "I have some great news." Mace rushed out to greet her while I stood up more slowly. My panties were soaking wet. I tried to rearrange my skirt as best I could, but I still felt the aftereffects of his hand on me, and I was wobbly in my heels.

"Oh, Josie," Tara said. I could tell from her face she knew immediately what we had been up to. The petty part of me was glad.

"I was just telling Mace that I took the liberty of finding him a new assistant," she said.

"You did?"

"Since Josie is so busy with the marketing project," Tara said, "you still need an assistant. I have the perfect person. She's just outside."

Mace nodded.

Tara poked her head out of the office door and called, "Come on in, Anke."

What? Uh no. Nope. This can NOT be happening. Except it was.

"Meet Anke," Tara said as Anke strutted into the room in a black dress with a hemline that skirted on unprofessional and a pair of mile-high stilettos. "She comes highly recommended."

"Recommended by whom?" I shot out.

Mace and Tara looked at me.

"Don't worry," Anke cooed. She had dyed her blond hair brown and wore a pair of glasses that I remembered she had talked me into putting on my credit card.

"I've worked with several international banks, and I'm very familiar dealing with high-powered men." She smiled coyly at Mace. "I'm interested to see how the Svensson males do business."

CHAPTER 44

Mace

Josie looked between Anke and Tara. I couldn't tell what was going on. Josie wasn't jealous, was she? My hand was just up her skirt, surely she could tell where my loyalties lay. But maybe not.

"Are you sure this is necessary?" I asked Tara.

"No," Josie interjected, her face dark.

"But you're busy," Tara said sweetly. "We need Josie to be successful with this marketing campaign. There's a lot of money riding on it. She shouldn't be splitting her time between you and the marketing push."

"It's just a temporary arrangement," I told Josie.

"Or maybe not!" Tara said with a laugh. "I suspect now that you've been bitten by the marketing bug, you won't want to go back to being Mace's little ol' assistant, will you?" Tara asked, turning to Josie.

Josie pursed her lips. "I just don't know if Anke is qualified."

"She has references from the Holbrooks," Tara said to me. "I talked to one of the assistants over there. I can put her on the phone with you…"

"Please don't," I said. "I would never hear the end of it if Hunter and especially Greg found out I was talking to the Holbrooks. He'd go on for weeks about us having to owe them a favor or something. If you've verified her experience, that's good enough for me."

I turned to Josie. "This could be a good thing. Your talents are much better spent elsewhere than organizing the supply closet or fetching coffee."

Josie nodded unhappily. I didn't understand what she was angry about.

"I need to go finish working on the marketing project," she said, not meeting my eye.

"But before you do," Tara said, "could you just give Anke a quick run-through of what you've been working on? Then, yes, please go back downstairs. We don't want to keep you."

Garrett knocked on the open door. Henry was next to him. For once the young boy was silent. He looked scared.

"We need to go down to the courthouse," Garrett said. "There have been developments. Meg finagled us an audience with a judge."

Tara grabbed my arm. "I hope everything is all right!"

"It will be," I assured her. Josie had a flat expression on her face. I wondered if she was mad about our naughty session. But I had other things to obsess over.

"Hunter's down there already," Garrett said as I picked Henry up and snuggled him to my chest.

"I don't want to go back," he said in a small voice.

"Hush," I said. "That's not going to happen."

Meg and Hunter were waiting in the lobby for us when we arrived at the ornate courthouse building. Our footsteps echoed in the marble floors and bounced off the high ceilings as we made our way to the courtroom.

When we walked in, Payslee was already there, sulking on one of the long wooden benches. Her lawyer was next to her, mopping at his face with a handkerchief. She called to Henry, but he shrank against me.

The judge was a thin woman. Though she was small, she perched in her seat like a bird of prey.

"Edna is Ida's sister," Meg whispered. "So I hope none of you pissed her or Ida off recently."

"As much as I loathe the Svenssons," the judge said after calling the courtroom to order. She peered at us over her glasses. "More so do I loathe women who dump their children off willy-nilly on unsuspecting citizens. I obviously do not have the authority to unilaterally terminate Payslee's rights as a parent at this moment. However, since the child was found technically abandoned in the train station, I am making him a ward of the state. Henry Svensson?"

"Yes?" my brother answered, his eyes wide and his voice small.

"You are now a ward of the city of Harrogate and officially in foster care," Judge Edna said. "Hunter Svensson, as his brother and a licensed foster parent, you will be a kinship placement while Payslee goes through reunification process."

"But that's not fair!" Payslee shouted. "He's *my* son."

"And you have to prove to this court that you are a fit mother," Judge Edna said, turning her piercing gaze onto Payslee. I winced, and Payslee shrank. I did not want that judge on my bad side.

"You need to have an apartment," the judge continued to address Payslee, "and a job and test negative for drugs. Until that time—usually it takes about four to six weeks—you will be allowed supervised visits with Henry."

"Sorry," Meg said after we left. "I know it's not exactly what we were hoping for."

"Please," I told her. "You were so helpful."

"Especially after what Hunter did," Garrett snapped. Hunter's jaw was tense.

Meg sighed. "It will buy you some time at least."

"That's all I need," Garrett said. I was glad he sounded confident because I wasn't so sure.

CHAPTER 45

Josie

"**W**hat is Anke playing at?" I hissed to Willow. I had grumpily shown Anke to her desk (formerly *my* desk) and helped her get situated. As soon as I was able, I escaped downstairs and dragged Willow into the women's restroom.

"I can't believe she's here. Surely it's not for a good reason," Willow said. "Are you going to tell Mace?"

"I can't!" I said, wringing my hands. If ever there was a time for hysterics and handwringing, it would be now. "I'd have to tell him everything. He's so stressed about his crazy family. Between his evil stepmother and a cult in the desert, it sounds like he has more on his plate than I do. I don't want to add to his problems." I slumped against the wall, and Willow petted my hair.

"Anke won't last here that long," Willow assured me. "It's too much work to be an assistant. I bet she misses some appointments and fades off into the distance."

"Or not," I said as my phone rang, displaying Anke's name.

"Darling, I need some help with the printer, then I'll let you get back to work," she said. Her voice with that lilting Slavic accent emitted from the phone.

"Why can't you call IT?" I growled at her when I walked into the office. Mace wasn't there, which was good because Anke and I were about to have it out.

She was sitting neatly at my desk, her legs crossed.

"I just wanted to have a little girls' chat," she said.

"Yeah? Well, so do I," I said, rolling up my sleeves.

"Darling, don't. We're not fighting over men," Anke said, rolling her eyes. "Besides I know you have your claws in him."

"I do not 'have my claws in him,'" I said, making air quotes.

"Please." Anke snorted. "You convinced him to let you move into his house. You smelled like sex when I walked in."

I resisted the urge to sniff myself. What did that even mean, smell like sex?

Anke smirked. "Don't tell me you're not thinking at least a little bit that he's going to ride up on his Bugatti and save you."

"No," I said, irritable. "I am not. One, Mace doesn't like motorcycles. He says they're unsafe. Two, I would never use someone like that."

"Josie, darling, trust your friend Anke. I'm not after your Mace. I promise on the grave of my mother," Anke said, holding up a hand. "I'm here to help you. Besides, there are plenty of Svenssons in the sea. You've got yours, and I have mine."

I relaxed slightly. Mace's brothers were smart—a lot smarter than me or any of Anke's other marks. They wouldn't let themselves get swept up in her lies. Hunter, Garrett, or even Archer would chew her up and spit her out. And I couldn't wait to see it happen.

"You just go right ahead," I said sweetly. "I wish you the best of luck." Maybe going after one of Mace's brothers would keep her distracted. I was going to give Anke just enough candy floss to hang herself.

My mood buoyed, I hurried back downstairs. Anke or no, I had a marketing project to finish. I felt even better when a text came in from Mace.

Mace: *Great news. Payslee isn't taking Henry. He's technically our foster kid now*
Josie: *We should celebrate*
Mace: *With lollipops*
Josie: *Blow pops*

I felt giddy and a little horny thinking about our celebration that evening. I tried to focus on meeting my daily goals. The website design was looking great, but we needed to work on the wording. We'd also had a draft returned from the videographer. I made detailed notes and sent if off. It was after dinner when I was finally done.

The lights were low in the house when I walked in. I assumed the kids had all gone to bed.

I didn't see Mace. I really wanted to surprise him. I walked into the guest bathroom and turned on the water. The place was stocked with all sorts of delicious-smelling oils. There was a mirror tray displaying several crystal jars of perfumes and creams. I knew from my snooping that it also had an impressive array of bath bombs.

I threw one in the tub and watched as the whorls of pink and blush spiraled in the steaming water.

I slipped in after setting my phone up on a towel. If Mace thought the lollipop picture was intense, this was going to make a banana split in his pants. I leaned forward in the water, my ass up in the air to better display the wet flesh between my legs. I was already hot and wet for him. Just thinking about him fucking me from the angle I posed at made my nipples hard despite the heat of the water.

I captioned the photo with, *I'm ready for my main course*, and sent it off. I lay back in the water, and not even a minute later, the door opened, and Mace stood there, shirt half undone.

"Did you run all the way over here?" I purred.

"I didn't know you were back," he said, slowly removing the rest of his clothes.

"Really?" I asked, rolling over to strike the same pose, hoping he would get the hint and stick his cock in my candy jar. "Is there someone else who sends you pictures like that?" I cooed.

"Hardly." His voice was low, and it echoed around the marble-clad bathroom. Almost as if he couldn't help himself, Mace crossed to me in two strides, grabbed my hips, and pressed his mouth against the flesh as dark pink as the water.

"You taste like cotton candy," he said against me. I moaned, wiggling slightly against him.

"I wish you had just fucked me in your office," I breathed.

"I will next time," he said as he licked me.

"I wanted you to fuck me," I moaned.

"And I wanted to stick my face in your pussy. Seems like neither of us got what we wanted today, and now that I have you all to myself, I'm going to enjoy making up for it."

Mace licked and nipped me, his tongue stroking from my clit to my opening. He sucked on my clit as he put two fingers inside me.

"You're so tight," he said, his fingers slowly stroking inside me.

"I'm ready for you," I whimpered. "Please fuck me."

"I told you," he said, his breath hot against me, "I wanted to lick your pussy today. There's a method."

I moaned as he grasped my hips, his tongue licking me into a frenzy. His mouth drew out the pleasure when I came, my legs trembling. He set me back down in the tub and removed the rest of his clothes while he watched me. My nipples rose slightly in and out of the pink water with every breath.

"I hope you're not already done," he said, an eyebrow half raised. His boxer briefs fell to the floor, and he stood before me, his abs glistening from the water that had splashed up from the bath. I felt a twinge between my legs.

"See anything you like?" he asked.

"I like every single piece of candy you're selling. It's like a French bakery display; I could just eat you up."

Mace pressed his mouth against mine before I could keep comparing him to various sweets. His mouth came down to suck on my nipples. He took one then the other in his mouth as one hand grasped my hip. The other slid down my wet skin, and I moaned as he stroked me.

"You're not going to join me?" I gasped, my head lolling to the side, my back arched.

"Yes," he said, "but first things first."

He pulled me out of the tub and leaned me over it, my feet planted on the floor, pink water dripping on the white bath mat.

"I can't believe," he said, kissing my neck as his cock pressed against me, "that I was jealous of a piece of candy." He opened a condom packet.

"You should be jealous of the blow pop in that picture," I said as his cock twitched against me. "Because when I was done taking the picture of it so close to my pussy, I put that blow pop in my mouth and sucked and sucked, letting my tongue roll all over that thick, hard piece of candy."

I squeaked the last word out as he entered me.

"I'm going to show you there are better things in life than candy," he growled in my ear.

I moaned as he fucked me. Any thoughts of a good comeback literally fucked off. I held onto the edge of the large marble tub, crying out every time Mace thrust into me.

"Your cock feels so good," I moaned.

"Better than a blow pop?" he asked, nipping my shoulder.

"So much better," I whimpered, pushing back against him. His large hands gripped my hips, and he pounded into me.

"Fuck me harder, Mace!" I begged, my cries echoing around the marble-clad room.

One of his hands came around to tease my clit. I bucked against his hand then back against his cock. I spread my legs wider for him, needing him to fill me. His fingers rubbed my clit in time to his thrusts.

My stomach tightened, and I came with a scream. Mace came a few moments later. He kissed me hard and rolled us both into the tub.

I straddled him, licking the pink droplets off his face.

"I can't believe you managed to even take those pictures at those angles," Mace said, pulling me down for a kiss. The bathtub water was still warm, and I relaxed against him.

"I am a marketing genius," I said, drawing a pink heart on his chest. "It's my specialty."

He kissed me again, and I felt his cock hard against me.

"I'm surprised your chocolate's not too melty," I said.

"The only thing you melt is my heart, Josie," Mace said with a crooked smile.

In that moment I realized that I loved being with him. Mace melted my chocolate heart. That was why I needed to do something about Anke. I knew she could ruin everything.

CHAPTER 46

Mace

It was jarring to walk into my office and see Anke sitting at what I thought of as Josie's desk.

"Are you finding everything okay?" I asked her.

"Perfectly charming!" she said in that slight lilting Slavic accent. "I've confirmed the hotel reservation for the conference and made dinner reservations with people Tara mentioned you may want to catch up with over a drink."

"Thanks," I told her and shut the door. As I sat down at my desk, Adrian came in.

"What?" I barked at my brother.

"Josie said she left some notes up here," he stammered and peered into the adjacent office. Anke looked at us and waggled her fingers at Adrian.

"Well go get them," I said tersely. I watched him slide the door open and scuttle inside.

"What can I help you with, darling?" Anke asked sweetly. Adrian blushed up to his forehead. He grabbed a stack of papers and fled.

But then he came up again right before lunch and again that afternoon under the guise of Josie forgetting something.

"Why don't you just take all of her stuff down with you?" I snapped at Adrian. "You're interrupting my meeting."

"It's just Liam," he said.

"Ah, yes, just Liam," my brother said dramatically. "I'm only the person who's investing almost a billion dollars into Harrogate."

"Sorry," Adrian said and scurried out.

"Teenagers," Liam scoffed. Then he smirked at me. "Adrian's got the hots for your newest assistant."

"I think Anke might be a lot for Adrian to handle," I said with a laugh. "Hopefully she goes easy on him."

"She'll chew him up and spit him out, I bet!" Liam said cheerfully. "Speaking of people sleeping with their assistants," Liam said casually.

I glared at him. "Vicious rumors."

"Dude, Remy said she's moved into the house."

"She's not dangerous."

"Hey, no judgement! *Tu casa, si casa!*"

"That's not even right," I said, crossing my arms. "Did you just make that up?"

"I'm behind on my Dora the Explorer," Liam said, leaning back in his chair and propping his feet up on my desk. I pushed them off.

"Greg wants us to nail down the factory," Liam said. "You know he didn't like the idea of the factory out here to begin with. He's thinking of nixing the whole thing, pulling the investment money."

I rubbed the bridge of my nose. "We'll figure something out."

"You better do it soon," Liam warned. "You know how Greg gets." He stood up and grabbed his bag. "I'm off to look at some other property in the next county over."

"That's not going to work," I said. "It's too far away."

"Keep an open mind," Liam said, shrugging on his coat. "It led you to great things with Josie."

Unable to help it, I smiled.

"You like her!" Liam said. "You better not screw this up. I want her to do some marketing work for Platinum Provisions. Jack thinks if he gets her and Chloe together in a room to come up with some product ideas, they'll basically start spinning gold."

I didn't like the idea of my brother having designs on Josie's time. I barely saw her as it was. She worked late every night on the marketing campaign.

I missed having her at home, and it wasn't just for her cooking, though the kids certainly missed it. After dinner, I went back to the office to meet up with Josie. She was waiting for me in the lobby.

"Are you too tired for a date night?" I asked after I kissed her.

"You mean a late-night date night?" she asked. "I've had a lot of coffee and chocolate, so I'm down. Where are we going?"

"Somewhere cool." I'd been plotting all afternoon. I drove her across town to the Mast Brothers' Chocolate factory. Using the code Archer had given me, I unlocked the padlock at the gate.

"Do you own this too?" Josie asked.

"Unfortunately not," I said. "It would be much easier if we did. Then Archer could just have it. He's going to have to convince the owner to sell."

"I hope he's not tearing down these cool old buildings," Josie said as we drove through the silent complex. "Did it belong to the Harrogates?"

"Two of Harrogate's sons had this chocolate factory. Mast Brothers' Chocolate doesn't exist anymore, but the building complex still remains," I said as I parked the car and grabbed the picnic basket out of the back. It was a smaller one than the big trunks we had taken to the train park.

"You packed snacks!" Josie said, wrapping her arms around me and kissing me.

"You're working really hard. You deserve a reward," I replied, pressing her close to me.

"If Archer turns this into a conference center, he has to make candy here in a little workshop or something," she said as we walked through the abandoned building.

"That's what they had," I explained, continuing my tour. "We moved here during their last year of operation before they folded. At one point they did have some exhibits." There was a dusty glass wall through which we could see some old candy-making machinery.

"I wonder if there's any candy left?" she mused.

"Please don't eat it," I begged.

Josie laughed, the peals echoing around the large space.

"This," I said, pointing to an animatronic weasel in a top coat, "is Mast the Meerkat."

Josie was silent for a good moment then said, "That's not terrifying."

CHAPTER 47

Josie

"This is a huge factory!" I exclaimed, twirling around in the abandoned lobby like I was in *Beauty and the Beast*.

"This is only one of the buildings," Mace said.

"And Archer is really turning this into a conference center?"

He nodded. "I think he wants to attract those huge international conferences—as big as the medical conference we're going to in a few weeks. Those attract tens of thousands, sometimes hundreds of thousands of people."

"And the town is going to be okay with that?" I asked. Judging from how the townspeople had reacted to PharmaTech's expansion, I wondered if they would accept this conference center.

"This is a little different because Archer would be restoring historic old buildings," Mace explained as he led me through the abandoned factory. "Those types of adaptive reuse projects are always more popular and well received. The bigger issue will be convincing the owner to sell. I think a lot of people have this idea that the factory is going to come back. They need to move on. The convention center would provide a lot of good jobs for people in this area."

He led me up the stairs to a roof deck and took out a blanket from the hamper, laying it out. We sat out there holding hands and silently admiring the view. I could see across the town to the Svensson PharmaTech buildings glowing on the hill. The tree-lined brick streets were strung out in a grid pattern, cut here and there by the vestiges of long-removed rail spurs. The train whistle sounded, and I snuggled next to Mace as we watched the train slowly crawl down Main Street.

"It seems like it's going a lot slower than it was when it almost hit me that time," I complained.

"No one else has ever had a problem with the train," he said. I could hear the smile in his voice.

"You don't even have any gates up for train protection," I said as I reached for the picnic basket.

"I have to confess that I didn't make any of that myself," he admitted when I opened the basket. "All of tonight's refreshments are curtesy of Grey Dove Bistro."

"Did you have it brought in?" I asked, mind-boggled that he could just have something delivered from a few hours away just because.

Mace shook his head. "My brother brought it. Chloe sends Liam back with food whenever he comes to Harrogate. We're lucky he didn't eat all of it."

I took out a cookie and inspected it in the faint light from the town.

"It looks like you!" I exclaimed, holding up the frosted cookie. Chloe had decorated it with a cartoon man's face. It had blond hair and was wearing a suit and tie. I took a bite. "Tastes as good as you too!" I joked.

"There's hot chocolate too," he said after he stopped laughing.

"You're speaking my love language," I told him around the cookie.

The hot chocolate was thick, and there wasn't so much sugar that it overwhelmed the rich bitterness. It also had a hint of cognac.

"So good," I said after I took a long sip. I held the thermos up to Mace's lips. "Try it! It's not that sweet. Besides, I think chocolate is supposed to be an aphrodisiac."

"I thought it had antioxidants," he retorted and took a sip.

I kissed him just to taste the chocolate mingled in his mouth. He pulled me back down onto the blanket.

"You know," I whispered, "it's too bad you didn't bring some chocolate sauce. I could think of a few things I'd want to dip in it."

Mace lay back on the blanket, hands behind his head, contemplating me. I reached for him and slowly undid his belt and unzipped his pants.

"You ever had a blow job on a roof?" I asked, making a kissy face at him.

"Can't say that I have," he said as I ran my thumb over the head of his cock.

"You only live once!" I said, winking at him, feeling smug when he hissed softly. "I want to lick you like a lollipop!" I sang, running my hand along the length of his rock-hard cock. Before I could go down on him, Mace reached and pulled me up to him. He kissed me, and I could taste the dark undercurrent in his mouth. His hand moved under my skirt.

"I want you," he whispered, his eyes bright in the dark. His fingers pushed at my panties. I closed my eyes, letting the pleasure wash over me.

"I want you just like that," he whispered as he put on a condom then pushed into me.

Our lovemaking was sensual and slow. The air was slightly chilled though it was close to summer, but Mace was warm, and his cock was hot in me. I bit my lip, stifling a moan as his large hands guided me up and down. I rolled my hips, letting his cock hit my clit. One of his hands moved to stroke my clit in time with our rhythm.

I leaned forward to press our mouths together as I came. Mace thrust into me a few times more, drawing out the orgasm. His abs tightened as he came.

"You're the best piece of candy here," Mace whispered in my ear. I could feel the grin on his mouth.

"I should cover myself in chocolate," I murmured, "and make you lick me all up."

"You don't have to cover yourself in chocolate for me to lick you," he joked.

CHAPTER 48

Mace

I spent the night after our rooftop date curled around Josie in my bedroom. She left even earlier than me to go to work. When I walked into my office, I half expected her to be there. But Anke was there instead. And so was Adrian.

"Anke has all these international contacts!" my younger brother said to me in excitement. "You said you wanted to branch out more into the Asian markets, right?"

"Yes," I said slowly, putting down my bag.

"I can put you all into contact, just to put feelers out," Anke offered. "I did something similar for the Holbrooks."

"Yes, that would be very helpful, Anke," I replied. Maybe she wasn't such a terrible assistant after all.

"Isn't she great?" Adrian gushed.

"Adrian, help Anke with anything she needs on that effort," I told him. He saluted me. "Sure thing, boss."

Adrian's crush was sort of cute. He was barely out of high school, and I knew he wouldn't act on it. It was more puppy love than anything else.

The conference was in less than a week, and Josie was scheduled to present the team's progress to me and my brothers along with Owen Frost.

"How's it looking?" he asked after shaking my hand when we met in the lobby.

"A lot better," I told him.

Tara and Anke were already in the room when I walked in. The first slide was up on the screen with the same thin blue circle logo. I admired how sharp it looked against the black background.

"I just want to say right off the bat," Owen began. "I've been to a lot of these types of conferences. This is by far the best thing I've seen. I love this logo."

Josie smiled.

"Yes, it's quite beautiful," Anke said. The expression on Josie's face seemed to grow dark, but then the smile was back. I must have imagined it.

"As you can see," Josie said, flipping through the presentation, "we have everything about ninety-five percent done. Mace will be speaking against these slides, so I'll run through what I've written for the presentation. Mace will need to memorize the final version after comments."

"I'm really impressed with what you all managed to accomplish in a short period of time," I said after she ran through the presentation.

"I've made a few more notes," Owen added, "but yes, I think this is quite good."

"There's a lot more!" Josie said. She closed the PowerPoint and brought up a website. It had the same black color with pops of blue.

It looked masculine and credible but still fresh. My brothers nodded appreciatively as Josie walked us through the website. Adrian elbowed Parker when his picture came up.

"You boys photograph so well!" Anke said with a laugh. Adrian laughed louder than anyone else.

"Shut up!" Parker hissed at him. Owen smirked. Josie didn't seem all that amused.

"Back to the topic at hand," she said, face serious. "As you can see, the website gives an animated walk-through of the gene therapy procedure. We have easy-to-digest information on how the various gene therapies work. We also have interviews with people who have used it. We also had a video produced."

She hit the play button. There were sweeping drone shots of the facility and images of Harrogate, the hydroelectric plant, and workers in the lab. The stunning visuals were punctuated by soft but upbeat music. Josie explained the story behind it as the video played.

"Svensson PharmaTech is all about innovation in health. We take a macro view of how our company integrated into and revitalized the town of Harrogate."

The screen showed videos and images of a run-down city that then transformed into the city as it was today. And when I said transformed, I didn't mean it just faded into another picture.

"How did you do that?" Garrett demanded. Josie grinned.

"It's such a cool effect, isn't it?" she asked, rewinding the video. We watched as an aerial flyover video of run-down Harrogate seemed to grow and brighten as new buildings popped up and trees sprouted.

"A guy I know does CGI for Hollywood movies. He rendered this graphic on the computer." She turned back to the video. "So you can see our innovation in Harrogate and in the fact that we developed this hydroelectric plant to power our buildings and the servers processing the genetic data. This technology is specifically tailored to each individual patient…"

There was a shot of Henry sitting in a medical chair, getting blood drawn.

"Did they have to bribe him to get him to sit still for that long?" I muttered to Owen. He snorted.

"We use a modified blockchain technology to parse the genetic data…" There was a shot of Owen in a tailored suit walking through one of his data centers. Then a shot of Parker at a computer talking to a random actress with Henry on her lap.

"I had a musician I know compose and record the background music," Josie said, "so that we aren't using the same stock music that everyone else has."

"Impressive concentration to detail, isn't it?" Owen whispered to me.

"One other question," I said. "It was great having you explain everything. Are you going to have someone narrate this video?"

She grinned at me. "Of course. You are. We have a recording studio set up."

"Mace is too boring to be a narrator," Garrett scoffed.

"He has a great voice," Josie countered. "Someone just has to be in the recording studio to help hype him up!"

I spent the afternoon going over the script. The writing flowed very well. I was excited to show her that evening, but Josie seemed stressed when she walked into my office late that night.

Anke had already left, and I'd stayed to work. I was behind on things between Payslee, my family, and my new whatever-it-was with Josie.

"What's wrong?" I asked her, wrapping her in my arms and rubbing her shoulders.

"Nothing." She sighed. "I just want the presentation to go well."

I leaned down to kiss her. "You've been working so hard," I whispered. "Let me give you a reward."

CHAPTER 49

Josie

Mace kissed me, and it wasn't soft and sensual. It was hard and promised a rough, quick release. I didn't know I wanted that until this moment.

"Fuck me," I gasped against his mouth. "I want you to fuck me hard."

He kissed me again, and I nipped his lower lip. Mace disentangled himself while I protested and went to the light switch.

"Unless you want to put on a show for the whole town," he said, "this is probably a better idea."

His gray eyes almost seemed to glow in the low ambient light from the parking lot. I saw the shadow of him unzip his pants and pull out a condom. He grabbed me, and I tangled my fingers in his hair.

"Please," I mewled.

Make me forget.

He turned me around, and I bent over the desk, my chest heaving against the tight blouse. My pussy was wet and aching for him. Mace pushed up my skirt and pulled my panties down. I heard the condom packet rip.

"Mace, I want your cock," I begged, "I want it rough. Just fuck me." Three fingers stroked me, then he was in me.

"Faster," I whimpered as I bent over the desk, legs spread as far as they could go while still hampered by my skirt. One large hand braced against the desk, the other held my thigh as he fucked me.

"You feel so good," I moaned. My nipples were hard. One of Mace's hands reached around to rub my clit, and I thrust against his hand and back against his cock.

"You feel so good," he said. "Josie, *fuck*, you're so tight."

It was over fast. He clapped a hand over my mouth, muffling my scream as I came.

"I was going to listen to your presentation," I said against his mouth as he kissed me, my legs still trembling, "but it's probably not going to be until tomorrow."

"Then let's go home," he said. Home with Mace. It felt cozy. I wrapped my arms tighter around him. I didn't want to let him go.

"I'm too tired to drive," I murmured.

"My chariot awaits," he said, grinning in the dark.

I rolled my eyes. "I need my car tomorrow."

"We have other cars at the house," he said. "I had the foresight to order a few more, just in case you lit any more cars on fire."

I swatted him. "That was an act of divine intervention," I told him. "Totally not my fault."

"Oh, absolutely," he said, helping me into my coat. "I don't know how gasoline got poured all over that car."

"Wasn't me," I said, taking his arm.

"I'm surprised you managed to get up this early," Mace commented the next morning as he drove me to the office.

"I'll have you know I can be a morning person when it's called for," I said, fiddling with the radio. "There's a lot of things you don't know about me."

"I think I know all of you," he replied smugly.

"Stop, unless you want to have parking lot sex and then do the walk of shame into the office," I warned as we drove up the road to the PharmaTech offices.

"I mean, it is early," he said, "and hardly anyone is here."

I shivered and picked at a lasagna stain on my shirt. I didn't have that many clothes. Maybe Marnie would let me borrow something of hers for the conference.

"So," Mace said as he parked the car. "Parking lot sex?"

"I'll have you know I've stooped quite low in my life," I retorted, grabbing my bag and opening the car door. "I'm not sure if I'm ready to stoop quite this low."

"What about bending over?" he said with a grin as he stepped out of the car.

"Depends on what's behind me," I replied as I came up next to him.

"I don't think you've had any complaints," Mace murmured. I slid my hand down his chest and hooked two fingers under his waistband. I felt the muscles twitch.

"I'll come oversee your narration this afternoon," I told him, giving him a kiss goodbye.

I didn't walk into the office with Mace. Instead I met Willow at my car.

"Ready to go proof the conference swag?" I asked Willow, who was waiting impatiently at the car.

"I don't know if we need to talk about Mace or Anke on the ride over," my friend said as she buckled her seat belt.

"I cannot believe she weaseled her way in. I keep hoping it's a bad dream," I said as we drove out of town to the manufacturer.

"Is she after Mace?" Willow asked, digging in my purse for some candy.

"Who knows? She claimed she wasn't, but she's just a lying liar," I grumbled.

"You sound serious about him," Willow remarked.

"I mean, I don't know. I think he's just having fun. I don't know if I can really make a big commitment. Isn't that what those billionaires are like? Maybe I'm just an easy lay—not that I'm complaining. This is probably the most exercise I've had in a while," I admitted.

"But do you like him?" Willow pressed.

I was silent for a moment. "I do really like him," I said carefully. "I just wonder, once he really knows me, maybe he won't like me very much."

The swag manufacturer was happy to see us when we arrived.

"These look great!" I complimented him as Willow and I inspected the proofs of the pens, T-shirts, bags, notebooks, and keychains I'd designed.

"Are you going to be able to have sixty thousand of each of these items done in time?" Willow asked.

"We have guys assigned to third shift to get all of this out for you," the owner assured us. "And we'll have it delivered to the conference center in New York City."

"We really appreciate your hard work," I told him.

"Absolutely! We'd like to have more of the Svenssons' business," the owner said. "I was talking to my pap, Marty. He said it was starting to feel like the old days a little. He worked at one of the Harrogate manufacturing plants making train parts. It's nice to have local customers. You know, we need a conference center here in Harrogate."

"I believe they're working on it," I replied.

CHAPTER 50

Mace

"When I get my conference center," Archer said, flopping on the couch in my office, "you guys won't have to go to New York City. PharmaTech could sponsor. We'd throw great parties, and I'll have a ton of hotels to house everyone. It would be sweet."

"As long as Hunter doesn't fuck it up with Meghan again," I grumbled.

"Still haven't found a spot for the factory?" Archer asked.

"Of course not."

"Josie's back and ready for you to record," Adrian said, coming into the office. Anke walked by and made a kissy face at him. Archer and I laughed as Adrian blushed.

"Make me proud!" Archer called as I grabbed my notes and went downstairs to the soundproofed recording studio.

Josie made me stand up, and she mouthed along with my words as I spoke, silently coaxing me to emote.

"Is it usable?" I asked as she played the recording.

"You didn't have that many ums," she said as we listened. "The sound engineer will edit it and put it in the video."

"Are we good otherwise?"

"I think so. The conference is in a few days. I had hotel rooms for us booked a day early so we could set up and familiarize with the venue."

I cupped her face. "Thank you so much for your work and expertise. We seriously could not have pulled this off without you."

She laughed. "The last thing I need to do is triage my outfits and do some laundry. Working eighteen-hour days has not been kind to my shirts. This is lasagna," she said, pointing to a stain. "And this is chocolate. And this is you. You got your candy floss all over my shirt."

"You can't walk around the conference with that all over your shirt," I said. She kissed me spontaneously, and I could feel her hard nipples through the fabric.

"You know, this place is soundproofed," I whispered, locking the door. I unbuttoned her shirt, sucking at her nipples through her bra.

"I think we should get you some new clothes," I told her, sliding my hand under her skirt to stroke her through the already wet panties, making her moan. "At the very least some new panties."

I hitched her skirt up, still stroking her as I rolled on a condom. I didn't bother taking down her panties, just moved them to the side and pushed into her. Her little whimpering moans in my ear were driving me wild, and she was shuddering and coming in my arms after a few minutes.

"Better than parking lot sex?" I asked her, making her laugh.

After checking to make sure the coast was clear, I followed Josie out of the recording studio.

"Honestly though," I told her, "you can get some new clothes."

"I don't know," she said uncertainly as we headed back to my office. But Anke was in there when we walked in. Suddenly I had no desire to sit in my office.

"You know what," I said to Josie, steering her away. "Let's go shopping."

"Right now? But your schedule!" she exclaimed.

"It's fine," I said. "The marketing stuff is all pretty much done, right? You can spare an hour for shopping."

"I don't have all day to spend shopping," she protested as I took her hand and pulled her to the car. "You know I have to dig through the sales racks and hope I find something in my size, then I have to check and see if it works with my coupons. Oh! I didn't clip any coupons!"

"The places we're going don't take coupons," I said.

She stopped. "I don't shop without coupons."

"You can't use coupons at a lot of the shops in Harrogate," I told her, exasperated. Why wouldn't she let me do anything nice for her? "They're pretty high-end, or so I'm told. I don't pay my employees peanuts, and they're the ones who shop there."

Josie was sitting stock-still in the car seat as we drove down Main Street and I parked the car. There was only light foot traffic, which was fine by me.

"They have suits and blouses and such here," I told Josie as I practically had to drag her into one boutique. I could tell this was a high-end boutique because, while it was clear the sales associate recognized me, she didn't immediately start fawning or make a curious face at Josie.

"She needs something to wear for a conference," I explained to the sales associate. Josie didn't say a word. I wondered what was up with her. I was just trying to do something nice.

"You don't have to buy new stuff," I told her. "But you were the one complaining about the state of your clothes."

"Right," she said and seemed to shake off whatever had been bothering her. The sales associate took Josie to a mirror and started measuring her.

"You have a cute curvy figure," she said. "This light-gray herringbone pattern will look nice against your skin tone."

"Here," Josie said, handing me her bag and jacket. "Hold these. You're just standing there, lurking."

"I'm not lurking."

"You are. If you weren't so attractive, it would be creepy," she teased.

"I mean I don't really have anything to add to this shopping expedition. I'm an engineer, not a designer."

"You manage to look nice," she said as the associate handed her blouses, soft sweaters, and skirts and blazers.

"Archer picks out my suits," I admitted.

"Your twin has excellent taste," she said, going into a dressing room.

Josie modeled every suit for me.

"I think this is conservative yet sexy," she said, posing in front of the mirror. "Perfect for a medical conference."

"You look great," I said, admiring the way the fabric hugged her curves.

"I can't believe how comfy it is," Josie gushed. "I always hated wearing business clothes because they were so scratchy, but this is so soft. Feel it!" she ordered, holding a sleeve out to my face.

"We'll have the alterations done in the next couple of days," the associate said after Josie had changed back into her old clothes. "I'll send it to your office, Mr. Svensson."

"My house is fine," I replied. I almost said our house. I wanted it to be our house.

The sales associate turned the iPad that doubled as a register around for me to swipe my card and sign.

Josie started to swear when she saw the total then turned it into a cough. "That is too much."

"You deserve it. You probably single-handedly saved my product launch," I told her as I swiped my credit card. "Besides, there's a lot of business that goes on at these conferences. You seriously cannot turn up looking like someone just scraped you out of a gutter."

"Do I look that bad?" she asked as we left the boutique.

"I mean, I don't have any complaints," I assured her.

"I know you don't," she said, bumping into me as she turned left and I turned right.

"Shoe store is that way," I told her, grabbing her shoulder and turning her.

"My shoes are fine!" she argued.

I looked down at her feet. There was a hole in the heel of one of her shoes.

"It was my stupid tiny house," she explained. "It has it out for me. I was going down the ladder, and my foot caught."

"You're lucky you didn't break your neck," I said. "Besides, why do you even need to be in there?"

"It's the only quiet place I can work without being interrupted. It's the tiny house or the bathroom, but in the bathroom all I think about was that time in the tub…"

"Thanks, now that's all I can think about," I said as I opened the door for the shoe boutique.

"Um, no, we need to go to a low-end discount shoe place," she said, balking in the doorway as soon as she saw the Louboutin sign in the window. "You saw how hard I am on shoes."

I gently shoved her inside.

"I can't believe Harrogate can even support a place like this," she whispered as we walked into the luxuriously decorated space. "It's so pretty." Josie patted one of the shoes on display.

"Whoa!" Josie said, turning to another display.

Whoa was my reaction. They were a pair of open-toe stiletto sandals that somehow turned into fishnet tights.

"That's… erotic," Josie said as we both studied the shoes. I wanted nothing more than to see her in them.

Focus. We're here for business professional wear.

"Is it crazy that I want those?" Josie whispered to me.

"Not crazy at all," I whispered back. "They would probably go very nicely with a shelf bra."

She turned her head into my chest to smother a laugh. "They totally would."

"Would you like to try these on?" the sales associate asked, coming up to us.

Yes, I thought.

"No!" Josie said, snickering. "I just need a basic black stiletto." She looked at me for confirmation.

"Get whatever you want," I told her.

"And a nude heel," she added.

Whoever had designed those shoes knew what they were doing, I decided as Josie walked back and forth in front of me, trying out the stilettoes. She looked elegant and sophisticated in them.

"I sort of want to wear these right now," Josie said as the sales associate carried the boxes to the counter. "But I don't think they go with lasagna stains." I handed the associate my card, and I knew Josie was itching to see the total.

"Don't worry about it," I told her, taking the bags and leading her out of the shop.

I'm coming back for you, I thought when I passed the fishnet stilettoes.

When we were outside, Josie looked down at her shirt then looked up at me.

"Want to go bra shopping?" she asked. "This is my only one left. My tiny house destroyed one, and Henry used another one as a slingshot."

I shook my head. "Henry needs to learn some personal boundaries. No one touches your bras but me."

"Well then, you and the tiny house are going to have to duke it out," she retorted.

"We should see if they have shelf bras," I said as we walked down the sidewalk.

She snickered. "For science?"

"For science."

"Somehow I don't think that's going to be sold in Harrogate," Josie said.

"Yeah that may be a bit much for the townspeople here," I said, wrapping an arm around her shoulder and tucking her next to me.

"I don't know. Ida might go for it," she said, laughing.

"That is an image I did not need in my brain," I told her, opening the door to the lingerie shop for her.

"It's probably a good thing," she teased. "You seemed like you were getting a little too excited!"

Josie did not model the lingerie for me. I was left holding the bag of shoes while she and the sales associate disappeared into the back room.

"You have to have a little mystery," the associate said.

I looked around the store while she was gone. They did not have shelf bras.

CHAPTER 51

Josie

While I did love to shop, going to the boutiques with Mace brought back memories of Anke. I had spent money I didn't have when I was with her. The high totals at the cash register brought back the sick feeling of realizing I was stuck with a bill of tens of thousands of dollars. What if something happened and Mace wanted me to pay him back for all of these new clothes? But I tried to keep a happy face on through the shopping. Mace was a good guy. He was trying to do something nice for me.

I tried to concentrate on finishing up the last touches on the marketing rollout. The swag was already at the conference center. The website would be live tomorrow, and the video had Mace's voice dubbed over. For once something in my life was going right. I had this strange feeling like everything was going to be okay.

Until I went up to Mace's office and Anke was sitting at my desk. I felt my eye start twitching, and I held a finger over it. Mace looked up at me when I walked in.

"Just seeing if you had any final comment on the video," I said. "Otherwise it's going up on the website."

He stood up and came over to me. "It looks great." He reached for me, and I looked over and caught Anke's eye through the glass. She winked at me.

What was her angle? She always had an angle. It didn't seem like she was going after Mace. And I hadn't seen her after Garrett, Hunter, or Archer.

"You're not upset about the clothes, are you?" Mace asked. He looked concerned. I wanted to kiss him to reassure him, but Anke was right there. Somehow after all she had taken from me, I didn't want to share this with her.

"It's fine," I said with a sigh.

"It's a gift," Mace said. "You've done a lot. You deserve it."

"I hope it goes okay," I said, crossing my arms over my chest.

"Owen's been showing it around," Mace said. "People seem impressed. I think it's going to go very well."

I was glad he was confident. Though, after all Mace had done for me, I felt like I hadn't done enough for him. I wanted to make sure his life was going as smoothly as possible. And I knew what I still needed to do.

Ida waved to me when I walked into the general store. "Any news?" I asked, grabbing a bag of candy and setting it on the counter.

"I did talk to my sister," Ida said. "She of course does not want to sell."

"If you could just get everyone in a room together," I begged. "I could pitch the big idea to them."

"Maybe canasta night?" Ida mused. "Art likes to bring his latest cider creation. Everyone will be a little tipsy. I'll try to convince my sister to come. The old bird's been grouchy lately."

"Thanks," I said. "I know you don't like the Svenssons."

"I love the Svenssons!" Ida said, clapping a hand on her chest. "They're the best kind of eye candy. It's just a woman has needs, you know?"

It was late when I arrived back at the estate house. I wanted to finish sending an email and opted to go to the tiny house instead of the main house.

I stripped off my top as soon as I walked in. Though I was still a little twitchy about the clothes, I had to admit having high-quality, comfortable business clothes was something I was looking forward to, especially now that I was going to have to spend the next three days at a conference. Speaking of which, I texted Marnie to make sure she had time to hang out.

> **Josie:** *Are you coming to the conference?*
> **Marnie:** *Part of it. I can't wait to see you!*
> **Marnie:** *Greg's been talking up your marketing presentation. He wants you to come do marketing for him on some real estate development. He doesn't want a repeat of Frost Tower*
> **Josie:** *I thought that turned out great though?*

Marnie: *Eventually, but it could have gone south and he doesn't want that to happen again*

Josie: *I guess after this marketing thing is done, I'll need something to do since Anke is now Mace's assistant*

Marnie: *I cannot believe the nerve of her. Is she trying to make a move on him?*

Josie: *She claims she isn't. I think she's after one of Mace's other brothers*

Marnie: *Good luck! Haha! I wish she would try her crazy tactics on Greg. I could use some amusement*

I jumped when I heard a knock on the door. Mace was standing outside of the tiny house. He was so tall and the tiny house so small, that even though he was on the ground, his head was about at the height of the door.

"Can I come in?" he asked.

"Or what? You'll huff and puff and blow my house down?"

"I don't think I'd even have to try that hard," he said, ducking to come into the tiny house. It wobbled when he stepped inside. "This house looks practically unstable. I'm shocked it hasn't collapsed yet."

"I guess I'll just have to huff and puff and blow you instead," I said. Mace looked as predatory as the big bad wolf. He came in and pushed me against the wall. His hands were everywhere, pulling at my clothes, tangling in my hair, hot on my bare skin. He pushed up my skirt and ripped my panties off.

"You can't keep destroying my stuff," I gasped as the zipper on my skirt ripped.

"I just bought you new stuff," he said then kissed and sucked at a freed breast. I grabbed for leverage on the railing to hold the ladder in place while Mace, still kissing me, undid his pants. The railing pulled out of the wall, bringing a tuft of insulation and splinters of wood with it. Mace ignored it. He rolled on a condom, then he pushed me back against the wall. I held onto him as he slid his cock into me.

The tiny house rocked as Mace found a rhythm. The lights shook, and the house creaked ominously. I cried out as he hitched me up higher, angling me so his cock rubbed my clit every time he thrust into me.

I kissed him to silence the screams. The house was not *that* soundproof. Mace responded by fucking me harder. I distinctly heard some of the wood paneling give as I came over the edge, Mace finishing close behind.

"We might have to move this into the main house," Mace said, kissing my temple and plucking bits of insulation out of my hair. "I'm not sure your tiny house can take much more."

CHAPTER 52

Mace

"I'm surprised that tiny house hasn't collapsed yet, what with all the abuse it's had to take," Archer said to me the next morning. We were at the Department of Child Welfare for Harrogate. Henry was having a supervised visit with Payslee. I knew Archer was trying to keep me from completely losing my mind.

"I wish the judge had just thrown her in jail," I muttered.

"Considering how much she apparently doesn't like Svenssons," Archer said, "we probably had the best possible outcome."

"I don't want to leave," Henry whined. He had been ill behaved the whole morning.

Payslee was in a glass-enclosed room. There was a table with a sad little basket of toys on it.

"Well hello, Henry," she said when I walked in carrying him. Henry ignored her, tensing in my arms. "I haven't seen you in years," Henry's mother said. "Didn't you miss your mama?" I set Henry on the floor. Archer was pacing outside the glass-enclosed room.

"Come here, Henry." Payslee's voice had that angry edge that all of my father's wives ended up developing, the outcome of too many ill-behaved boys, too little money, and not enough time, energy, or resources to go around. "Henry, your mama is talking to you," she yelled. "Why don't you come and tell me how your day was?"

I clenched my fist. Henry shrank from Payslee.

"Don't you ignore me, boy!" Payslee raised up her hand like she was about to hit him.

"That's it!" the social worker said, throwing open the door. "This is a supervised visit. You do understand that, Payslee, correct? This is all being videotaped."

The tension in the room sent Henry over the edge, and he started screaming like someone had set his favorite toy on fire.

"We have to end the supervised visit for Henry's safety," the social worked informed me, ushering Henry and me out of the room.

"Of course," I said smoothly, but inside I was relived. This was one more mark against Payslee.

"Surely the judge will see she is unfit," I said to Archer while Henry screamed in my arms.

Archer winced. "He's almost purple. Are you sure he's okay?"

"He's just stressed," I answered. "He was up all night."

We watched as Payslee stomped out.

"That's *my* son," she yelled at us as she left. "I will have him back!"

"I just don't understand why she wants him back so bad," I remarked to the social worker.

"Probably money," she replied, sounding disgusted. "But I'm requesting that she takes some parenting and anger-management classes before another visit with Henry."

Another reprieve.

"You know, there are people who genuinely want to be better parents," the social worker said. "And then there are people like her. I'm just mad we're wasting resources on her when they could be better used helping someone else."

"On that note," Archer said to me, "I'll see you in New York."

"Are you coming to the conference?" I asked him as we walked out the door.

"A good chunk of my hotels are booked solid for conferencegoers," he told me. "Of course I'll be there."

"Schmoosing and boozing," I said, slipping on my sunglasses.

"You'll have so much fun you'll want to move back to Manhattan," Archer said.

"I don't know. It's a little hectic for me. I like a slower pace," I said.

"You are so old," Archer said, adjusting my tie from where Henry had yanked on it. Now that we were out in the sunshine, my little brother had started to calm down.

"You want to go to the park?" I asked him. Henry shook his head. "A snack?"

"No," my little brother said.

"What do you want?"

"To see Josie," he said as I wiped off his face.

"Well isn't that convenient?" I told him. "Me too. Great minds think alike."

Josie was in the conference room. Boxes sat on the table, and the marketing team was laughing and joking.

"Anything else we need to add? It's your last chance," Josie said as I walked into the room. Henry ran to her, and she picked him up, cradling him to her chest as she talked to me. "We've been testing the website. The swag and brochures are on-site. Plus we have the iPads for the people manning the tables to do demonstrations on."

"It all looks great," I told her and the rest of the team. "Thank you all for your hard work. I have a good feeling about this. We'll let you know how it goes. Willow, Josie, and Adrian will be at the conference in case there are last-minute changes. The rest of you, go get a drink and expense it to us, please. I really appreciate all your work. It looks fantastic."

"I haven't seen you in forever!" Josie told Henry after the team had left for a bar.

"He's had a rough day," I explained.

"How was it with, you know?" she asked.

"Over before it even began," I replied. "Seems like there's another extension."

"That's good," Josie said, smiling.

"Yeah," I said, watching her nuzzle Henry's nose and make him laugh. "It's good."

CHAPTER 53

Josie

"**M**y new clothes arrived!" I announced, waltzing into Mace's bedroom that evening with the bags of clothes on hangers.

"The tiny house let you leave without ripping anything?" Mace teased.

"Please! I didn't take them anywhere near the tiny house," I said. "They're all staying here."

"I have another surprise for you," Mace said, wheeling out a brand-new suitcase from his closet. "I didn't want to risk you showing up with all your things in some sort of grocery sack."

"I'm shocked you think so little of me," I told him. "I would at least use a garbage bag. Not a cheap one either—one of those stretchy ones that smell like marzipan and have the plastic ties." I looked over the suitcase. It was nice, with a built-in hanging bag to store my suits.

"I have a little surprise for you," I said.

"Did you find a shelf bra?" he asked, the corners of his mouth quirking.

"No shelf bras in Harrogate, but they did have this nice little surprise. Close your eyes," I said. Mace closed them, and I took off my skirt and went to stand in front of him. I took his hand and put it at the V where my legs met.

"Keep your eyes closed," I said, spreading my legs slightly, "and see if you can find the surprise."

His hand moved down, warm against me. He pressed his hand against the panties, then he felt it.

"These have a hole in them," he remarked. "I thought you bought new ones."

"It's not a hole," I said, shoving him slightly. "They have a built-in slit for easy access."

He grinned wolfishly then, in one smooth motion, bent me over the bed to lick at the slit. I arched against his mouth.

"I should wear these at the office," I gasped as his tongue licked my clit, still covered by a bit of the sheer fabric. "It will give you easier access." My head dipped down as he put two fingers inside of me. He ripped a condom packet with his teeth. I spread my legs wider, inviting him, needing him to fuck me.

Mace entered me in one smooth motion and pushed me into the bedspread, a large hand tangled in my hair. The hand moved down to circle my breast, pinching at the nipple as he fucked me through the slit in my panties.

I bucked against him when his hand moved down. The panties ripped, giving him better access to my clit. His fingers teased me while he filled me with his cock. I let out screams and moans every time he moved in me.

I came in a jumble of *ohmygods* and curse words. Mace grabbed my ass, fingers tight as he came in me.

Nuzzling my neck, Mace said, "The nice thing about these old houses is the plaster is two inches thick. I can make you scream all I want."

All through the morning drive down to New York City, Willow texted me complaints about Tara. Willow had left for the conference yesterday. She stayed with Marnie and was already on-site setting up. Tara was overseeing the general booth for Svensson PharmaTech, and Willow was working on the one specific to the gene therapy.

> **Willow:** *Anke's here. She's talking up a storm with Tara. I wouldn't mind her getting ripped off by Anke*
>
> **Josie:** *As much as I can't stand Tara, I'm not sure even I could wish Anke's destruction on her*

"Who are you texting?" Mace asked, looking over.

"Just Willow about the booth," I said. "She says it's all ready to go."

Our rooms were in one of Archer's hotels near the large conference center. We dropped off our bags then headed over to the conference center.

"Badge, badge," Anke said, handing them out. Mace went off to talk to Owen, and as soon as he was gone, Anke turned to me.

"Isn't it wonderful to be back in New York City?" She squeezed my hand. "Simply marvelous. Just like old times, isn't it? We should go out. I know a great place."

"I can't, Anke," I said through gritted teeth.

"You aren't still mad at me, are you?" she exclaimed.

"Of course I'm still mad at you," I hissed, brushing her off to look at the booth setup.

"Look who finally decided to show up," Tara snipped while I walked around. "Too busy screwing the boss to show up on time, I see."

I stopped dead in my tracks. She smirked as I struggled to keep the shock off my face.

"You weren't all that careful," she said. "I saw you two together."

I leveled my gaze at Tara. "I guess that's the closest you'll ever get to sleeping with him."

"You're a slut," she spat.

"Better than a conniving bitch who is shitty at marketing yet claims to be a pro," I retorted.

"You're going to pay for that," she snarled and stomped off.

"You seem pretty confident," Willow said, linking arms with me as we went off to look around the rest of the exhibition space.

"I got laid last night," I said, grinning. "And the night before that and the night before that. This conference is finally happening. Mace bought me some new luggage, and I have a drawer full of candy in his bedroom."

Willow stopped short, and I jerked to a halt. "Wait, is that some euphemism for sex toys or like edible underwear or something?"

"No," I said. "I literally have a drawer full of candy."

"You're an addict," my friend said and laughed.

"Hey, I had to survive this past month somehow!" I said.

"Do you think Tara is going to make your life miserable?" Willow asked in concern.

"She can try."

After looking at exhibits and watching a few sessions, we went to meet up with Marnie for a drink.

"Did you see any of the presentations?" Marnie asked after we had all hugged.

"Our stuff looks a thousand times better," Willow said, looking at the cocktail menu.

"Agreed," I said.

"Not to pat yourself on the back!" Marnie said with a laugh. "Look," she continued, her tone serious. "I've reached out to the FBI. They've already been looking into Anke."

"For defrauding people?" I asked, feeling sick. "I thought it was just you and me."

Marnie shook her head. "Not just people—banks. The agent wouldn't give me specifics, but it sounds like Anke has been running some sort of lending scheme where she convinces a bank to give her a loan for a fake business idea or investment. They give her the loan. She spends the majority of it and uses the rest as collateral to secure another huge loan."

"Like how much?" I asked, feeling faint.

"Millions of dollars," Marnie said.

I looked down at the table. The server brought our drinks. I took a big swig of mine, but I could barely taste it.

"You should go to the FBI," Marnie urged.

"What's the point?" I asked finally. "It's doubtful they care about what happens to me. The banks are going to get their money back first." The drink was sour in my stomach.

"The only thing that's going to happen is that my name is going to be attached to the whole scandal. People—*Mace*—will know I'm a complete idiot. I'll never see a penny of that money. I'll have to testify. There will be stress eating and drinking." I took another sip of my drink. "I just don't see why I should."

"Just think about it," Marnie said.

"I will," I told her, easing off the barstool. "I have to go. Mace's presentation is tomorrow. I have to make sure he's ready."

I trudged back to the hotel.

And things had been going so well.

Surely if the FBI was involved, Marnie would have told her boss, Greg Svensson, what had happened with Anke. Word would get back to Mace soon. It was only a matter of time before my charade disintegrated faster than the cotton candy in that viral video of the raccoon washing it in a puddle.

As I headed back to the hotel, I noticed through the window of a little French restaurant someone who looked like Anke. She was talking to a rich-looking older couple along with a doughy, sweaty man I thought I recognized from somewhere. I couldn't place him.

I wanted to stare longer, but I didn't want them to look up and see me. I didn't know what Anke was doing, but I knew, I just *knew*, she was up to no good.

CHAPTER 54

Mace

My presentation was that morning at eleven a.m. I was up at five a.m. to make sure I wasn't late.

"It's so early," Josie murmured when I turned on the light. She pulled the covers over her head, and I kissed her through the sheet. She was naked under them. I knew because I had taken all her clothes off last night. "Go back to sleep," she mumbled.

I ran my hands over her through the sheet, kissing down her torso and sucking on a nipple through the soft cotton. She moaned slightly. "Or I could wake you up," I said. "Morning sex is better than sugary cereal to get you moving."

"It is?" she asked, her breath slightly hitching. I reached one hand under the sheet. She was warm and still slick from our lovemaking the night before. I drew my fingers through the wetness. Her back arched slightly, and she pressed back against my hand.

"You might need to prove that theory," she gasped. I rolled on a condom, my other hand still stroking her.

"We'll have to have a lot of morning sex," I told her. "You have to have several data points."

I kissed her neck then slid into her, feeling satisfied as she whimpered through her nose. I moved in her slowly and methodically, stroking her clit in time to my thrusts. She ground her hips against me, then I flipped us over so she was on top of me, riding my cock.

"Now are you awake?" I asked.

"Yes," she said and moaned.

I held her hips as she rode me. I moved her up and down, feeling her tighten against my cock as I stroked her clit. She tipped forward on her knees over me, and I thrust up into her, hearing her high-pitched little moans every time my cock rubbed against her clit.

Her nails dug into my shoulder as she came. Then she collapsed on top of me. Her breasts were soft as she rested against me.

"You know what would make this perfect?" she asked as her breathing slowed.

"What?"

"A bowl of cereal."

"Maybe that wasn't such a good idea," Josie said as we headed downstairs. The hotel connected to the conference center through a sky bridge, which was convenient. I looked at her in concern.

"I mean," Josie clarified, "I hope I didn't take all of your mojo. You need some to spare for the presentation."

I pulled her into a niche and kissed her. "I always have more in reserve."

After doing the sound check, I waited backstage with Josie, Tara, Adrian, and Anke while we watched as people filed into the large hall.

"Ready?" Josie asked as she adjusted my suit. I didn't think I would ever tire of having Josie fuss over me. "You got this!" she said, clapping her hands. "Who's the best? You're the best!"

"What are you doing?" I asked in confusion.

"Hyping you up!" she exclaimed. "You need to have a ton of energy, and you won't eat sugar, which is the best booster there is!"

"Funny," I said. "My brother swears by bulletproof coffee."

"Which brother?"

"Several of them actually," I said. One of the stagehands motioned to me.

I walked out on stage and looked back, just a quick glance. Josie was making a heart sign with her hands. My heart jumped, and it wasn't just from the adrenaline.

My presentation was short. Josie had worked to keep it under ten minutes. Then Owen and Parker joined me onstage, and we did a roundtable discussion about the product with one of the conference hosts. I led it so that I could steer the conversation to the relevant points we were supposed to hit.

That was also Josie's idea. She said it would be more engaging than a forty-five-minute presentation. After taking several audience questions, our hour and fifteen minutes were up. The audience filed out slowly to go to lunch while Owen, Parker, and I went backstage.

"That was fantastic!" Josie crowed, pumping her fist. "The audience was super engaged."

"I'm so glad that's over," Parker said, loosening his tie.

"Please," I snorted. "You enjoyed it."

"I'm just glad you sounded interesting for once and I didn't have to stand up there under one of those vomit-inducing PowerPoints," my younger brother shot back. "I'm going back to the booth. I'm sure people will have questions, and I want to make sure that there are no rumors or misinformation."

"You have a lunch with the hospital heads," Anke reminded me and Owen.

The lunch went well. The hospital administrators put us through the wringer with questions, but Josie's pamphlets, website, and other collateral were helpful in explaining the concepts.

"Stop by our offices anytime to see the labs, or we can send someone out to give a presentation to your people," I said after thanking one president of a large regional healthcare system.

I was never a big people person. Archer was the one who always was gregarious and fun and extroverted, but I felt great today. I knew it had a lot to do with Josie. I couldn't wait to see her.

I saw her from afar as I headed back to the booth with Owen.

"You got lucky with her," Owen said gruffly.

"She's great!" I said. I couldn't help but smile when I thought of her.

"Don't screw it up," he warned.

"Please," I snorted. "As if."

"You should buy her something nice for helping us out," Owen said. "There was no way we would have been able to get another firm on such short notice."

"I already have it covered," I said, trying not to grin when I thought about the present I had found for Josie.

The Svensson PharmaTech booths were busy. Parker was doing a live demonstration of sequencing genomes at the booth along with geneticists specializing in various cancers and other diseases who were there to talk about how they used the information.

"Any interest?" I asked Josie, touching her lightly on the waist.

"There's been a steady trickle of people," she told me. "People seem very interested, especially with the speed and relatively inexpensive cost."

"You helped make it easy to understand," I told her.

"So the rumors are true!" I heard a man say behind me. I turned to see my brothers Weston and Blade.

"There are more of you!" Josie exclaimed.

"Nice to meet you," Blade said solemnly, extending his hand. "I told him not to come bother you," Blade said to me.

"I'm assuming from the names you're all Mace's full brothers?" Josie asked as Weston swept her into a hug. I shoved him off of Josie.

"Of course!" he said, batting away my hands. "Though we're the younger, fresher models."

"You aren't that young," I told them.

"Are you guys twins?" Josie asked.

"Irish twins," I explained. "Born the same year but nine months apart."

"*Exactly* nine months," Blade said. "It's actually quite fascinating when you look at the probability of that occurring."

"Your name shouldn't be Blade. It should be boring," Weston retorted.

"You're boring!" Blade shot back. How they managed to run a successful company was beyond me.

"I'm the fun one,'" Weston told Josie as he put a palm on Blade's face.

"Is Archer around?" Blade asked. "I was wondering if there was any news on the conference center."

"The chocolate factory?" Josie asked excitedly.

"You've been there?" Weston demanded. "How does it look? Could we hold retreats there?"

"Their company, ThinkX," I explained to Josie, "is a consulting company. They do logistics and a type of fake engineering called industrial engineering."

"It's real!" Blade protested.

"Please," I scoffed. "While I was studying inorganic chemistry, you guys were partying. All you do is make spreadsheets."

"Don't knock a good spreadsheet!" Blade said.

"Also, who designed your whole software system?" Weston demanded. "And who developed your whole supply chain?"

"All right! All right!" I said, waving my hands. "Correction—they do a little bit more than spreadsheets."

"We're a big competitor with Holbrook Enterprises," Weston bragged.

"I think we do better work than them because their conglomerate is a catchall for a variety of industries," Blade said, "whereas we mainly focus on logistics, software systems, and back-end processes to make your business run more smoothly and make more money."

"You have a pretty good sales pitch," Josie said.

"But you could make it so much better," Weston said, grabbing her hand.

"What my brother means to say," Blade said, pulling Weston back before I tackled him, "is, how much is Mace paying you because we'll pay you three times as much?"

"And I'll pay you five times as much." A tall dark-haired man in a dark suit clapped me on the shoulder and shook my hand.

"Wes Holbrook," he said, extending his hand to Josie. "Also I'm probably the only Holbrook the Svenssons can stand."

"Greg can't stand you," I corrected.

"Can Greg really stand anyone?" Blade mused.

"I think he's kind of funny," Josie said. We all gaped at her.

"You think Greg is funny?" Blade asked, peering at her like she was some sort of strange sea creature.

"He has a dry sense of humor."

"Maybe she has him mixed up with someone else?" Weston asked. "Are you sure it was Greg? Tall, blond, mean as a snake?"

"Are he and Hunter around?" Wes asked.

"They were at the presentation, but I think they're off on investment meetings," I told him.

"Phew. I don't think I can handle them right now."

"How's business?" I asked Wes.

"We have this new product..." Wes bounced slightly on his feet and looked at Josie.

"Are you serious?" I asked, looking around. "All of you want to hire her?" They nodded.

"*Hell. No,*" I snarled. They all started yelling at me at once.

"You can't say that!"

"I'll pay you ten times the amount!"

I waved them all away.

"Just think about it!" Wes said over his shoulder as he left.

"You have so many handsome brothers," Josie said, nudging me. "But don't worry, you're the best looking one!"

I stayed at the booth the rest of the afternoon—people seemed to like that Owen and I were there to talk and answer questions. When I wasn't talking to people, I watched Josie. I wondered if she was happy.

It was clear I couldn't have her go back to being my assistant, especially since now Anke was my assistant. Did Josie want to continue to live in Harrogate? We had amenities, yes, but it was nothing like Manhattan. Maybe she would be happier working on slick marketing projects at ThinkX with Weston and Blade. Or maybe she would want to work with Wes Holbrook. His robotics company was hot right now, and tiny robots were always cool.

I knew I should encourage Josie to build her career, but I didn't want to lose her. I wanted her to always be in my life—not just in the tiny house but in my home.

CHAPTER 55

Josie

The flow of people trickled off as we approached cocktail hour.

"Two days down, one to go," Willow said.

"I could use a drink," I said as I strung the cable lock through one of the TV screens.

"I'm meeting up with Marnie," Willow said to me as we powered down the iPads. "You coming?"

"No," Anke said, coming up beside me and wrapping an arm around my neck as if we were old friends and she didn't scam me out of my life savings and tank my credit score. Willow glared at her. I longed to ask Anke what she was doing in the restaurant yesterday evening. I wished I could remember who that man was.

"She has a hot date," Anke said. "Mace had me clear his schedule."

"He didn't say anything to me about it," I replied.

"Stop playing coy," Tara snapped, setting down the box she was carrying. "You came in here, flirted with Mace, and took advantage of him. You don't care about him at all."

"Of course I care about him!" Her words hurt. She made me sound like Anke, like I was just using Mace.

"When he finds out what you did, he's going to drop you," Tara sneered.

"And you're going to be there to pick up the pieces, *right*?" Willow said, rolling her eyes. "Josie's ten times the woman you are, and Mace sees it."

Tara glowered and looked me up and down. "Ten is an overestimate, but she's definitely twice my size." Tara shoved the box under one of the tables, grabbed her bag, and left.

"She's just being mean," Willow assured me. "You're curvy. Guys like that. It's more to grab onto."

My phone buzzed.

"That's him, isn't it?" Anke asked. She had watched the whole exchange between me and Tara in bemusement. I looked at the screen. Marnie had sent me the contact info of the FBI agent on the case and told me to contact him about Anke.

I still couldn't quite believe she was back. She was like a hurricane or a tornado. I didn't even know where to begin to fight her. It seemed like I just had to curl up in a ball and let her pass over me then pick up the pieces later.

My phone buzzed again. This time it was Mace.

Mace: *I want to thank you for your help*
Josie: *Publicly or privately?*
Mace: *Both*

He sent me a picture of himself, cropped at the neck. The bulge was prominent through his boxer briefs.

Josie: *Is that a chocolate bunny in your pants or are you excited to see me?*

Mace: *Very excited*

"Ooh," Anke said, peering over my shoulder. "He wants you. Well done." She blew me a kiss. "I have my own Svensson to wrangle."

"Ugh," Willow said after Anke left. "She's such a snake. You need to talk to the FBI about her. She should be in jail. You heard what Marnie said."

"I know I will, just, it's too much to think about," I fretted. "I want to have one nice evening with Mace."

"I don't think he'll hate you or think less of you when he finds out," Willow said. "Everyone makes mistakes."

"But it's such a stupid one," I countered. "And I feel like I'm making an even bigger one by letting her just hang around here."

"Keep your enemies close," Willow stated. "Now you can tell the FBI exactly where she is when it's time for her to be arrested."

But I was afraid of what Mace would think. He was so perfect. If I was organized enough to make a spreadsheet of my top qualities for a man, he would check every box. Thoughtful, cared about family, employed. Also did I mention smoking hot?

Mace was waiting for me in the lobby bar when I came down from my hotel room. The light lit the burnished bronze of his hair. He looked every bit like a suave billionaire. His suit was perfectly tailored to accentuate the sharp lines of his torso and back. He finished his drink, tipped the bartender, and sauntered over to me, an easy smile on his face.

"Reveling in your success today, Mr. Big Shot CEO?" I teased him.

He rubbed his jaw then leaned in to kiss me. "You're the one who should be basking in the glory of your awesomeness," he replied. "This seriously would not have happened without you." He leaned down to kiss me again. "I had Anke make reservations at this place called Salt House. She said it was fairly new but had good reviews."

I tensed up at the mention of Anke. To FBI or not to FBI—that was the question.

"Or we could go somewhere else," Mace said, furrowing his brow. I forced myself to relax and squeezed his bicep.

"That sounds perfect," I assured him. I was going to put Anke out of my mind. There was a perfect evening planned with a perfect man, and I was determined to enjoy it.

The Salt House restaurant was busy when we arrived, but the hostess led us to a private room upstairs. There was a table set for two at a large window overlooking a cozy courtyard.

The waiter poured us a glass of wine each. Mace picked up his glass.

"To you, Josie. Thank you," Mace said solemnly.

"You're so serious!" I joked.

"It is serious," Mace said. "I'm so glad I met you."

"Even though I poured chocolate sauce all over you and set your car on fire?" I asked, swirling the dark liquid around in my glass.

"I thought you said it was an act of God," he said with a smirk.

"It was totally an accident," I corrected.

I wanted to tell him how much he meant to me but couldn't find the words without sounding sappy and clingy. Fortunately I was saved when a charcuterie tray arrived.

It displayed a variety of cheeses—creamy brie, fresh goat cheese. There were little dabs of honeycomb and jams—not plain jams but interesting ones like peach and jalapeño, tomato jam, and fig and orange blossom jam. The meats were savory and salty, a perfect counterpoint to the sweetness of the jam and sharpness of the cheese. There were salamis, cured venison sausage, and duck prosciutto.

"This is so good," I said. "I love a charcuterie tray."

"Salt House is known for it, hence the name," Mace replied as he took a slice of cheese with the little bamboo knife.

"Crap," I said.

"What?"

"I didn't take a picture," I said. "I should up my Instagram game. Chloe's Instagram looks amazing. Mine used to look amazing."

"What happened?" he asked. I stuffed some cheese in my mouth to delay. I couldn't believe I brought that up. I didn't want to give him a hint of my stupid YOLO lifestyle with Anke.

"Eh, you know," I said, waving my hand.

"It's probably better you don't take pictures," Mace said. "I've eaten with Chloe before, and she spends a bit of time framing the perfect shot."

"Wait!" I told him before he picked up another bite of the peppery salami. "I need a picture of that meat. When I'm cold and alone in my tiny house, I want to look back fondly on this moment when I had a whole charcuterie platter all to myself."

"I thought I already sent you a picture of my meat?" Mace said casually, eating a piece of cheese swiped in tomato jam.

"No, you sent me a picture of a bowling ball in your underwear. But if you do happen to send me a picture of your salami, please try and be a little imaginative in your presentation? Actually," I amended as I built a little tower of sharp sheep's milk cheese, peach and jalapeno jam, and a sliver of duck prosciutto on a cracker, "imaginative isn't maybe the exact word I was looking for."

"Good because I was thinking of putting a little hat on it," Mace said.

"One guy sent me a dick pic and put googly eyes on it."

"I hope he's not in this state," Mace said, his voice dangerously low.

"No," I said. "He's Dutch, and he went back home."

Mace was still glowering. I stuffed the cracker tower in my mouth. He watched me chew and swallow.

"Oh no, you're so jealous!" I said. "It would be funny if you didn't have billions of dollars and a pack of wild brothers to send after the Dutch guy."

"My brothers aren't crazy. Well, not all of them," Mace said. "Though maybe I could convince Garrett to go all Liam Neeson on your European charcuterie."

I bashed down the thoughts of traveling with Anke and spending money I didn't have.

Trying to keep my tone light, I said, "It was a very small sampling. And while Europe may be known for their cured meats, I think I prefer American sausage the best."

CHAPTER 56

Mace

"You want the last of the honeycomb to wash down all that American sausage?" I asked Josie, scooping up the gooey golden chunk of waxy honeycomb with my finger.

She leaned over the table, her mouth slightly open. I could see the curves of her breasts threatening to spill out of the low-cut dress she wore. Her lips wrapped around my fingers, and I grunted. The touch of her tongue against my skin sent shocks down my torso.

"Yum," she said with a moan, "the big finale!"

Good thing the door to the private dining space opened because I think I was about to jump across the table and crush her mouth to mine.

"We will be bringing up the main course shortly," the server said as his colleague cleared away the empty charcuterie board. "The chef is preparing filet mignon, with truffle macaroni and cheese, broccoli chard, and a Spanish red wine to pair. How would you like your steak prepared? Rare?" His tone was hopeful.

"Yes, thank you. That would be perfect," I assured him. We both looked at Josie.

"What?" she asked, confused. "Of course I want it rare. How else would you eat it?"

"Thank God," the server said with obvious relief. "There was a woman downstairs who asked for her steak well done."

"I hope you told her to leave," Josie exclaimed.

"Of course not. That would be rude," the server sniffed. "We simply told her it wasn't possible, that the grill doesn't get that hot."

Josie tipped back her head and laughed, and I decided it was the most wonderful sound in the world.

I poured her more wine and sat back, regarding her. "So you've helped kick off a multibillion-dollar launch, and you have several owners of large, powerful companies begging for you to come work for them. Do you have any plans to move up in the world?"

I tried to play it casual, but my heart was yammering. I had to know if she wanted to leave. I didn't want to hamper her, and I knew that if she took work with Wes Holbrook or with my brothers at ThinkX, she could hop from one major project to the next and write her own paycheck.

Josie looked thoughtful for a moment and swirled her wine glass around. I could barely breathe. "I guess my marketing contract with you is over," she said slowly, "and you have—" She took a sip of the wine. "Anke as your assistant."

"That doesn't mean we don't have work for you," I said.

"What about Tara?" Josie countered.

"I know she was tough at first, but I think she's warmed up to you," I said earnestly.

Josie gave me a critical look. "I don't know. She doesn't like me moving in on her turf." She frowned slightly.

"There are several good opportunities in Manhattan," I pressed. "I could help you find a job."

"Trying to get rid of me?" Josie asked, still looking at her wine. I reached over the table and plucked the glass from her hand, setting it aside.

"Josie," I said, taking her hand. "I am not trying to get rid of you. In fact, I want you to stay. Maybe we could fix up one of the cabins on the property." I looked into her eyes. "Or maybe you secretly hate my family and that would be too many brothers-in-law."

She gave me a crooked smile. "Your family is one of the things I adore about you," she said.

"And the easy way you can just *be*, not just with my family but with me as well, is one of the things I love about you," I told her honestly.

She smiled at me, and maybe it was the wine, but it seemed a little sad.

"Whatever you decide for your career, I want to be there with you," I told her firmly.

"I want that too!" Josie said then started to cry.

"Holy smokes," I said, getting up to go to her.

She motioned me to sit back down and dabbed at her eyes. "Sorry," she said. "I didn't mean... I'm just stupid."

"You're not stupid," I told her.

She sighed. "At the very least, if I'm not working at PharmaTech," she said, taking a big swallow of wine, "we could have a real, open relationship."

"We have a real relationship," I said, taken aback. "We went on a date. We went on several dates." Her eyes flicked up to the ceiling then back down to my face.

"Sure, but I was still sleeping with the boss. It doesn't really stir confidence in other employees."

"I'm sorry. I didn't want to make things difficult for you," I said.

"I'm a grown woman. I can make my own choices," she said sharply. Her expression softened. "Besides, we were having fun—no need to make things serious or difficult." She smiled brilliantly at me.

I wanted to howl that this was serious for me. I wanted the difficulties and the struggles and to go through them with her. But I had already practically ruined the evening.

During the last few days, my biggest concern had been that I might lose her. It hadn't even occurred to me that this wasn't something serious for her. Were there signs I missed? Maybe normal people in normal relationships didn't send pictures like that or decorate themselves with candy.

My brothers always joked that I liked to immediately jump to the worst possible conclusion. Maybe I was doing it here. Josie hadn't given any indication that this was just a flight of fancy for her.

Just be normal, and make this a pleasant memorable evening, I ordered myself as the waiter opened the door and walked in with a large oval tray.

"This looks fantastic," Josie said as the sommelier came in with a new bottle of wine. He poured the dark-red liquid in the glasses and faded out of the room with the rest of the wait staff, leaving Josie and me alone.

"To you," Josie said. "Thank you for a wonderful evening."

"It's my pleasure. I really like you a lot, Josie," I said as she inspected her steak.

"Because I saved your marketing bacon?" she joked.

"Well that and you're just an amazing woman." It seemed like the compliments were making her uncomfortable. I tried to steer the conversation into a more lighthearted mode. "Most importantly," I told her as she cut a slice off of the dry-aged beef, "you eat your steak rare. If you had ordered it well done, I don't think we could have been friends anymore. I'm from the American West. We are very serious about our beef."

"There's no way I could have it well done," she said. "I like my meat red and raw." She took a comically slow bite, her teeth clanging on the tines of the fork, pulling it out of her mouth in an exaggerated gesture.

"If you're going to eat like that this whole time," I said, "I'm going to have to end this dinner early and take you somewhere for your private present."

"But then we would miss dessert," she said innocently.

"I wouldn't miss it. You're my dessert."

The lighthearted jokes worked. The rest of the dinner went smoothly, with an easy rhythm.

"I would say that I didn't have room for dessert," Josie sighed, as the servers cleared away our plate, "but I always have room."

The servers set down a plate in front of us.

"This is the tallest piece of cake I've ever seen!" Josie said, clapping her hands.

"It is a seven-layer heartthrob cake," the waiter explained.

"From Grey Dove Bistro," Josie cut in. "I saw this on Instagram! It has white pound cake, lemon curd, raspberry mouse, another layer of pound cake, raspberry and lemon compote, white chocolate mouse and another layer of pound cake and finally a layer of chocolate ganache."

"Yes," the server said. He seemed a little miffed that Josie had stolen his thunder. "It's a cake developed by Chloe exclusively for Salt House."

"I always wanted to try it," Josie gushed.

"There was also a special request made in-house for you," the waiter added.

"For me?" Josie squealed. Another server put down a plate with a single round ball of fried ice cream and a small little pot of chocolate.

"Aw!" Josie said, jumping up and coming around the table to sit in my lap and throw her arms around me. "It's like the first time we met!"

"Just please don't dump the chocolate sauce all over me!" I said.

"So that was my public surprise," Josie said after dinner when we were in the car. "And where's my private one?" she whispered in my ear.

I just wanted to rip her clothes off right there in the back of the car. Instead I settled for kissing her in the dark and letting my hand slide up her leg to the wet, warm panties I knew were waiting for me. She spread her legs slightly, and I just wanted to pull her on my lap and fuck her. But I controlled myself.

"This isn't the hotel," Josie said, confused when we pulled up to our destination.

"I wondered when you would figure out we're going the opposite direction," I teased as I helped her out of the car. She swung her legs out, and I wanted to kneel down and bury my face in between them.

"I had a lot of wine," she said, giggling as she leaned against me. "And I have a terrible sense of direction. The only reason I don't get lost in Harrogate is it's a giant grid, and if you go around in a circle, you end up back where you started."

She leaned on my arm as we walked into the renovated old brick warehouse building.

"Is this one of Archer's hotels?" Josie murmured against my mouth as I kissed her in the elevator.

"It's a condo building," I told her. "It was the first major real estate project that Svensson Investment did."

"Airbnb-ing it?" she commented. "Swanky."

I looked down at her. "It's *my* condo."

"But you live in Harrogate," Josie blurted as the doors opened to a private lobby.

"I could fit three tiny houses in here," she exclaimed. "It's huge! But where's your kitchen?" She looked around.

"This is just the lobby," I told her as I punched in the numbers on the keypad and the large metal door slid open.

"Welcome to my Manhattan residence," I said to her, sweeping my arm out.

"Wow!" Josie said, slowly walking inside. "This is enormous."

"Sorry," I told her. "It's very masculine. If you want to redecorate, you're free to do so."

"Like right now?" she asked. "I mean... yes, I would like a craft room and a candy wall and the ceilings painted the color of bubble gum."

"Why would you glue candy on the walls?" I asked.

"Not glue," she said, walking into my kitchen. "I would put the candy in jars and arrange it on shelves."

"What would you do with a whole wall made out of candy?" I asked, following her.

"Eat it?" She looked at me incredulously. "Don't turn up your nose. You eat my candy, and you like it!"

She crooked her finger. I picked her up easily and set her on the polished concrete counter. Josie wrapped her legs around me. My pants were tight as her hips rolled against me.

"This is a nice surprise," she purred. "Giving me your nine inches of heartthrob in the biggest condo in New York."

"It's not that big," I said, kissing her neck.

"It's not the size that matters. It's how you use it," she quipped. Her hand palmed the bulge in my pants, slowly pulling down the zipper. "And you use it very well."

As much as I wanted to fuck her there on the counter, I had something better planned. "Your surprise," I groaned.

"There's more?"

"There's always more."

I went into the never-used dining room and picked up the packages. I'd had them delivered to the condo. Both boxes were wrapped in metallic wrapping paper and decorated with large pink bows.

Josie clapped her hands when she saw the boxes. "They're so shiny!" She carefully unwrapped them. "I want to save the paper," she explained. She opened the box and immediately started laughing.

CHAPTER 57

Josie

I pulled the tiny strip of black lacy lingerie out of the tissue paper. "Is this what I think it is?" I asked, laughing.

"While they don't sell shelf bras in the small, wholesome town of Harrogate, they do sell them all over the place in Manhattan," Mace said. From the expression on his face, I knew he was salivating to see me in the shelf bra.

"You have a dirty mind, Mace," I teased. "I knew someone who fixated on schedules was up to no good."

"Getting you off in the office didn't clue you in?" he asked innocently.

"Dare I ask what's in this box?" I said as I wriggled the top off then gasped. In the box were a familiar pair of fishnet stockings attached to a pair of black open-toe stilettoes. "You didn't!" I said, laughing.

"I can't believe they sell these in Harrogate but no shelf bras," he said, grinning. "Seems like they should go hand in hand."

"Where is your bathroom?" I asked, picking up the items. "I'm going to try these on."

"Down the hall, take a right into what looks like a sitting room but then keep going through the master bedroom, and it's on your left."

I blinked at him.

"On second thought," Mace said, picking me up as I shrieked. "Let me just take you there. Can't have you getting lost."

I shooed him out of the bathroom when he set me down. Partly because I had to sit on the floor with my legs up in the air to put on tights and partly because I needed to have a mini orgasm, looking at his bathroom.

It was huge—at least three times the size of my tiny house. It was white and gray, with similarly polished concrete countertops to the kitchen and a large plush rug in the center of the room in front of the tub.

I did some quick yoga poses just because I could. Even though Mace said he was never here, the whole place smelled like him. I stripped, and when the slightly chilly air hit my nipples, they went pebble hard.

Laying back on the rug, I slowly eased my feet in the shoes then rolled the black fishnet tights up. Though surely the designer didn't expect people to go commando with these shoes-tights, underwear would look dumb. I was just glad that I had mowed the lawn before I came to the conference.

I put on the shelf bra. It was soft, softer than it looked with all the lace. It must have been expensive. It was like a pushup bra, with the cups missing. I turned around to look at myself in the mirror, thinking I was going to look stupid, but actually I looked, well, it was really erotic. The high heels on the shoes perked up my butt. The waistband on the fishnets sat at the narrowest part of my waist, accentuating the curve. Though the shelf bra was small, it did live up to its name. My boobs were pushed up, the nipples high and erect. On the back of the shoe-tights, there was a black ribbon down each leg like you would see in the vintage tights from the forties. It was like a landing strip from my feet to my happy place.

I swung the bathroom door open and sauntered out. Mace stood up off the bed and said, "Fuck."

"That's the idea," I told him. I walked up to him. He brought up his hands but didn't touch me, just ran them down the airspace around me. I could feel the warmth radiating off them.

"You are so fucking hot," he growled. His voice was low and deep; it rumbled around the room. Mace looked at me like I was a dessert buffet and he wasn't sure if he wanted to start with the macarons or the mousse.

"You're wearing too many clothes, Mr. CEO," I told him. Just seeing the desire on his face was making me wet and hot.

I reached up to loosen his tie. That contact jumped the spring, and Mace crushed me to him, devouring my mouth, his hands running up and down my body, cupping my ass, stroking my breasts. He kissed his way down my neck to a breast, putting it in his mouth, rolling the nipple with his tongue.

"Your tits are so amazing," he whispered as his fingers traced the lace edges of the bra. I let my fingers comb through his hair, and Mace undid the buttons on his dress shirt while he teased my nipples.

When his shirt fell to the floor, he stood tall before me. His large hands rested on my hips, his thumbs running along the narrow black waistband of the fishnet tights. I let the palms of my hands rest on his collarbones then travel down over the slight curve of his pecs then over the ridges on his abs to his belt.

As I undid it slowly, my nipples, high and perky because of the shelf bra, brushed against the skin of his chest. My pussy felt hot and wet, and I just wanted him to touch me. I wanted his hand and his tongue and his cock.

Instead of giving me what I craved, he was making this infuriatingly slow motion of running his fingertips over the wide fishnet pattern. I threw his belt to the floor then undid his pants.

"You going to fuck me with this?" I breathed, slipping my hand into his boxer briefs. "Or are you going to stand there?"

He grinned. "I'm trying to decide if this fishnet pattern is wide enough to fuck you through it or if I'm going to have to rip them," he replied in a dangerously low voice. "I'm pretty sure I can get my fingers through."

I shivered as his hand moved down, down, the other caressing my ass. The lower hand slipped between my legs. I widened my stance.

"You look so fuckable in those shoes," Mace said, then his fingers pushed through one of the holes of the tights. There was a seam down the center, and though he was able to work around the fishnet, it wasn't enough for me.

"You're just teasing," I gasped.

"You said you didn't want me to rip these," he said, his tone infuriatingly mild.

"I wanted to wear them more than once," I said breathlessly as his mouth went back to my tits, teasing the nipple.

Mace stepped out of his pants, pushing me back a few steps and spreading my legs wider apart.

I groaned as he kissed his way down. His tongue poked through the fishnet, and the pressure of his mouth rubbed some of the fishnet fabric against my pussy, a delicious friction. My legs were about as stable as a Fruit by the Foot, and I leaned against Mace. He held me up, his hands on my hips as his tongue traced the pink folds.

Mace stood up abruptly.

"Don't stop," I groaned, reaching for him. Mace picked me up, large hands on my waist, and put me on the bed. "You going to fuck me?" I begged, chest heaving.

"Yes, but I think I'm going to have to rip these," he said and reached down. The fabric pulled then ripped.

"They should have just made these with a strategic opening," I said as his mouth went back down. My legs were spread. My feet were on the floor in the heels, the height of them bringing my hips up at an angle.

Mace took full advantage and slid two fingers in my opening to stroke me as his tongue sucked at my clit. After all the teasing, it didn't take long for him to bring me to the edge. I dug my nails into his scalp as I came.

"Fuck," I whimpered as I watched him slide on a condom.

"That's happening next," he said, giving me only a slight breather before he slid into me. I moaned as his cock, thick and long, filled me. He stood in front of me and lifted my hips up and fucked me. I couldn't reach to grab him, so

I twisted my hands in the sheets as he thrust into me, his fingers digging into my ass through the fishnets.

I felt like I was almost about to come, and I reached up to pinch my nipple, needing more stimulation. Mace stopped and pulled me upright, kissing me, his tongue claiming my mouth.

"It's so hot when you do that," he said, his mouth moving to my breast.

Mace picked me up and pushed me back farther on the bed. I spread my legs, and he kissed from my tits down to the waistband of the fishnets and lower. The heels of the stilettoes dug into the mattress as he went lower, his mouth teasing my clit.

"I thought you were going to fuck me," I said, desperate for his cock.

"I love making you come," he said, then his mouth was back. He teased and nipped as I begged him to fuck me.

I came, cursing him. I pulled him up to me, my nails digging in the ridges of muscles on his back. "Fuck me," I mumbled against his mouth.

"One day," he said, ignoring my orders and instead teasing me with his cock, stroking it on my clit then teasing my opening but not giving me what I needed, "I want to watch you on my desk, your legs spread, stroking yourself, telling me all the dirty things you want me to do to you."

"You want to watch me play in my candy jar?" I kissed him then bit his lip. "You fuck me with that big cock, and I'll put on the best show you've ever seen," I promised.

"Well, when you put it that way." Mace winked. Then he thrust into me, and I moaned, arching up against him. Every time he thrust, my nipples brushed the muscles on his chest, and his cock rubbed against my already sensitive clit. I rolled my hips against him, seeking the friction. It didn't take me long to come. But it was small. I felt it roll through me, and even as it happened, I knew he could make me come again.

I whimpered as he stopped, kissed my mouth, and turned me around.

"This is quite the view," Mace said. I was on my knees in front of him, resting on my forearms, and he stroked me with his fingers. Then he rammed his thick cock into me; my back arched, and my breasts rubbed against the soft sheets. I had to brace myself against the headboard as he fucked me. One of his hands reached to rub and tease my clit.

He hooked a hand in the waist of the fishnets, braced the other against the headboard, and then fucked me hard and fast. I couldn't do anything but moan his name.

"Josie, you're so hot and tight," he whispered. "You feel so good." I whimpered as my legs widened, inviting him to claim me. High-pitched pants came out of my mouth in time to his thrusts.

"I need you, Mace," I said, my voice hoarse. "Your cock feels so good."

His rhythm grew more erratic, and I felt his hand tighten at my waist. Mace ground against me as he came. The thought and the reality of him coming in me made my belly tighten, and I felt the spasms of pleasure wash over me.

"I think I'm basically just a puddle of melted chocolate," I slurred as he took off the condom.

"And I'd lick you all up," he whispered in my ear.

I woke up the next morning feeling amazing. Mace was wrapped around me, his hand cupping my breast.

"I think I ruined your shoes," Mace said. He sounded self-satisfied and not at all sorry.

"It's not like I was going to wear them to work or something," I told him.

"I wouldn't mind you wearing them to work," Mace said.

I was about to push the tights down when he stopped me.

"I just need one more." He kissed his way down. I could feel his mouth through the ripped fishnets.

"You always make me so wet," I moaned as he licked me. "I want it hot and dirty." He teased me as he put on a condom.

"Yeah, you want my thick cock," he said as he entered me. I moaned, arching back against him as he pushed into me. I was slick from his tongue and from last night, and I hung onto the headboard as he fucked me, his balls slapping my ass with every thrust. He reached to pinch my nipple.

"Your pussy is so hot and tight," he said, still fucking me.

"I need to come," I whimpered. "I want you to make me come." His fingers moved to my clit, and he rubbed me, stroking me in time to the thrusts.

I screamed as I came, my body still spasming. Mace's thrusts became more erratic; his large hands dug into my hips as he came.

"Fuck, that was good," he said, burying his face in my hair. "I could fuck you all day."

"But there's breakfast and the conference," I said as my heart rate started to slow. He kissed me but let me leave to go to the bathroom.

I wanted to take a bath in the huge tub. Seriously it was like a small swimming pool. Mace could have fully laid down in it with room to spare, and he was not a small man. But I took a shower instead.

I was standing under the spray, letting the hot water wash off the effects of our lovemaking. A shadow crossed over the steamy glass, and the door opened. There was a bench in the shower, which was good because all the sex in those ridiculously tall heels was making me wobbly. Mace stepped through the spray and bent down, sucking my nipples, making them hard as his hand slipped between my legs.

"I told you I wanted to fuck you all morning," he said over the rush of the water. He lifted my hips up, kissing down, down, the flesh still sensitive from a few moments ago. I whimpered as he slowly stroked me with his tongue. I turned around and leaned over the bench.

"Is this an invitation?" he whispered.

I heard him roll on a condom. Then he slowly entered me. I moaned deep in my throat as he fucked me steadily. One leg was up on the bench, and his cock slid in me as he stroked my clit, the water mingling with my own wetness. I closed my eyes, leaning back against his broad chest as his other hand moved up to my nipples. He kissed my neck and my collarbone with little kisses as he slowly fucked me.

Mace bucked against me and increased the rhythm of his thrusts and the hand on my clit. He pinched my nipple, and I felt my chest tighten. I pushed back against his cock and then against his hand.

"I know you're about to come," Mace whispered, nipping my ear. "Your pussy gets so tight." My body rippled in response, the pleasure washing over me. In a few short thrusts, Mace came too.

"I love fucking you in the shower," Mace said, tipping my head back and kissing me deeply.

"You love fucking me everywhere," I replied with a smile.

"You have the sweetest candy," he said, turning off the water, wrapping me in a towel, and snuggling me in his arms.

"I guess we should go back to the hotel. I need some clothes," I said, rubbing my nose against his bare chest. He smelled so freaking good.

"Our stuff is here. I had it packed up and brought over," Mace said.

"Just like that, huh?" I said.

He grinned. "There has to be some benefit to having all this money."

Reluctantly we headed back to the conference for the last day. Mace's car was also magically in the condo garage, and he put our bags in the trunk. He slipped his sunglasses on then sat in the driver's seat, staring at the parking deck wall.

"Earth to Mace? Did I break you last night?" I joked.

He turned to me and pushed the sunglasses up on his head. His expression was serious.

"When I said yesterday that I liked you, I didn't mean it," he said.

"Okay, what the hell—"

"I love you," Mace said, grabbing me. "I know you think this is just a fun fling, but I don't work that way. I don't want to live without you. Even if you take a job in Manhattan, I will tell my brothers that you can't be there all the time and that you need to work remotely."

"Okay," I said. I was slightly shocked. I didn't know how to respond, so I pulled him down for a kiss. All the while my thoughts were racing.

I couldn't tell him I loved him, even though I guess that was the right response. But did I love him? I was basically lying to him about Anke. And despite what Willow said, I knew when he found out that this perfect thing with Mace would all come crashing down. You don't lie to people you love.

CHAPTER 58

Mace

I took a huge risk telling Josie that I loved her. And she didn't say it back. Did I miscalculate? I had to tell her—it was the truth. Maybe she didn't want anything permanent, but I did. I shouldn't have fallen in love with her. But I did. What was going to happen? Would she move to New York City? She couldn't live in a tiny house on my property forever.

I avoided Josie as soon as we stopped at the booth. I dropped my stuff and basically spent the rest of the time in meetings or attending sessions of potential big clients. All through the remainder of the conference, my thoughts spun. Had I blown it? Was she just going to stay in Manhattan and not even come back to Harrogate? Was she mad? Did she hate me?

I was a complete wreck late that afternoon when the conference was officially over. I paid the tab at the coffee shop in Archer's hotel after meeting with the CEO of a large research university that wanted to partner with PharmaTech, and someone nudged me.

"Dude," my twin brother said. "You look like a wreck. Late night?"

"I think I ruined my life," I whispered.

"You are the most dramatic, emotional person," Archer scoffed.

"I'm not emotional," I snapped. A few people turned around to gape at us.

Archer grabbed me by the suit coat sleeve and pulled me to his office. He had one in every hotel that he and his cofounder and our half brother Mike shared. He shut the door and took out a bottle of whiskey, pouring me two fingers. "Drink that and don't puke on my carpet," he ordered. "This is an imported alpaca shag rug made by the nicest little old Peruvian lady."

I sipped the whiskey.

"Let me guess what happened," Archer said, leaning back in his chair. "You did your crazy Mace thing and told Josie you couldn't live without her and you loved her to the moon and back."

"I didn't say it like that," I growled.

"And then I bet you freaked out and didn't give her a chance to process it, and now you think she's already found someone better, richer, more handsome than you in the last, oh, five hours and is already planning on running off to southern France with him. Is that right?"

I scowled at my twin.

"Wait, of course it is! I know exactly how you think." Archer leaned over the desk. "Your thoughts devolve into the worst possible scenario. You overreact. It's a good trait for a CEO who makes products that could literally kill people if not designed and manufactured perfectly. However, it makes the rest of life unnecessarily stressful."

My twin poured me another drink.

"Let me reassure you," Archer said. "I am the only person better looking, friendlier, and better in bed than you, and I have not seen or heard from Josie today, so you're safe on that front." He leaned back, a self-satisfied smile on his face.

I stared at him. "You're terrible," I said finally.

"And you're paranoid and crazy," Archer said affectionately. "With you and Remy bouncing around out there in that huge estate house, it's a good thing I'm planning on building that conference center. I'll have more time to make sure you two aren't building matching bunkers."

"What do I do about Josie?" I asked through my teeth. I loathed admitting I didn't have control over a situation, but I was willing to throw all my rules to the wind if it meant I wouldn't drive Josie away.

"Just act like a normal person. You threw down the big L word. Though you're crazy, you have a lot of positives in your favor," Archer said, waving his arms around. "She'll talk to her friends. She'll tell them she's freaked out that some guy she only met six weeks ago says he loves her and wants her to move into his creepy compound out in rural New York. Her friends will of course tell her she's crazy for thinking that's a good idea and tell her to dump you."

"What?" I shouted, jumping up.

Archer held up a hand.

"Then one friend will be like, 'But he's so handsome!' and another will say, 'But he's rich!' and Josie will say, 'You're right. Also he's not a serial killer, and he's good with children!' and then her friends will all be like, 'Yeah, you should totally move to his compound!'"

"I don't have a compound!" I yelled.

"Bro, it's totally a compound," Archer said, finishing off the whiskey in my glass. "But I mean, it's like a high-end, glam compound."

Josie didn't act like she was getting ready to flee when we drove back to Harrogate that night. She kept up a stream of ideas about a general marketing direction for Svensson PharmaTech.

When I pulled the car in front of the house, I cut her off.

"Josie," I said. She looked up at me; she was chewing on her lip. I leaned in to press my mouth to hers. "I didn't mean to put a lot of pressure you," I told her.

"I know," she said. She looked down at her lap. "You're a wonderful man."

"But," I said, more forcefully than I intended. "There's always a but, isn't there?"

"But nothing," she said and shrugged unhappily. "You're amazing and perfect, and I'm not."

"You are," I insisted. She shook her head.

"So this is the, 'It's not you, it's me'?" I said sharply.

"No," she countered. "It's the, 'You have a lot on your plate with your family and your business.'" She looked sad, but maybe it was just the shadows from the moonlight.

"I really like you, and I do want to spend the rest of my life with you, but I'm afraid that you don't actually know me, and when you do really get to know me, you won't like me anymore." Josie pushed the car door open and hurried out.

I let her go and pulled the suitcases out of the trunk. I took them up to my bedroom, but when I looked out through the windows to the backyard, I saw the lights on in her tiny house.

I set my bag down and took hers to the house. I knocked on the door.

"Josie?" I called. She didn't answer. "I have your bag."

I waited a beat, and when the door didn't open, I turned to go back to the main house. But I heard the door creak, and she called out to me.

"Thanks," she said. I could see tears in her eyes. I went to her, ducking under the doorway, picking her up, and pushing her back against the small couch.

"I love you, Josie," I told her. "I already know you, and I know you're perfect for me."

Our hands were all over each other. I ripped at her shirt, and she gasped as several of the buttons popped off and I pulled her breast out of the lace bra. Suckling on a nipple, I rolled it over my tongue. She moaned as I pushed up her skirt, my fingers pressed against her soaking-wet panties.

"Still have a hankering for raw meat?" I joked. Josie laughed then whimpered as my fingers slipped under her panties to tease her clit and stroke down to her opening. "You like that, don't you?" I whispered to her as she ground against my hand.

"I want you to fuck me," she whispered back. The sadness in her face was thankfully gone. I was pleased to see it replaced by wanton desire. I pulled her panties down and threw them to the floor. Not bothering to take off her skirt,

I pushed it up around her waist. She spread her legs, begging me to fuck her, as I undid my tie.

"Not yet," I told her. I grabbed her hand, licking her fingers, then I took them and pressed them to the hot, wet flesh between her legs. "I want to see you touch yourself," I growled. "Give me a good show."

Her hand moved slowly as the other stroked her breast, circling and pinching the nipple.

"I want your cock," she said breathlessly as her hand moved in the silky warmth. I slowly undid my shirt, letting it fall to the floor as her fingers dipped into her opening. Her legs spread wider, and she moaned slightly. "I want your big, thick cock thrusting in me, making me scream," she said, her voice throaty. I kicked off my shoes and grabbed Josie's hips, pressing my face to her, licking her clit, sucking on the flesh. I slipped two fingers in her opening. She was already halfway gone, and she bucked against me as I stroked her and sucked her, making her come.

"Shit," she said, panting as she watched me take my pants off. Free of the constraints of the boxer briefs, my cock was erect and stuck straight out. Josie's hands shook as she took off her skirt. She half turned to throw it up on the loft along with her bra. I grabbed her from behind and pushed inside her. She was hot and wet and so tight. She hung onto the ladder as I fucked her.

Her breaths came out in high-pitched whimpers as I slid inside her, one hand on her clit. I felt her come again, and she moaned, her body tightening around me.

Every time I thrust in her, she made a little high-pitched breath that made me wild. I felt her body tighten for another orgasm, and it sent me over the edge. She leaned her head back, and I kissed her, swallowing the scream as she came.

I gathered her to me, and we curled up on the couch.

"I guess this couch has seen some shit," she said. "Should probably flip the cushions."

"Just burn down the tiny house," I told her, nibbling her ear. "I don't want you nomadizing off anywhere. This is your home. Stay here."

"Okay," she said, eyes half closed, her breath slightly cooling my skin. "I'll stay."

Josie didn't seem like she was having second thoughts the next day. She smiled at me when she sat down in the car, turning around in her seat to poke at Henry.

"Now that I'm back, we can go have lunch outside!" Josie told him excitedly.

"You're done with the conference?" Henry asked.

"Almost done," Josie said. "There are still a few things I need to wrap up. There are some changes I want the developers to make on the website." As we drove down Main Street to PharmaTech, I saw Payslee and her lawyer walking down the street.

"I don't like them," Henry said defiantly, glaring out the window and kicking at his car seat.

"I don't think anyone likes your mom and her skeezy lawyer," I told him. Josie was ramrod straight in her seat, staring out the window at them as we passed.

"Don't worry," I assured her. "Payslee didn't make a good impression on the social worker last visit. Hunter's pretty confident everything's going to work out."

Josie wiped at her face and said in a faint voice, "Sure."

CHAPTER 59

Josie

I couldn't believe it. Anke had been meeting with Payslee's attorney? I knew Payslee wanted Henry back for some reason. I would bet my tiny house that it had something to do with Anke.

"What am I going to do?" I asked Willow over the phone. She was still in New York with Marnie. I was holed up in a conference room with a bag of chocolate chips. Things were crashing down around me. I should have come clean about what a dangerous person Anke was when she first reappeared.

"Talk to the FBI," Marnie said firmly, coming on the line. "This is crazy."

"But Mace said he loved me," I told my friends faintly. "I know Mace is going to hate me when he finds out I let Anke mess with his family." I felt sick. I shoved a handful of chocolate chips in my mouth, hoping it would settle my stomach, but it didn't.

"If you care about him," Willow said firmly, "you'll talk to the FBI. If Mace's brothers want you to come do marketing with them in Manhattan, you definitely can't just leave Anke in Harrogate to run whatever scam she has brewing."

"I know," I said, chewing on another handful of chocolate chips. "I'm so stupid," I said, the tears starting to stream down my face. "This is all my fault."

"Nothing's happened yet," Marnie said. "The last time I talked to the FBI agent in charge of the case, he said they were compiling evidence. Just tell him what you know, the people she's come in contact with, and your speculations. They'll sort it out. They're professionals."

"Okay," I said, voice shaky.

When the call ended, I dialed the number for the FBI agent. He seemed interested in talking to me and said he would drive out to Harrogate and meet me in a few hours.

My phone buzzed with a text.

Mace: *Lunch?*

It came with a picture of Henry holding a drawing of pizza. I smiled and wiped my face.

On the way upstairs to Mace's office, I heard a familiar laugh. Anke. I looked around wildly then found her in one of the conference rooms. Adrian was with her.

"Darling!" she called and waved. "Have you recovered from the conference? It was something else, wasn't it?"

Adrian leaned back in his chair. "We're just going over some potential accounts," he told me.

"Okay." I looked between them. Nothing seemed amiss. "I'm going to have lunch with your brother. You want to come?" I asked him, still feeling suspicious.

"Nah, we're just going to finish this," he replied.

"Go along to lunch," Anke said. "Adrian and I will order in here."

Something about them felt off. But surely Anke wouldn't be going after Adrian? He was barely out of high school, and he didn't run a company. I didn't think he even had money. He still lived at home.

I chewed on my lip as I walked into Mace's office. Henry ran to greet me, and Mace stood up, smiling warmly at me. My heart ached. Would he still want me when my house of cards, more crappily built than my tiny house, came crashing down?

We ate pizza at a small shop on the second floor of one of the many old historic buildings.

"Is the train coming?" Henry asked excitedly.

"Not until this evening," Mace told him. "Sit down and eat. You like pizza."

"It's good pizza, Henry," I told him.

"Not as good as yours," he said.

The FBI agent texted me as we finished lunch. He was in Harrogate and wanted to meet in ten minutes.

"I'll meet you guys at the office," I told Mace as we walked out of the restaurant. "I need to run by the store."

"I can drop you off," he offered.

"No thanks!" I said brightly. "I'll just walk. It's a nice day."

"I'll see you later," he said, pulling me close and kissing me.

I pretended like I was walking to Ida's General Store then cut to a side street to the café where the agent wanted to meet me. He was standing outside. He was a tall square-jawed dark-haired man who looked like every stereotypical Hollywood FBI agent.

"Detective Donley," he introduced himself when I walked up. "You're Josie?"

I nodded. We sat at a table outside, and he took out a laptop and pulled up a document.

"Can you tell me when you first met Anke?" he asked.

I told Agent Donley everything in great detail, how I had met her at a club, how effortless she seemed, how she always seemed to have all this money, how we took trips, how slowly she stopped paying upfront and started having me front the money.

"She would always pay me back," I said, starting to cry. "Until she didn't."

"I see you filed a police report," he said.

"They said it was a civil matter," I said, hiccupping. "And refused to pursue it."

"This is more than a civil matter," Agent Donley said. "Anke has defrauded various banks in Europe and America out of millions of dollars."

"She has another scheme," I told him.

"Yes, her position at Svensson PharmaTech," he said.

"I don't know what she's up to. I think she's trying to convince one of the Svensson brothers to marry her or be her sugar daddy or something," I told the FBI agent.

Agent Donley snorted. "Well don't tip her off. If she's there thinking she's going to be the next Mrs. Svensson, it will be easier to nab her."

"She does have a tendency to drop off the radar," I warned him. I twisted my tissue. "There is one more thing." I described seeing Anke talking with Payslee's lawyer and the well-off older couple.

"Hmm," he said. "I'll look into that. They may be potential investors of some kind. Or it could be some sort of other scam."

I gave him the name of the restaurant and the time I had seen them.

"Here's my card," he said when we got up to leave.

"What am I going to do?" I asked, trying not to cry.

The FBI agent looked at me sympathetically. "Cheer up," he said. "To be perfectly frank, you probably won't get your money back. But Anke is definitely going to jail. She did an astounding amount of illegal activity for someone so young."

I looked down at my shoes. The FBI agent pulled a piece of saltwater taffy out of his pocket and handed it to me.

"The elderly woman at the general store gave this to me. I'm not a big sweets person, but maybe this will cheer you up. She also wrote her number on it and told me to call her."

I tipped my head back and laughed. "Ida is a character."

"These small towns are great, aren't they?" Agent Donley said with a grin and patted my shoulder. "Just let me know if anything changes or she moves. Also, don't talk about this with anyone. I don't want to tip off Anke. Especially in a small town, word gets around."

I mimed zipping my lips. "I won't say anything," I assured him.

On my way back to Svensson PharmaTech, I felt lighter than I had in weeks. The authorities were taking care of Anke. I had done my part. I knew Agent Donley had said not to talk to anyone, but I felt like I needed to come clean to Mace. It was his company, and he should know. I walked into his office, fully intending to tell him. But he wasn't there.

"He left already," Anke said. She and Adrian were in her office.

"It was really weird," Adrian said. "Usually he doesn't leave that early. But now we have the office to ourselves." He smiled at Anke.

"Oh," I said. "Okay."

"What did you want to talk to him about?" Anke asked, blinking up at me.

"Just about the website," I lied.

She looked at me assessingly. "I see."

I stayed late at the office, working on the pitch presentation for the landowners of the parcels that the Svenssons needed in order to move the factory. I lost track of time and didn't get back to the Svensson estate until after dinner. I was excited about the presentation. It was going to be very convincing, I hoped.

The house was dark when I came back. I wondered what had happened with Mace. Maybe it was a family emergency?

I half expected him to come knock on the tiny house door, but he didn't.

Where was he? I wondered as I curled up alone in the loft of my tiny house.

CHAPTER 60

Mace

Henry wouldn't stop talking about the trains after we left the pizza restaurant.

"You're obsessed with them, aren't you?" I asked him.

"Train! Train!" he chanted, twisting in his car seat.

Remembering what Josie had said about spending time with Henry and letting his energy out, I took him to the train park. I pretended to chase him around the locomotives as he shrieked.

We drove back late to Svensson PharmaTech. As I cut back through town to the road that led up the hill to my company's offices, that was when I saw it—Josie and a tall, handsome man. She was laughing at some joke he told her. He even gave her a piece of candy. She was the flirty, sensual woman who had made me fall in love with her. I gripped the steering wheel, resisting the urge to swing the car around, run over there, and beat the man to a pulp.

Set a good example for Henry, I ordered myself and kept driving.

So that was what it had been about. *That* was why she didn't say she loved me. *That* was why she said she wasn't good enough for me. She had been cheating on me this whole time. My whole body was tense when I pulled into the parking lot. I dragged Henry upstairs and sat at my desk, staring at the wall.

What am I going to do? My whole world was crashing down. *How could she do this to me?*

The whole office reminded me of her. We had made love on that desk. There was the couch that she put all that stuff on. There was the window she broke. I could still smell the smoke from the fire she had started. I opened the drawer of my desk and was confronted with a small container of saltwater taffy.

"I can't be here anymore," I muttered. I grabbed Henry by the arm. "Pack up your crayons," I ordered him.

"I want to stay!" he protested. "When is Josie coming back?"

"Never," I spat. "She is never coming back."

Henry did not like that answer, and he started wailing. Garrett left his office and stalked across the hall.

"Why is he yelling like that?"

"I don't want to go!" Henry cried.

"I'm leaving," I told Garrett.

"Leaving where? What are you talking about? Have you finally lost your mind?" he exclaimed.

"I'm done," I said. "I'm just done." I picked up Henry and all his crayons and walked out.

"You forgot your jacket," Garrett called after me. Everything sounded fuzzy, and I didn't feel like I was quite there. I heard Garrett swear.

I was on autopilot on the drive home. I took Henry up to the clubroom with me. I pulled out a bottle of whiskey while he spun the antique globe. I knew he would probably break it, but I didn't care. Part of me wanted him to just destroy the whole house.

Eventually Henry wandered off. I sat in the chair, staring out the window. It grew dark. Josie didn't return. Was she with him? When had she met him?

I was furious and heartbroken. I sat in the pitch-dark room. I saw a dark figure creep across the yard, and the tiny house lights turned on. She must have been with him. That was why she stayed out so late. Was that why she had stayed out late the past few weeks? How long had this been going on?

It was after midnight when the door to the clubroom cracked open and Hunter walked in.

"Henry said you were possessed by a zombie," Hunter said, coming over to me.

"Josie's cheating on me," I rasped.

"Uh-huh." My older brother collected the bottle and the glass.

"She is!" I insisted.

"She doesn't really seem like the type," he said.

"I saw her; she was with another man."

"Is that what this was about?" I heard Garrett snap from the doorway. "You just spiral into the worst possible scenario. Did you see her kiss him, stick her hands down his pants?"

"Don't be crass!" Hunter scolded.

Garrett ignored him and scoffed, "Is this like that time you were convinced you had smallpox but really you were just so stressed you gave yourself hives?"

"She was laughing with him, and he gave her a piece of candy!" I yelled at my brother.

"Candy? Like a euphemism for a sexual favor?" Hunter asked.

"No, he gave her a piece of saltwater taffy," I said.

"Let me get this straight," Garrett said, his mouth quirking. "You saw Josie with a guy on the street, and she was being her usual Josie self, laughing and being friendly and eating candy."

"But she lied and said she was going to the store," I insisted.

"Maybe she went to the store and then met this guy," Hunter said in a patronizing tone. "He could be a friend from work."

"He doesn't work for me!" I yelled at my brother.

"We really don't seem to have a lot of information here," Hunter commented to Garrett.

"We have one piece of information," Garrett retorted. "Mace is well-known for being an overreactive, worst-case-scenario type of person. The canned food always has botulism. It's always about to not just rain but catastrophically flood. You saw something you have no context for, threw away everything you knew about Josie, then refused to act like a grown adult man and instead came in here to drink and sulk."

"I am not sulking," I said, glowering at my brothers. They really were the worst.

"This sounds like a classic case of Mace overreacting," Garrett said, turning to Hunter.

"Except—" We turned to the door. Greg was standing there, a dark look on his face. He walked in. "Except this time, Mace is not overreacting."

"I'm not?" I asked, shocked.

"No," Greg replied, pouring himself a drink. "This time you are actually underreacting." He took a sip of the scotch. "It's worse. It's so much worse than he ever imagined."

CHAPTER 61

Josie

I left early the next morning. Mace clearly wanted some space.

I went to a cute little coffee shop and sipped a hot chocolate while I made a few edits to the presentation. I hoped it was enough to convince the property owners to sell to Mace and his brothers. I also tried to do some research into the couple I had seen with Anke but didn't find anything. I had nothing to go off of.

On my way to the PharmaTech offices, I stopped by Ida's General Store to pick up some snacks.

"I have mochi balls," Ida announced when I walked in. "Made locally. It's green tea ice cream wrapped in a Japanese sweet rice paste. Dottie's granddaughter has started making desserts. She's inspired by Chloe and the Grey Dove Bistro."

"Aren't we all?" I replied.

"Great news on the property front," Ida said as I brought my snacks to the register. "I convinced everyone to come to the meeting. Believe it or not, they said they were open to it. I talked you up," she said proudly. "Bert said he wouldn't mind selling if it meant keeping the green space. The rest of those old fools seem to think they're going to take their little dilapidated parcels with them to the great beyond." She snorted. "I know you'll set them straight. Especially my sister."

"Thank you so much," I said to Ida.

"It's next Tuesday," she said, "at the bingo hall. Harrogate is on the rise, but we need to be better. We need more young people here, and they don't want to have a bunch of vacant lots and burned-out buildings around. No one wants to raise their kids in a place like that."

"Harrogate is nice," I protested.

"It could be better," Ida sniffed. "You should have seen it in its heyday. It was something else. I was talking to this couple about it. His father was from Harrogate, worked at the chocolate factory. He and his wife are trying to adopt. They're an older couple."

"Uh-huh." Ida sure did like to talk my ear off.

"I mean, they seemed pretty old to be adopting, just between us," Ida continued, "but they said they had an almost-five-year-old boy they were going to take. So props to them for looking at an older child. They said he was healthy, blond, gray eyed. Said he was real cute. They were so excited! They had a GoFundMe up. They convinced a bunch of people from their church to donate." She pulled up a page on her phone. "Would you look at that?" she exclaimed, shoving the phone in my face. "Eighty thousand

"Time for you to finally be thrown out," she said.

"Mace, listen to me. I have to tell you—"

"Is it about Anke and the fact that she was involved in a plot to sell my little brother to a rich infertile couple? Or was it the fact that she manipulated Adrian into handing over hundreds of thousands of dollars to her. Or was it the fact that you knew that she was dangerous, knew that she was a scam artist, and let her waltz around here, setting her traps and wreaking havoc on my company and my family."

"I can explain. I just—" I looked wildly around. "She scammed me too—"

"Then why didn't you say anything, Josie?" he asked, his mouth a thin, angry line. "You lied to me."

"I didn't lie," I said in a small voice. "I just didn't tell the truth." I fought back the tears. "Is Henry okay?"

Mace's eyes narrowed. "Henry is safe," he said. "No thanks to you."

"I am so sorry," I cried, the tears spilling down my face.

Tara had a triumphant look on her face. "I told you she was no good," she said to Mace.

"The worst of it is," Mace said to me, "I trusted you. I loved you. I let you around my family. But that's my fault. You told me you were a terrible, no good, untrustworthy person. And you were right."

"I am so sorry," I begged. "I can make it up to you, I—"

"I don't want to hear it," Mace interrupted. "I heard all about how you and Anke were two peas in a pod. It shouldn't surprise anyone why you two got along so well. You're the same conniving, manipulative person."

"I love you," I said. But the words sounded hollow to my ears.

"No, you don't," he sneered.

dollars over their goal. Isn't that something? I should start a GoFundMe."

"Wait," I said, grabbing the phone. I zoomed into the picture. It was the couple. The ones who had the meeting with Anke and Payslee's lawyer.

"I have to go!" I said, running out of the store.

"But your snacks!" Ida called after me.

"I'll come back for them!"

I ran to the car and texted the Agent Donley the link to the GoFundMe page. Then I raced to PharmaTech. I had to tell Mace about this. Henry could be in danger. I knew exactly what Anke was up to. She was trying to sell Henry to that couple. Somehow she had convinced Payslee that it was a good idea and she could make way more money than Hunter would ever bribe her with. With the GoFundMe plus whatever money the rich couple had, Anke would be walking away with a tidy sum.

I parked crookedly in one of the visitors' spots and sprinted into the building. I was huffing and puffing and sweaty when I stumbled into his office. Mace was sitting at his desk, writing in a notebook.

"There she is," he remarked, not looking up. It was not said in a playful manner. I stopped short.

When he finally raised his head, Mace's expression was menacing. He steepled his hands in front of his face. I looked over at the assistant's office. Anke wasn't there.

"I need to tell you something," I urged.

"I bet you do." His face was cold.

"Where's Henry? It's important!" I pleaded.

Tara walked in. "Good morning," she said brightly. She turned to sneer at me. "Is it that time already?"

"What time?" I asked, confused.

I sobbed as Tara looked on. Having her witness my fall to rock bottom just made it so much more painful.

"Shall I have security escort her out?" Tara asked, her voice dripping with satisfaction.

"No," Mace barked. "Tara, Josie lied by omission, but you flat-out lied. Why did you recommend Anke come work here?"

"I—" she stammered, and I looked up at her.

"You knew that letter was a forgery," Mace continued.

"No, I didn't—"

"Yes, you did," Garrett said, walking in. "You said that you checked with the Holbrooks. A perusal of your phone records indicated that you did talk to one of the Holbrook secretaries that you knew. However, I talked to her last night. She said she told you she had no idea who Anke was. And you told Mace to hire her anyway."

"You were trying to get me fired!" I screeched at Tara.

"She said she knew Josie," Tara protested. "I was just trying to show everyone the truth."

"By bringing someone who committed multiple felonies into this office?" Garrett scoffed.

"I was trying to save you," she pleaded with Mace. "Josie had you under her spell. I was trying to expose her."

"Well, congratulations, you did," Mace said. Tara seemed to breathe a sigh of relief. But it was short-lived. "You're both fired," Mace said. "Turn in your electronics. Your things have already been packed. The boxes are at the reception desk."

I was numb as I did the walk of shame through the office. It was crawling with FBI agents.

In the lobby, Agent Donley was talking to the receptionist.

"Did you get my message?" I asked tearfully.

He nodded. "We already found the couple last night. They are in custody along with the lawyer. If you hear anything from Anke, or Payslee for that matter, please let us know. They have both disappeared."

Disappeared? That didn't sound good. But I had just been fired and had bigger problems than Anke to consume my thoughts. I needed to figure out where I was going to go.

Tara took her box and stomped out of the office. I followed slowly behind her with my own. The only things it held were the shirt that I had worn on my first day and two jars of candy.

I sobbed as Tara looked on. Having her witness my fall to rock bottom just made it so much more painful.

"Shall I have security escort her out?" Tara asked, her voice dripping with satisfaction.

"No," Mace barked. "Tara, Josie lied by omission, but you flat-out lied. Why did you recommend Anke come work here?"

"I—" she stammered, and I looked up at her.

"You knew that letter was a forgery," Mace continued.

"No, I didn't—"

"Yes, you did," Garrett said, walking in. "You said that you checked with the Holbrooks. A perusal of your phone records indicated that you did talk to one of the Holbrook secretaries that you knew. However, I talked to her last night. She said she told you she had no idea who Anke was. And you told Mace to hire her anyway."

"You were trying to get me fired!" I screeched at Tara.

"She said she knew Josie," Tara protested. "I was just trying to show everyone the truth."

"By bringing someone who committed multiple felonies into this office?" Garrett scoffed.

"I was trying to save you," she pleaded with Mace. "Josie had you under her spell. I was trying to expose her."

"Well, congratulations, you did," Mace said. Tara seemed to breathe a sigh of relief. But it was short-lived. "You're both fired," Mace said. "Turn in your electronics. Your things have already been packed. The boxes are at the reception desk."

I was numb as I did the walk of shame through the office. It was crawling with FBI agents.

In the lobby, Agent Donley was talking to the receptionist.

"Did you get my message?" I asked tearfully.

He nodded. "We already found the couple last night. They are in custody along with the lawyer. If you hear anything from Anke, or Payslee for that matter, please let us know. They have both disappeared."

Disappeared? That didn't sound good. But I had just been fired and had bigger problems than Anke to consume my thoughts. I needed to figure out where I was going to go.

Tara took her box and stomped out of the office. I followed slowly behind her with my own. The only things it held were the shirt that I had worn on my first day and two jars of candy.

CHAPTER 62

Mace

After instructing Remy to hook up Josie's tiny house and pack up her things, I sat back at my chair, feeling numb.

The FBI agent in charge knocked on my door and came into my office. "We have all of the electronics Anke used and the ones your brother used to transfer the money. We have a forensics team looking at where she sent it."

"Thank you," I told him.

I sat at my desk after he left, staring at the opening where the window used to be. Garrett appeared in my field of view, and I shook off the cobweb feeling.

"How was Adrian able to transfer half a million dollars with no oversight?" I asked Garrett, proud of myself for how calm I sounded.

Garrett's jaw popped as he clenched it. "He was a Svensson, and the bank just *authorized* the payment."

There was a knock on the door. Two men in coveralls stood there.

"We're here to fix that," they said, pointing to the window. I nodded at them.

"Talk in my office?" Garrett asked. I followed him wordlessly across the hall.

I stood at the door, watching as the repairmen carefully lifted the heavy piece of glass and fitted it in the opening.

"I talked to the bank," Garrett said. "Anke sent it to an account in London and had it transferred from there to somewhere in Asia, it seems. Depending on where it is, we should be able to recover some of the funds."

"I don't even care about the money," I said. "I just don't understand why everyone has *lost their fucking minds*!" I wanted to pick up a chair and throw it, but I knew Garrett would be mad if I broke a window in his office.

"*Mace?*"

I whirled around. "Adrian," I spat. My younger brother shrank back. He reminded me of me when I was younger and my father would fly into a rage. I didn't want my little brothers to be afraid of me. I went to Adrian and pulled him into a hug. "It's just money," I told him. "I just don't want to lose you. Anke is dangerous. She could have really hurt you. That's why I'm upset. It's not the money."

"*I'm* upset about the money," Garrett retorted. "What were you thinking, Adrian? Half a million dollars to some random account?"

"I'm sorry! I don't know what's wrong with me." He sat down on the sofa. "You should fire me."

"I'm not firing my little brother," I said, patting his head.

"But you fired Josie," he said sadly. "It wasn't her fault. It was my fault."

"All of this would have been avoided if she had just come clean," I said.

"Yeah, but you don't know what Anke is like," Adrian said. "It was like she had me under a spell."

"You can't just use that as an excuse," Garrett snapped.

"It will never happen again," Adrian promised.

"It better not," Garrett told him. "Whatever the bank doesn't recover, you're going to work to pay back. Blood, sweat, and tears."

"Absolutely," Adrian said.

"You will start by getting lunch," Garrett said.

An hour later, Adrian was organizing the supply closet. He had ordered me a sandwich, but it sat untouched on my desk. The window was fixed. It was like Josie had never been there. I wondered if I had been too harsh. I was willing to give Adrian another chance, after all.

But Adrian is my brother. And he's not even twenty. He's just a kid. Josie should have known better.

I shook off the regret. It was 1:15, and I had a conference call.

I spent the rest of the day distracting myself with work. At 3:20 I left the office. My younger brothers would be back from school, and I wanted to spend time with them. It was unnerving that Anke had so easily found a couple to basically buy one of my brothers. I did have a lot of brothers, but I wouldn't trade a single one away.

I made Adrian come home with me. Payslee and Anke were still at large. The FBI hadn't found them, and Payslee's lawyer didn't know where either of them were. I had the whole house on lockdown. Several of my other brothers had come into town to make sure the kids didn't wander off. They were all cooped up inside and restless.

"Is Josie coming back?" Isaac asked when he saw me.

"No," I told him.

"Seriously? I need her to help me with a presentation!"

"She promised she would help me make a logo for my business," Otto whined.

"What business?" I asked him. "You're twelve."

"I'm making T-shirt designs to sell online," Otto boasted.

"What?"

Weston shrugged from his spot on the couch. "Kid's an entrepreneur."

"What's for dinner?" Theo whined. "I'm hungry."

"Josie was going to make pizza tonight. She promised," Billy said, looking at me, annoyed.

"Well she's not here, is she? And she's not coming back, so find something else to eat," I barked.

"I don't see why," Isaac persisted. "It was Adrian's fault."

"It wasn't Adrian's fault," I said.

"I mean, it kind of was Adrian's fault," Archer said. He was eating a muffin and sharing pieces of it with several of the kids.

"Did you bring that back from Chloe?" I asked.

"No, actually Josie made this," he said. "It's really good. She said they were from some health-food recipe someone had posted online. She modified it because she said applesauce was no substitute for butter. But hey, it's got fiber and like half a zucchini in a single muffin. You can't even taste it. You should try it. It's good," he said, holding out a piece.

I ignored my twin. "I don't want Adrian being blamed," I told my brothers. "Anke is the person at fault."

"Then why isn't Josie here?" Arlo shot back.

"I don't want to hear anything more about it!" I yelled at them. "We'll have baked chicken and steamed vegetables for dinner."

"I want pizza!" Henry screeched.

I left them to their complaining. My suit suddenly felt constricting, and I needed a drink. I looked out of the large windows of the clubroom over to the spot where Josie's tiny house used to be.

"This sucks," I said to the glass.

The door opened, and one of my brothers walked in. "I'll start dinner in a little bit," I said, not turning around.

"I don't see how," Hunter said, taking my glass away from me. "The chicken's all frozen."

"I need that," I said, halfheartedly fighting him for the glass.

"You need to go find Josie," he countered.

"She almost got Henry kidnapped!" I shouted.

"You're the one who said Anke was to blame. Josie's also a victim. She lost eighty thousand dollars to Anke," Hunter said.

"She showed bad judgment," I snarled.

Hunter sighed and took a sip from the glass. "I know she did, but trust me, from someone who's been in her position, she is very, very sorry."

"I can't—"

"Let me be perfectly blunt with you," Hunter said sharply.

"Aren't you always?" I joked.

"No. Quite often I temper my thoughts because I know your weak little minds can't handle it."

I glared at him.

Hunter ignored me. "Let's look at the facts. You have a weirdly large family, personality quirks that would send most sane women running, and enough money to attract all the crazy ones. You don't date. You don't play the field, yet someone basically perfect just fell in your lap. You think you're going to find someone else just like her but who doesn't have a checkered past? You won't. Never mind the fact that you grew up in a polygamist cult in the middle of the desert."

I scowled.

"Josie is the best you're ever going to do," Hunter said. "In these types of situations, pride is not your friend. If you don't go after her, you will regret it every day of your life. Trust me. And when you find her, get on your knees and beg her to come back."

CHAPTER 63

Josie

When I returned to the Svenssons' estate house, my tiny house was already parked out front and hitched up to my truck. Sobbing, I moved my bag and box to the front seat of the old truck.

"I'm so stupid," I whispered to myself. How could I let this happen?

I didn't know where I was going to go. In a daze, I trundled down the driveway. Thunder boomed. It was going to rain soon. I looked up at the hole in the roof of the truck.

"Mace put that hole there," I sobbed.

My phone rang, and I put it on speaker phone. I hoped I didn't get a ticket. "I can't talk long," I said, my voice shaking with emotion.

"Aww, Josie." Marnie's voice came out of the phone.

"Josie, what happened?" Willow asked.

"I screwed up!" I said, choking out another round of sobs. "He fired me and kicked me out."

Marnie said sympathetically, "It seems like an overreaction. The Svenssons were furious. Just give them a bit to calm down. You didn't do anything wrong. You even went to the FBI."

"I lied, and I let Anke around them," I sniffled. "She was going to kidnap Henry."

"Do you know where she is?" Willow asked.

"No and I never want to see her again. She ruined everything good in my life."

"Look," Willow said. "There's a tiny house village about an hour's drive east. You remember Homer? I told him you were coming. He says they have a spot for you to park the house."

"Thanks," I told Willow. "I have to go. I'm not supposed to use the phone and drive."

I hung up, and my phone beeped. I set Google Maps to the address Willow had given me. But it had barely calculated the route before the battery died.

"*Crap!*"

I had been relying on the phone Mace had given me since it was brand-new and could run for a day on one battery charge. My old phone could not. And of course the ancient truck had nowhere to plug in an adaptor.

"Okay, Josie," I pep-talked myself. The sky was dark overhead, and thunder rolled. "The village is... that way. I think." After driving for over an hour, I didn't find it.

I pulled into a gas station.

"Oh no," the attendant said when I told her the address. "That's the opposite direction. You need to go back through Harrogate and keep driving east."

"Thanks," I said dejectedly. I bought a few gallons of gas then slumped in the truck.

"Why does this have to happen to me? Why?" I whispered, banging my head on the steering wheel. I grabbed a handful of candy from the jar, trying to forget about all the times I had teased Mace about eating my candy.

My heart ached from missing him. I hated myself for hurting him. The cold anger on his face when he had looked at me and said I was fired was going to haunt me every night for the rest of my life.

My nose ran as I headed back toward Harrogate. I knew I looked like a wreck. I was an ugly crier on a good day, and I had been crying nonstop since this morning. My face was puffy and swollen. I rolled down the window to bring the cold air in. All I got was a face full of dirty water from the windshield.

"I hate my life!" I screamed as I drove at a crawl down the road. The tiny house was swerving dangerously, like there was something heavy on top of it. Maybe the tiny house would actually kill me. But I didn't want it to flip over. Then I would be a jobless, *homeless* disgrace.

As I drove, a car came my direction and blinked its headlights at me.

"What the—my lights *are* on! Why is everyone out to get me?" I screeched.

As the car passed, I looked out the window to yell at the driver, and I jerked the wheel in surprise. "Mace?"

"Pull over!" he called out to me. I navigated the truck and tiny house to a wide shoulder on the road and sat there, the spray from the rain coming into my car through the window and dripping from the plastic garbage sack I'd stuffed in the hole in the roof. I half wondered if I was hallucinating. The only thing I'd had to eat that day was candy. Maybe my sweet tooth was about to do me in.

But Mace was very real as he ran up to the driver's side of the truck and opened the door.

"What are you doing here?" I asked. I wanted to cry, but I was so exhausted. Mace pulled me out of the car, bundling me in his arms.

"You're freezing," he said.

"Why did you come find me?" I asked and sneezed pathetically.

"Come into my car. You're going to get pneumonia. You shouldn't even be driving this truck. You could have had a wreck and died," he said, ushering me to his car.

As I sat in his car and sipped the water he'd given me, I stared out the front windshield at the back of my tiny house.

"I am so sorry, Mace," I said, turning to him.

"No, I'm the one who's sorry," he said.

This time I did start crying. "Stop being so perfect! I screwed up," I cried.

"Yes, but not as bad as Adrian, and I didn't fire him." Mace swept a hand through my tangled, wet hair.

"I'm a mess," I said.

"Yeah, but it's adorable," he said with a smile.

"No," I shook my head. "I'm really a mess." I took a deep breath. Time to come clean. "Anke cost me all of my life savings. She convinced me to pay for all our expensive stuff like hotels and her clothes and fancy restaurants. I went along with it because I wanted to finally, for once, live a glamourous life. At the end of it all, I had maxed out all of my credit cards, and I had a *lot* of credit cards. I had to start paying off the debt, and I used up my life savings just to keep the credit card companies from taking me to court. I'm still up to my tits in debt."

"I could have helped you," Mace said, stroking my arm. "That's what family does—we help each other."

"I'm not after you for your money," I snapped. "I really like you. In fact I think I love you. That's why you really should find someone better than me. I love you, but I don't deserve you. You are a good man. I'm a mess."

"But was it real?" Mace insisted.

"What?" I was confused.

"I don't know, all of it—being with my brothers, with me, going out, joking. Was it real?"

"Of course it was real!" I said, insulted he would think I would fake that.

"Then it will be okay," Mace insisted. "Henry's fine. Adrian will hopefully be fine if I can keep Garrett from throwing him down a trash chute or something. I told you I didn't want to lose my family." I nodded, and he stroked my cheek. "You're part of my family. I don't want to lose you."

"I'm going to screw up," I said. "I always screw up everything. I don't want to mess you up."

"Josie," Mace said. He sounded a bit exasperated. "Have you met my family? I think I'm already messed up. But you make me less messed up. Just come home. I miss you. Also my brothers miss you, and I think there will be a *Lord of the Flies* style revolt if I show up without you. So either we're both going to wherever you were going to take that horrible little tiny house, or you have to come back with me."

The look on his face was so open. I couldn't help but smile, and Mace leaned in to kiss me. He pushed me back into the seat. "I love you, Josie," he murmured as he broke the kiss.

"I love you, Mace," I whispered.

Motion caught my attention, and I looked past his shoulder. The door to the tiny house shook, then the lock popped, and the door opened.

"What the—" Mace turned around, and we gaped as Anke shut the door, saw us in the car watching, then sprinted to the pickup truck cab.

"My purse is in there!" I shrieked.

"And apparently your keys are too," Mace remarked as the truck roared to life, and the tiny house groaned as Anke took off down the road.

"She's stealing my house! Where's your phone? I'm calling the police!" I hollered.

"There's no need," Mace said.

"She'll get away," I insisted as Mace drove after Anke.

"No, she won't," he said. "Look." He pointed up ahead. I could see flashing lights in the distance. "The FBI set up roadblocks on the main roads leading into and out of Harrogate to try and catch Anke and Payslee."

Anke saw the roadblock, but I knew from experience that there was no way she was going to turn the tiny house around on the highway. Instead she gunned the engine.

"She's going to ram them," I gasped.

"She can try," Mace said grimly.

There was a pop and a screech. "They shredded her tires," Mace said. Sparks flew as the axles on the truck and the tiny house trailer scraped against the asphalt.

"You mean they shredded my tires," I groaned.

CHAPTER 64

Mace

"I can't believe they confiscated my house!" Josie complained when we returned home from giving our statements at the police station. "All my worldly possessions were in there."

"Not everything," I said, nuzzling her neck. "I still have your shelf bra and your shoes."

"As hot as that was, I can't make dinner in that outfit," Josie said.

"All your conference clothes are here too," I offered.

"Are any of my yoga pants here? Or my comfy T-shirts?" Josie asked. "No. Why the FBI needs all of that is beyond me. Where do they even store a tiny house? And they have my purse! My driver's license is in there. And all my candy."

"Your priorities seem a little out of whack," I told her.

"Josie!" my little brothers yelled when we walked into the kitchen.

"We have everything chopped for pizza," Henry said proudly.

"And we took the extra dough you made out of the freezer," Adrian said.

"Oh, Adrian, I'm sorry," Josie said, hugging him. "I never should have let Anke near you. She hinted that she was after a Svensson brother, but—"

"You just thought it was one of the awesome ones and not one who has no common sense and can barely function in society?" Archer interjected from his spot at the large island.

"Stop being mean to Adrian," I told him, "or I can scrounge up that vegan bread, and you can eat that for dinner."

"Is that still around?" Josie asked, grimacing. "I thought we threw that away."

I watched as Josie washed her hands and started making pizzas. Her clothes were kind of wrinkled, and her hair was frizzy from the rain and then air drying in the Harrogate police station. She was messy and amazing.

Hunter came and stood beside me. "I told you so."

"Ever think about taking your own advice?" I asked him.

He scowled. The doorbell rang, and Otis and Peyton raced to answer it. "The mayor is here!" they exclaimed, racing back into the kitchen.

"Mayor Barry?" I asked.

"No, the pretty one!"

Hunter's scowl got even deeper.

"Something smells good," Meg said as she entered the kitchen.

"I'm making pizza," Josie replied, waving a floury hand.

"Stay for dinner?" I offered. "There's plenty of food."

"Is there?" Archer asked.

"You can have some of Hunter's pizza," Garrett said casually.

You could freeze something with the look Hunter shot Garrett.

"I came by to bring you your purse," Meg said, holding out Josie's bag.

"Did you get her tiny house out?" I asked Meg.

"Unfortunately, the FBI is impounding it."

"What are they going to do with a tiny house?" Archer mused.

"Agent Donley is probably going to take his love interest there," Josie said as she rolled out the dough.

Meg laughed. "He is quite attractive, isn't he? He has that whole dangerous-yet-protective FBI aura going on."

Garrett was struggling to maintain a straight face, and Hunter was quietly dying of unrequited love beside me.

"I think I'll take my hot blond guy though," Josie said, winking at me.

Meg leveled her gaze at Hunter. "I suppose blonds do have more fun."

CHAPTER 65

Josie

I wondered what was going on with Meg and Hunter. She seemed a lot more relaxed with a glass of wine in her at dinner. I might have to drag her out to a bar one night and make her spill. I loved a good story. From the way Garrett was looking between the two of them, he must have thought there was something there too. If he was going to push those two together, or back together, whatever the case may be, I wanted in.

But first I needed to fix my own love life.

"I thought Mace said he forgave you," Willow said as we bounced along in the school bus. One of Mace's brothers had commandeered my car, and Remy was nice enough to chauffeur.

"He did, but he's such a sweetheart, and I still haven't forgiven myself. Hopeful this will fully redeem me. I also don't want his brothers to think badly of me."

"I thought you were going to be doing some work with Weston and Blade though, right?" Willow asked. "So they can't think you're that bad."

"I need to do this for me," I reiterated.

"And me," Adrian said, piping up from a seat behind us.

"Did they recover the money?" Willow asked.

"Apparently Anke's trying to include the return of the money in a plea deal," I explained.

"She always has a scheme going," Willow said, shaking her head.

"It doesn't matter. My brothers think I'm dumb. I should have known better," Adrian said dejectedly. "If Josie needs to redeem herself by convincing all of Ida's crazy old friends to sell their property, then I want some of that goodwill to run my way."

"No promises," I warned. Adrian had snagged my presentation off the PharmaTech servers. I was feeling confident when we walked into the bingo hall.

"You're here!" Ida exclaimed, hugging me. "Art brought cider, and I brought snacks and wine. They're nice and marinated for you."

"I hope not too much. I need them to actually remember the presentation," I joked.

"Mrs. Ida." Remy greeted the elderly woman with a big hug then headed off to fill up a plate with cheese and fruit.

"Now there's a man!" Ida said.

"What about Bert?"

"Oh, lassie, I'm just looking. He's too young for me. Couldn't keep up! Speak of keeping up"—her voice went into a stage whisper—"I saw the car chase on TV. So much drama for Harrogate! It was on the national news and everything."

"I hope it wasn't too salacious," I said with a grimace. "There is such a thing as bad publicity."

"Can we get this show on the road?" complained a tiny older woman wearing a neat suit.

"Judge Edna, also known as my sister," Ida said, rolling her eyes. "We're waiting on the deputy mayor."

"I'm here," Meg said. She shook my hand. "As much as I like fucking with Hunter, we should try and come to a resolution."

Ida elbowed me as Meg went off to shake hands with the judge and other attendees. "Fucking Hunter, eh?"

"You have a filthy mind," I told her and walked to the front of the room to start the presentation. There was one word on the screen.

Heritage.

"Harrogate's heritage is fundamentally about working people," I began. A picture of smiling factory workers from decades ago flashed up. "It is also about a heritage of industry and development." A sepia picture of two of the Harrogate men in top hats and waistcoats standing in front of a factory came up on the screen. "Harrogate's architecture reflected these values." I showed a picture of one of the restored buildings on Main Street.

"Even in its heyday, there were still issues." The next slide was a picture of the old town dump, a haze of smog in the air.

"Things changed. Factories closed," I continued and flipped to an image of the closed chocolate factory.

"New families moved in, and the dump was turned into a new research complex with factories and jobs for a new type of resident." There was a drone picture of the Svensson

PharmaTech facility. "And this, too, is part of Harrogate's heritage." I clicked to the next slide.

"But part of Harrogate's heritage is the land." There was a picture of Mace spinning Henry around on the large meadow where he wanted to build the new facility. "We don't want to lose that either," I told the gathering. "You don't want that, and the Svenssons don't either. They're willing to put non-noxious, light industrial factories, research facilities, and office space in downtown Harrogate. While strides have been made to not just restore Harrogate to its heyday but to surpass it, there's still a number of vacant lots. The Svenssons would like to redevelop those lots, obviously keeping any historical structures," I said, nodding to Meg.

"But they need a large assemblage of land on a rail spur." I put up a satellite photo of the parcels Adrian had outlined. "This is where you come in. The spirit of small towns is working together. I know we all want to preserve the green space. This is a viable solution." A few people were nodding along.

"However, while the Svenssons will buy the land at a fair market value, you can't inflate the price a ridiculous amount," I warned them. "Or they won't go for it, and they'll just build their new factories and facilities on the land they own."

Meg nodded and stood up. "Full disclosure—the city can stall the project, but eventually the woods and meadows will get torn up to make way for the new buildings."

Ida stood up. "I'm selling."

"I'm old," Marty said. "My son says the Svenssons give his company a lot of work—saved them really. I know my son wants me to sell."

"At the presentation a few weeks ago, they mentioned a data center," Ernest said. "Where will that go?"

"We'll find a spot outside of town for that," Adrian said. "Obviously a data center doesn't belong in the middle of town. But the rest of the uses will fit right in."

"Sounds fine by me!" said an older woman with blue tightly permed hair. "My kids don't seem to have any interest in the land. As long as the price is fair. Maybe they could throw in another little park somewhere? I love to take my grandbabies to the train park."

"We will absolutely include some green space," Adrian said. "We'll work with the city on the best location."

Bert smiled. "I'll sell as long as the meadow and the trees are saved. I'm all for it." Several people nodded in agreement. One older man looked pensive.

"Art," Ida warned.

"My distillery," he said. "I was going to build it in that old warehouse on my property."

"Platinum Provisions makes that type of equipment," I said, or I was sure they *could*. "How about they throw in a custom distillery set for you instead?"

"I guess so," he said. "Fine, I'll sell."

"Sis," Ida said.

Judge Edna had a look on her face that I'm sure had hardened criminals shaking before her. "For me it all hinges on the money. I think they need to pay more than whatever the market value is worth," she said.

"They aren't going to pay an exorbitant—"

The judge held up a hand to cut me off. "However, I don't want the money to just go into our pockets and to be frittered away on bird-watching equipment, trinkets, and alcohol." She looked to her sister, Ida. "I propose that for those who are interested, instead of paying us, the money could go into a trust for Harrogate. Some of us in this room who are responsible"—she glared at her sister—"would sit on the board to provide some oversight and to make sure the money's flowing back into the town in the form of job training, investments, aesthetic improvements, and such. Then we could ask the Svenssons to kick in a little bit more money, with the understanding that it goes to make Harrogate a more attractive place."

"That's a fine idea, Your Honor," Remy said. "I think we should go tell them right now. I know all my brothers would be happy to hear it."

CHAPTER 66

Mace

My brothers and I met that evening at the PharmaTech offices. Most people had gone home for the day.

"We need to figure out this factory," Greg said. "We can't just spin our wheels."

Liam pulled up a satellite view on the large screen in my office. "I found a good spot in the next county over. It's on a train line, though it's a different company from the one that runs to PharmaTech."

"It just seems far away from our research facilities," I told him. "It's an hour and a half by car. It's difficult to collaborate."

"But it has a large amount of land," Liam said.

"The city will let us build it here eventually," Garrett said. "Especially if Hunter stays out of those meetings with Meg."

"It's been years," Greg stated. "And she hasn't let up on him. Just locking him in a closet doesn't mean she won't try and block the project at every turn. It would be simplest and quickest to buy this land and build it there."

We heard what sounded like gunfire coming from outside.

"What if that's Payslee?" I yelled and raced to the window. "She's still loose! She could have kidnapped one of our brothers, and there could be a hostage situation outside."

"You are literally the most useless person," Garrett said, pushing me aside and looking down into the parking lot. He sniffed. "It's just a school bus."

"Did you have a school group coming here?" Liam asked.

I stared at the bus. It was painted a familiar green. "It's Remy."

"And it looks like he brought half the town with him," Archer quipped as the doors jerked open and several senior citizens, including Judge Edna, filed out.

"Are they protesting?" Greg demanded as we hurried downstairs. "This is why I want to put the factory somewhere else. You can't have protests going on during business hours."

"This isn't a protest," Josie called out as she scooted around an older woman with a walker and came up to hug me around the waist. "These are all members of the new Harrogate Trust."

"Trust what?" Archer asked.

Josie laughed. "They want you to put the money you're going to pay them in a trust, so they will sell their land on the block with the five-story brick warehouse building by the old rail spur across from the park."

"Remember?" Adrian asked me. He was still a little gun-shy and looked at me slightly worriedly. "We had thought about buying land downtown for factories and facilities."

"It was too expensive," I countered.

"How does this number sound?" The judge handed me a slip of paper.

I handed it to Greg, and he and Garrett mumbled over it. Garrett nodded, and Greg extended his hand.

"Deal," he said, shaking Judge Edna's hand.

"Wonderful. I'm sure us lawyers can figure this all out." Edna looked between Meg and Hunter.

"And the city is okay with selling your parcels?" I asked Meg. She nodded.

"Why are you helping me, I mean us?" Hunter demanded.

"We can lock him back in a closet if you prefer," Garrett said, scooting between Meg and Hunter.

"Because the trust will be a nonprofit for the benefit of the city," Judge Edna said. "It would also be a nice gesture for your company to make up the difference in the tax write-off you get by paying the money to a nonprofit."

"I think that's perfectly reasonable," Greg said.

I was still a bit shocked that Josie had managed to organize all of this.

"The foundation will obviously be reviewing the design choices. We have a board member who is very particular about design," Edna continued.

"You?" I asked. The judge pointed at Josie.

"I'm not on the board," she exclaimed.

"There are three people with sense in this room," Edna stated. "You, me, and the deputy mayor, and no, Ida, I was absolutely not talking about you."

"I can't be the chairwoman," Josie protested.

"Meghan can't. She's the deputy mayor." Edna snorted. "I hear you're unemployed. You're the perfect choice."

"That means Josie will have to be in Harrogate for large amounts of time," I said, a grin spreading over my face. "We approve."

CHAPTER 67

Josie

"I can't believe you managed to do that," Mace said. He had sent his brothers back home, and he and I had returned to his office.

"I felt like I owed you," I told him.

"Don't," he said. "Everything's fine. I overreacted."

"So do you want me to call them all back and say never mind?" I teased.

"No! No," he said in a rush. "This is good."

"I also have something else that I hope will make it up to you," I said.

"You already did more than enough," Mace answered.

I shook my head. "That was the public makeup. Now I have a private one." I flicked off the lights to the office. The only light was from the parking lot below. I undid my skirt, letting it fall to the floor. Then my panties followed.

"You don't have to…" Mace whispered, but he looked like he really wanted me to.

I walked slowly to his desk and perched on it, spreading my legs.

"Shit," Mace groaned.

I undid my blouse slowly and took it off.

"Did you have that on the whole day?" he asked as he gazed hungrily at my breasts, perky from the shelf bra.

"Nah," I told him. "Changed in the bathroom. I don't think the judge would have been impressed if I gave my whole spiel in a shelf bra."

Mace visibly swallowed and unzipped his pants. I touched my nipple, rolling it in my fingers. My other hand trailed up my thigh. I rubbed my hand in the slickness, playing in my opening then bringing it up to my clit.

"I know you wanted to watch me play in my candy jar," I purred, rubbing slow circles on my clit. My breath hitched. Mace looked on, gray eyes dark with lust.

"It feels so good when you stroke me with those big hands as you tease me with your cock," I whispered to him. "Sometimes I play in my candy jar, thinking about you sucking on my tits, my hard pink nipple in your mouth, then you bend me over, your big hard cock teasing me as my hot pussy gets so tight and wet thinking about you. I just stroke myself and tease my clit, wishing it was your cock."

I leaned my head back. The Adam's apple was prominent on Mace's throat, and his body was as tight as a spring as he watched me.

I closed my eyes and moaned. "My pussy gets so hot and wet thinking about you. I want you to bend me over the desk and—"

I shrieked as he grabbed me and kissed me, his mouth crushing mine. His cock rubbed against my clit.

I moaned. "Just like that."

He kissed me, sucking my breasts. I heard him roll on a condom, and he pushed into me. I wrapped my legs around him as he fucked me, his cock rubbing against my clit. Mace kissed my mouth, his tongue tracing my lips, then he moved back down to suck my breasts.

The smell of him enveloped me as his cock filled me. I threw my head back, and he kissed me again, swallowing my cry. His mouth stayed on mine as he fucked me.

"You're mine, Josie," Mace whispered against my mouth. "You're mine to fuck, and you're mine to love."

"I love you, Mace," I told him, my arms around his neck. "I want to be yours forever."

We came together, wrapped in each other's arms.

We had a relaxed, easy rhythm together the next morning.

"How are you?" he asked, planting a kiss on my neck as I was halfway through cracking three dozen eggs for breakfast.

"Nothing like hot office sex," I quipped. "Too bad my tiny house is still impounded. I could go for some hot tiny house sex."

"I think I still have a crick in my neck from the last time," Mace said, rubbing his shoulder. "How about some hot high-end, historically accurate renovated mansion sex instead?"

"You don't have to twist my arm," I said, tilting my head back so he could kiss me. He cupped my face as I held my hand straight out. "Sorry you're doing all the work," I whispered. "My hands are covered in egg."

"I'll always do all the work," he joked.

The kids were antsy at breakfast. Mace wanted them to stay inside because Payslee was still at large. He didn't even want them to go out on the estate grounds.

"I want to go to the park," Henry whined.

"No," Hunter snapped at him over his newspaper. "You're at the table; make polite, civilized chitchat."

The doorbell rang, and ten of the youngest all sprinted to the door, chairs clattering to the floor.

"That is not appropriate behavior!" Hunter yelled as he stood up to go after them. "You all need to march back in there and—"

He stopped short, and we all looked to the doorway as Meghan walked in.

"Sorry to interrupt breakfast," she said.

"Not an interruption at all," Garrett replied, righting one of the chairs. "Have some omelet. There's a free seat next to Hunter."

A tendon jumped in Hunter's neck, but he sat down next to Meghan after making sure the kids fixed their chairs.

"I brought by some paperwork about the land deal and the trust," Meg said as Garrett set a plate of eggs in front of her. "But I also just received a message from Agent Donley. Payslee has been spotted in Pennsylvania. The state troopers there are telling him they have her in custody. He's going down there to take her in. You're home free!"

All through cleaning up after breakfast, Henry chanted, "Park! Park!"

"I'm going to take them out," I told Mace, giving him a quick kiss on the cheek. Henry and Otis cheered.

"Maybe we'll get some frozen yogurt," I told them. "Vegan frozen yogurt," I amended when Mace frowned. "Remember that vegan shop where we first met? They have a vegan frozen yogurt stand."

"That doesn't seem your style," Mace said.

I showed him my candy jars in my purse. "I have a little something to add onto it."

I was relaxed on the drive to the park. Everything was going well. As soon as Meg had given us the news, Mace seemed to completely relax.

"Are you excited to see the train?" I asked Henry and Otis.

"It's coming soon," Otis said. "We have to hurry." I parked the car, then we went to the best spot to watch, according to Otis.

"Here it comes!" Otis yelled as, in the distance, the train chugged down the street.

I was watching the train and not paying attention until a thin, haggard-looking woman jumped out at us. It was Payslee.

"That's my boy!" she yelled.

Henry screamed.

Momma-bear instincts I didn't even know I had reared up. "Stay away from him!" I shouted and swung my bag as hard as I could. It hit Payslee's head with a *thunk*. Payslee fell, and the train, the conductor seeing the commotion, screeched to a halt a few feet away from where Payslee lay knocked out cold on the tracks.

CHAPTER 68

Mace

Henry was clinging to Josie when I arrived at the train park. The train engineer milled around as Otis peppered him with questions.

Susie was on-site loading Payslee into the back of the police car. "The FBI's coming to take her into custody," Susie said, her mouth pursed.

"Are you all right?" I asked my brothers.

"Josie knocked her out, *bam*," Otis said, miming what had happened.

"I don't know what you have in that bag, ma'am," the train engineer said. "But I sure wouldn't want to meet you in a dark alley."

"It's just candy jars," she said with a laugh. "They aren't even broken."

"We make good strong women out here in the rural areas," the engineer said. "You should count yourself lucky, Mr. Svensson." He shook my hand.

Susie gave him the go-ahead to continue on his route, and he climbed up into the cab, blowing the horn as Otis and Henry cheered.

The next few days were spent catching up on work, doing police reports, and trying to nail down the land deal.

"We have to move now," Greg said. "I don't want them to change their minds."

"That's part of why we're having this big Memorial Day cookout," Josie said as she loaded Greg up with boxes of ground beef, hot dogs, and condiments from the car.

"It will foster some goodwill," she said as she followed us into the house with several large boxes of buns.

"You're not going to cook all of this food by yourself, are you?" I asked Josie as I surveyed the boxes in the kitchen.

"Of course she's not!" someone sang out, coming into the kitchen.

"Oh, hey, Chloe," I said, greeting Jack's girlfriend.

"Hey, Chloe?" Josie looked at me, irate. "It's Chloe Barnard, my freaking idol, and you're just like, 'Hey, Chloe, what's up?'"

Chloe ran over to hug her, and Josie burst out crying. "Oh my God, I love you so much! You are an inspiration! I follow you religiously."

Jack walked into the kitchen after his girlfriend. "This is a regular occurrence," he said to me, putting down a huge box of what I assumed from the smell was desserts. "It'll calm down in a second."

"All right, big strong men, I have two carloads of food outside," Chloe said, clapping her hands. "And they're big vehicles, not those prancy little sportscars you boys like to drive. We drive trucks in the Midwest."

"Amen," Josie said.

The driver of the other car, Liam, was standing there, contemplating the packed trunk.

"We had to take out all the seats to fit everything in here," he said as I unwedged a box. It took us a few trips, but we brought everything inside.

"This seems like a lot of work for just two people," I said, surveying the towers of unloaded boxes in the kitchen.

"Wrong answer, dude," Jack said. "Wrong answer." He handed me an apron. "Best get to chopping. Knives are to the left."

"So is the land deal official?" Jack asked as he mixed onions, ground beef, and cheese for extra-special burger patties.

"The foundation is still being formed legally," Greg told him as he sliced onions with neat precision next to me.

"I'm still shocked Josie managed to convince them to sell. I wish I had been there to see your faces!" Jack said with a laugh.

"They were pretty surprised," Josie said, coming by with a large bowl of potato salad to put into one of the fridges.

"I think at this point," Greg said, "all is more than forgiven. And I'm sure we can fix your debt situation."

"Nope," Josie said, shutting the fridge door. "At the end of the day, it was my decision. I went to Morocco. I used the hotel. I bought the fancy clothes and the expensive drinks. I need to pay for it. I have a plan. I'll pay it off in three years and four months. Garrett made me a spreadsheet."

"I already forgave her," Liam said.

"Yes," Jack added, "we need you to spearhead the marketing effort for some of our new products."

"So you'll be spending a lot more time in Manhattan, then?" Greg asked. "Because we have some real estate deals that could use your eyes."

"What? Wait," I told my brothers. "She's not moving to Manhattan. She has to stay here."

They immediately started arguing with me.

"You fired her and kicked her out."

"You don't get to have any say on her time!" Liam yelled.

"I can go back and forth," Josie said.

"It's a quick train ride to Harrogate, and the drive wasn't that bad," Chloe added. The short blonde bounced on her heels, grinning.

We all looked at her.

"I also want your thoughts on some marketing. I'm thinking about a franchise in Harrogate!" Chloe said in a rush. The two women screamed, and Josie hugged her.

"And if Chloe's opening a franchise here, then hopefully Jack and Liam will be spending more time in Harrogate," Josie said. She had a slightly guilty look on her face.

"Why do you need them here?" I growled.

"Ah, there was one other part of the land deal," she said. "I promised Art a top-of-the-line custom distillery from Platinum Provisions."

"A distillery!" Liam said loudly. "Count me in!"

"I'll still be here, Mace," Josie said, hugging me. "Don't worry!"

"At least move into the cabin so you're not sneaking around in sin," Greg snapped.

A horn blared outside. We could hear it through the window.

"That better not be another bus," I said, not bothering to take off my apron before racing outside.

"You can't let Remy run roughshod over everything," Greg told me. "Hunter said he's been talking about getting goats."

We pushed through the large glass doors out onto the terrace in time to see Archer in the green school bus towing a brand new, large—

"Tiny house!" Chloe yelled. "Oh my God, it's so cute! We should get a tiny house, Jack!" Jack didn't seem all that enthusiastic about the idea.

My little brothers, who Adrian had all organized to clean up the expansive back lawn, stopped what they were doing and looked over at us.

Hunter walked out from the study off the opposite side of the terrace, trailed by Remy, who was saying, "They'll be good for the land, and you can make cheese..."

"I'd pay good money to see Jack Frost live in a tiny house," Hunter said.

"Did Hunter Svensson just make a funny?" Jack asked, biting back a grin.

"I think that was a threat," I remarked.

"I found this on craigslist," Archer said proudly, gesturing to the house.

"How'd the bus do?" Remy asked.

"Great towing capacity," Archer replied. He looked between Hunter and Remy. "Are we going to be proud new goat parents?"

"Absolutely not," Hunter replied.

CHAPTER 69

Josie

After we spent most of the evening cooking, the guests started trickling in the next day around lunchtime. I'd had Remy hang American flags from the windows and place a giant one down the exact center of the house for Memorial Day. Judge Edna, Ida, and a pretty brown-haired woman were the first to arrive.

"I told you we were early, Edna," Ida complained to her sister. "You have to arrive fashionably late to these things."

"This is Olivia, the architect who worked on the estate house," Mace said as I shook the young woman's hand.

"And she's my granddaughter," Ida boasted.

"She's more so *my* grandniece," Edna sniffed. "She takes after me."

"You did a wonderful job on this property," I gushed.

"You're going to have to come back and work on the cabins," Mace told her.

"Are you two moving into one of them?" Olivia asked. "I really wanted to work on those the last time, but—" She gestured to the house. "This place is so huge. We had to phase it."

Chloe was a huge hit at the Memorial Day cookout, and so were her desserts.

"I'm so glad she's opening a bakery here," I told Willow.

"I know. The only reason I agreed to stay in Harrogate and help you with your marketing work was that I had heard rumors she was opening a shop here. And now it's true!" She sighed happily and took a big bite of the slice of orange creamsicle cake Chloe had baked. "I could just eat this all day, every day," Willow said, shoving the rest in her mouth. "She made so much food, and it all tastes fantastic."

"I love cooking for huge amounts of people," Chloe said, coming up beside me and hugging me.

"I know! I always wanted a big family."

"Seems like you got it," she said as we surveyed the crowd. In addition to most of the town, the majority of Mace's brothers were there. Tall and broad shouldered, I could see them towering above the crowd. Mace's younger brothers raced around, periodically getting yelled at by Hunter.

"Is this the famous Josie?" asked a woman. She was tall with a long platinum-white braid down her back. Her blouse was sleeveless, and it looked like she never skipped shoulder day.

"Belle!" Chloe exclaimed, hugging her. "You came!"

Chloe turned to me and joked, "Don't you just feel short and inadequate around her?"

Belle rolled her eyes.

"She's Jack's sister," Chloe explained, "and I have a special pair of extra-high-heeled shoes I usually wear when she's around."

"You're hardly inadequate," Belle sniffed. "The inadequate thing here is Romance Creative. Organizationally it's a mess. I'm trying to get them to solidify a brand, but they keep jumping around to different reality show formats." She jerked her head over to where Dana Holbrook and Gunnar Svensson were in an animated conversation with Ida. I heard the words "bondage bachelor" and shuddered.

"See?" Belle demanded. "So, Josie, do you do consulting? I've been trying to get my brothers to put me in contact with you, and of course both Jack and Owen are completely useless. If you want something done right, you do it yourself."

Meg waved and headed in our direction. "The famous Chloe," Meg said. "The rumor mill says you're opening up a shop in Harrogate."

"News sure travels fast here," Chloe said, grinning.

"Small town," Meg replied with a shrug. She was about to take a bite of the cookie she held when she looked over and yelled, "Get away from them! Excuse me."

Meg handed me her cookie, then she marched over and dragged away two young teenage girls who were very obviously flirting with Isaac and Bruno Svensson.

"They're just friends from school!" one of the brown-haired girls complained when Meghan hauled them back over to where we were standing.

"There will be none of that," Meghan scolded her little sisters.

The girls looked longingly at Isaac and Bruno, who elbowed each other and laughed. Meg scowled in their direction.

Hunter, who seemed to have a nose for when anything was amiss with the younger Svenssons, strode over and handed them each a bag. "Don't stand there, gawping," he growled. "Go pick up trash and be useful." He smiled slightly in Meghan's direction. She kept scowling.

"Don't think," she said to me, "that just because I let that land deal slide through that the Svenssons are just going to run roughshod over the town of Harrogate."

"I wasn't planning on it," I said, backing away slowly. I fled to the terrace, where Remy was manning the grill. He had his Marine Corps Veteran hat on. Susie was there talking to him. Every time she would laugh at something he said, he blushed straight up through his beard to his forehead.

"They're swapping stories about the service," Cliff, the fireman, said when I came up.

"Making sure Josie doesn't set anything on fire?" Mace asked from behind me.

The fireman laughed. "That and this is where the hot food is! It barely seems to make it to the table before it's scarfed up."

"My brothers eat a lot," Mace said sheepishly.

"No kidding!" Cliff replied, saluting to Mayor Barry, and headed across the lawn to go talk to him.

"This turned out really nice," Mace said, handing me a plate. "Did you even eat? You made all this food."

"You helped!" I took the plate with a hot dog smothered in cheese, chili, and minced onions.

"That's the best way to eat a hot dog," Mace told me. I bit into it and gave a thumbs-up.

Otis, Nate, and Peyton ran up to the grill and started jostling for food.

"Don't fight around the grill," Mace reprimanded them. Two of his brothers, I think it was Carl and maybe Mike, were in some sort of drunken argument about the latest football game. Isaac and Bruno were standing by them, watching them wave their arms.

"Hey!" Hunter yelled across the lawn. "You are not done yet." He stormed over to them, collecting Otis, Nate, and Peyton on his way. He handed the three of them trash bags, then he handed Carl and Mike trash bags as well and pointed them to opposite corners of the large lawn. Then he went to keep Henry from sticking his whole face in the potato salad.

"Are you sure you want to wake up to this every morning?" Mace asked me after a moment.

"You mean to you and this awesome house and the wonderful—" Henry screamed at Hunter, and Hunter scolded him. Mace and I winced. "Sometimes wonderful people." I smiled up at him. "I couldn't think of anything I want more." He leaned over and kissed me, causing me to almost spill the plate of food.

"Don't let me lose that!" I shrieked, lunging to catch my cupcake before it fell. Except I overcorrected, and the cupcake ended up smooshed on Mace's neck and part of his cheek. "You look good enough to eat," I said as red, white, and blue sprinkles dripped off him. Mace stood there in shock.

"It's like both of my great loves all in one delicious sugary package," I quipped. A grin spread slowly across Mace's face, and he grabbed me, wrapping his arms around me.

"You're smearing cake in my hair!" I shrieked as he nuzzled me.

"You know," Mace said, "I think I'm starting to be on board with your life philosophy."

"YOLO?"

He shook his head then kissed me, the sweetness of the cake lingering on my lips. He pulled back and said against my mouth, "If it's covered in candy, eat it!"

The End

A SHORT ROMANTIC COMEDY

HIS *Candy Crush*

CHAPTER 1

Josie

Follow your passion, and you might end up hanging upside down from the roof of a tiny house. At least that's what Mace's little brothers seemed to have concluded.

They were playing on the new tiny house Archer had parked haphazardly at the edge of the lawn near the carriage house. It had been sitting there since the Memorial Day picnic. Now it was the middle of summer. Mace's younger brothers were currently swinging on the rooftop porch railings of the tiny house on wheels.

Forget you only live once—I was afraid they were going to only live a little bit longer. Otis was hanging next to the edge, and I sucked in a breath. Spending the last few months with Mace had given me a greater appreciation for why he always acted like the world was about to end. All of the young boys in the house seemed hell-bent on self-destruction.

"We should do something about that," Mace said to me, gesturing to the tiny house.

"I'm shocked it took you this long to say something," I replied. We were lounging out on the terrace, enjoying the summer morning sun.

"I'm afraid it's going to tip over and crush one of the kids if they keep climbing on it," Mace said.

"It has been convenient to use to store product samples for the cabin renovation," I told him. "Who knew how much went into renovating a building on the National Registry of Historic Places?"

"As I recall, it was a nightmare with the estate house," he said and turned to me with a grin. "I'm glad you're the one handling it and not me."

I leaned over and kissed him. "I wouldn't have been able to do anything without Olivia. It's good she specializes in historic architecture."

Mace pulled me closer to him, and I snuggled against his chest.

"She's nice," I continued. "We should find one of your brothers to fix her up with."

"I like her too much to saddle her with one of my brothers," Mace said with a snort.

"Aww, they aren't that bad," I said. Mace silently jerked his chin toward the tiny house. Archer was hanging off the little metal balcony railing by his knees, and Henry and Theo were swinging from his arms. There was a *crack* and a *crunch* as the railing gave way, and Archer tumbled down.

Mace jumped up, and I followed close behind him.

"I'm good!" Archer shouted, springing to his feet.

"You look like you fell right on your head," Mace said to his identical twin brother.

"He looks fine to me," I said as Archer struck a pose.

"We should burn this tiny house," Mace said, looking up at the dangling railing.

I leaned up to kiss him. "It's going to have to wait. I have to meet with Chloe." I couldn't believe I was saying that. Chloe and I were basically friends now. Well, sort of.

"We're going to have a meeting with Jack at Platinum Provisions to go over that distillery equipment," I explained as he followed me into the main house.

"For Art right?" he asked as I collected my bag.

"Yep. Jack and Liam said they wanted to sell the equipment, so we're doing a bit more work on the marketing and design side."

"Too bad Chloe's bistro isn't open yet," Mace said with a sigh. "You could meet there instead of having to travel outside of Harrogate."

"Olivia says that due to the health codes for food prep, permitting a restaurant is complicated. But I get to go to Manhattan, so I'm not complaining."

"Are you driving or taking the train?" Mace asked.

"Probably the train," I said. "I want to work during the trip."

"Don't get lost," he said, grabbing his car keys.

I snorted. "You have the Find My Phone app. If I do get lost, you'll have to come save me."

I waved to Mace after he dropped me off at the train station. I felt very glamourous going into the city. Though my original tiny house along with all my possessions was still impounded, I had let Mace buy me some new clothes.

Admiring my reflection in one of the shop windows in the train station, I looked glamourous and mysterious, if I did say so myself. Which was fitting, because I wasn't *actually* going to see Chloe about the distillery. I had something else in mind…

CHAPTER 2

Mace

I wished Josie hadn't had to travel today. I tried to tell myself that I was lucky Josie hadn't permanently moved to Manhattan. Still, she traveled to New York City at least a few times a week. Between the time she spent working on marketing projects at my brothers' companies and then just generally dealing with my little brothers, it felt like I hardly ever had her to myself.

"I feel like you're handling this like a mature adult," Archer said in the car on the way to the PharmaTech offices. Archer had set up a de facto headquarters for his conference center in Josie's old office. It had been months, and though I loved my twin, I was ready for him to move out of my office.

"Did you secure your conference center yet?" I asked him.

"Ugh, I need Josie to come save the day. I can't believe that guy won't sell," he complained. "My life is in shambles right now."

"This wouldn't have anything to do with one of your many ex-girlfriends being here, would it?" I teased him as I parked the car.

Archer grimaced. "Girlfriend is a strong word."

"She seems to think you two are getting married," I said as we walked into the PharmaTech offices.

"Just because the perfect woman fell out of the sky into your lap doesn't mean you are suddenly some expert on love," Archer scoffed.

Archer flopped down on the couch in my office as soon as we walked in. I tried to do work, but Archer's moping was distracting. Actually that was only partially true. Mainly my thoughts were consumed with Josie. She hadn't called or texted.

Mace: *Everything ok? How's NYC?*
Josie: *Fine. I'll be back tonight*
Mace: *You didn't get lost did you?*
Josie: *Haha*

I put down my phone then picked it back up. I wished I had gone with her. But she would be back soon. The last train to Harrogate was at 11:30 p.m. I knew she wouldn't be on that one. Maybe she would take the 6:45 train? Or the 7:15?

I wondered if I should go surprise her. But no. She was working. And so should I. I tapped my fingers and checked my calendar. I had a call with Jack about the factory.

"Did you have a chance to look over the documents?" I asked him when he picked up the phone. "Josie said that the Harrogate Trust is going to want to have a meeting soon about the site area improvements."

"I did," Jack said. "Everything looks good. The dimensions of the buildings are what we need, and they seem to have the mechanical and data systems we're going to need. Maybe we can have a conference call with Josie soon? There were some questions I wanted to ask her."

"Maybe you can talk before or after your meeting about the distillery equipment," I suggested.

Jack was silent for a moment. "I don't have a meeting with her today…"

"She said she was meeting you this afternoon," I growled. "She said you, her, and Chloe were meeting about it."

"No, we're basically done… uh I… crap."

"What?" I shouted.

"I have to go. Talk to you later," Jack said in a rush and hung up.

"What the hell?" I muttered. I couldn't believe Josie had lied to me.

I snatched up my phone and quickly navigated to the Find My Phone app. I tried to calm my heart rate as the map centered on the blue dot of Josie's phone. I felt bad for spying on her, but I had to know what she was doing.

The blue dot definitely wasn't at the Platinum Provisions offices, and it wasn't at ThinkX's offices, which was my brothers Weston and Blade's consulting firm. She wasn't even at the Grey Dove Bistro. Instead, the app said Josie was in a residential apartment building. Who was she meeting?

The revelation completely obliterated my concentration for the day. All I could think about as I forced myself to sit through my afternoon meetings was that Josie must be unhappy with me. Why else would she lie? I racked my brain trying to think about what I had done the last few weeks to make her angry. I didn't think I had done anything, which left the only conclusion I could draw, which was that she was fundamentally unhappy with me. I must have gotten complacent in the last few months and not been as attentive. Resolving to be a better boyfriend, I went to the store after my last meeting to buy her favorite candy.

"There's the most handsome man in Harrogate!" Ida called out when I walked into her general store.

"Hi, Mrs. Ida," I said with a wave.

"Don't you Mrs. Ida me. I'm not that old," she scolded. "You can call me sweet cheeks or honeybun. That's what Bert prefers."

I gulped. I still didn't quite know what to make of Ida.

"You know," she said thoughtfully, "you do look sort of glowing. I can't tell if it's the hair or if it's because you're a man who's getting laid every night."

"I... ah..."

"It takes one to know one," she said conspiratorially. "Now that Bert isn't so stressed about your company tearing up the green space, he's really on his game."

"Glad I could be of assistance," I said diplomatically.

"You can assist me anytime," Ida said with a wink. "Though I wouldn't do that to Josie."

"Speaking of Josie," I said, hoping to change the subject from Ida's bedroom escapades, "I wanted to pick up some candy for her."

"Getting frisky in the bedroom, eh?" she asked. "I know what Josie likes!" Ida loaded me up with English toffee, chocolates, and other candy.

I put them away when I returned back to the estate house then played with my little brothers.

"Is Josie making dinner?" Peyton asked me.

"I'm not sure," I admitted. I had expected her to be back by now.

Mace: *You coming home for dinner?*

Josie: *OMG I lost track of time! I'll miss it I'm sorry I'll make it up to the boys!*

What was she doing? I paced around the kitchen, trying and failing to concentrate enough to make dinner for my brothers. A singular terrible thought crossed my mind. *What if she's found someone better?*

You're jumping to conclusions, I told myself. But what if I wasn't?

CHAPTER 3

Josie

I met Chloe at her friend Nina's apartment.

"I can't have all the décor in mine and Jack's apartment," Chloe said as we walked in. "Mace will sometimes randomly come there. Plus other Svensson brothers show up from time to time, and you can't trust a single one of them to keep a secret. They're like puppies that just stole your socks."

"But they'll be at Mace's surprise party, right?" I asked her.

"I have invitations going out tonight," Chloe promised. "Hopefully they won't spoil the surprise. It's not like any of them have anything better to do this Saturday, and they're all local."

I surveyed all the decorations and supplies Chloe and I had gathered over the last few weeks for the surprise party for Mace's and Archer's birthday.

"Nina helped me pick out a lot of these party favors," Chloe said. "Want to see?"

"They go with the black-and-white theme," Nina said as she showed me the hats, balloons, streamers, and giant letters we would use to decorate the house and backyard.

"I think it's perfect!" I said, clapping my hands. "This is going to be an amazing party!"

Nina led me into her tiny bedroom. On the bed were two huge stuffed animals, a black cat and a white cat.

"I feel like it's fitting for Archer and Mace," Chloe said. "One is wholesome and wakes up early to exercise and eats healthy, and the other is up all night and is hungover during the day."

"These are awesome!"

"Chloe and I were thinking we would make black-and-white cupcakes and then also a half-cholate, half-vanilla cake with a ton of candles," Nina told me.

"Great idea," I said, "especially since we're going to have a lot of people. Just with the Svensson brothers it's over fifty, plus all our friends and some of the townspeople. It's going to be a crowd."

"At least it's warm," Nina said. "Chloe showed me pictures of the backyard. Our friend Maria is coming by to help decorate."

"That's nice of her!"

"She is going to help me run the Harrogate franchise," Chloe explained. "So she wanted to go out there anyway."

We discussed layouts, menu, and logistics for the next few hours over wine and cheese. I lost track of time and didn't realize how late it was until Mace texted me.

"Crap," I said, grabbing my bag. "I need to go."

"You better!" Chloe said. "We don't want him suspecting anything."

I barely made the train, but I did miss dinner.

"I'm so sorry," I told Mace when I arrived back at the estate house.

"It's okay," he said, kissing me. "I heated up some of the frozen lasagna you made."

"That industrial-sized freezer came in handy, didn't it?" I asked, tapping him on the nose. "We should buy two more."

"How was your meeting?" Mace asked.

"It was good," I said. Mace gave me an odd look. He didn't know, did he? "It was very productive," I continued. "Chloe talked the engineers into adding in some more design work."

"Are you happy?" Mace asked, expression serious.

"Of course! You make me very happy," I assured him. Then I lowered my voice. "In more ways than one."

"I'm sorry I'm taking over your space," I told him as I sprawled out on his bed. I would never be tired of all the extra space and the attractive man I shared it with.

"Really? Because you don't look all that sorry," he said with a smile. My clothes were strewn around his room. I watched as he picked up my shoes.

"I need to get you a box or something," he said. "You know, I have several drawers cleared out for you and space in the closet."

"Er, yeah."

Mace opened a drawer and peered inside. "Is this candy?"

"I had to put my stash somewhere," I said. "I think Remy's been eating my candy."

"I'm the only one who's allowed to eat your candy," he growled and jumped on the large bed, straddling me.

I wrapped my arms around him. "And you're such a sexy candy eater," I said, kissing him from his strong slightly stubbly jaw to his sensual mouth. "Though having all this space is a big bonus in your favor. I'm never going back to tiny house living."

"I can't tell if you're here because you like not living in a coffin on wheels or if you like me for me," he said.

"None of the above. I'm totally after your lollipop," I joked.

He kissed me and lazily unbuttoned my blouse.

"Someone's in a candy mood," I said, my breath hitching slightly.

"I always want your candy," Mace replied, his breath against my nipple making me shiver. He lovingly kissed my breast, circling the nipple with his tongue, pinching and teasing the other with his fingers. His other hand trailed down between my legs.

"You're so wet," he breathed. A small cry escaped my lips as he stroked me. Mace kissed his way down. Spreading my legs, he licked me. His fingers dipped into my opening, and I bucked against him. He held me down with his free hand so he could lavish me with his tongue. My body clenched, and I whimpered as his tongue teased my clit, sucking it then licking down the length of the slit to my opening and back up again.

"I want your cock," I whimpered as his fingers moved in me while he sucked my clit, bringing me close to the edge. He ignored my request, content with licking me into a frenzy.

I came with my fingers tangled in his hair, and his tongue drew out the waves of the orgasm.

"Just give me a second," I wheezed. "You really were on your game tonight."

Mace laughed softly and gathered me into his arms. "Don't worry about it. This is more than enough for me."

CHAPTER 4

Josie

I went with Mace to the PharmaTech offices the next morning. I lied and said it was because I wanted to spend some time with him, which I did, but more importantly, I wanted to talk to Garrett.

I made sure Mace was out of his office before slipping into Garrett's office and explaining the situation.

"Wait," Garrett said. "You're throwing Mace a party?"

"Yes," I said. "A surprise party. It's for Archer too."

Garrett made a face. "Mace doesn't like surprises. Also we don't really do birthday parties in our family."

"You what?" I exclaimed. "The shock! The horror!"

"There are so many brothers," Garrett said. "And in the cult, it simply wasn't done. Why have a party if the world was going to end soon? Also there were so many of us our parents probably didn't even know our birthdays."

"That's sad," I said, feeling bad for the Svensson brothers.

"It isn't practical," Garrett said. "We would have a birthday party a week."

"And?" I said. "What's the problem with having birthday cake and ice cream twice a week?"

"It's too much."

"I can't believe you don't celebrate birthdays," I said.

"In all the time you've been here, you didn't notice that there was never a celebration?" Garrett asked, irritably tapping his pen against his desk. "Did you even run a probability calculation on the number of brothers versus the number of potential birthdays?"

I shrugged. "It's not like all of your brothers are here, just the two dozen or so youngest. I figured maybe everyone was born in the winter, you know, like goats."

"That is one, completely inaccurate, and two, Hunter doesn't want anyone to talk about goats," Garrett said.

"What if I give Mace a goat for his birthday?" I asked, waggling my eyebrows. That earned me a smirk from Garrett.

"As amusing as that would be, best not."

I smiled, glad he was finally in a better mood. "I've already planned the party, and Chloe sent out the invites. But I need someone to keep Mace and Archer occupied," I said in a rush.

Garrett groaned dramatically. "I can't really be expected to—"

"Who else would I be able to trust with such an important task?" I demanded. "Between Archer and Mace, one of them will sniff something out! Though I suppose maybe Adrian would do it if you aren't up for it."

"What? No. He wouldn't be able to keep them away for ten minutes. He's too dense to understand the delicate logistics of such an operation." Garrett glared at me. "I know you're trying to appeal to my ego."

"And is it working?" I asked hopefully.

"Yes. I will keep them occupied tomorrow."

True to his word, Garrett had Mace and Archer out of the house bright and early at ten a.m. sharp. Remy was on the roof with binoculars and radioed me the all clear when the car was far enough away.

"Bring in," he said dramatically, "the baker!"

Chloe, Nina, Maria, and Jack all pulled into the roundabout, their SUVs loaded with food and decorations. Liam and a few of Mace's other brothers pulled in a few minutes later.

"Unload! Unload!" I yelled to the younger Svenssons I had enlisted to cart everything to the kitchen and backyard.

"How long will Garrett keep them occupied?" Weston asked me.

"Well, Mace is going to know something is up," I said. "But I'm hoping they stay away at least a few hours. We have to cook a lot of food."

"We might not have that much time," Chloe said, glaring at Jack.

"You didn't tell me that Josie was coming in and I was supposed to cover for you!" Jack protested.

"I don't know, Jack," Chloe said, rolling her eyes. "I mean, I've only been planning this party for *weeks*."

"Mace isn't dumb," Liam said. "He'll be back here in thirty minutes. Watch."

"I have faith in Garrett," I said. "Come on, people. Let's move it! This needs to be the best surprise party ever!"

CHAPTER 5

Mace

As soon as we left the house, I knew something was up.

"Why are we going to look at property?" I asked. "I thought Archer already found the chocolate factory for his convention center."

"Yes," Garrett said impatiently, "but I think that Meg will shut it down out of spite because, well, you know."

"Ah, yes, Hunter's terrible decision-making skills," Archer growled from behind me. My normally upbeat brother didn't look that excited to be out and about. This was clearly an unplanned outing.

"Why do I have to sit in the back?" Archer complained.

"I'm taller," I stated.

"No, you aren't," he scoffed. "We are literally the same height."

I looked out the car window. "I just don't understand why you're taking the time to do this, Garrett. And why I'm here." *Especially since I would rather be with Josie.*

"We need your opinion on the conference center," Garrett said.

"No, we don't," Archer countered. "If we needed anyone's opinion, it would be Josie's."

"You're planning something," I said to Garrett.

He huffed, "There is no ulterior motive here."

"There's always an ulterior motive with you," I said. "Take me back to the house at once!"

"Stop being so histrionic," Garrett snapped, pressing his foot on the gas.

He drove us far out to the next county. We were surrounded by miles of fields when he finally stopped the car.

"You want me to put my conference center here?" Archer asked, peering over his sunglasses at the half-collapsed, former county farming exhibition hall.

"It's out in the middle of nowhere," I said.

"Yeah, and it's ugly!" Archer complained. "What am I supposed to do with this?"

"Why did you take us all the way out here?" I demanded, advancing on Garrett. "This has something to do with Josie, doesn't it? She was lying to me about where she was two days ago, and now you're acting weird."

"Forget about Mace's paranoia," Archer said. "I'm tired and hungry."

"Why don't we go eat lunch?" Garrett suggested.

Archer and I both stopped and looked at him. "A lunch date? Who are you, and what have you done with my brother?"

"Remy said he saw an alien," Archer commented, crawling back into the car and lying down on the seat. "I can't believe I wasted my Saturday on this."

"We have other sites to look at," Garrett said.

"Take me home!" Archer yelled.

"Give me the keys," I demanded, holding out my hand.

"No," Garrett said, backing up.

Considering his hungover state, Archer jumped out of the car faster than I would have expected.

"I'm going to tickle you if you don't give us the keys!" Archer sang, walking toward Garrett, arms outstretched. It was a serious threat. Even when he was a child, Garrett hated being touched. Tickling would earn you a black eye.

"Don't touch me!" Garrett spat.

We both advanced on Garrett.

"You're going to be sorry," he warned.

"Yeah, probably, but it's worth it to know what you, Josie, and Jack are hiding," I said.

In unison, Archer and I both tackled Garrett. Archer held Garrett down while I snatched the keys from him and ran to the driver's seat, starting the car.

"Get in," I ordered my younger brother.

Garrett scowled the whole ride back, periodically texting someone. Did it have something to do with Josie? But when I pulled into the driveway, nothing seemed amiss. There were a few more of my brothers' cars than usual, but it was the weekend, and sometimes they came into Harrogate to visit.

"I don't know if I can deal with Greg right now," Archer said, waking up when I parked behind our older brother's car. "I came out here to escape him."

Garrett seemed antsy as we walked into the house. It was completely dark.

"Are all the lights out again?" Archer asked, stretching and yawning as we walked into the dining room. "You should buy one of those smart home systems so you can clap and say, 'Turn on lights.'"

As if they had heard Archer's command, all the lights suddenly flooded on.

"Surprise!" Over a hundred of our friends and family jumped out. Jack and Liam walked out with a huge black-and-white decorated cake that said HAPPY BIRTHDAY on it. Josie ran up to hug and kiss me.

"You did all this?" I asked in amazement. She nodded.

"Why?" I asked.

"It's your birthday, silly!" She placed a party hat on my head. "And yours too!" she said, hugging Archer and giving him his own hat.

"Blow out your candles," Jack said. "Before this cake catches my suit on fire."

"Did you use thirty-four candles?" I asked, looking at the cake. It was awash in a layer of flames.

"Actually we have sixty-eight because of both of you," Josie said.

"I think Archer's been drinking too much to blow all these out. He'll probably act like a flame thrower," Liam joked as I tried to decipher the best way to blow out the candles without catching the house or Jack and Liam on fire.

"You act like I'm a drunk," Archer complained.

"You certainly aren't straight and narrow," Greg commented.

"The candles!" Jack urged. I gathered my younger brothers to help me blow them out.

"Wonderful. Now the cake is going to have germs all over it," Garrett said as we blew out the candles with only minimal singeing of Jack's suit.

"Don't tell me you're still mad that we didn't run around the countryside with you," Archer commented.

"I had to allow enough time for decorating and cooking," Garrett said. "We should have stayed away two more hours. The grill's barely hot."

"You kept them away long enough," Josie assured Garrett. "Though the hamburgers and hot dogs aren't done, so we might have to eat dessert first."

"Fine with me!" Chloe said. "And I have cupcakes, too, for the paranoid amongst us." We inspected the cake.

"On second thought, I think that layer of wax probably protected it," Garrett said.

"We'll doctor it up," Cloe said. "I always do cake deliveries with some extra icing."

Henry grabbed my hand. "Open your presents!"

I followed him outside to see my brother Carl helping one of Chloe's friends tack up the final party streamer.

"Sorry," I said to Josie. "I should have stayed away longer. I guess I sort of ruined the surprise."

"Hardly!" Josie said. "You seemed very surprised!"

"Yeah," I said. "I was."

"You can open presents while Remy starts grilling," she said. There was a table stacked with nicely wrapped packages.

"The big pile is Mace's," Liam announced.

"I'm hurt, you guys," Archer said, clutching his chest.

"Don't be too excited," Josie said under her breath. "The younger kids wanted to each get you a gift, or at least wrap something, so I can't vouch for what's inside."

Though the presents were all nicely wrapped, some of my younger brothers had given me some weird stuff. Henry's package, for example, was a professionally wrapped box that held a crayon-scribbled note and a single piece of dried-out pizza.

"Geeze, Henry," Hunter said, taking the box and throwing the pizza in a trash bag. "I didn't realize that's what he had put in there."

"It's one of my favorite things," Henry said seriously.

"I wondered what that weird smell was," Liam said.

It wasn't as weird as the gigantic stuffed cats.

"Aren't they awesome?" Josie asked, laughing.

"They're so soft," Archer said. He had taken multiple party hats and had them all stacked on his head, alternating white and black. "I'll put it in my love den."

"No," Hunter barked.

My favorite presents were the ones Josie gave me.

"These are actually supposed to be from everyone," she said, "but of course the kids wanted to get you something themselves as well."

Inside the boxes were several nicely composed photographs of my brothers in various groupings. There was also a large one of all of us at the Memorial Day cookout.

"You could put some of these up in your office," Josie said. "It needs a personal touch."

"Thank you," I told her, feeling touched. I also felt a little ashamed I had ever doubted her. I pulled her close to me. "This was a wonderful birthday."

"Thank you, Josie!" Archer said, joining the hug. "Not to third-wheel and make this awkward or anything."

CHAPTER 6

Josie

The food was finally ready after Mace and Archer opened all the presents. It was also good timing because several of the townspeople I had invited had started to show up.

"It was a surprise party?" Ida exclaimed when she walked into the backyard. "You didn't tell me that! We missed the big reveal."

"Mace showed up early," I explained.

"And of course she's not going to tell you it's a surprise party," Edna, her sister, sniffed. "You can't keep a secret for anything, Ida!"

I left them to argue and found Mace surveying the party.

"It's your party," I said, wrapping an arm around his waist. "You should be down there. Look at Archer."

He had dragged Ms. Dottie and Mrs. Levenston, two of the town senior citizens, onto the temporary dance floor we'd set up.

"I'm just amazed that you did all this for me," he said. "I'm just—I'm really touched." I hugged him, and he leaned down to kiss me.

"You do a lot, not just for me but for your family as well," I said. "You're a good man, and you deserve to be celebrated."

He pressed his mouth against mine for a deep kiss. I was panting a little when he pulled back. "I love you, Josie," Mace said. "You really are the best thing that's ever happened to me." A crafty smile on his face, Mace looked around and tugged me away down a path.

"Where are we going?" I asked.

"We're going to christen the cabin," Mace said. "This seems like as good a time as any."

We slipped through the front door of the cabin. There was primer on the walls and a table in the middle of the living room, but it was otherwise pretty bare.

"They're going to miss us," I whispered.

"Guess we'll have to be quick," he said in a low voice. His hand snuck under my skirt. "Good thing you're already wet."

Mace pulled out a condom. "Prepare for any contingencies," he said with a wink. My heart was racing. I would never get tired of Mace looking at me with unbridled desire. He undid my shirt enough to expose my lacy bra and sucked my nipple through it then pulled it out.

"I love your tits," he mumbled against my skin. I heard the rasp of his pants zipper, then I moaned as his hand pushed under my skirt and into my soaking-wet panties.

"And I love your cock," I whimpered as he stroked my clit. In one smooth motion, he turned me around. I leaned against the table, chest heaving as Mace pushed my skirt up and pulled down my panties. I moaned as he entered me. The cabin was well soundproofed, so I let my cries sound around the empty room as Mace thrust into me.

"Your cock feels so good," I moaned as he fucked me, his large hands digging into my hips. I bucked back against him, needing him to fill me. One of his hands reached between my legs, spreading them further. Using two fingers, Mace teased and played with my clit. My breath came out in begging pants as he thrust into me.

"Harder," I begged, needing the release. His rhythm sped up. Egging him on, I moaned, "I love it when you fuck me with that big cock."

His teeth nipped my neck, and his hand left my hip to come up and pinch my nipple. I bucked against him, every motion sending pleasure sensations through me.

"I love fucking your tight, hot pussy. I love how wet you get for me," he growled in my ear as he fucked me. My legs were trembling, and my body clenched.

"Come for me, baby," Mace whispered in my ear as my body spasmed around him. I felt him come, then I collapsed over the table.

"That was so good," I half-moaned half-whimpered, the aftershocks of the orgasm making me a little dizzy. "You know just what I like," I said, turning around to face him.

"I do?" he asked. Mace swept the hair out of my face and kissed me. "What are your favorite things?"

"Cock and candy!"

The End

Acknowledgements

A big thank you to Red Adept Editing for editing and proofreading.

And finally a big thank you to all the readers! I had a great time writing this hilarious book! Please try not to choke on your wine while reading!!!

About the Author

If you like steamy romantic comedy novels with a creative streak, then I'm your girl!

Architect by day, writer by night, I love matcha green tea, chocolate, and books! So many books…

Sign up for my mailing list to get special bonus content, free books, giveaways, and more!

http://alinajacobs.com/mailinglist.html

Made in the USA
Monee, IL
08 November 2020